The El

by Catherine Gigante-Brown

Cover design by Lisa Ponder
Author photo by Barbara Nitke

Published by Volossal Publishing
www.volossal.com

Copyright © 2012
ISBN 978-0-9886262-8-7

For my father,
all my love, always

Table of Contents

1 Borough Park

They lived in a neighborhood called "Borough Park." Only there were no parks, just rows and rows of wooden houses tiredly leaning against one another, as wearily as the people who lived inside them. The sidewalks were cracked in many places. The cobblestones paving the streets were uneven and coming up in spots, tipping to one side or another like loose teeth. The weather did that—the endless snow in the winter, the rain that came down in dirty rivulets in the spring and autumn, and the summer sun that pounded down soullessly, making the streets themselves steam and stink.

But the El rose above it all.

That's what everyone in Borough Park called the elevated train—the El, for short, like the nickname of an old, familiar friend. The El saw everything and said nothing. It coursed three stories above the streets, through the heart of the neighborhood, like hot blood through chilled veins. The El connected everyone, yet at the same time, tore them apart. It took them to strange and wonderful places they'd never before been and to ordinary places they were weary of and wished they'd never have to return. To work, to play, to Manhattan and beyond. The El ferried them to alien neighborhoods with curious, daunting names like Bushwick and Gravesend, linked them to other train lines like the Sea Beach. And it led to the ocean.

But as for Tiger, he preferred the trolley. Tiger preferred the trolley because his father worked on the El. Not as a motorman, sheparding the train along the tall, undulating network of wood and steel tracks. But instead, as a conductor, opening and closing the doors with the pull of a lever.

It was a suitable job for a drunk, straightforward, uncomplicated, doable even if you've tipped back a few. And if you were smart about it when you worked nights, you could even drink on the job and still take home a decent paycheck, thanks to the Transport Workers Union which had been formed two years earlier. Sometimes Tiger's father would have a drink on them, toasting his good fortune and his Union job. Other times, he'd curse the God-damned T.W.U.

Tony would steal sips from an old cough medicine bottle which he filled to the brim with whiskey. Every fifth stop or so, he'd take a slug. He'd make a game of it, counting off New Utrecht Avenue, 62nd Street and so on. The soothing brown liquid bathed his throat as he slammed and unslammed the doors, gave the motorman the "all clear" signal then clattered toward 18th Avenue.

Tony's drinking game varied from night shift to night shift, just to keep it interesting. Sometimes, he devised a diversion where he would tap his makeshift flask whenever a pretty blonde stepped into his car or if a dark-eyed woman smiled at him. This was a far trickier and riskier game of sport, left entirely up to chance instead of the predictability of numbers, not so fool-proof as the "Five-Stop Rule."

But women smiled at Tony often for he cut a handsome figure in his crisp blue uniform and stiff-brimmed hat. He had the kind of aquamarine eyes that spoke of an ocean but not any ocean around Brooklyn. The waters around Coney Island were slate-gray, like his daughter Kewpie's eyes, and sometimes just as cold.

Somehow, Tony's drinking game made the numbness of his job even more numb. But this was a deadness he could control the depth of, depending how much he drank. Tony knew his work was something a chimpanzee, even a dimwitted chimp, could have done, probably better than he did. Tony also knew that his son was probably embarrassed of him because his Pop didn't do something as magnanimous as drive the train. Opening and closing doors wasn't nearly as impressive as fitting ships with weaponry like Tiger's grandfather did.

Still, Tony was lucky to have a steady job, especially in 1936. His family had just enough—and then some—while others went hungry. Others who lived on the same block, even. But just enough wasn't nearly enough for Tony. Never was.

This particular day, Tiger watched his father fill his medicine bottle flask in the kitchen as he did every afternoon before he left for his shift. Tony stood on the checkerboard-patterned linoleum which was scrubbed clean on hands and knees by his wife. Rosanna was hanging laundry from the clothesline strung outside the kitchen window. She always seemed to turn her back on Tony's alcoholic ritual in one way or another. She knew full well what was happening but didn't want to acknowledge it just the same. Kind of like what went on with Kewpie.

Legs slightly apart, lips whetted in anticipation, hand steady as he poured, Tiger glanced up at his father as the boy played with his lead soldiers beneath the oilcloth-covered kitchen table. Tony peered down at his son, winked and smiled. "It's our little secret," he whispered. Tiger said nothing, just turned away.

The flask would have to last Tony's entire shift or else everything would be ruined. Tony would return from work, squinting in the unkindness of daylight, wobbly and mean-spirited, yelling at Rosanna for no reason at all. Or backhanding Tiger for leaving a stray soldier out on the linoleum for him to crush underfoot. Or stealing into the kids' room before dawn, fumbling under his daughter's soft sheets laundered thin and sheer from too much use. "It's our little secret," he'd whisper, his breath hot and rancid like something that came out of a sewer. Kewpie would say nothing, just turn away.

Tony was usually too drunk to do much besides grumble, then stumble away, but still, Kewpie couldn't sleep afterwards. She would hold her body stiff and wooden, afraid to move, scared to breathe freely, fearful he might return. The sour stench of him lingered long after he was gone. Kewpie couldn't get rid of it, even after scrubbing herself raw the next morning with a washcloth in the big, deep tub which stood on lion's paws in the bathroom.

Kewpie swore her mother knew. She swore everyone knew. She imagined Rosanna lying awake in her own bed, holding her breath and straining to hear the muffled words, then sighing with relief when Tony plodded into their room and heaved himself onto their sagging bed, still wearing his shiny work shoes.

The Martino Family lived in what was known as a "railroad apartment." This meant that the rooms of the flat were strung together like railroad cars, each connected to the one before it like the cabs of a train: kitchen and parlor followed by two bedrooms. Kewpie shared a room with Tiger. It was sandwiched between their parents' bedroom and the second-story porch, bordering the porch being its one redeeming quality.

Kewpie tried to concentrate on the sound of Tiger's breath buzzing in the slight space between his front teeth and ignore her father's thick mumbling in the next room. Then Kewpie heard the rustling of cloth, her mother's hushed voice of refusal, more rustling, pawing, soft rebukes and then finally, silence. A silence that was broken by the rumble of the El in the distance and followed by a quiet even more profound.

The next morning, it was as though nothing had happened. Rosanna was already up and in the kitchen, the faint aroma of the match she'd lit the pilot light with still smoldering in the air. The battered teakettle boiled away on the grate. Tiger chomped enthusiastically on his buttered toast. Her father could be heard snoring two rooms off the kitchen. Kewpie passed the dark mound of his body hunched under the covers as she moved quickly through the railroad rooms, careful not to wake him.

"Shush," Rosanna said, without even looking at her daughter, who hadn't made so much as a peep. "Shush."

The tracks of the El ran rose in front of the Loews 46th Street Theater on New Utrecht Avenue, less than a half block away from the Martino home. The wheels screeched and scraped along the wide turn as the train came into the Fort Hamilton Parkway station. Steel against steel, metal grating metal. Sometimes the sound was barely audible but others, it was so earth-shattering that it seemed as though a train would soon come barreling into their second-story apartment, crunching through the porch's newly-painted white posts, shattering the window glass, spoiling Rosanna's neatly starched, hand-sewn curtains, shoving its way through Kewpie and Tiger's bedroom, pounding past the clump of Tony's sill-soused slumbering form, bursting through the parlor's fringed lampshades and worn velvet sofa, coursing into the kitchen and taking the icebox along with it until the train came exploding out the other side of the apartment.

This was one of those times. The El sounded so loud this morning, it was almost unbearable. Kewpie clapped her hands over her ears until the train passed. Rosanna was taking the tea ball out of the pot with her back to her children, so only Tiger noticed.

But then again, Tiger noticed everything.

2 Crooked Rooftops

As her cup of tea cooled on the counter, Rosanna stood at the kitchen sink gazing out the window, hands immersed in tepid water. Past the crooked rooftops, some dotted with pigeon coops, others crisscrossed with clotheslines and still others studded with old kitchen chairs, she saw the El flashing in the morning sunlight. Its windows flickered like fleeting gold as the train sped along the tracks, a treasure that was headed far away from her. But what Rosanna didn't see were her daughter's hands clapped over her ears, so hard the girl's long, graceful fingertips were turning white.

Rosanna heard the wheels scream around the turn as the El faded into the distance. It was a sound that brought her husband both to and from her. A sound that kept him occupied and mostly out of trouble during his shifts, sometimes seven days a week. And for those 12 hours each day, Rosanna felt light and free inside, even if she were only visiting the greengrocer or chatting on 13th Avenue with Sadie Lieberwitz.

Sometimes Rosanna found herself humming as she strolled. Sometimes she felt so good that she bought the kids a miniscule box of Seven-Layer Cookies from Piccolo's Bakery, even though they really couldn't afford it. 'Everyone deserves a little sweetness now and then,' she told herself. 'Whether they can afford it or not.' Tiger called them Rainbow Cookies and ate them methodically, stripping them layer by layer and counting before he devoured each color, just to make sure there were indeed seven layers. It was as though the boy didn't trust anyone's word, not even a baker's.

As Rosanna rounded the corner onto 47th Street, everything changed. Her spirit sunk and she had to keep reminding herself how to breathe. When the house came into view, she had to will herself to keep walking toward it. A nice enough place with its well-tended front garden and careworn front porches, but sometimes she could hardly bear the place because he lived there, too. And Tony was either inside, sleeping off a drunk or would soon be home to spoil everything.

Nothing, not even the sight of her mother sitting at the wooden table on the porch, writing a letter to some almost-forgotten friend or carefully flipping cards in a game of solitaire, not the comforting smell of Poppa's cherry-scented pipe tobacco or the feel of Tiger's scrawny arms hugging her neck, then reaching for the box of sweets in her shopping bag, could lift her spirits.

And now, staring at the gray dishwater that swallowed her puckered fingers, pushing the rag in and out of chipped teacups and jelly glasses, Rosanna tried not to think of the day ahead. She tried to forget the night before, but couldn't. The muted voices, the brush of bed sheets, the knowledge of what was but then sharp denial a heartbeat later.

Kewpie couldn't bear to look at her. And Rosanna couldn't bear to see her daughter's face, her firmly set jaw, her silent rage, as the girl chased her cereal around the bowl with a teaspoon. So, Rosanna looked at the back of her daughter's head, the golden-brown locks, freshly let down from pin curls. She studied Tiger's cowlick and his profile, lined in concentration, as he moved from toast to toy soldiers. He looked up at her and smiled.

Rosanna turned back to the window and the drab tapestry beyond it. There was no doubt about it: the windows were dirty. No matter how often she cleaned them with a solution of vinegar and warm water, and painstakingly dried them with wads of newspaper, the grime always seemed to return the next day. Perhaps this grimy cast was just the color of the streets or maybe it was the shade of her spirits.

Tony shifted in their bed a few rooms away. Rosanna shuddered. They would be alone today. No kids to protect her. Both Tiger and Kewpie would be in school soon and she would no doubt be summoned to her husband's side to do what no decent woman did in the middle of the morning. 'For crying out loud, I just washed,' she'd think as he groped her. 'I've got the kitchen floor to mop and shopping to do. And my parents...'

Rosanna imagined her father sitting in his own parlor on the floor directly below her bedroom, thoughtfully turning the pages of the *Brooklyn Daily Eagle* as plaster dust sifted down into the fold. Calmly puffing his pipe, occasionally relighting it, he'd pause to brush the powder from his shoulders while high above his head came the thump, thump, thump of his son-in-law's relentless, hangover hump. Rosanna could see her mother in the kitchen, paring potatoes onto the sheaves of yesterday's *Eagle* in rhythm to the thump, thump, thump. Her bright green eyes momentarily dimmed, the bad eye turned slightly inward, a scowl on her usually-smiling lips.

The door slammed as the children left for school after hurried good-byes. And not three seconds later came a growl from the bedroom. "Roe...Roe..." She had to go. She was his wife, after all. And maybe it would keep him out of the kids' room. But Rosanna knew this wouldn't be the case. Tony's actions had nothing to do with desire and everything to do with meanness, pure and simple. They weren't hinged on what Rosanna did or didn't do but had everything to do with him.

Rosanna put down the dishrag, dried her hands on her housedress and went into the bedroom.

She had been christened "Rosanna Maria" but everyone, including her parents, who named her, called her "Roe," for short. The oldest child in a string of six, she was sharp and dark and serious, even as a toddler.

Rosanna had lived in or near Borough Park all her life, first on Chester Avenue, in the shadow of Green-Wood Cemetery, then here on 47th Street. Green-Wood was the only park that she and her siblings had ever known. They played tag among the statues of shrouded death and sobbing angels, climbed the weeping mimosas and flowering forsythia, whose stalks were so stout that they resembled trees instead of bushes. They scaled the walls of the little granite houses which encased entire dead families and lay their heads on marble pillows atop the grave of Hiram Pardee, watching the clouds change face. They patted the head of Rex, the loyal bronze dog who stood watch over his master's plot, then ran off screaming bloody murder when Kelly told them Rex had just licked his hand. Kelly did this every single time they visited Rex; his brothers and sisters expected it, looked forward to it even, and gave the same hysterical response each time.

Perhaps this is why Rosanna was so serious—some of the somberness of Green-Wood had rubbed off on her. But none of her siblings were. Not Margaret, who later changed her name to Astrid. Not Julius, who would take long walks with a sketch pad wedged under his arm and a charcoal pencil shoved into the pocket of his knee pants to mount the foreboding staircase of the Brooklyn Museum on Eastern Parkway, sit cross-legged on the cold marble floor and draw the Egyptian artifacts he saw there. Julius was taciturn but he wasn't nearly as solemn as Rosanna. Nor was Camille, who forced Margaret to entertain her with tap-dances as she sat on the privy. Nor were Jo or Kelly, or her parents, for that matter.

When Rosanna was five, her family moved to the house on 47th Street. It had a wide, wooden wraparound porch and another porch on the second floor. While her mother wanted to put a statue of the Blessed Mother in the little garden out front, Poppa wouldn't hear of it. He couldn't see wasting so much space on "Mary on the Half Shell." With a half smile, Bridget scolded her husband for his sacrilegious sentiments but he held fast, insisting that they'd do fine without Mother Mary watching over their front yard. And they did. He opted for a cherry blossom tree instead.

When it was very hot, she would sleep out on the upper porch with her brothers and sisters, staring at the stars until they grew foggy and her eyes grew heavy. It was spacious on the porch compared to the bedrooms that grew more and more crowded with the arrival of each new child. If you were the counting kind, you would note that there was a space of 14 months between each Paradiso sibling.

Now, you might think that with six children, there would be a shortage of many things in the household but this was not the case at 1128 47th Street. Although money was sometimes tight, Poppa had good skills and was a hard worker. They usually had plenty of everything to go around, not the least of which was love. There were several certainties you could expect when you visited: laughter and joyful mayhem and a great, noisy commotion of some sort, always a high-strung dog or two clamoring underfoot, mostly Pomeranians with pointed faces and jittery nerves.

Bridget always had something bubbling on the stove that smelled delicious, and was delicious. More often than not, her suppers didn't include meat but they were healthy and savory just the same. Lentil and macaroni soup so thick you could stand a spoon in the bowl. Creamy pasta dishes. Plenty of fresh vegetables seasoned with onions and garlic, sparkling with robust olive oil. Thankfully the children were healthy and solid, and they were also kind and polite. Loving parents, it was true, but Poppa and Bridget were also strict parents. They insisted on good manners and looking presentable, even if the hand-me-downs were a bit shabby by the time they reached the youngest.

Poppa was fortunate to have secured a job at the Brooklyn Navy Yard when he was a teenager, soon after he came to this country. Dependable, determined and smart, he worked his way up in the ranks until he finally made shipwright and in 1922, after the kids were grown, became a member of the International Association of Machinists. He never missed a dues payment until the day he retired.

Before the elevated train tracks shadowed Borough Park, Rosanna recalled it as a place of unpaved streets and farms. There were horse-drawn carts everywhere, fresh milk still warm from the cow and fresh eggs, too. It was a time of simple pleasures, when games like "Ring-O-Levio" and "Kick the Can" could occupy entire afternoons. As would amusements like picking up clumps of dried horseshit and throwing them at each other. Rosanna remembered when cows roamed past the house on the way back to the dairy barn nearby. Pigs and chicken freely wandered the roads, too. But then cobblestones replaced the dirt and Rosanna began to change as well.

Her body erupted into a series of curves and people—men, especially—started to look at her oddly. The trolley car operator, the fellow who drove the milk wagon down the rutted streets, the junk man and even old Mr. Jacobs, who ran the grocery store. Rosanna herself noticed that there were soft pads of flesh where there used to be straight lines. And she began to smell differently, not bad, just different. Like something fertile, wild and strange. This was soon followed by the monthly flow of blood that came hand in hand with pain.

Rosanna's cotton undershirts no longer contained her new body and her mother insisted she wear chemises, which made her itch. She favored twisting her long dark hair into a pair of braids that trailed down her back. People said it made her look like an Indian princess but she felt from a princess these days, especially with Tony pounding away, raining rivulets of fetid sweat onto her cool, dry skin.

When Rosanna was a girl, she loved to run—and she felt like running now. Running and running and never coming back. In grade school, her specialty had been relay races and she was good at them, too. In fact, she still had the medals to prove it, hidden in a half-forgotten box under her bed. She liked the feel of a baton in her hand—hard and warm and almost alive. Rosanna thought of this as she lay in bed with her husband, reluctantly taking him in her hand. Firmly, as you'd hold a broom handle, and without emotion. It was simply a job that had to be done, like cleaning. But not nearly as rewarding. And just like cleaning, the dirt would pile up and sooner rather than later, you'd have to do it again.

Tony was on top of her now, not even looking into her face. His shoulder was wedged just under her chin. She could see all the way into the kids' bedroom windows from the high mahogany bed. Just outside the middle window, beside the old

ginkgo, was a flowering pear tree, its clusters of delicate white
flowers a gift of springtime. She traced its fragile lines with her
eyes as Tony absently pounded, pushed and cursed under his
breath, then was quiet.

When Rosanna was a child, they had a real pear tree in the
front yard and a peach tree out back. Both were long dead. At
night, they would gather on someone's porch and harmonize to
popular songs of the day. "Smile Awhile" was one of her
favorites and it sounded so lovely in the still, warm darkness.
Her father had the first crystal radio on the block. The neighbors
would huddle around it and take turns listening, good-naturedly
grabbing the headphones from each other when a particularly
rousing boxing match was broadcast. She smiled into her
husband's heaving chest, in spite of herself. Those were
happy days.

Peeling herself out from under Tony's body, Rosanna was
soon at the sink again, thinking of how very different things were
now. *She* was different. She had long stopped running. She had
weathered and matured. She had become cracked and wounded,
just like the streets and the crooked rooftops. And there was dirt
everywhere. No matter how hard or how long she scrubbed,
she just couldn't seem to get it clean. But she also couldn't
stop trying.

She started with the windows.

3 Downstairs

"You dirty stink! I'll break your nut!" Bridget said, tripping over a fluff ball of a dog as she hoisted a steaming pot of gravy from stove to tabletop.

Tiger loved being downstairs in his grandparents' apartment. There was always something happening, something good. Either Butchie and Ted were in a tizzy or his grandmother was making meatballs or maybe Aunt Astrid had stopped by, straight from her job as a milliner, with wispy feathers clinging to her shoes and skirt. The radio was always crackling either with music or with a serial: "Who knows what evil lurks in the hearts of men? The Shadow does."

And Tiger did, too.

The very air seemed different downstairs. Laden with happiness, hope and adventure. At any given moment, anything could change. His grandfather might shuttle him off to the Navy Yard to survey a destroyer—Poppa had worked on a slew of tugs, cutters, light cruisers and battleships, including the *U.S.S. Arizona*, which was built there—or his Uncle John might take him to work with him at the projection booth in the Sanders or the Minerva in Park Slope. You never could tell.

It was Easter morning. Hidden eggs found and bright baskets of sweets discovered, Grandma Bridget was now making manicotti. She let Tiger stir the batter for the shells, which she made from scratch, or "from scraps," as Poppa said. Tiger carefully blended the egg, flour and water into a sunny paste. Rosanna never let him help cook, explaining that he was too messy. And his father said it was women's work, something only sissies did. But downstairs Tiger was free to do all sorts of magical things he couldn't do upstairs.

Already, there was a ham baking in the oven, glazed pink with a lovely concoction of honey, black-strap molasses and orange juice, speared with canned pineapples rings and maraschino cherries. Bridget let Tiger stab the pineapples and cherries into the ham with toothpicks, albeit a bit too violently, but in the end, he did the job just fine. There were mashed, candied sweet potatoes too and when it was time, Bridget would let him cover the dish with marshmallows. This she would cook to perfection until the marshmallows were toasted a delicate brown and never burned.

"How's school?" Bridget asked as she flipped a manicotta shell effortlessly in the cast-iron frying pan.

"School's school," Tiger shrugged. "It's okay." He was in the fourth grade at Public School 131 down on 43rd Street and Fort Hamilton Parkway.

"You do good in school, you do good in life," she told her grandson.

As Bridget lightly fried the manicotti shells, Tiger rolled ovals of salami into little tubes for the antipasto and piled them onto a plate. When he and Bridget were finished with the manicotti, together they would assemble the wonderful salad, the first course of their Easter dinner. Antipasto was generally the opener for every big family meal at the Paradiso house, always delicious yet always slightly different. Sometimes it was dotted with pepperoni, roasted peppers or cured olives, other times it was festooned with deviled eggs, celery and carrot sticks, which Bridget let Tiger pare and cut all by himself.

"Who else is coming?" Tiger asked his grandmother. He sat at the table with a bowl of ricotta, a pan of spaghetti sauce, cubes of mozzarella and an empty tray in front of him. Bridget eased her pleasantly-rounded body into the kitchen chair beside him. Tiger could feel her shelf-like chest softly pressing into his arm as she leaned forward slightly, silently presiding over the proceedings. He could also smell a hint of anisette on her breath. "Just a small glass," Poppa had told her earlier, "to ring in a pleasant holiday." And that's all she had, half of a dainty shot glass worth. His father would have guzzled half the bottle.

Tiger gently lifted a flimsy pancake, still warm from the frying pan, and placed it on the tabletop. "Just the usual..." Bridget answered thoughtfully, "and your father."

Tiger cautiously spooned a dollop of ricotta cheese, beaten silky with egg and mixed with grated cheese, onto the manicotti pancake. "If your dad makes it home in time," his grandmother added.

Bridget guided Tiger's spoon back into the ricotta. "A smidge more...Don't be stingy," she told him, smoothing down her apron. "It won't be the same since Sophie, Kelly and the kids moved out to Arizona, but..."

"It will be a lot more quiet," Tiger said.

"Maybe a little too quiet," Bridget smiled.

Tiger sprinkled a generous handful of mozzarella onto the mound of creamy ricotta and spread it flat with the back of the spoon and wondered, "How about Aunt Jo and Uncle Harry?"

Bridget stirred the gravy she'd transferred from the large pot to a smaller one. "You know she hasn't been right since she lost the baby. Says she can't come out yet because all she sees is babies, babies everywhere. But just give her time, though. She'll come around." Bridget took a deep breath, then continued. "And as for your uncle, he's working overtime but might stop by for dessert with Sully."

Tiger thoughtfully rolled up the first manicotta and placed it on the tray, lifting it tenderly as one might cradle a newborn kitten. Then he started working on another manicotta. When they finished an entire tray, he would smother the manicotti with his grandmother's sweet tomato sauce. Then they would build another tray.

"*Nu*? What's this?" It was Dr. Lewis. He lived across the street and loved making house calls to 1128 47th Street, especially on Sundays. Today, Kewpie was sick with stomach cramps again. She was curled up in bed and claimed she could barely walk. Said she felt too bad to hunt for Easter eggs so Tiger found them all and split his booty with his sister. Dr. Lewis had been summoned to check on her.

Bridget looked over her shoulder at the squat, pear-shaped man. His horn-rimmed glasses always seemed on the verge of sliding off the slope of his potato-like nose, which dipped toward his mouth. Dr. Lewis had been the family doctor since the Paradiso Family moved to the block. "How about a meatball?" Bridget asked.

"Is it Kosher?"

"About as Kosher as you'll get in this house," she concluded. "The meat's from Adler's but with cheese and bread soaked in milk…"

Bridget poked around in the gravy pot. Dr. Lewis was already making space for his black leather bag on the crowded table and pulling up a chair. Bridget plopped a heavy meatball into a flowered cake plate and handed Dr. Lewis a fork. He was digging into the meatball before she even set down the plate in front of him.

"How's Kewpie?" Bridget wondered.

"The usual," Dr. Lewis told her between bites. "Hot water bottle and an aspirin and she'll be good as new."

"Did Rosanna settle up with you?"

"This will do," Dr. Lewis said, pushing the empty plate toward her.

"Thank you, Morris," she said quietly. "How about another?"

Dr. Lewis tugged at the tip of his prominent beak. "Well, I really shouldn't…Eva is making a brisket…" But Bridget had another meatball in the plate before he finished explaining and he gobbled it up almost as quickly as the first.

Astrid and Sam came into the house as they generally did, arguing. Upon Astrid's head was one of her latest creations. This hat was big as a serving platter and appeared to be just as hefty. It was piled high with ostrich plumes and covered with fake orchids that dripped over its wide brim, much like Dr. Lewis's proboscis drooped toward his mouth. Astrid looked a great deal like Rosanna, except for her nose, which was tiny and upturned. Before Tiger was old enough to remember, Astrid had her nose fixed. It was around the same time she changed her name and became a blonde.

"Hmmm, you nose didn't look broken to me," Poppa quipped when she showed up one day all bandaged and bruised. "But now it does."

"There was nothing wrong with your nose," Bridget insisted And indeed, there wasn't. This was a family of proud, long, bumpy, Roman noses, and to admit there'd been something awry with Astrid's former muzzle was to criticize their own.

"I think you had a fine nose," Rosanna snorted, for Astrid's old nose had been an exact replica of her own. But Astrid waved them all away and waited expectantly for the unveiling of her corrected snout.

When the swelling finally went down, Astrid's nose looked strangely unfinished, too small for her face and for her abundant personality, which admittedly, was not a good one, yet it was a personality just the same. Astrid was as happy with her store-bought nose as she would be with a nicely-tailored $15 dollar suit from Abraham and Straus. And she wore her new honker just as proudly. Although she never told Sam about her nasal augmentation, he probably knew just the same. How could he not? Why would she be the only one in the Paradiso clan bestowed with a button nose?

Sam was helping Astrid out of her jacket of mouton lamb when Rosanna walked into the dining room, carrying a large platter. "Nice of you to show up when all the work is done," Rosanna huffed, instead of hello. She put the antipasto onto the almost-filled dining room table and disappeared into the depths of her mother's kitchen.

Astrid admired the pretty pinwheel pattern of food: tomatoes, mozzarella, circles of hardboiled egg. Rolls of Genoa salami sliced through it like the spokes of a wheel. Little heaps of marinated carrots and cauliflower were interspersed throughout, as were olives of two colors: khaki green and shiny black like the coal in the cellar bin. When Astrid reached forward to sneak a taste, Rosanna smacked away her hand. "Jeez Louise, you're always prowling around like a cat," Astrid complained.

"You'll ruin it," Rosanna told her, then put down a basket of bread. "Besides, you have to wait for Grace."

"Is Grace coming too?" Sam wondered and caught Rosanna around the waist.

When she brandished the bread knife at her brother-in-law, Sam released Rosanna in mock fear. "Heathen," she smiled and headed back toward the kitchen. "And it wouldn't kill you to help set the table, Margaret," Rosanna called to her sister.

"It's Astrid," she called back.

Tiger came in with a slab of butter on a plate and made space for it on the table beside the bread. "You make this?" Sam asked his nephew, gesturing toward the antipasto as Astrid slipped a tube of salami between her fire-engine-red lips.

"I helped," Tiger admitted.

"Nice." Sam patted Tiger on the head and pretended to pull a dime from behind his ear. "Buy yourself something you're not supposed to have," Sam told the boy surreptitiously, handing him the coin.

The kitchen was a flurry of activity. Boiling pots were everywhere. Two trays of manicotti cooled on windowsills. The gorgeous, glistening ham waited tolerantly on the table. Camille put the marshmallow-covered sweet potatoes mixture into the oven as her husband John, wearing an apron over his shirt and tie, dipped a heel of Italian bread into the gravy.

"Not yet, Camille," Bridget said. "Tony's not..."

Rosanna broke in. "Don't wait for Tony."

"We eat as a family, Roe."

Rosanna couldn't look anyone in the eye, not even Tiger. "He didn't come home last night," she said to the glazed ham.

John rested one hand on his sister-in-law's shoulder and unfastened his apron with his other hand. He felt her flinch slightly. "I'll go look for him."

Rosanna shook her head.

"But he could be dead in the street somewhere," Camille protested.

26

Tiger's heart did a joyful flip. He lived in hope.

"No, John," said Rosanna. "Not this time." She went into the hallway to call for Kewpie then continued down the hall to the front porch to let Poppa know supper was ready. He laid down his pipe and newspaper on the card table and followed her inside. In a minute, they were all there. All except for Tony.

Dinner was a blur of plates being passed back and forth, of food being swept up, swallowed and replaced. There was a certain poetry to the meal, a particular order. Not in the stuffy, Emily Post sense, but in a natural, humanistic manner. Everyone made sure the others had enough to eat before digging in for more themselves.

For example, you asked if someone wanted the last of the marinated mushrooms before swishing it onto your plate. If you knew someone liked eggplant as much as Poppa did, you pushed the remainder onto his dish without asking, like Bridget did just now. If you remembered that Sam enjoyed the curl of pigskin Bridget always put into the gravy for extra flavor, simmered to a succulent orange tendril, you offered it to him first. And there were no false niceties, no polite "Oh no, I just couldn't..." Because you could. Of course, you could. You were with family and there was no sense pretending.

Rosanna herself was tired of pretending. Pretending could be an extremely exhausting business. She was sick of acting as though everything was all right when in reality, it wasn't. Even though she tried her best to hide it, to cover for Tony's shenanigans, the whole family and most of the neighbors knew what was going on. Only they were too polite to say anything.

Kewpie toyed with the manicotti on her plate until the center oozed out, all white and creamy in a sea of red sauce. She knew that her grandmother beat the ricotta smooth with egg and added a pinch of Parmesan when most people just plunked the cheese, straight from the container, into a store-bought shell. Bridget, in turn, knew that manicotti was Kewpie's favorite. This is why she made it instead of lasagna, her grandson's first choice. These days, Kewpie seemed to need a little more of a pick-me-up than Tiger did.

Sunday was the only day Rosanna allowed the kids soda, insisting always upon milk for strong bones and teeth. But Bridget put her foot down at serving tomato sauce with milk at any time; the very thought made her ample stomach do flip-flops. Poppa poured Tiger a glass of root beer without asking. Then Poppa, the keeper of the soda vault, returned the sacred bottle to the spot on the floor beside his feet where he guarded it like Cerberus.

Conversation swirled around Kewpie's head, moved through her like smoke:

"Take that damn thing off your head, Astrid...It looks like a pigeon gone beserk..."

"I'll have you know this is the height of..."

"Tiger, elbows off the..."

"Where'd you get the sausage, Momma? It tastes..."

"So, then I said to him, 'If you don't like it..."

"Sam, you told this one at least a million times before. How many..."

"The Kloppenbergs are a very good-looking people..."

"Are you kidding? Minna with that *faccia cavallo*?"

"...Spencer Tracy. They say it's the best picture he ever..."

"Stop being such a *gavone*, Johnny..."

"Lettie, Julius and the boys are at..."

"Kewpie, you hardly ate."

Pasta plates were cleared away, washed and put back onto the table. The sisters swiftly left and returned with new platters: ham, sweet potatoes, escarole, corn, boiled white potatoes tossed in butter and fresh chopped parsley. Sounds began blending together: cutlery scraping china, chewing, bread being torn into chunks, sighs of culinary ecstasy and brief silence broken by the screech of the El's brakes in the distance.

Then came the sound Kewpie dreaded most of all: the sound of a key in the door. His key. First, the jingling, which could have been the noise of the dogs' tags ringing against their collars as they begged frantically for table scraps. But no. It was him. Next, came the scrape of key in lock, then the shove of a firm shoulder against the front door.

John glanced up from his plate and saw his niece's shoulders slump forward, as if in defeat. Tiger's body noticeably stiffened as his father's drunken footsteps tapped closer and echoed down the hall. Rosanna didn't even look up, just placed her fork in her plate and waited.

Tony stood in the doorway a moment before coming in. He was still wearing his uniform. "Happy Easter, everybody," he bellowed. Although he tried to regulate the timbre of his voice, his volume control seemed to be busted. He balanced a sack of cookies from Piccolo's precariously on the edge of the table. When it fell to the ground, he didn't even bother trying to pick it up. Probably because he knew there was a very good chance he'd topple over.

On shaky legs, Tony navigated his way to his empty place setting at the table. Rosanna bolted up. "I'll get you some manicotti."

He grabbed her wrist, a little too roughly, in protest. "No, you sit. Eat. Enjoy," he told her. But Rosanna couldn't eat; he was still holding onto her right wrist. She wilted back into her seat without mentioning it.

Tiger turned away from his father and instead, concentrated on the candied sweet potatoes. He examined the toasted marshmallow crust until his eyes watered. Perhaps if he could have just a spoonful, a smidgen, a taste, it would miraculously set everything right again. "Dad, could you please pass the sweet potatoes?" he asked his father, trying to involve him in the meal.

Rosanna tried to wrestle her wrist out of Tony's grip. "I'll do it," she said.

Tony finally released her arm. "What? I can't take care of my own son?" the tipsy man asked rhetorically.

Still standing, Tony leaned forward, a little too forward because he fell directly into the sweet potatoes, face first.

Easter dinner was officially over.

4 Naming Names

It seemed to Tiger that everyone in his family had more than one name. First, there was your given name, the one handwritten in script on your birth certificate. "*Remember thy Creator in the days of thy youth*," it said in a fancy scrolled flourish near the bottom of his, which was from Methodist Episcopal Hospital on Sixth Street. The scroll curled around an oval which depicted a cartoon-like Christ Child hugging an equally crudely-drawn Mother Mary tightly about the neck.

Your Christian name was the one the nuns at religious instruction at Saint Catherine's insisted on calling you because they only recognized Saints' names. "I never heard of a Saint Tiger, Anthony Joseph Martino, Jr.," Sister Patrick Maureen constantly reminded him. (The kids dubbed her Sister Patrick Moron behind her back, which was definitely not her Christian name.) Who ever heard of a woman called Patrick? Maybe she wasn't really a woman at all. And under all those black and white robes, assorted hoods and mysterious layers, past the calamari collar that ringed her neck, beyond the clinking strand of rosary beads as frightening and foreboding as Jacob Marley's chains in *A Christmas Carol*, who really knew?

So, in addition to your Christian name, there was your nickname. Tiger's grandfather was responsible for most of the family monikers and they were always perfect. In fact, Poppa had given Tiger his and that's one reason the boy liked it so much.

Named after his father, Tiger was known as Junior until he was about six. Small and scrappy, Tiger fancied himself a big bruiser, even before he was christened with his formidable handle. As the story goes, one day the boy was proudly displaying his miniscule bicep for Poppa. Tiger stood on a dining room chair, chest puffed, flexing his spaghetti-thin arm. He flexed it so hard that his knickers fell down. Poppa laughed so vigorously that he fell into a chair. "You're a real Tiger McPunch," he said, wiping the tears from his eyes, thus christening the nondescript boy with a pugilist's name. Tiger would certainly have to be tough with a father like his, Poppa reasoned silently to himself. Maybe having a strong name would help. But then again, probably not.

Poppa was also the one who started calling Tiger's sister Angela "Kewpie." It came to him the first time he ever saw her, swaddled in a pink blanket Bridget had crocheted herself, as Rosanna carried the baby into the house straight from United Israel-Zion. The child was so chubby and peachy that her skin resembled stuffed plastic. She reminded Poppa of a Kewpie doll from Coney Island: plump, rosy-cheeked, with enough hair for a topknot. Everyone else agreed, and from then on, Angela was known as Kewpie.

Even though Kewpie no longer resembled her namesake, the soubriquet, as Aunt Astrid would say, still remained. In recent years, Kewpie had grown into a tall, slender teenager, willowy even in cheap clothes and slacks. Her hair was honey-blonde and bone straight, coaxed into a flutter of waves by pin curls laboriously fastened to her head with bobby pins every night. Her fair skin was dusted with freckles. Her eyes were brilliant and laughing, except when she was home. Except when her father was home, was closer to the truth. That's when they became dark, gray and clouded, as though a storm had rolled in. And indeed, one had.

Then there was Kelly. Born Nicholas, he was one heck of a ball player. The first time Poppa saw his son whack a hardball two sewers away with a broomstick handle and watched him round the trashcan-cover bases to home plate (an empty feed bag), he yelled, "Slide, Kelly, slide!" It was a popular cry from an old song of the same name which originally referred to Mike "King" Kelly, the Chicago Nationals' flamboyant catcher-outfielder. Though it had been many years since Nicholas played stick ball, he was still known as Kelly.

Veronica, the nice Jewish girl Kelly had taken for a wife, also possessed a handful of handles. At her naming ceremony eight days after her birth, the rabbi proclaimed her Sophie but Veronica was the name she herself chose when she converted to Catholicism to marry Kelly. Although Kelly had fallen in love with a buxom gal named Sophie, he still loved Veronica, or Sophie Veronica as she was sometimes called, perhaps twice as fiercely. But Kelly was also fond of referring to his wife as "Dear Old Girl" in private. Despite the fact that she wasn't old—she was a few years his junior—she was still dear to his heart. Few people knew of Veronica's lovely nickname but Tiger heard Uncle Kelly slip with it once or twice, and the boy smiled each time.

Now, Tiger's grandmother's Christian name was Margarita in Italian, Margaret in English, but no one ever used either. Some close friends and longtime neighbors didn't even know her real name. As far back as anyone could remember, Poppa called her Bridget, short for "Bridget O'Flynn," after the song, because she looked more Irish than Italian, with her startling green eyes, creamy ivory skin and light hair. Her hair was threaded with three shades of gray these days but was still beautiful. So, people either knew her as Bridget or Mrs. Paradiso, if they didn't know her very well. And her children called her Momma, even when they were grown.

Poppa himself had a slew of nicknames. The grandkids, even his own kids and wife, referred to him as Poppa. As the unofficial mayor of 47th Street, he was affectionately known as

Uncle Mike by most of Borough Park and simply as Mike at the Brooklyn Navy Yard. He spoke smatterings of eight different languages, even Chinese to Mr. Wong who ran the chop suey place under the El. No one called him Michael Archangel, his given name, except for Bridget, every so often in the dark, in a whisper so faint he could barely hear it. But he could feel it. And it sounded just like it did when they were young.

Harry's patrol partner and best friend Sully was christened Patrick Sullivan. "We were so poor, they couldn't afford to give me a middle name," he liked to quip to Tiger. But no one called him by his real name either. He was always Sully, except to Rosanna, who dubbed him Paddy, sometimes Patrick, but never Sully. And she always said his name with a slight smile curling her lips, as though it felt good just to say it.

Even the El had many names. Officially, it was known as the West End Line but few called it that. The El was shorthand, a secret code. To some, it was simply "The Train." Yet, the El was so much more than just a train. It was majestic, precarious, dangerous, rising impossibly above the streets like an urban snake. Rectangular concrete blocks more than two foot by three foot anchored its girders of steel to the street below. Its massive wooden railroad ties took four strong men to lift. Spikes, now beginning to rust, plates and rails held the ties in place. Then there was the slick, smooth, scary third rail. One touch of your boot sole could turn you into a crispy critter.

How did they build the El? How did it stay up there, so solid and true? Why didn't it just crumble and collapse? Tiger had seen a Packard plow into the footing once, shatter a corner of concrete, and the El didn't so much as shudder. It boggled his mind and even frightened him a bit. Sometimes he lay awake at night, across the room from Kewpie, listening to the El's oddly-soothing grumble in the distance, worrying that if just one girder popped out of place, the whole thing would come crashing down, collapsing like a row of dominoes from Ninth Avenue where it rose up out of the tunnel, all the way to Coney Island, raining steel and wood onto New Utrecht Avenue, maybe even spearing through the roof of his house.

But the crash never came. The El ebbed and flowed out to Coney Island like the ocean, bringing his father away and back again. How many times did Tony go back and forth during the length of a shift? On the last go-around, Tiger's father would be ushered almost to their doorstep via the El, sometimes coming straight home but more often than not, stopping at the no-name bar under the El to take the edge off.

Tony's footsteps were sometimes light and brisk, but mostly, they were weighty, stumbling up the brick steps at some ungodly hour. There were only five front steps in all, but they could be tricky as they tended to slip and move and shift underfoot after he'd tipped back a few.

The house's outside door was kept unlocked, however, the inside door was a challenge because it involved fitting a tiny, unruly key into a shrinking slot. The weathered wooden staircase to the Martinos' second story railroad flat seemed as insurmountable as Everest, at least to a drunk. The winter before, Harry and Kelly had carpeted the stairs with a runner of red roses, a pattern which Bridget had picked. But instead of muffling Tony's late night entries, the rug only seemed to magnify them. Try as he might, Tony could never make it up the steps in one shot. Awake in his pitch black room, Tiger could hear the banister creak rebelliously as Tony leaned against it or else he'd hear the stairs groan if his father had chosen to take a seat and rest his swirling head.

Once, Tony had tumbled down the staircase headfirst, cracking his skull on the hall radiator. He'd lain there, knocked out cold, blood trickling from the open wound in his head until Bridget discovered him with a gasp the next morning. Dr. Lewis rushed across 47th Street with his trench coat hastily belted over his nightshirt and put two stitches in Tony's forehead.

After that, Tony didn't hesitate to crawl up the stairs on his hands and knees if necessary. On those nights, he was too plastered to find his way into Tiger and Kewpie's room, even into his own bedroom. Often, they'd find him curled up on the kitchen floor with a tablecloth pulled up to his chin like a sheet. Those were the times Tiger hated him most. But Rosanna did her best to see that her husband was securely tucked into bed before the kids got up in the morning. She didn't want them to see him like that.

Yes, everyone in the Paradiso Family had nicknames. But not as many as Tiger's father had. Anthony Joseph Martino, Sr.'s litany of names were whispered harshly under the breath or uttered sadly with a shake of the head. Or else they were shouted, sometimes accompanied by a fist pounding upon a table. But never in front of Rosanna or the children.

Here is a sampling:

The Bastard. (Poppa)

Low-Life Drunk. (Uncle John)

S.O.B. (Bridget; she never cursed.)

Good-For-Nothing. (Aunt Astrid; she didn't swear either.)

Fuckface. (Uncle Sam; he cursed like the sailor he used to be.)

What's in a name? A name says it all. Tiger was named for his father, which is why he preferred his nickname.

But not even the nuns at St. Catherine's understood.

5 Stillborn

It was already May and Aunt Jo still hadn't been to the house. And she only lived three blocks away, on 44th Street. While Uncle Harry stopped by regularly after his shift to pick up leftovers for their dinner, Aunt Jo wasn't leaving the apartment and she wasn't cooking either. He said that she barely ate. Bridget and Rosanna tried to visit her most afternoons but sometimes, she wouldn't let them in. "She'll come around," Bridget said knowingly.

And one day, she did.

Poppa was at work. Bridget and Rosanna were up at 13th Avenue, grabbing a quick bite at Kresge's then picking up a few things for supper. Tiger was downstairs in his grandparents' apartment, flipping baseball cards against the breakfront. He was ten after all, and could be left alone for an hour or two. The women promised him a cannoli upon their return.

When Tiger heard the front door open, he thought it might be his delicious crunchy pastry shell stuffed with sweetened ricotta cheese and chocolate chips. But instead, it was Aunt Jo, christened Josephina, but no one ever called her that. Of all Tiger's aunts, she was his favorite. Maybe it was because Aunt Jo was so unlike any of the others. Where they were dark and angular, Aunt Jo was petite, slightly pear-shaped and peach-colored. Even her hair was lighter, more like his sister's. In fact, Kewpie looked more like Aunt Jo's daughter than Rosanna's. His aunt also had an easy laugh and a healthy sense of humor.

Aunt Jo closed the door quietly behind her. She was wearing a pale green suit and a matching hat that slouched on top of her head. A sheer black net came down from the hat's brim, obscuring the top half of her face and shielding her eyes. Aunt Jo let out a startled "Oh!" when she saw Tiger. After a moment he ran to her and wrapped his arms around her waist, which was still nicely plump from the baby. But he tried not to hug her too hard because he knew she'd been in the hospital. Only he wasn't exactly sure what had happened.

"I missed you, Tiger McPunch," she said softly, rearranging his cowlick, which popped right back up again.

"I missed you too, Aunt Jo."

She held him at arm's length so she could take a good look at him. Pleasantly bony, worn knee pants, hand-me-down shirt, socks that never stayed up, scuffed shoes. He looked exactly the same as she remembered him. "Hmmm," Aunt Jo told Tiger. "You've gotten bigger."

"Think so?"

"I know so." Aunt Jo looked past the dining room into the darkened kitchen. She listened for movement upstairs but there was nothing, just the El, slicing above the streets a distance away. "Where is everybody?" she wondered.

"Shopping. Working."

"Sleeping off a drunk?"

Tiger just shrugged.

"Ah, so he's disappeared again."

"Don't know where he is." Then he added, "Don't care." But she knew he cared. How could a boy not?

When Aunt Jo sat on the red tufted sofa, it looked like Christmas between the color of her outfit and the shade of the couch. The cushions and backrest were worn to a comfortable rosy sheen. She pulled a hat pin from her amber curls then lay the hat on the sofa arm and pierced it with the pin. Tiger wondered if the hat was one of Aunt Astrid's creations but didn't ask. It didn't matter anyway.

Josephina O'Leary (nee Paradiso) seemed more relaxed now as she fished a pack of Lucky Strikes from her purse, then reached for Poppa's box of matches on the coffee table. She slid a cigarette between her lips and sighed. "Smoke?" she asked Tiger, offering him one. He laughed it away, shaking his head.

On the wall above Aunt Jo's head was a painting called "The Innocents." A crusty old relative in Cosenza had sent it to Poppa and Bridget as a wedding gift forty some odd years ago. It depicted a young boy and a young girl curled up in the ecstasy of sleep. Their arms and legs were wrapped around each other. Their nightshirts were rumpled. The girl's sun-colored curls were sprawled out on a squishy green pillow beneath her head. A doll in a faded pink dress stared out into Poppa and Bridget's parlor. The painting had an odd, other-worldly quality which Tiger didn't like. It made him feel strange, unsettled.

When he was boy, Uncle Julius painted everything in sight. At some point, he'd done a copy of "The Innocents," which hung upstairs above Rosanna and Tony's bed. Tiger always wondered if his mother were trying to recreate the tranquility and sweet madness of the apartment downstairs by hanging a reproduction of the painting above her own marriage bed. Rosanna's feeble attempt failed miserably, however.

That afternoon, Aunt Jo took note of the painting, which had hung there for decades, practically ignored. "You see?" she said. "Babies. They're everywhere." Then she started to cry.

Tiger didn't know what to do. When the cigarette fell from Aunt Jo's fingers onto the parquet floor, he picked it up and placed it into the carved, glass ashtray. A trail of smoke drifted toward the ceiling. Tiger sat awkwardly on the couch beside his aunt. At first, he couldn't understand a word she said but he just let her go on talking anyway. Then he suddenly understood her babble. Her baby. Aunt Jo was crying for her baby.

"The doctors told me not to talk about it," she sobbed. "They said I should just forget it. Forget it! And it wasn't an 'it.' It was a baby. My baby." Tiger had never seen anyone cry this hard before, let alone a grown-up. Sometimes he heard Rosanna or Kewpie sobbing faintly in the night but these were always such haunted, hidden sounds, more like hiccoughs than hysterics. But the way Aunt Jo wailed was truly terrible, so deep and desolate that it made him want to cry himself.

Aunt Jo wrapped her arms around herself, rocking slightly as one might do to comfort a child, and she kept right on crying. Tiger took a balled-up handkerchief out of his pocket. It was a little grubby but Aunt Jo took it gladly, blew her nose and swabbed her tears. Her face was still awful, though. Much worse than Lon Chaney's in *The Phantom of the Opera*. They'd played the old silent film at the Loews 46th last Halloween and it scared Tiger so much that it gave him nightmares.

Like the Phantom, Aunt Jo's face was horrifying, except hers was streaked with black and beige makeup. Her Cherry Chanteuse lipstick appeared to be bleeding and now it was all over his handkerchief. Tiger would burn it in the alley so Rosanna didn't see.

"They wouldn't even let me name her, Tiger," Aunt Jo sobbed. "Could you imagine that? They wouldn't even let me name my own daughter."

In the framed painting above the sofa, The Innocents pretended to sleep but they were really listening. Tiger knew they were wide awake and that they heard every word.

The boy waited a moment then said, "But you did name her, didn't you?"

"How did you know?"

"I had a feeling," he told her softly.

Aunt Jo cleared her throat. "Hope," she murmured. "I named my daughter Hope." She smiled slightly, remembering.

"I like that name," Tiger told her and squeezed her hand.

"Me, too," she said, patting it.

It was so quiet that Tiger could hear the clock from the Ansonia Clock Factory ticking on the wall. On its face was the sun, a crescent moon, a handful of stars and some clouds. Poppa gave Tiger the job of winding this clock with a brass key every morning and the boy never once forgot. "What did she look like?" Tiger wondered.

Aunt Jo's face seemed to brighten, then fog over. "Oh, she was so beautiful. She was perfect...every finger and toe. Her mouth was like a rosebud. She was so chubby and beautiful, even had hair like mine. She was perfect..."

"What happened?" Tiger asked like the little child he was. "No one would tell me exactly what happened."

Aunt Jo's mouth trembled but she didn't cry anymore. "Nobody knows what happened," she told him. "They think the cord...They said...They said I shouldn't blame myself, but I do. Maybe if I took better care of myself, if I ate better, if I got more rest, if I worried less..." Her voice trailed off. "I didn't start smoking again until afterwards," she said, then ducked out the stub of the Lucky Strike in the ashtray.

"I heard Aunt Astrid say something about you losing the baby," Tiger struggled. "Where did you lose her?" His honest green eyes pleaded for an answer.

"That's just something people say when a baby dies, Tiger. My baby...Hope just...died. That's all. It happens sometimes, I suppose."

Tiger finally understood. "Then it's nobody's fault. Is it?"

"No," Aunt Jo repeated. "It's nobody's fault."

The Ansonia clock on the wall struck four. Both Tiger and Aunt Jo jumped slightly. "Do you believe what they say about unbaptized babies, Tiger?" she asked. "That they don't go to heaven, I mean?"

Tiger considered this for a moment. "No," he said firmly. "No. I don't. I don't think God would do that to a tiny baby. It doesn't seem right. But don't tell Sister Patrick Maureen I said so."

The Catholic Church taught that all unbaptized souls, babies and otherwise, went to a place called limbo. Nobody knew exactly what limbo was like, only that it wasn't quite heaven, wasn't quite hell. The very name made Tiger imagine an endless line of infants, Jews and Chinamen alike, dancing under a very low, very long stick to a jaunty Calypso song that was perhaps sung by Billie Holiday rather than Ethel Merman. But all in all, limbo didn't sound like a very nice place.

"I think there's a special part of heaven for babies like Hope," Tiger told his aunt.

She smiled. "I think so too," she said.

Aunt Jo lit another cigarette and took a long drag. This time she didn't offer one to Tiger. "I never told anyone this," she began. "Not even your uncle. But I held her. The nurse asked if I wanted to. Of course, I did. She also asked your uncle but he said no and left the room fast. The baby felt so good in my arms. Her little body was still warm. The nurse must have read on my chart that I was Catholic. She asked if I wanted to baptize my daughter and I told her 'yes.' Together, we baptized her. It wasn't the same as Father Dunn doing it but I guess that counts for something."

After not being able to talk about it for so long, Aunt Jo suddenly couldn't stop talking about it. She kept right on talking after they heard the outside door open and click closed. "But what gets me is that some people don't appreciate what they have," she said. "They have three, five, nine kids and they treat them like dirt. And here, I can't even have one. It's just not fair."

Aunt Jo glanced at the partially-open door and met the angry gaze of Tiger's father as he stomped past Bridget and Poppa's apartment and up the stairs. Tony wanted to tell his sister-in-law that life itself wasn't fair but he figured she already knew that.

6 Child of the Streets

Tony didn't know why he was the way he was, only that he was. All his life he tried to fight his cruel nature and evil intentions—and lost. He'd never known his father and he had no good memories of his mother, no matter how hard or how far back he thought. Even his remotely-pleasant recollections about her were rimmed with bad.

Philomena Martino was a severe-looking woman with one solid eyebrow running across her furrowed forehead. She finally died the year before last but Tony didn't shed one tear or feel a sense of loss. Good-bye and good riddance summed up his sentiments. He and his brothers bought the cheapest pine box they could find to lay out Philomena at Joe Bruno's. Only a handful of people attended her wake. Tony stood at the back of the room, snickering with Paulie and Tommy. Their sister Marie didn't even bother to come.

Tiger, who was a very warm, affectionate boy, didn't like his Grandma Phil. He said she scared him and squirmed at the very thought of visiting her. Often he had to be forced to kiss her hello, even with the promise of a sweet as bribery. At age five, he quipped that she reminded him of the Witch from Hansel and Gretel, only meaner. Tony didn't scold Tiger when the boy confided this to him in private because it was true.

When Tony was a child, Philomena operated a speakeasy of sorts in their run-down tenement apartment. This was even before Prohibition. A true visionary, she saw profit in catering to other people's vices and began making wine in the cavernous bathtub that stood in the middle of the kitchen. As an adult, Tony tried to reason that his mother was merely doing the best she could to raise four brats on her own, that she resorted to any means necessary to support the family single-handedly. There weren't many options for a husband-less woman at the turn of the century. But deep inside, Tony knew this wasn't the case. His mother was mean and cold-hearted, and she didn't give a stinking rat's ass about anyone but herself.

Philomena had no problem letting her offspring go about hungry and dirty while she herself was fat and perfumed. She'd throw the kids out of the apartment whenever she entertained customers or when she was throwing a party to reel in more clients. Her forte was selling drinks to drunks and introducing non-drinkers to the decadent pleasures of her cheap, strong wine—and other things.

Like most shady addresses, the apartment Tony grew up in had two means of egress. In this case, it was the front door and the fire escape. The latter led to a narrow alley between two crumbling tenements. The front door opened onto New Utrecht Avenue and the tracks of the El. The train sped past their parlor windows, which served Philomena's purposes just fine. The El was so loud that the neighbors couldn't hear anything that went on in the apartment and the clacking cars of the West End Line moved too quickly past the Martinos' third story windows for riders to process what they saw. But the dark, gritty curtains were usually pulled tight even in the stark light of day.

Soon after her brainstorm of selling rotgut wine, Philomena realized another decadent pleasure she could procure. You see, Tony's mother preyed on the weak of all varieties and these folks came in all sorts of ugly and pretty packages. There was no shortage of lovely immigrant girls in need and hideous old men who desired them. Perhaps these young ladies made it successfully through the rigors of Ellis Island but their family did not. There they were, strangers alone in a strange, frightening land with no one to look out for them. And that's where Philomena came in.

She had come to America unaccompanied herself, betrothed to a man she'd never met, promised in a marriage her parents had arranged when she was just a child. She knew what it was like to be afraid and isolated in an alien land. To these young women, Philomena served as sordid mother figure. She was a mother to all but her own children, who ran wild in the streets. Ask anyone. They'd tell you the same and they weren't being spiteful gossipers; it was just plain fact.

Perhaps these young ladies Philomena befriended were lucky enough to secure a menial job in a factory and then, to their dismay, received unwanted advances from their bosses. So, in addition to working in a sweatshop, they had to contend with the floor manager pressing up behind them between racks of clothing, kneading their breasts through their starched uniform, grinding against their body until he was through. All for no extra pay. And what could they do? They needed this rotten job to feed the hungry mouths in their house or to help bring more family members over from the Old Country and into squalor. After all, squalor was better than starvation.

Philomena was very sensitive to this dilemma, even reveled in it, then ultimately profited from it. Her scheme began as hiring a girl to help cook for her brood or clean the apartment. Although Philomena's children were filthy, her threadbare apartment was always spotless—it was a place of business, after all. Or perhaps these poor girls were brought in to work nights after their factory shifts to make a few extra pennies. At first, they would do easy work like filling wine bottles, tasks that couldn't be trusted to the clumsy, careless fingers of her children. Whichever method Philomena used to reel them in, it wasn't long before these girls were fulfilling other tasks.

Whoring was effortless work compared to the sweatshop. At least they could sleep till noon if they chose instead of getting up for a 12-hour shift that began at seven in the morning. At least they weren't doing a factory job they hated plus getting mauled besides. At least they were calling the shots—up to a point. And the take for one night on your back or on your knees was more than they'd earn a week in a sweatshop. As long as they brought in the bucks, Philomena was happy.

Romanians, Poles, Syrians, even Finns and Norwegians in need...Philomena employed them all. However, she drew the line at using her own people. Italians or Sicilians, for that matter. The darker the man, the lighter his preference in women, she noticed, so Nordic girls were choice especially among Jewish and Italian clientele. If Scandinavians were scarce, then a fair-haired, blue-eyed Polack would suffice.

Tony lay on top of the neatly-made bed thinking back on his childhood, not knowing why but remembering it just the same. His uniform pants were down around his ankles. In broad daylight, in the middle of the afternoon, anyone could walk in but he didn't give a damn. Tony hadn't been home for two, maybe three days—he'd swilled so much hooch, he couldn't be sure. He was dirty, still drunk, needed a bath and a shave, but there he lay on Rosanna's nice, clean bed, doing nothing but remembering.

Even as a kid, Tony's brother Paulie had a lot more sense. When Philomena threw him out on the street at night, Paulie would find a place to flop, taking their brother Tommy with him. Tommy wasn't right in the head, was born that way, and Paulie always looked out for him. Their sister Marie was born sickly and had a gimp leg besides. Polio they suspected, although Philomena never bothered taking her to the doctor to find out. There was always a place for Marie at one or another of her friend's homes. But Tony was a loner and he loved wandering the streets.

Sometimes Tony would sneak out a bottle full of his mother's wine, which the woman would sell to her teenage sons, but not give them. After all, business was business, even with family. To help pass the evening, street kids would play all sorts of cruel games in the cover of night. Sometimes they would throw a drunk a beating or set fire to a hobo's satchel. Sometimes Tony would put Marie into a shopping cart and roll her onto the trolley tracks. He'd leave her there, gaping at an oncoming vehicle wildly clanging its bell until she pissed herself in terror. But he always rescued his sister seconds before the trolley smashed her to bits, pulling the cart away in the nick of time. It was great fun, but how often could you do that?

Then the Martino children would disburse to their various friends' abodes, leaving Tony by himself. He couldn't go back to the apartment or his mother might beat him heartily with a belt, humiliating him in front of her customers. Many nights, Tony was so tired he'd make his way up the fire escape, curl into a ball and try to sleep. Other times, he just walked and walked until he felt he would drop.

One night, the curtains to the fire escape window were open and Tony saw Justina on her back, lying on the foul bed he shared with his brothers. Legs spread, Justina's skirts were turned up and Mr. Meyer, who owned the dry goods store, was hunched over her body. Justina's usually-appealing face was hardened in disgust until she turned her head and saw Tony watching her. Then she smirked. Before Tony knew what was happening, he was stiff, then spurting.

Justina's smile widened as the front of Tony's knickers darkened. He thought the reason for her grin was because Mr. Meyer had finally finished with her. The ancient Jew had let out an exhalation in Yiddish and suddenly stopped pounding. But Justina's smile was all for Tony. When his mother let her children back into the apartment that night, Tony buried his face in the used, still-damp bed sheets, smelling the young whore in them. He managed another sticky spew before Paulie and Tommy came home.

The next time Tony saw Justina, he was in the apartment alone. He was so exhausted that he'd skipped school just to sleep. Tony awakened midmorning, brandishing an impressive hard-on and was stumbling into the bathroom to pee. Justina was in the kitchen, delicately pouring blood-red wine into long-necked bottles. She stopped what she was doing, said nothing, approached the boy and reached into his drawers. There were rings of muck on his thighs and splotches of soil on his belly but neither deterred her.

"So stout," Justina noted. "And so dirty." She kept her hand wrapped around his shaft as she spoke. "Let's give it a quick wash and I'll put it in my mouth," she promised. Justina was soon busy with an enamel basin, a shake of Kirkman's soap flakes and a washrag. Even in the cold water, Tony stayed erect. As Justina splashed his cock and thighs, the water darkened with mud. One, two, three strokes and Tony's seed was floating, then sinking in the basin. Justina laughed and threw the gray mess out the kitchen window.

Another time, Tony encountered Justina and a red-haired, freckled Irishwoman by the name of Susie. He had just come into the apartment following a rare appearance at school. "You've got to see this," Justina giggled to her friend, tearing Tony's suspenders from his shoulders so his knickers fell. He sprung to life as the girls oohed and aahed.

"And he ain't even full grown yet," Susie marveled.

Right there on the kitchen floor, Tony took them one after the other. Crisp crumbs of bread and bits of unnamed, long-forgotten food clung to his knees. Tony slid in and out of their fleshy receptacles slick with other men's juices. They laughed as he fucked them each in turn, guffawing harder and harder the more desperate and urgent his movements became. When Tony was done, they grabbed the bucket and mop and washed the wet spots from the floor so Philomena wouldn't notice anything awry.

It was only a game to Justina but Tony fancied it love. Though the boy was nice enough, she saw seducing him as a way of getting back at her stone-hearted employer. She could lash back at Philomena by tainting her son, just as Justina herself had been ruined by others. Why not drag someone else down with her, like her old boss Mr. DiSanti had dragged her down and her Uncle Jake before him. It was a circle of hate and soon the boy was drowning in it. Tony was surrounded by people who corrupted others for fun and profit, and before he knew it, he was one of them.

Now a grown man, now so far gone he hardly recognized himself, Tony cleaned his body off on his shirttail. He didn't care whether or not Rosanna noticed the stain, but he knew she would, for nothing ever got past her.

There was the click of a door closing; Tony hadn't even heard it open. Kewpie bounded into the house, fresh from the candy counter at Kresge's. Her face dropped when she saw her father on the bed but she didn't scream or gasp. She was already gone and running back down the stairs before Tony realized what had happened.

7 Dairy Queen

"Go on, tell them, Tony," Rosanna urged her husband.

"But they've heard it all before," Tony told her.

"Come on, tell us again, Pop," Tiger begged. "Please?"

It amazed Tiger how his mother kept trying, no matter what. No matter how many times his father came home drunk. No matter how many nights he stayed away. No matter how many mornings he returned as though nothing had happened. No matter how many bruises she tried to hide. Rosanna kept forgiving him, kept trying to keep the peace, kept hoping. For without hope, what else was there?

They were all four in the kitchen, the center of Tiger's universe. The boy was doing homework. Tony was guzzling a cold beer. Kewpie was flipping through *Hollywood Revue*. Rosanna was chopping onions and garlic for peas and pasta, the dish she was making for dinner that night. It was a cheap, easy, delicious meal that pleased everyone—except Kelly's little girl Billie, who despised it. Chewy elbow macaroni cooked just right, sweet, wrinkled canned peas, chicken broth glistening with a thin sheen of olive oil on the surface. Rosanna found herself feeling almost happy as she minced.

"What do you think, Kewpie?" Tony asked. "Should I tell it?" Kewpie wasn't really listening. She was scrutinizing pictures of Myrna Loy as Billie Burke, surveying the miles and miles of silk Rayon used in the number "A Pretty Girl is Like a Melody." Kewpie was a pretty girl and she definitely was not like a melody, even on the best of days. She closed the magazine and picked up *Screen Gems*. "Sure," she said absentmindedly.

Tony cleared his throat then took another sip of his Schaefer. He wasn't officially drunk yet but well on his way. There was a fine line between jovial and jerk, and luckily, he had a few more bottles to go before he entered the Fiefdom of Stupidity. "Well," Tony began, "believe it or not, there used to be a dairy not far from here, out near Green-Wood."

"That's right," Rosanna added. "Borden's Dairy, and they had a big barn for the horses."

"Horses?" Tiger said in wonder. "They milked horses in those days?"

"No, dummy," his father said. "For the horses that pulled the delivery wagons."

Rosanna winced at Tony's comment then patiently explained to Tiger, "They delivered the milk in wooden wagons instead of trucks. Can you imagine that?"

Tony gave an exasperated laugh. "Who's telling the story, Roe?"

She reddened and smiled slightly. "Why you are, Tony. Go ahead."

Rosanna's smiles were so rare these days. Even in photographs, the grin she reproduced for the benefit of the camera looked wounded and guarded, as though she were afraid someone might guess her most terrible secrets. Tony vaguely recalled the young girl whose dark eyes seemed to glow whenever she smiled, smiled at him especially. "Why, you could light up the Great White Way," he used to tell Rosanna and this would make her beam even brighter.

Whatever happened to that girl? Tony wondered. But immediately, he knew the answer: *he* happened to her.

"Go ahead, Pop, we're waiting," Tiger said.

Tony drained the amber-colored bottle, still moist with perspiration from the icebox. He tried to wait to take another Schaefer but he could think of little else than how good the next one would feel going down. "Yes, a big barn this dairy had," he continued, "with cows and horses. Cows for milking and horses for pulling the wagons."

"And what did you do, Pop?" Tiger already knew the answer but he played along.

"I drove a milk wagon, son," Tony said proudly.

"It was a good job, especially back then," Rosanna added. Tony raised his eyebrows slightly and she was quiet. He grabbed another Schaefer from the icebox.

"It was a good job," Tony echoed. "Despite the horse shit and the pain in the ass Jew bastard bosses." He popped the bottle top and tossed the cap into the sink. "I was never the kind of guy who could work inside, know what I mean? I need to be out and about. That's the way you see the world, meet people."

Tony looked at Rosanna and nodded, then took a deep slug of beer, draining almost half the bottle. He smacked his lips. "That's how I met your mother," he said. "This house was on my delivery route. First time I laid eyes on her, I stopped dead in my tracks. The horse did, too."

The intoxicating scent of garlic sizzling filled the small, crowded kitchen. Rosanna gave it a stir then added some chopped onion, sliding the onion into the pan from the cutting board, which was shaped like a pineapple. Tiger had made it in shop class the year earlier. "Gertie," Rosanna said firmly. "The horse's name was Gertie."

"Gertie was a good girl, a fine animal," Tony nodded. "She knew my route by heart. So even when I had a few..." He mimicked knocking back a beer bottle for emphasis.

"Gertie could finish it?" Tiger asked.

Tony lifted the real bottle to his lips then took it away without taking a sip. "Not only that but she knew the way to your momma's house."

"That's how much your father came to visit me," Rosanna blushed.

"I kept thinking up excuses to pass by the house," Tony agreed. In a second, he was on his feet. Tony grabbed Rosanna around the waist and waltzed her from checkerboard to checkerboard across the linoleum. She protested slightly, wooden spoon (also made by Tiger in woodshop) in hand, but let her husband take her anyway.

Tony sang a made-up, nonsensical song about Rosanna Banana, his Brooklyn dairy queen. It was all going so nicely— even Kewpie couldn't help but smile—until Tony spilled a ribbon of beer down Rosanna's back. She gasped and pulled away, feeling the sudsy mixture slip down her spine then soak the seat of her bloomers. It even rained down onto the linoleum before Tony realized what he'd done.

Without warning, the clouds rolled back in. It always happened like this, as sudden as a summer thunderstorm. "Go on, finish the story," Rosanna told him, shaking the wet beer from her clothing then running a dishrag along the floor with her foot. "And let me finish making dinner," she sighed.

Back at the stove, Rosanna picked out the few blackened bits of garlic that could ruin a dish with bitterness. She added two quarts of chicken stock which she'd rendered from a half-price bag of necks and wings from Moskowitz's market the day before. Tony obeyed his wife and sat back down at the table. He took another mouthful of beer.

What had he seen in her all those years ago? Oh yes, the light. There was also a cleanness, a purity in Rosanna unlike any other woman he'd ever met, and he'd known quite a few. In her, there were no hard edges like his mother had. There was no scrappy survival instinct like his sister possessed and no jaded whore sensibilities like Justina and the others. Rosanna even smelled clean. Maybe if he could have her, could touch her, could make her his wife, she would make him clean, too.

But instead, Tony ruined Rosanna, pulled her down into the mire with him. It was plain to see that she was valiantly struggling to swim, fighting to keep her head above water, and was losing the battle.

Tony looked at Tiger. The boy was waiting expectantly for him continue, so he did. "If I talked to your mother too long,"

Tony began, "Gertie would come in and get me." Tiger's eyes widened in disbelief. Kewpie considered Fannie Brice as "Baby Snooks" in *Screen Gems*.

"It's true," Rosanna contended, stirring in the can of peas.

"The horse would nudge the front gate with her nose, open it, walk through, wagon clanking and all, and tug on my coattails," Tony recalled. "Hard. Gertie would pull at me until I came with her to finish my deliveries." Although Poppa had long gotten rid of the gate (said it was unwelcoming) and replaced the surrounding fence with hedges, Tiger tried to envision this scene just the same.

Five beer bottles were lined up on the drain board. Tony opened a sixth. By now, his speech was slightly slurred. His head bobbled like a spent boxer's in the ring, though he tried to control it. "Your folks hated me," Tony shot suddenly at his wife. "Hated me."

"They didn't hate you, Anthony. And they don't hate you now. They just..."

"They said I came from the wrong side of the tracks," he nodded at Tiger. "And they were right. Said I grew up on the streets. Right again."

Although Rosanna knew what was coming next, she didn't know how to avoid it. No matter what she said, it would be the wrong thing. He would twist and turn her words no matter how good-intentioned they were, looking for a fight.

Rosanna's hand trembled as she struck a match and lit the second front burner. She put a pot on the boil for the macaroni. When preparing this dish, some people made the mistake of adding the uncooked pasta directly to the soup. This caused too much of the precious broth to be absorbed by the macaroni and what you ended up with was a thick, gluey mess. Rosanna never made this mistake. She'd made others in her life but never this one.

"Your Pop had a rough childhood," Rosanna explained to Tiger, trying to smooth over Tony's inebriated rage. Tiger was the only one still listening.

"Rough? You can't imagine how rough. You kids got it easy," Tony hollered. "We were lucky if we even ate or slept in a bed.

My fucking mother put us out in the street every God-damn night." Tony had officially crossed the line of reason and it was a frightening, unpredictable place to be.

Kewpie got up and left the room. Tiger bit his lower lip in anticipation, like he did listening to a tense moment in "The Green Hornet" on the radio. Rosanna didn't bother telling her husband to mind his tongue because then more crude talk would follow. The water was boiling now. Rosanna added four handfuls of elbow macaroni and stirred so hard that water splashed onto the stovetop.

"I didn't have it easy like you did, Roe. I didn't have a family who loved me. And you still got it easy," he shouted.

Rosanna just looked at Tony, too scared to say anything. But he knew. He knew the truth: that she didn't have it easy at all. In fact, just the opposite was true: she had it hard because she was married to him.

Rosanna's helpless expression was enough to set Tony off. When the back of his hand came in contact with her cheekbone, she didn't flinch. Her eyes were downcast as she continued stirring the peas and pasta. She prayed silently to Saint Jude, the patron saint of hopeless causes, that Tony wouldn't hit her again. She prayed to Saint Teresa, the Little Flower, that there wouldn't be a bruise but there was. There always was.

Tiger didn't move or cry; he knew it would only make things worse.

Tony hurled the beer bottle into the deep enamel sink. Amber glass shattered everywhere. Slivers covered the floor, the kitchen table and flew into the soup Rosanna had been cooking with such care. Tony stormed out of the apartment, slamming the door behind him. He slammed it so hard that it popped back open from the force. Hopefully, he'd be gone for a while, only he always came back. Eventually he came back. Rosanna's desperate prayers to dead saints had been heard, as least temporarily. But she was certain that her parents had also heard and that Mrs. Rosenkrantz across the alley had surely heard as well.

Kewpie came into the kitchen, closed the door quietly and locked it, then began helping her mother clean up the mess. They strained the glass encrusted soup through a colander in the sink, then dumped the solid bits into the dustbin. It was Tiger's job to deftly wrap the broken chunks of beer bottle into pages of *The Brooklyn Daily Eagle*. He then put the sharp, sodden wad into a brown paper sack and threw it into the trashcan in the alley so no one would get hurt.

That done, there was now the question of supper. There wasn't much money to spare this week and Rosanna was all out of ideas.

8 The Promise of Summer

Spring was Bridget's favorite time of year because it made even the cracked concrete sidewalks of Brooklyn seem poetic and beautiful. Perhaps the reason for this was the flowers, which grew easily here, as did the trees. First the crocuses came up, forcing their way out of the cold, crusty earth, often when the late winter snow was still on the ground. Nothing could stop their determined yellow, white and purple heads from breaking the surface. Nothing. This was even before the waxy daffodils gathered their courage to sprout, before the tulips found their bravery to bloom.

Then the forsythia would come to life. It seemed that one day, their woody branches were brown and bare, the very next they were studded with hopeful green buds and the day after that they were covered with tiny yellow blossoms. And the azaleas were such a deep fuchsia it almost hurt the eyes. Let's not even begin to discuss the lilacs, their heavy blossoms drooping downward, heady scent reminiscent of what heaven probably smelled like.

The flowering pear trees were always such a pleasant surprise for Bridget. In the winter, they resembled most other trees, half-dead and void of leaves, but in the springtime they exploded with elegant white blooms in fireworks clusters of stars. This was the flowering pear's gorgeous secret. Each year, Bridget forgot how lovely they were, and each year, was happily reminded. She even forgave the flowering pear tree for its nasty secret—despite such deceiving, dainty ivory flowers they gave off an odor that was reminiscent of wet cement.

However, Bridget's favorite tree of all was the cherry blossom. Their depth of color was so rich, it seemed unworldly. Their scent was a gift from above, impossible to capture in a bottle or jar. Bridget would close her eyes and just breathe, grateful for the gift of cherry blossoms, though their blooms were fleeting. The breeze would easily coax the flowers from their clusters and leaflets would fall like pale pink confetti, carpeting the ground, softening the concrete underfoot, sometimes resting upon Bridget's shoulders and her hair as she passed beneath. They had a cherry blossom tree in their front yard along with the roses, lilies and hostas. And a magnolia, with its plump petals, carpeted the pavement in front of the DeMeo's place down the block.

That afternoon, Bridget sat on the porch which ran the entire length of the house. The slats beneath her feet were freshly painted, yet the gorgeous perfume of the cherry blossoms overpowered the strong scent of enamel. Glasses perched on the tip of her nose, sweater draped over her rounded shoulders, right ankle (the bad one) wrapped for support, Bridget sat at her little card table which was set out near the railing. Poppa had covered it with a fresh piece of oilcloth, as he did every spring. The cross around her neck, the one her father had given her some 50 years earlier, hung around her neck, reflecting the sunlight.

Bridget was alone. The other mismatched wooden chairs all sat empty and were arranged haphazardly around her. Poppa dozed in the parlor with the *Eagle* softly sliding from his lap, page by page. Tiger and Kewpie were still in school. Rosanna was grocery shopping and Tony was working on the El, or so he said.

Bridget reveled in the solitude of the afternoon. She was writing a letter to an almost-forgotten friend in the town where she was born, in a language she almost never spoke, except with Poppa sometimes, late at night when they were alone. She looked at the lined pad in front of her. Four pages were already filled. 'Everyone here is fine,' she wrote in delicate Italian curlicues, even though everyone really wasn't fine. Astrid and Sam bickered like fiends. Jo still mourned her lost child. Kewpie was fading away. Each day for Rosanna was a struggle, and Tony was drinking himself cruel. But Tiger, Tiger seemed fine.

'And then, there's the promise of summer,' Bridget wrote, followed by three dots. She signed her name, her real name, Margarita, folded the pages into an onionskin envelope and sealed it tight.

But Tiger was not fine.

Even at ten, the world didn't make much sense to him. He had lots of questions and no one seemed to have any answers.

Even at ten, Tiger didn't think life was just. First, there was the Lindbergh baby, then Aunt Jo's Hope. What did God have against babies anyway? Or children? His mother liked to say that God looked after drunks and kids but he knew this wasn't true. Like any other child, he was doomed, along with Hope, despite the fact that he'd been baptized the real way.

Just last week, Frank Fusco's cousin had been run down by a car on Fort Hamilton Parkway. The eight-year-old was killed on his way back from mass at St. Catherine's. Little Sal was hit so hard that he was knocked out of his Sunday shoes. It was the first (and last) time Sal's mom gave him permission to walk home alone. She figured he was old enough since he recently received two sacraments (Confession and Communion) and he promised to look both ways. He did look both ways but the car sped through the stop sign and mowed him down anyway.

At religious instruction the following week, Sister Patrick Maureen pointed out that since Sal's soul was clean and shiny after being given Confession the night before, he probably flew straight to heaven. (Minus his shoes, of course.) Sister Patrick Maureen said it was God's will, and that maybe Jesus just needed another little altar boy up there in heaven. But Tiger knew this was a lie. Didn't she see the way Sal's mother sobbed at Bruno's Funeral Home, how she tried to crawl into that polished wooden box with her son's broken body? What kind of God would do this to his children?

When Tiger asked his mother why this happened to Sal, she threatened to wash his mouth out with soap and spank his coolie. He didn't notice the tears in her eyes and it didn't matter that she apologized and hugged him right after she scolded him. Tiger never asked Rosanna anything of remote significance again. He couldn't ask his father because his father was "under the weather" and under the covers. And Kewpie, Kewpie had her own problems.

Then there were those ragged farm families in the Dust Bowl with their hollow, hungry, hunted eyes. Not to mention the terrible things that were happening in Spain, which also worried Tiger. As did talk of that cartoon-character looking Chancellor of Germany. To Tiger, Hitler resembled a skinny, angry Oliver Hardy more than he represented a "threat to world peace" as they said on the newsreels. But still, Hitler worried him, too. And he didn't want to even begin to think of Mussolini.

Tiger couldn't ask Poppa to explain all of this because his grandfather was away at the Brooklyn Navy Yard from early morning until suppertime. He was putting in long hours since they were on deadline, working on the *U.S.S. Brooklyn*. They'd laid the light cruiser's keel more than a year ago and it was scheduled to be launched in November. There never seemed to be a shortage of ships which needed guns welded onto them.

As foreman, Poppa was in charge of his own personal army of immigrants, Panamanians mostly, with skin as dark and shiny as coffee beans. Poppa loved them like his own children—and they loved him back—plus he respected them besides. He learned pieces of their language so he could better communicate with them but they taught him curse words, too. A mild, polite man, Poppa still enjoyed collecting colorful epitaphs in a variety of foreign tongues.

Even though he worked his gang—and himself—hard, Poppa still treated his men at the Navy Yard kindly. As a result, everyone was clamoring to be part of Mike's crew. So for Poppa, summers meant that he was as busy as a one-legged man at a butt kicking contest. That is until he took his two week's vacation, no matter what, last week of August, first week of September.

Sometimes the promise of summer was the only thing that kept Tiger going. The thought of school ending, and running wild outdoors from morning until the street lights blinked on, was an attractive one. And at the end of May, Coney Island officially opened for the summer. Memorial Day weekend, to be exact. When his father felt particularly beneficent or guilty or when he wanted to get Tiger and Kewpie out of his hair, he'd give them five bucks and they could spend the entire day down at Coney. There, they could buy, eat and do anything they desired, plus come back with change.

Yes, there was always the promise of summer. And somehow, it carried Tiger through the other months.

For Tony, summer always meant more. More daylight, more overtime, more opportunities to drink, more riders on the West End line, and as a result of the shattering heat, more flesh. Garments would drop piece by piece, like the cherry blossoms discarding their petals, for the train's overhead fans just didn't cut it in the dog days of August.

The El was the quickest, easiest, cheapest gateway to the beach, much faster than the trolley. In Brooklyn, everybody and their Aunt Tillie went to the beach in the summer. There was always a breeze, no matter how high the mercury, and you could always cool down there. People didn't just go to Coney Island but also to Manhattan Beach and Brighton. However, Coney was more accessible and more exciting with the rides and midway. Besides, you didn't have to trudge along street after street through fancy neighborhoods like Manhattan Beach just to reach a crowded rectangle of sand. At Coney Island, the beach was just a block from the Stillwell Avenue station. A few even walked that extra mile or so to Sea Gate beyond Coney Island if they knew someone who could get them past the wrought iron barrier to Sea Gate's choice private stretch of sand.

Tony loved watching the women heading for the seashore, bare-legged, almost naked under their light cotton shifts. Some, he imagined, didn't even wear bloomers. Just the scent of cocoa butter alone, the suggestion of warm, brown sun-kissed skin, moist and gently sweating, was enough to get him aroused. And sometimes, when these women struggled with their straw bags bursting with sand toys, blankets and snacks, a spaghetti strap slipped from a shoulder, unveiling an errant pale, pink nipple or a round, enticing globe of a breast which he spied beneath a naked armpit.

It made Tony's life worth living.

Summer also meant couples, often too stimulated to ferry their lust back home, or perhaps with no place private to go. They would be groping between cars, grinding and grabbing and gyrating, sometimes pulling the elastic leg band of a swimsuit aside to reveal a flash of fur or to release the pressure of a straining erection. The movement of the train, speeding to the next station, might be enough to bring them off. Body pressed against body, the train would do all the work, swaying and pumping on its own. All you had to do was remain standing. Tony had to remind himself to concentrate on his work rather than what was going on between cars, but it wasn't easy.

If he weren't careful, he'd jam the doors square on some big chooch's shoulders or catch an unsuspecting woman's skirt between the doors' rubber edges. Although sometimes he did the latter on purpose, just to see the startled look on their faces or perhaps get a glimpse of a well-turned thigh or the wisp of a lace-trimmed slip. In return, the women received a hearty apology, a flash of Tony's easy smile and twinkle from his turquoise eyes. This seemed to suffice.

Just the week before, Tony had noticed a nice dish getting on at Union Square. "A real hot tomato," the motorman later noted, as the dame sashayed onto the Stillwell Avenue platform. A skirt so tight "you could see what she had for breakfast," the motorman added in the locker room. "But she looks like a bad girl. And you know what I say: bad girl, bad news."

But Tony couldn't be deterred. "Maybe she just needs a bad boy is all," he concluded.

Still, Tony couldn't forget how the salmon-pink fabric of her skirt—the same color as her sex, maybe—hugged the woman's ample hips and behind, how the jacket of the same shade caressed her breasts. Or how her white-blonde curls brushed her shoulders and her tongue lightly moved across her cotton-candy colored lips when she eyed him. Tony remembered all of this in the bathroom stall at the train depot, before he even clocked out. Jerking off on T.W.U. time was an aphrodisiac on its own.

Yes, there was always the promise of summer, and Tony lived for it.

9 Dish Night

Every Wednesday night was Dish Night at the Loews 46th. Tiger loved going to the movies on Dish Night, and not just for the picture show. Sometimes the show in the audience was even better than the one onscreen.

At 15, going on 16 in a few months, Kewpie said she was getting too old to go to the movies with her grandparents. Besides, she was working as much as she could at Kresge's to save up for a real beauty salon perm. However, Tiger looked forward to Dish Night with Grandma Bridget and Poppa. You might even say it gave his life purpose.

Although his grandmother was famous for her sumptuous meals even during the week, on Dish Night, she and Poppa were content with leftovers. "Planned-overs," Bridget liked to call them, for she planned not to cook on Wednesday nights. She simply made more on Monday or Tuesday and kept the leftovers stored in the icebox until then.

For Tiger, there was nothing better than walking along 47th Street with his grandparents on either side of him. He couldn't imagine ever growing too old to walk down the block hand in hand with them.

Bridget got all dolled up for the occasion, "going out on the town with my men," as she called it. A touch of rouge on her cheeks from a fancy brass compact, a daub of lipstick, her long silvery hair fastened into a bun with rhinestone hairpins, even a spritz of Evening in Paris perfume, which had become something of her trademark scent. Tiger thought her the most beautiful grandma in the universe. And perhaps she was.

Poppa would wear a tie, suit jacket and would take his pocket watch. It was as though they were going to Radio City Music Hall in Manhattan instead of just walking around the corner to the Loews 46th. But to Tiger, this theater was even better than Radio City because it was his.

Now, there were lots of movie houses in Borough Park in those days, and all over Brooklyn, for that matter. The Elton, the Beverly and the Marlboro. The Minerva and the Sanders in Park Slope. The Dyker and the Harbor in Bay Ridge. One every couple of blocks it seemed. Some poorer households didn't even own a radio but just about everyone could afford to go to the moving pictures once in a while. The movies were a source of joy and sorrow, laughter, information and news. And dishes.

Bridget couldn't get enough of those dishes. It was her goal to build a full set. Three full sets, to be exact. That's why they went to the Loews 46th religiously each and every Wednesday night. With an adult priced ticket you received one piece of flawlessly simple white bone china. The dishes looked great with anything on them, especially Bridget's uncomplicated masterpieces like earthy escarole and beans soup and perfect golden-brown roasted chicken whose toasty skin crackled in your mouth when you took a bite. And these china dishes were high quality, too. They were as good as the ones they sold for top dollar at Abraham & Straus downtown. With any luck, Bridget would have three full sets by Christmas.

If Poppa was in a good mood—and he was always in a good mood—he would let Tiger get a handful of rainbow cookies at Piccolo's, which was right around the corner, under the El. He and the Mrs. preferred the woody sweetness of *pignoli* cookies, which were studded with pine nuts. "Old folk's cookies," Poppa would concede, snatching the white bag from the counter, after exchanging a few niceties with Alfonso Piccolo, the owner and baker, in Italian.

"You two aren't old," Tiger would tell his grandfather.

Bridget and Poppa would glance at each other, gray and pleasantly weathered like cedar furniture that had faded in the sun. "You keep us young," his grandmother would tell the boy. Poppa handed her the cookies, which she stowed in her oversized handbag.

Walking under the El, Tiger would hope they didn't run into his father. He would double-cross his fingers, still nestled in Poppa and Grandma Bridget's hands, and make a wish. Seeing Tony would ruin everything. Maybe he would still let Tiger go with them if he were a happy drunk, but more often than not, his father would make a scene, ending with, "I don't need your charity!" and Tiger being pulled down the block by his shirt collar. His bottom still hadn't healed from the strap the week before.

But this beautiful evening at the end of May, the coast was clear. "The Mayor of 47th Street" nodded hellos to friends and neighbors with practically every step in their short *passeggiata* to the Loews 46th. There was a word or two in Chinese to Mr. Wong as they passed the restaurant, a laugh in Polish with Sol Kaminski, who worked in the *kielbasa* shop (his wife Harriet knew Kewpie from Kresge's), and so on. It impressed Tiger to hear Poppa slide effortlessly from one tongue to another as they walked the space of a block and a half. It impressed his wife also, even after all these years.

Poppa knew the girl at the ticket booth—her uncle was one of the best welders on the job. He knew most of the ushers, too, and Pete Acerno, the manager. Poppa seemed to know everyone everywhere, at least in Borough Park.

Stepping across the threshold of the Loews 46th was like slipping into another world. Of all the theaters in the neighborhood, this was Tiger's favorite. He couldn't stop staring at the twinkling lights and frothy clouds painted on the ceiling. Even after the house lights went down and the newsreel began,

Tiger would keep on looking up until his neck started hurting. The stars were smiling down on him. More stars than you could ever see in a real Brooklyn sky.

In the lobby, Poppa let Tiger hand Wally, the ticket-taker, all three stubs. Tiger gave them back to his grandfather, who put them in his pocket, beside his watch. Next came the best part of Dish Night—the ushers standing on chairs by the sets of double doors, reaching into deep wooden crates, doling out the treasures one by one, littering the floor with straw and strips of newspaper printed in cities they would never visit.

Tiger, Poppa and Bridget always got on Augie's line. Technically, every adult ticket holder was entitled to a free dish, but Augie, an usher who was sweet on Kewpie, always gave them an extra plate for Tiger's child's ticket. Kewpie, in turn, rolled her eyes at the sound of Augie's name every time her grandparents mentioned his kindness.

Tonight they were presented with a gravy boat. The week before, it had been a cup and the week before that, a saucer. Tiger thought the gravy dish looked silly, like a genie's slipper, but Bridget thought it was just wonderful. *Tres elegant*, as Aunt Astrid might say. By Sunday, one gravy boat would grace Bridget's table, filled to the brim with her marvelous spaghetti sauce, mellowed to a rich magenta, its surface dappled with olive oil. The other two gravy boats would be packed away in a box in the basement. One for Kewpie when she got married—"I'm never getting married!" she'd loudly inform them—and the other for Tiger's wife, whoever she might be.

Tiger took his usual seat in a row toward the center of the theater, not too close to the screen, and one seat in. Bridget took the aisle seat so she could stretch out her bad leg. She kept the next empty seat for Tiger and Poppa took the one beside him. Once they were all settled in their places, they handed the gravy boats to her for safekeeping. She guarded them on her wide lap, scooped her hands around them like a mother duck protecting her charges under wing.

Unbeknownst to Poppa, Bridget slipped Tiger a handful of penny candies as soon as the lights went down. And unbeknownst to Bridget, Poppa slipped Tiger a Hershey's bar, which the boy would do his best to chew secretly. It was impossible to clandestinely chomp on a Tootsie Roll, which is why Poppa switched to Hershey's. These treats were in addition to the cookies from Piccolo's. Yes, life was sweet for Tiger, sandwiched between his grandparents.

When the house lights went down, everyone in the Loews 46th began to cheer. There were the customary announcements, asking ladies to please remove their hats and the usual advertisements featuring a procession of dancing candy bars and prancing popcorn buckets to whet appetites. A hush came over the movie house as the newsreel began. Almost all the seats were taken. Tiger looked out over the sea of heads as the news of the day floated by. Someone named Haile Selassie had run off to a place called Aden. Italy formally annexed Ethiopia. Tiger wondered if any of his relatives were involved in this terrible thing then immersed himself in studying the outline of Polly Flynn's intricate corkscrew curls as she sat two rows in front of him.

"Dead Jockey Rides to Victory!" headed the wacky news. There was Ralph Neves, full of life, as he recounted how the horse he was riding tripped and he was trampled by four others at a race track near San Francisco. They went so far as to toe-tag him down at the city morgue but then Neves got up off the slab and took a taxi back to the racetrack, bare-chested and missing one shoe. In the jockey's room, they were busy collecting money for his widow, who promptly fainted upon seeing her recently-deceased husband arrive, very much alive. Neves wanted to ride again that very day, explaining "I don't feel dead!" but they wouldn't let him. The following day, however, "The Portuguese Pepperpot" rode to victory five times.

The next news item was even more unbelievable. It seems that a Japanese prostitute cut off her lover's something or other. "What's a prostitute, Grandma?" Tiger asked aloud, and those sitting within earshot let out soft chuckles. At that point, Bridget grasped Tiger by the hand and took him to the bathroom, even though he didn't have to go. By the time they returned, the opening credits for *Little Lord Fauntleroy* were rolling and Poppa was already dozing.

Even though Tiger didn't like Freddie Bottle-Ass, as Poppa called the highly-annoying child actor Freddie Bartholomew, the movie had potential in Tiger's eyes. A rags-to-riches story was always a winner is his book. The picture opened in Brooklyn, where the unwitting Lord of the title (he of the Bottle-Ass) was growing up. However, it was a much cleaner, shinier Brooklyn than the one Tiger knew. But after only a few minutes, this story of "A Poor Brooklyn Boy Destined for Greatness!" succeeded in angering the bona-fide Brooklyn boy in the audience who was comfortably wedged between his grandparents. In Tiger's opinion, Poppa wasn't missing much.

Tony, who didn't like picture shows to begin with, would have declared this one "a crock of shit" and in this case, Tiger would have to agree with him. What was with the cheesy English accent? Freddie would have gotten his Bottle-Ass kicked daily if he talked like that in Borough Park. He would have been thrown a beating just for having a Sissy Mary name like "Ceddie," as his character had unfortunately been christened. And finding out your dead father was actually a British nobleman, what a load of crap. Thank God for Mickey Rooney, who, thankfully, saved the picture.

Poppa stirred beside Tiger, opened his eyes and muttered, "Mickey Cooper."

"It's Mickey Rooney, Poppa," the boy corrected. "And Gary Cooper."

"Sure, it is." Poppa tried to watch the movie but his eyes grew heavy again and his head began to nod toward his chest. Bridget sighed. Tiger smiled as she handed him the bakery shop bag, now freckled with darkened spots from the butter which had leeched onto the paper.

Tiger smiled as he chewed which wasn't an easy feat, and didn't drop a crumb. He was in heaven at the Loews 46th. He didn't even mind when the El thundered by every 15 minutes or so, shaking the balcony seats above them. It was so loud that you could hear its roar above the movie soundtrack. Tiger wished he could stay there forever, nestled in the darkness of the Loews 46th, safely snuggled between his grandparents. But he knew this wasn't possible. Soon, the picture would be over and he would be thrust back into the harsh reality of the railroad flat around the block.

A loud crash made Tiger jump. It was the familiar sound of china breaking. This was soon followed by wild applause rising from the audience. It happened from time to time during Dish Night, at least once, usually more. A plate fell from an unsuspecting lap as the owner fished for a sleeve of Necco wafers. Or like Poppa, someone had drifted off to sleep, their gravy boat slipped from their lap and a porcelain explosion resounded through the aisles. Bridget leaned in close to Tiger. "Haven't lost one yet," she whispered, patting the pile in her lap for emphasis. Her breath was warm and smelled like pine nuts from the cookies. Tiger nodded.

If Augie had extra pieces and Mr. Acerno wasn't around, he'd sneak the person a new dish while he made a quick cleanup. That's just the kind of guy he was. If only Kewpie could see this side of him. But she seemed to favor bad boys, the ones who smoked cigarettes and did things they weren't supposed to do. What Kewpie didn't realize was that it was just a matter of time before bad boys did something bad to you.

So, Tiger sat in the comforting false night of the Loews 46th, studying the fake stars twinkling on the ceiling, the painted clouds only shadows. He sat there not paying much mind to the picture show, counting the minutes until the spell was broken and he'd have to go home.

When the movie ended, the theatre's side doors as well as its front doors were flung open so everyone could file out easily into the night. No matter which exit Tiger and his grandparents took, Augie was always waiting there for them with a small gift or treat for Kewpie. Sometimes it was a box of Black Crows from the concession stand. But this night, it was the sugar bowl they'd given away at Dish Night a few weeks earlier. "I figure she could keep jewelry in it or something," he shyly told the girl's grandmother, who accepted his gift graciously, as usual. They could hear a trinket clinking around inside the depths of the sugar bowl but didn't peek, though Tiger wanted to.

"It's private," Bridget explained to him.

Poppa put a gravy boat in each deep jacket pocket as they

walked. Tiger was entrusted with the other while Bridget carried Kewpie's treasure.

On the slow walk home, it was just as Tiger had suspected— the stars in the real sky didn't seem to shine as brightly as the pretend ones at the Loews 46th. The boy could hear his father's slurred yelling when they were two doors away from the house. He didn't want to go upstairs, but he had no choice. His grandparents watched him from the foot of the stairs, somewhat sadly, practically holding their breath. Tiger mounted the steps, carefully holding Kewpie's present in front of him, like a peace offering or a shield and opened the door.

10 The Beat

Harry was a Queens boy, Elmhurst to be exact. But if the truth be told, he much preferred living in the shadow of the El to growing up beside the specter of the Elmhurst Gas Tanks. He'd been a patrolman almost ten years now, a beat cop. Although Harry was good at what he did and his superiors told him he'd make an excellent commander, he had no desire to move up in the ranks. Sitting behind a chipped city-issue desk with a sergeant's badge or a detective's shield clipped to a suspender strap was his idea of hell on earth. Harry preferred the stark honesty—and dishonesty—of the streets. Devilishly hot in the summer, demonically frigid in the winter, smelly, dirty or swept clean with an old broom, the streets were what they were. Either you dealt with it or you died. He liked the cut and dryness of it.

Harry's beat was Borough Park. That's how he met Jo, in fact. He was pounding the pavement one evening as she was coming home from the insurance company where she worked downtown. Crossing the trolley tracks under the El, one of Jo's heels became wedged between the track and the cobblestones. He spotted her across New Utrecht Avenue, trying to finesse her foot out of its trap, laughing. The autumn sun was setting behind her, all gold and pink and bruised purple. "November sunsets are the most beautiful," she always said. And it was true.

Perhaps it was her musical laugh, light and holy as church bells, or then again, it could have been her shapely gams, but Harry found himself smitten on the spot. He liked the confident way she rested her weight on his shoulder as he slipped her foot out of her shoe. "Like a real Prince Charming," she'd recount to her sister Camille later. He noticed that her toenails were painted a bright coral. It startled him, yet excited him. This gal seemed so reserved, but the tarty toenails sure threw him for a loop.

For Harry, the very touch of Jo's hand was intensely intimate. It felt as though they'd known each other for years instead of just minutes. He admired the way her front teeth overlapped slightly, one crowding the other. It gave her mouth a vulnerable, kissable look. Jo was easy on the eyes, it was true, but she also seemed the sort of girl who'd be easy on the mind, not demanding much in earthly goods but expecting her beau to give his all in devotion. And this was quite all right with Harry.

Jo's shoe was salvageable but the heel had become unglued when he'd wrestled it free. "You don't know your own strength," she cooed. Harry blushed as he handed Jo back her shoe with an apology. Pucci, the shoemaker, could—and would—fix it, she assured him. Harry offered Jo his arm, which she gladly took, grasping it firmly and surely. He helped his Cinderella limp down the block to the house full of sisters and brothers and wonderful smells in the middle of 47th Street.

From then on, Harry was what his partner Sully indelicately called "stupid in love." That head over heels, can't eat, can't sleep, can't think of anything else but her, terrible, wonderful sort of adoration. The kind of devotion George and Ira Gershwin made millions writing songs about. Harry would deny it up one side of Fort Hamilton Parkway and down the other but he knew it was true. And Jo loved him back just as hard.

As burly, brawny, wide-shouldered and thick-necked as Harry was, this wisp of an Italian girl with the tawny curls turned his heart into *polenta*. *Polenta* was a delicious sort of Guinea mush he discovered during one of his many meals at her parents' bustling and bountiful table. Bridget liked Harry immediately because he was a good eater. Poppa liked him immediately because he had a steady job and didn't appear to have a sore elbow from tipping back too many.

Harry and Jo were married three months later. Much to the chagrin of Harry's sergeant Phil Gataletto, whose biggest pet peeve were Italian maidens with vivid surnames like Paradiso trading them in for bland, nondescript Irish ones like O'Leary. But Josephina took Harry's name willingly and proudly, and regardless of her colorless surname, Sergeant Gataletto danced with Mrs. O'Leary at her wedding dinner, which was held at Rex's Tavern.

For Tiger, having an uncle like Harry prowling the streets had its good points and its bad points. For one thing, nobody would mess with Tiger, steal his Milky White marble or filch his brand-new baseball. If anyone so much as tried, Uncle Harry would appear out of nowhere, looming, brooding and silently threatening. He was like Tarzan, only larger and scarier.

But then again, Tiger couldn't get away with anything either. If he even thought of lifting a piece of penny candy from Dora's Luncheonette or considered throwing a firecracker at an unsuspecting alley cat, Uncle Harry seemed to sense it and was there in a flash. What was worse, if Uncle Harry didn't magically appear, his buddy Sully did.

It was Sully who showed up with Uncle Harry when Tiger's father got too rough or too rowdy. It was Sully who helped Uncle Harry home with Tony, soaked from dirty gutter water as he lay passed out in the street. Other times, Tony would be seen walking shakily between the two cops, his shirt inexplicably torn or his eye mysteriously blackened from saying the wrong thing to the wrong person. Sully and Harry saw to it that Tony didn't get his ass kicked any more than it needed to be.

It was Sully's Irish eyes, blue as the skies above the County Cork, which welled up with sympathy for Rosanna, whose own eyes shamefully avoided his, as well as her brother-in-law's. It was Sully's giant yet comforting ham hock patting Tiger's shoulder and his street-roughened voice softened with empathy as he told the boy knowingly, "It's okay, kid. My old man was a drinker, too." It was Sully who first noticed the florid bruises on Rosanna's forearms and detected the slight limp in her step one winter. "I slipped on the ice," she'd explained, chuckling with embarrassment, never looking at him. But Sully knew better.

Sully had grown up in South Brooklyn, a few train stops away from Borough Park. His sister Irene knew Rosanna from school and from the inter-borough relay races they'd both been good at when they were girls. Irene, who now lived in Queens with her lawyer husband and three sons, sometimes sent gently worn hand-me-downs for Tiger or tomatoes from her garden. Rosanna always accepted these with grace and shyness, as if they were gifts from Sully as well as from his sister.

Sully remembered Rosanna from those relay races but doubted that she even noticed he was there. He would watch the olive-skinned, solemn woman-child with the long braids trailing down her back, muscular legs pumping under her baggy gym tunic, pumping until she was victorious across the finish line. Sully always marveled at the way Rosanna's braids took flight as she ran. Thick as horse tails, lifting off her strong back like a fragile Wright Brothers craft at Kitty Hawk, then gently touching down when she stopped running. The sight alone was enough to take his breath away. Yes, Sully loved Rosanna even then, but didn't dare tell her.

It wasn't long before the dairyman started courting her. That snotty, flashy street urchin with the smarmy liar's grin. Before Sully knew it, Rosanna married the shifty milkman and they had a baby on the way.

But what Sully didn't know, never knew, was that Rosanna had noticed that shy, skinny fellow with the pleasant smile who never missed one of her races, even if his sister wasn't running that day. Rosanna always wished he'd come up to her and say something, anything. But Sully never did, and now it was too late.

Yes, Harry liked his partner, and his beat just fine. Although some preferred the day shift, he liked the cover of night. It always amazed him how dimness changed the face of everything. The outline of a rosebush in a front yard might take on the shape of a hunchback. A rolled-up carpet on a front stoop might resemble a rabid mongrel, ready to spring to attack. Inviting backyard paths were transformed into murky alleyways. Friendly neighbors huddled in overcoats against the chill became potential thugs, reeking of menace. And it was Harry's job to sort one from the other.

There was mischief in the most unlikely places. Beneath the massive girders of the El, for example. The trolleys that ran there were few and far between during the evening hours and revelers could avoid being caught in the glaring lights if they took the trouble to learn the trolley schedule. The crash of the West End Line overhead, surging into the Fort Hamilton Parkway station, could mask a multitude of sins and sounds.

Not a night went by when Harry didn't glimpse a couple grappling amongst the girders, spy rolled-down hose showing beneath a lifted skirt or the glint of a bright white buttocks glowing above dropped knickers, pumping in and out of the gloom. Harry often looked the other way if these were young lovers with nowhere else to go. The small-time working girls, he didn't mind either. It was getting harder to put food on the table in these tough times, and they deserved a break. Harry would rap his nightstick against a metal post in warning and watch the goodtime girls and their Johns scatter like rats. Once, he thought he'd seen Kewpie disappearing into the shadows.

It was the men, the fancy Manhattan swells, tumbling with young street scullions who were so hungry they'd do just about anything for a Baby Ruth, which Harry couldn't abide by. He'd let the boy go with a swift kick in the pants but he'd throw the man a beating he wouldn't soon forget. "Not in my backyard," he'd snarl through gritted teeth, as he raised the billy club overhead. "Not on my watch." The man would go stumbling off, never to be seen or heard from again, and glad for the cop's beneficence.

Although they weren't supposed to, Harry and Sully sometimes split up during their beat, walking separately, then coming together at a designated time and place. Usually the skell bar on the corner of 46th Street, where some lush or another always managed to cause trouble. Occasionally, it was Tony. But

Harry's errant brother-in-law usually preferred The Pink Pussycat on 39th Street, where his brother Tommy worked as a bar back and Tony could get loaded for practically nothing. Although Rosanna knew his watering holes, she never sought out her husband. She never even sent Tiger to fetch him like some of the more desperate wives did. What was the point? It was more peaceful when he was gone, anyway.

Harry would post himself beneath the El's girders, trying to nab a pervert, while Sully, more often than not, would find himself on 47th Street. There was a narrow driveway on the left side of the Paradiso house and an even narrower alley on the right. The alleyway was pitch black, shielded by the house beside it and Sully would be safely masked there. He wouldn't look; he'd just listen. Listen for raised voices, for crying, for furniture being shoved aside like matchsticks. When he was satisfied that all was well, he would move on.

Sully would smile in the dark on the rare occasions he heard Rosanna singing. He guessed she was probably sewing at the kitchen table. First it began as a low hum which graduated into a bona-fide song. Sometimes it was a popular tune of the day like "Pennies from Heaven" or "You're the Top." But more often than not, it was a song from their youth. She favored both "Rose of Washington Square" and "Second Hand Rose." Rosanna loved roses—all the Paradiso women did—and sung about them in a soft, wavering, hesitant voice you had to strain to hear, especially from the alley. But she never sang when anyone else in the house was stirring. The kids had to be asleep and Tony had to be out, or out cold, before she would comfortably warble.

Only Rosanna didn't sing much anymore. There wasn't much to sing about.

As summer approached and the nights grew warmer, Rosanna took to sitting on her second story balcony and rocking in her favorite old chair. It had graced her parents' porch when she was a child and lately, lay neglected and piled with gardening tools. One day, Rosanna rescued it from obscurity, lugged it upstairs and pushed it out onto her own porch. And there it waited.

With its worn green paint and sagging wicker seat, to her, being in the chair was like sitting in the lap of a beloved friend.

Rosanna rocked in the cool of the evening, sometimes with an afghan she'd knitted warming her lap. Sully would listen to the chair's familiar, rhythmic creak as she rocked to and fro, staring at something out past the crooked rooftops. Sometimes he swore she knew he was there but Rosanna never let on. Neither did he. This was Sully's favorite part about the night shift.

Perhaps Harry's favorite thing about working nights was being home with Jo during the day. She'd quit her job at Prudential on Court Street since marrying him—no wife of his needed to work—and was home all the time now. Harry enjoyed sleeping while it was light, waking midday to the scent of Jo's strong coffee, feeling her ease under the sheets beside him in nothing but a full slip. Always black, never white as you might suspect. Jo was still full of surprises, like her lacquered toenails, for example.

Sometimes they would just talk in secret whispers but others, he'd lift the black slip's lace hem over her lovely buttocks and take her from behind in the starkness of day. Other times, he'd have her on her back so he could study her face, which changed like the sky, painted with shade, then light.

But these days, since losing the baby, Jo seemed to just want to hold Harry quietly, just hold him. She was crying less often but still couldn't bear to be penetrated, not just yet. Dr. Lewis said her body was ready but Jo claimed her spirit was not. This was all right with Harry; he had plenty of time. He expected to spend his whole life with Jo, maybe longer if what Father Dunn said was true. A few months' wait was nothing he couldn't endure.

Until she was ready for him, Jo didn't mind taking her husband in her hand and steadily, stealthily coaxing him onto her belly, leaving a puddle like thick, spilled milk. Now, it was her turn to study his face, which for Jo, was a constant source of fascination. It amazed her how this tough-talking beat cop could curdle so easily around her gently clenched fist, how his features tightened with an urgency, how his face reddened and puffed slightly, and finally, how this big man trembled like a scared kitten in a drainpipe. All from a rub and a tug.

Jo didn't even mind when Harry slid himself between the crack of her upturned bottom, satin bloomers pulled down to her knees like a harlot's, hips propped on a pillow, like an offering on an altar. His sure, knowing hand hooked beneath her, searching, seeking and finding, always finding. Finding and unraveling her like a long, shimmering flag unfurling in the steady wind.

But Jo still couldn't let him inside her, not just yet. And Harry understood. Besides, he was pretty good at waiting.

11 "Cheek to Cheek"

Tony officially met "the blonde bombshell," as the guys referred to her, a few days before his birthday. Oh, he had noticed her several times before, getting on at Stillwell and getting off at Union Square, and vice versa. Speculations on her whereabouts were always a hotbed of conversation between Tony, the motorman and trainman. On the long, slow ride to Manhattan, he often studied her sturdy crossed legs, one of which usually bounced rhythmically as she read a dime-store novel. She seemed to go through a couple of books a week. Every few days there was a new trashy cover nestled between her neatly-manicured fingertips. Thus, a fiery redhead was traded for a sultry brunette and a strapping knight for a shirtless farmhand. Although Tony was far from being either, she still noticed him.

It was on June 9th that he finally spoke to her.

"Miss, you dropped something," was what Tony said when he saw the book she'd left behind on the wicker seat. She was the last one in the train car at the last stop and he was due for his break.

Without even looking back, she responded, "I didn't drop it. I finished it." And stared Tony down, challenging him with her blue bedroom eyes.

"That's littering," he told her, a grin starting to crinkle the corners of his mouth.

"So, arrest me," she said, holding out her hands in front of her, waiting for him to clink on a set of imaginary handcuffs. The girl tossed her platinum curls in expectation. They looked like the sort of ringlets an angel might have, but Tony figured this chippie was far from being an angel.

At this point, they both laughed. "I figured someone else might like a read," she explained, "and I'd save them the chump change."

"Just being a good neighbor?" Tony pressed.

"Yeah," she agreed. "Something like that."

It was well past the evening rush, nearing eight, and the sky was beginning to dim. "Working late at the office?" he wondered.

"You writing a book?" she wondered back.

Tony adjusted his hat, which he imagined made him look taller, slightly regal, even. The deep navy of his work suit was flattering, he'd been told by more than one bar floozy. Although he wasn't supposed to drink in uniform, he sometimes did. It couldn't be avoided.

Tony shrugged at the blonde before him. "I was just thinking…" he began, "that it ain't safe for a woman like you to be walking home alone after dark."

Shifting her weight onto one red pump, then the other, she straightened the seams of her dress. "And what would you know about a woman like me?" she challenged. Tony didn't know what to say. Without missing a beat, she added, "You offering to see me home?"

"Why, sure," Tony said.

"How do I know you're not a masher?" she queried. The hopeful arch of her eyebrows said that maybe she wished he was.

"I got a wife and kids at home," he explained.

She rolled her eyes, "Ah, the worst kind." And held out her arm. Tony took it. They exchanged names. Hers was Denise.

Tony didn't care who in the signal house saw. There was an unwritten code of dishonor among transport workers: whatever goes on in the yard, stays in the yard. And it held true for what went on in the trains and on the platforms, too. Unless you were a "beakie," a plainclothes rat hired by the Brooklyn-Manhattan Transit to drop the dime on employees. Otherwise, motormen, guards, trainmen and conductors alike knew how to keep their lips buttoned when it came to delicate matters like dames. Or drinking, gambling, what have you. And Tony liked to partake in all of the above.

In his twisted mind, however, Tony had never been unfaithful to Rosanna. Well, technically speaking, and not that he remembered, anyway. Oh, sure, a couple of times he woke up in a strange bed with a strange head on a strange pillow, but that didn't count. He'd been tight, his judgment was impaired and he doubted that anything had happened, anything of significance anyhow. Tony had cloudy recollections of late-night visits to his kids' room but what actually went on there, he hadn't a clue. And besides, Kewpie was family so if anything happened, it didn't really count. It hadn't counted with his sister Marie when they were growing up and it didn't count with his daughter now either.

Tony marveled at how gracefully Denise moved on such high heels, swaying like a jungle cat, riding one hip then the other. She sashayed along the platform, wiggling her way down the steel-capped steps, never once losing her footing. Tony felt grand walking down Surf Avenue with his arm linked through Denise's. "It's such a nice night," she sighed, "and I do feel like walking." So they did.

Denise and Tony made their way toward Sea Gate, past Nathan's Famous, whose many sets of double doors were thrown open to the warm evening. Several lines of people crowded both the inside and outside serving areas. Everyone patiently waited their turn to order at the shiny countertop. Even in the dead of winter, Nathan's was busy. People constantly craved those wonderfully salty franks that crunched when you bit into them.

Their crinkle-cut fries were like manna from a greasy heaven. But Tony'd never sampled their fried frogs' legs, which were also on the menu; he couldn't get his head around them.

Tony asked Denise if she wanted to stop, his treat, but she shook her head. "Nah, bad for the figure," she told him. Rosanna would have jumped at the chance and scarfed down one, maybe two dogs, a cup of French fries plus a Coca Cola to wash it all down.

Tony and Denise continued along Surf Avenue past Phillips Candy Shop, which was still open and also packed. But Denise refused even a bag of milk chocolate raisin clusters. "It goes right here," she noted, patting her curvy hips for emphasis. Rosanna would have gladly accepted a bag and then bought another for her parents. There would have been no stopping her. But then again, these days, Tony so rarely took his wife to Coney Island, or any place else for that matter, that she was ravenous for entertainment when he did break down and step out with her.

"We're almost halfway there," Denise remarked when they crossed West 27th Street. "It's a long walk. You sure you're up to it?"

"Oh, I'm up to it," Tony insisted.

"Good," Denise told him. "I like a man who can rise to the occasion." This racy remark made Tony walk even prouder. He gave Denise's arm a little squeeze as they continued their stroll. Out of nowhere, a song popped into his head and he began to whistle "Cheek to Cheek." In the coming weeks, it would become their anthem of sorts.

Denise smiled in the darkening night. "You know, you kinda remind me of Fred Astaire," she said. Tony puffed up like a rooster in a barnyard full of prize hens.

Beyond Denise's padded shoulders, past the Riegelmann Boardwalk in the distance, the sunset illuminated the clouds in an odd light so that they looked to be outlined in yellow crayon. In the background, above the voices and the rest of the street music, the crank of the rides, the scream of people being plunged down metal rails, the rhythmic beat of the ocean breaking upon the shore could be heard. It was early in the season so the streets weren't yet clogged with people, although there was a decent crowd.

Denise tip-toed down Surf Avenue, gently guiding Tony. It was the way a woman might move on a dance floor, a proficient dancer anyhow, letting the man believe he was in charge but in reality, it was she who controlled him. The steady breeze rustled Denise's crinoline skirt, making a soft crunching like a squirrel through crisp autumn leaves. Tony would remember this sound long after he left Denise with a hearty handshake at the gate which gave "Sea Gate" its name. He would recall the sound in the cramped stall of the men's room, which was just beyond the locker room. Hunched over on the toilet, he brought himself off with his fist at her expense again, seeing Denise on her knees in front of him on the damp, smudged bathroom tiles this time. Tony could practically feel her upturned crinolines scratching his thighs as he came into a wad of toilet tissue.

Tony walked Denise home the next night, too, and the next. She made sure to get into his train car each evening as she made the pilgrimage home after work. Well after business hours, Tony noted. What did she do until seven or eight every night? Knock off a few drinks before heading home? Or knock off her boss? Tony didn't want to know, just wanted to see her was all. His heart quickened at the sound of her heels clicking toward him on the concrete platform. His body stiffened at the sight of her unbridled curves coaxed into a nubby business suit even though there hadn't been more than a peck on the cheek between them.

Tony had taken to skipping dinner and walking Denise home on his break. Even though conductors weren't supposed to eat in the train cab, Tony did, for he thrived on doing things he wasn't supposed to. He'd sneak bites of Rosanna's leftover meatloaf on crusty Italian bread and wash it down with a swig or two of scotch, neatly folding and saving the tinfoil, just as his wife instructed. Eating on the run didn't sit well with his delicate drinker's stomach but Tony decided that Denise was well worth the indigestion of a stolen meal.

They'd met on a Tuesday and each night since then, Tony got a little closer, went a little further with her. Denise wasn't a whore after all, she'd assured him, just a nice girl trapped in a naughty girl's physique. On Wednesday, the guard at Sea Gate's Surf Avenue gatehouse nodded his approval as Tony passed through its opening with Denise. He escorted her to a grand-looking house complete with castle turrets on Lyme Avenue. She rented a room at the top of one of those turrets from an Orthodox Jewish woman named Marilyn who insisted everyone call her Aunt Mimi.

Tony had the displeasure of meeting Aunt Mimi on Thursday night. With a grimy kerchief covering her sheitle-less head, she reminded him of a loony maiden aunt who bunked with a dozen cats or the batty wife from a Brooklyn production of *Jane Eyre*. Wild-eyed and unkempt, Aunt Mimi was bedecked in a long striped skirt and a flowered sweater with holes at the elbows. She said hello to Tony in the hallway then disappeared furtively into her apartment. There was a long, lingering kiss from Denise in the vestibule. She slipped her cool, sweet tongue into his mouth then was gone. The hall door swished shut before Tony even opened his eyes.

By Friday night, Denise and Tony were necking beneath the sprawling maple tree in Aunt Mimi's front yard. The evening was moonless but the bright white of her summer dress shone whenever the beacon from the Nortons Point Lighthouse fell on their bodies. Her dress's red poppy print was lost in the shadows while the deep hue of his uniform faded completely into the darkness.

Denise liberated Tony with a deft unzip of his trousers. He was hot in her hands in the temperate air, swaying hard and heavy like an elephant's trunk. "You're a big, healthy boy, aren't you?" she growled, echoing the sentiments of Justina many years earlier. Tony didn't answer her; didn't have to.

He gathered Denise's skirts up past her hips and lifted the crinolines in a cushion around their bodies. He felt the tabs of her garters making little indentations in his legs, felt her stockings scraping his skin. Denise spread her legs even wider, grinding the heels of her pumps into the dirt. She eased him between her legs so that he could feel the silk of her tap pants. Though he tried to get inside, she wouldn't let him. But for now, Tony was content with sliding along her dampening crease. He could feel her heat radiating through the sheer, soft material. Denise stood on her tippy-toes, as though trying to reach a high shelf. And finally, she did reach it, whimpering and moaning and cursing and trembling all over him. Tony reached it also, a beat behind her, spilling his seed onto the dry grass behind them.

Denise didn't say anything afterward, just straightened her skirts, her hair, adjusted her lipstick with a fingertip and left.

Tony had to walk quickly down Manhattan Avenue through the Surf Avenue gate, practically running down Surf to Stillwell. It was a little over a mile but he didn't mind for it was worth the walk, the run, even. Luna Park was a blur of brightness as he hurried past, all towers and Arabian architecture and millions of light bulbs. He'd have to remember to give the kids a few bucks so they could get lost there some Saturday.

If Tony had more time, he would have stopped at Phillips Candy for a sack of those licorice whips Tiger liked. Hell, he was already late and five minutes wouldn't make or break him. Besides, he didn't give a damn. They could dock his measly pay if they wanted to, and probably would.

Tony pushed open the candy store's glass door and was immediately surrounded by sweetness.

12 The Girl with the Chestnut Mane

On Saturdays, Tony knew Denise didn't work, so there was little chance of seeing her. Because of this, he was in a bum mood from the get-go. Kewpie was at Kresge's—anything was better than being home when her father was there—and he could hear Tiger outside with his friends. His son's joyful voice raised in play and the boy's careless, goofy laugh made its way up to the open kitchen window. Jimmy Burns was running around in his Superman cape again, threatening to jump off the garage roof. Tony peered out the window in disgust. "I don't know why his damn fool mother encourages it," he growled, "making him that stupid cape and all."

"Aw, Tony, it's harmless," Rosanna tried to tell him.

"Won't be harmless when he falls and breaks his neck," Tony said. He was sitting at the kitchen table with a cup of tea set in front of him, his tender stomach unable to tolerate toast, cereal or especially not eggs fried in olive oil. Although Rosanna offered several times, Tony insisted only on tea, black, no milk or even sugar. Cream would surely curdle in the whiskey he'd added

surreptitiously from the medicine-bottle flask. He thought
Rosanna wouldn't notice, except she did.

There was something different about Tony, but Rosanna
couldn't put her finger on it. He'd come in during the wee hours
from the night shift, humming. Cole Porter, Irving Berlin, she
couldn't quite make it out. He even had bags of sweets for the
kids and the raisin clusters her parents liked. But that afternoon,
he woke up like a grizzly in a bad humor. Tony was no stranger
to black moods, but this wasn't the same.

Each time he lifted the gilt-edged teacup to his lips, Tony
smelled Denise on his fingertips. A vague scent of the sea mixed
with a hint of Joy perfume. (It was extremely expensive, a gift
from an old beau, and was supposedly Mae West's favorite,
Denise had told him, breathlessly.) He could even smell *eau de
Denise* distinctly above the vapors of the liquor in his tea.

Rosanna was posted a few feet away at the stove, chopping
something, always endlessly chopping. She wore a baggy
housedress, the pattern long faded and indistinguishable. There
was no chance of seeing blossoming poppies or vibrant blue
roses on this baby doll. Rosanna wore once-fluffy bedroom
slippers. The skin on the heels of her feet was cracked and dry.
There were no patent leather pumps, red or otherwise, within
sight. Tony wondered if his wife had ever worn red in her life.
"It's a color for clowns and hussies," he remembered her
saying once.

Tony studied the shapeless form that was turned away from
him, bent over the cutting board. Garlic. She was chopping
garlic. Rosanna popped each clove from its papery sheath and
sliced it wafer thin before bringing the blade down again and
again until the garlic was almost translucent. Her fingers always
smelled of the stuff, even after she scrubbed her hands several
times with Kirkman's. Tony doubted if Denise even knew what
a head of garlic looked like or could identify its bin at Moe the
greengrocer's. And there was something very attractive about
that thought.

Rosanna chopped. There was an art to it, she believed, a
science to chopping the garlic just right, releasing the vapors so
that they were almost intoxicating. When she was a girl, waking

to the scent of Bridget's garlicky gravy simmering on the stove early on a Sunday morning was one of her favorite things. To her, this smell was more pleasant, more evocative than coffee brewing. Wedged between sister and brother in that big, warm feather bed, the aroma would gently nudge her awake. Rosanna would slip out from between slumbering siblings and sneak into the kitchen. She would tear off the end of the Italian bread, dip the heel into the sauce until it was beautifully soggy then let it drip onto her tongue like Holy Water.

Bridget would smile when she spotted Rosanna creeping into the kitchen. She was expecting her, counting the minutes until her cooking roused her eldest child, because it always did. Rosanna Maria (as she was called in those days) would rest her head on her mother's belly, usually rounded from one pregnancy or another, and smile into the warm, familiar flesh. Bridget would smooth down the girl's hair, which trailed her spine, long and thick and shiny as a horse's mane. Together, they would chop and knead and stir and laugh, before anyone else was awake. It was their special, stolen time when Rosanna didn't have to share her mother with anyone. These were perhaps her most pungent childhood memories—the mornings she spent alone with Bridget, learning to cook.

Rosanna could feel Tony staring at her back and hoped he wasn't thinking of anything dirty. Not with Tiger playing right outside. She could hear her son's laugh, like music, in a voice much higher than the other kids. His laugh was so unguarded and free, a laugh she never heard indoors. In the apartment, Rosanna heard herself saying things like: "Shush, your father's under the weather," or "Why do you have to laugh so loud? You know he's sleeping." Imagine, telling your child to laugh more quietly? Quiet was against the very nature of a laugh.

Rosanna wiped away a tear, hoping Tony wouldn't see. If he did, she could say it was from the onions she was now chopping, only it wasn't true. She was crying because she couldn't remember the last time she'd laughed like that.

Tony kept replaying last night's movie in his head: the sound of the surf plunging against Nortons Point jetty, the feel of Denise's hair between his fingers, lacquered and crisp with hairspray, the momentary glare of the lighthouse light, the crests of her nipples, round and hard as the cherry drops at Phillips Candy shop, the heat of her skin, the smell of it, the sensation of her silk underdrawers bringing him off.

Rosanna always wore baggy cotton bloomers, once white, now dingy, despite the bleach she added and the spirited scrubbing she gave them. Her hair was now a drab brown but was once so vibrant it almost seemed alive between his fingertips. Practically everything about his wife had lost its sparkle. Had he done that to her?

The first time Tony saw Rosanna, he was making deliveries with Gertie faithfully pulling his dairy wagon. He spotted a lovely girl from the vantage point the wagon's high bench gave him. When called her "The Girl with the Chestnut Mane," it made her laugh out loud so that her whole face shone. Tony even made up a comical song to go with the name which made her smile even more dazzling.

Rosanna had been walking down the dirt road with a little sister in hand, maybe Camille or Josephina. He remembered thinking that she looked so scrubbed and pure compared with everything else around her. Tony had never seen a dress so white, or hair so lush and bright, caught in a big, creamy ribbon. The Paradiso Girls were on their way home from Saturday afternoon confessions at St. Catherine's, and he remembered thinking, 'What sins could this creature possibly have?'

These days, he would have to answer, just the sin of marrying him.

Rosanna figured that maybe if she made the perfect meal, if she scoured the kitchen floor a little harder, if the windows shone a little brighter, if she prayed more fervently, then he would stop. Stop drinking, stop hollering, stop hitting, stop breaking, stop ruining. That he would stop, just stop. But what Rosanna didn't realize was that it wasn't her. It was all about him. And he was broken long before she met him.

In their own charitable way, Poppa and Bridget had tried to tell her this before she and Tony got too serious, but Rosanna refused to listen. This Anthony fellow came from a different place, Poppa had said, from a place where you didn't have three

simple but square meals a day, where nobody mended your
clothes, where no one cared whether you were safely tucked in at
night, and no one looked after you at all. They'd heard gossip
about Tony's mother, which turned out to be true, about how she
made a living, and it horrified them.

Always a headstrong child, Rosanna simply could not be
swayed. She was tired of being "the good girl," tired of always
doing what was expected of her, tired of always being safe. So,
without anyone's blessing, she married the ne'er-do-well.
Rosanna's parents did their best to embrace their son-in-law
and welcome him into the family, but like a stray dog taken into
a caring home, you never knew when that dog might turn on
you. But one thing was for sure, they always did. It was just
a question of when.

And seventeen years later, Rosanna was tired. She was tired
of being "the good girl who married the bad boy." She was tired
of constantly trying to make things work, yet for some reason
she still tried. Only now, she had given up on trying.

Tony's head was pounding. His stomach was in knots. The
bicarbonate of soda Rosanna served him did nothing. The aspirin
didn't help either. And then there were the kids, those damn kids
screaming in the alley. "They're only playing," Rosanna told
him, trying to make light of it. Tony pushed her aside. He flung
the window open as wide as it would go and banged his head on
the sash.

"Get the hell out of here," Tony shouted out the window,
rubbing the top of his head. The children scattered like mice.
Tiger looked embarrassed and afraid before he disappeared
with them.

Almost on cue, Mrs. Rosenkrantz's son began practicing
his violin in the house next door. The sound grated across
the alleyway, the song of a tortured cat. "Ti-tu, ti-tu," Tony
mimicked. "Shut the fuck up!"

Bertha Rosenkrantz yelled an epitaph in Yiddish before
clapping her window shut but the muffled noise of a strangled
Stradivarius could still be heard.

When he came away from the window, Tony realized that his
wife was cringing. Rosanna didn't dare look at him but she

didn't stop chopping, no matter how badly her hands shook. By accident, she brought the paring knife's sharp blade down onto her knuckles. Blood immediately began to flow. She ran her hand under cool tap water then wrapped it in a dishtowel until the bleeding stopped. Her husband left the room without asking how she was.

It was Tony's birthday and Rosanna wanted to make a special meal, even though he had to work that night. Munitsal, his favorite, in which little hunks of pork fat and potatoes floated in a soupy broth. The kids hated it but she was making it just the same. People deserved to have their favorite dish on their birthday, she reasoned. Rosanna had bought all the fixings while he slept. There would also be *scungilli*, snails cooked in red sauce and served over spaghetti. The kids weren't too crazy about this either, but too bad. She would serve them plain pasta tossed in grated cheese and butter. They would have sautéd green beans on the side and Icebox Cake for dessert. How could someone be grumpy with a feast like that, even if they had to go to work?

As the tomato sauce simmered on the stove, Tony reappeared in the kitchen, fully dressed in his uniform. "But it's so early…" Rosanna began then stopped when she saw the dour expression on his face. She took a deep breath and tried again. "It's your birthday," she told her husband.

"I know what day it is," he barked.

"I was making you a special supper," she said in almost a whisper.

"I'm going to work," he informed her.

And that was that. Tony was gone without so much as a peck on the cheek, without even opening the gifts she and the kids had gotten him.

Rosanna sat down at the kitchen table. The girl with the chestnut mane crumpled up and cried, and there was no one to even comfort her. Not the laughing children, not Mrs. Rosenkrantz, who opened her window again to shout more Yiddish curses. Rosanna didn't even lift her head from the table when she heard the splash of cold water against warm concrete. At least once a day, Mrs. Rosenkrantz threw a big pot

of water onto rowdy, happy children to chase them away so
Ti-Tu could practice his violin undisturbed. But it never worked.
It only made the kids laugh harder and play louder.

At first, Tony was surprised to see her getting on at 42nd Street.
He immediately felt lighter, happier. Denise was a vision in black
satin, her dress cut low, fabric dripping off her shoulders. Her
black pumps sported matching rhinestone buckles that mimicked
the one between her breasts. There were even rhinestones clipped
to her ear lobes. But then Tony saw him—an older gentleman
in a dress suit and hat, stinking of money. The guy's fedora
alone probably cost more than Tony made in a week. 'What's
the cheapskate doing taking the subway anyway?' he wondered.
But Tony realized how hard it was to get a cab to venture into
Brooklyn, let alone all the way to the ass-end of the borough to
Sea Gate. Maybe Denise insisted they take the train, just to get
his goat, Tony decided. The bitch-whore-cunt.

Denise strolled into the subway car without so much as a
glance into the conductor's cage but Tony knew she spotted him.
He knew because his ears burned. The guy followed her like
a cocker spaniel and obediently sat beside her in a two-seater
bench directly across from Tony's box. Even though the
overhead fans were going full blast, Denise fanned herself with
a *Playbill* that read *On Your Toes*. She wanted Tony to notice,
and he did.

Even as he pulled the lever, opening and closing the doors,
attempting to concentrate on his work and trying not to pay her
any mind, Tony heard snippets of their conversation. Denise was
speaking a bit too loudly: "Don't you just love a Rodgers and
Hart musical"… "Isn't that Ray Bolger just divine?"… "And
George Balanchine…does he know a thing or two about dance!"
She thought "Slaughter on Tenth Avenue" was the show's
highlight, while the little runt's ballot was cast for "There's a
Small Hotel." Tony was so distracted that he slammed the door
on an old lady's foot at Ninth Avenue. He could have sworn he
heard Denise giggle. When she and her fancy man stepped onto
the platform at Stillwell Avenue, Denise looked over her
shoulder and blew Tony a kiss.

The brakes of an incoming Sea Beach train shrieked through the silence.

Earlier that afternoon, after Tony had left so abruptly, as the fat soup bubbled furiously on the stove, a chorus of screams and then a thump roused Rosanna from the kitchen table. The girl with the chestnut mane forced herself to get up and go to the window. A handful of children stood on the Rosenkrantz's wooden garage roof, peering over the side. Another cluster of kids gathered around a small, broken body on the concrete below. Rosanna held her breath and then realized that it wasn't Tiger. The fallen form was shrouded in a Superman cape.

Someone clopped up the hall stairs and the apartment's front door flew open. Tiger's face was streaked with dirt and sweat and tears. "Mamma!" he cried but didn't even have to finish the sentence. They were out the door, down the stairs and across the street at Dr. Lewis's in a matter of seconds. He moved quickly for a man shaped like a bowling pin, pulling the linen napkin from his shirt collar as he ran, grabbing his black bag from his cluttered desk, forgetting all about the leftover stuffed cabbage his wife Eva had left for lunch.

By the time they arrived in the backyard, a crowd had already formed on the cracked concrete. Sully's hulking frame was already hunched over Jimmy Burns' body, trying to breathe life into him. When Sully felt Dr. Lewis's hand on his shoulder, he moved aside, making room for "the senior man," as he'd put it, the man with more training. With Sully, there was no ego, no pretenses, just what was the right thing to do.

But the doctor told Sully to keep going. Rosanna felt a surge of pride as the large cop brought the boy back to consciousness at Dr. Lewis's urging. "Look at him, big strapping lug that he is," Dr. Lewis would later say. "He has more air in one breath than I do in three. *Kineahora*." This meant, "God bless him" in Yiddish, without uttering God's name, which religious Jews like the good doctor believed was a sin, unless, of course, you were praying.

Jimmy Burns stirred on the ground, coughing and crying at the same time. "My arm," he said, grabbing it and writhing.

Jimmy looked like a fallen bird as Sully scooped him up and carried him across the street to Dr. Lewis's office, dragging the Superman cape in their wake. By this time, word had reached Jimmy's mother, who ran down from 12th Avenue sobbing and wiping her hands on her apron.

The crowd disbursed and life on 47th Street pretty much went back to normal in the shadow of the El. But for many years to come, they would talk of the time Jimmy Burns tried to fly off the Rosenkrantz's garage roof and Sully saved him. At least the Girl with the Chestnut Mane would.

13 Blue Knight

After the incident with Jimmy Burns, it became apparent to Rosanna that her good child could very easily become a bad child if left to his own devices. Even though Tiger seemed to possess nothing of his father on the surface, the man was in his blood. And it was all too easy to be swayed from one side to the other. Given the same bleak upbringing, you could either choose to be a Sully or a Tony. Rosanna hoped and prayed her son would be a Sully. Not that Tony was around much anyway, but she was damned if she'd let what happened to him happen to Tiger.

The sight of Jimmy Burns lifeless on the concrete then screaming in agony put the fear of God in Tiger. As Sully shuttled the boy across the street to Dr. Lewis's, Tiger silently reached for Rosanna's hand, something he hadn't done since he was in diapers. And she took it. She took it and squeezed it hard, brought it to her lips and kissed his dirty knuckles. Tiger burrowed his face into his mother's housedress, not wanting his friends to see him cry.

Once inside, tears dried, hands washed, Rosanna let Tiger help put the finishing touches on the Icebox Cake. After he crumpled up the graham crackers into a fine dust, she showed him how to scatter them on top of the pudding cake, like a layer of sweet sand. "Am I doing it right?" he wondered.

"Just perfect," Rosanna smiled. She watched her son's face as he worked, his brow wrinkled in concentration. She smiled at the way he bit on the tip of his tongue, which protruded slightly, as he accomplished this relatively easy task. But to Tiger, being entrusted with topping the Icebox Cake was the most weighty, awesome responsibility in his tiny universe.

In Tiger's mind, that dessert was pure bliss: chocolate then vanilla pudding layered over graham crackers in a square glass pan. The heat of the cooked pudding, then the rapid cooling in the icebox softened the graham crackers to a lovely, pillowy consistency so that you didn't even have to chew. Tiger wanted so much to do right, sought approval and beamed when he got it. "Just perfect," his mother repeated.

When the Martino family retired to their kitchen to eat Tony's birthday supper without him, it was a meal none of them particularly enjoyed. Except for the creamy, delicious Icebox Cake, which they had just before bed. When Tiger, Kewpie and Rosanna sat to finally sample it in the dim kitchen far past the kids' bedtime, it truly seemed the most wonderful Icebox Cake Tiger had ever tasted. Rosanna even allowed them a cup of tea with a splash of milk and honey, and took her best teapot from the cupboard, the one with the gilt-edged roses, for the occasion. Each wonderful mouthful simply slid down from mouth to throat to belly like a dream. They didn't bother to put a candle in the cake or even speak of Tony's birthday.

By the time they had his cake, Tony was on his meal break, standing in the streetlamp's glow beneath the windows of the Half Moon Hotel on Surf Avenue. He was wondering which room Denise and her fancy man were in, cursing under his breath. Tony tried his damndest to give that rich, rat bastard the *malocchio*, hoping the evil eye Tony cast upon him would wilt his erection and the man's wrinkled dick would wither in defeat.

Nearing the middle of June, it was already as hot as August. The rooms of the narrow railroad apartment were stuffy and airless. Rosanna let Kewpie and Tiger sleep out on the porch this warm, clear Saturday evening. She dragged out the bedrolls, beat the dust from them and set them out on the clean, wooden slats of the upstairs decking. The slats themselves sagged slightly but that was all right. The stars and the glory of the night more than made up for it.

Kewpie was tired from work and from her chores but Tiger was excited at the sheer thought of sleeping outdoors. "Do you think we'll see a shooting star?" and "What's that sound?" and "Can God see us better now?" were some of his questions. Although Kewpie answered her brother with a weary groan, this still didn't seem to matter to Tiger. He just kept right on talking.

Then he was quiet for a long time. Kewpie thought that maybe Tiger had fallen asleep but he was just busy thinking. The blanket of darkness had given him the gift of bravery. "I hope he goes away and never comes back," Tiger said plainly. "Not dies but just leaves."

"How would we manage without him?" Kewpie yawned.

"We'd get by. I know we would."

An airplane rumbled softly overhead. Tiger watched the winking lights make their way across the sky. Voices drifted up from the sidewalk below as two or three people moved past the house. Tiger held his breath, hoping one of them wasn't his father, but the tones faded into quiet and there was no sound of feet shuffling up the steps, no crash of the door.

"Do you think Poppa will die soon?" Tiger wondered.

"Jeez, I hope not," Kewpie told him. "Why do you think about these things?"

"It's just that he and Grandma Bridget are so old and..."

"Quit worrying and go to sleep," Kewpie said to her brother, exasperated. She turned to one side in the bedroll, feeling like a cloth caterpillar, while Tiger lay on his back staring at the stars. It made him dizzy even though he was lying down. It made him feel tiny and insignificant even though his mother told him that everyone mattered. Everyone and everything. A little boy was as important as the stars, she said. He wanted to ask Kewpie about this but then he heard her gently snoring. He wanted to tell Kewpie about the shooting star he saw, slicing a bright arc against the bleakness then disappearing. It was splendid to watch. And no matter what his mother said, he knew a shooting star was far more important than any of them.

Tiger soon drifted off to sleep and didn't hear the following sound: two sets of polished black patent leather shoes striking the pavement, the sound of those shoes climbing the house's brick steps then creaking across the wooden porch.

Neither did Rosanna, who sat at the kitchen table, darning a pair of Tony's work socks. Did she hear a knock or was it just her imagination? Poppa or Momma would just come in, without bothering to rap on the door, and Tony wasn't due home until morning. There it was again. Rosanna stood and opened the unlocked door to find Sully with his cop hat in hand. Harry stood at the foot of the staircase, about to drop into her parents' for a brief hello. He nodded up at Rosanna, signifying that he knew Sully was visiting her alone and that it was okay with him.

For such a large man, Patrick Sullivan seemed very small as he stood in the hall. His wide shoulders practically filled the doorway as he remained there solid and firm like a blue knight. "I just wanted to ask about Tiger," he faltered. "He seemed really upset about what happened today with the Burns kid. I wanted to make sure he was okay."

"Yes," said Rosanna. "Yes, he's fine. Thanks for looking in on us. Tiger was little shaken up but he's fine now. And Jimmy?"

"Doc Lewis says it's a pretty bad break. Could have been a lot worse. That kid must be made of rubber."

Rosanna smiled and looked at the welcome mat outside the door and at the hallway itself, freshly swept. "It was pretty amazing what you did," she told Sully. "You brought that boy back to life."

Sully looked into her eyes and then at her feet. Her right was placed on a white linoleum square and her left, on a black one. Sully felt his face grow warm and imagined that he was reddening to the tips of his ears. "Just doing my job, is all, Roe," he said, shrugging. "I'm glad I was close enough to hear the screaming."

"Me, too," Rosanna told him. "It's good to have you looking out for us. All of us, I mean." There was a silence which she soon filled. "Yeah, Tiger was pretty shaken. Took him a while to settle down but he finally did," she added. "He's sleeping now. They both are. I let them bunk out on the porch tonight."

"It's a nice night," Sully agreed. "Warm but nice."

Rosanna stepped aside so that her clean but weary kitchen came into view. "Please, come in, Paddy. I was going to have another cup of tea."

As if on cue, the battered teakettle began its high-pitched wail. By force of habit, Rosanna ran to shut the burner underneath it so the sound wouldn't wake the children, but they were so far away it didn't matter and there was no husband sleeping off a drunk to worry about either. She'd conditioned herself to quickly silence noises that might provoke Tony to fly off the handle, although tonight he was nowhere in sight. It was a hard habit to break.

Sully remained in the doorway. "I couldn't," he said.

Rosanna shoved the socks, needle and thread into the sewing basket on the floor. "Sure you could," she told him. "It's just a cup of tea, Patrick." Although Sully still hadn't moved, Rosanna set two saucers and two cups on the table. Her good china, he noticed. She took the teapot from the drain board, plunked in the tea ball and drowned it in steamy water. Only when she took out the Icebox Cake, did Sully finally step over the marble saddle and into the apartment. They left the door open while they sat.

Talk never came easy to Sully but when he was with Rosanna, the words just flowed. Her compassionate brown eyes and kind manner made him feel at ease, maybe because she was safe—she was another man's wife and he was a gentleman. But Sully's feelings of comfort could have stemmed from the fact that they'd known each other most of their lives. "You both come from the same place," his sister Irene liked to say, quoting one of Bridget's favorite phrases, and it was true. Not just geographically but the same place of heart. Sully had known Rosanna since she'd worn her hair in braids and she'd known him since he was in patched knickers. She was certain and she was true and she was safe.

By the second cup of tea, Sully noticed the nasty bruise on Rosanna's arm. He held her thin limb lightly between his chubby fingers. "You slip on the ice again?" he asked. Rosanna wriggled out of his gentle grip to add more hot water to the teapot.

"I'm clumsy," she said with her back facing him. "I walked into..."

"His fist?"

Rosanna's doe-eyes flashed with emotion then softened. "Into the doorway. I walked into the doorway, Patrick. It was my fault."

"Sure it was," he told her.

Sully wanted to throw the bastard a beating, take to him with his billy club, but it would only make things worse for Rosanna. So he did nothing. Just sat there in her snug kitchen, sipping tea in a pretty cup that was too delicate for his thick fingers. He scraped his fork on the flowered plate, scooping up the last bit of pudding cake, as Rosanna eased another sliver onto it. Before he could refuse she told him, "Just a drop more. It's a sin to waste."

Sully laid his hand on top of Rosanna's on the table, his big pink paw completely covering her small, slender hand. "If you need anything, Roe," he began. "Anything at all, just say the word and I'll..."

Rosanna put down the empty Pyrex cake pan and patted Sully's hand gingerly. "I know, Patrick. But there's nothing you can do. There's nothing anyone can do. But thanks," she said, smiling sadly.

14 "This is it... This is Nash"

It had been two weeks and still no word from Tony. Not that Rosanna minded his not being around but she did miss his paycheck. Or at least the part he didn't drink away each week. Rosanna knew he was still showing up at work but the Transport Workers Union said she wasn't entitled to any of his pay without a signed document from him, and that wasn't happening since Rosanna had no clue where he was. Kewpie gave what she could from working part-time at Kresge's but it wasn't enough to get by. Poppa and Bridget helped out in other ways.

The Jimmy Burns incident managed to put the whole block on edge. Jimmy's broken arm and was healing nicely, but his Superman cape was retired to the attic. To keep Tiger out of trouble and to bring in a little something extra for the Martinos, Poppa started taking the boy with him to the Navy Yard. At first, Rosanna wasn't very receptive to the idea. "He's just a kid, Pop," she said. "He should be running around and playing and having fun during the summer."

"And he will," Poppa told her kindly yet firmly. "But two or three days a week isn't gonna kill him. And I could really use his help."

Rosanna wiped her hands on a dishtowel. "But what about Tiger taking work away from a grown man who needs to feed his family?"

Poppa looked around. The kitchen was well-worn but spotless. Rosanna did the best with what she had, which wasn't much. Poppa rested his hand on his daughter's shoulder, which seemed to be sagging with responsibility. "Anthony will be helping to feed his family," Poppa stressed. "Besides, this is different. Boy's work, not men's work. A man couldn't feed his family on this. But a boy, a boy would be a great help. To you and to me."

If the truth be told, Rosanna worried that her whole world was slipping through her fingertips. In some ways, she felt as though she had already lost Kewpie and now her little boy was going, too. Tiger looked up at her expectantly, his green eyes ablaze. She smoothed his cowlick with one hand and rested the other on his waist, feeling sinew and ribs. "Please say yes, Ma," he begged. "Please?"

Tiger couldn't decide which he liked better: walking along the street with his hand tightly clasping Poppa's or driving alone with him in the Nash. "You make me feel like a cabbie!" his grandfather protested as Tiger slid into the car's cavernous back seat. Tiger loved being swallowed up in the dark, tufted leather, barely able to see out the windows. He watched the tops of houses roll by, both brownstones and wood frame. He watched the water towers, chimneys, wisps of clouds and swirls of pigeons pass the rolled-down windows. Maybe he did like riding in the Nash a little better than walking beside his grandfather. Yes, it definitely was the Nash.

And as much as he belly-ached, Poppa enjoyed driving the boy. He liked peering at his grandson's bright face in the rear-view mirror without Tiger knowing, studying the slender features that were so like his daughter's and so like her husband's. Tiger was dark and serious like Rosanna but had emerald eyes like

Tony's. Being ferried about in the Nash and playing stickball were some of the boy's rare, free moments when Tiger's features were unmarked by the furrows of concern that have no business being in a ten-year-old child's face anyhow. These were times of pure, unencumbered joy, and the old man was glad he could give this to Tiger, even fleetingly.

The Nash was barely a year old and still smelled new. Its burgundy skin gleamed like the dark wine Poppa sipped with Sunday dinner. Twinkles were built into the paint, Tiger noted. This car was Poppa's pride with its bug-eyed headlights and small, secretive back windows. He polished as religiously as Bridget and Rosanna went to Mass, giving Tiger the important job of scrubbing the whitewalls, as snappy as spats on a gangster. Its insignia, like a general's epaulet or the flag of a bold emerging nation, was perfectly centered in the car's gleaming grille. A nameplate proclaimed "Nash" in a rectangle of ebony which was mounted within the lush red and gold shield. "This is it! This is Nash!" the slogan went. And it certainly was.

Tiger knew that his grandfather had paid almost a thousand dollars for the car. He knew because he'd heard his parents arguing about it in the bedroom one day as he did his homework at the kitchen table. And Tiger was sure, that in their apartment downstairs, his grandparents had heard, too, despite the fact that Bridget always made the radio louder because she couldn't bear the sound of Tony and Rosanna's fights.

It had gone something like this:

"Almost a thousand fucking bucks!" Tony shouted. "Do you know what I could do with a thousand bucks?"

Tiger wanted to suggest, 'Drink it away?' He knew his mother was probably thinking the same thing, but instead of uttering it, Rosanna said sweetly, "But it's his money, Tony. He can do what he wants with it."

"While we're living like dogs upstairs," Tony yelled.

"We don't live like dogs, honey," she tried to explain. "Look, we pay almost no rent. Why, on your salary, we should..."

"What? We should have a house by now? Say it."

"I wasn't going to say that."

"Like your sister Jo and her crooked cop husband?"

"Harry's not crooked…I just mean that…"

"I know exactly what you mean. I can spend my money the way I like, too. I can piss it away if I want. Just like my inheritance."

When Philomena died, she had more than $26,000 in a bank account, an unheard of sum in those days. Marie wanted no part of Philomena, not even her money, so the woman's three sons divided it amongst themselves. Tony squandered his share on who knows what and managed to swindle some of his brother Tommy's money away from him as well. Rounds of drinks at Jerry's and the Pink Pussycat, an ill-fated second honeymoon (with both kids in tow) to Niagara Falls, and so on.

Rosanna chose not to follow Tony's lead. It was safer that way. "My father worked hard his whole life," she decided to say, then realized it probably wasn't her wisest choice of words.

"Like I don't work hard?" Tony screeched.

"I didn't mean…"

"Oh, sure you did. Sure you did, Roe."

This was followed by the sound of movement, of shuffling feet, of furniture being bumped. Tiger thought he heard his mother's muffled cries but he couldn't be certain. Tony stormed out of the apartment without saying good-bye. After finishing his homework, Tiger put himself to bed, passing his mother's form clumped on the mattress.

The following morning, Tiger spotted a fresh mark on Rosanna's wrist. It spread across her skin like a blossoming flower. She tried to cover it, tugging down the sleeve of her sweater whenever she remembered, but the material kept pushing back as she lifted her arm to stir Tiger's farina. The ugly bruise was eye level as she plopped his breakfast into a bowl before him. Tiger couldn't stop looking at his mother's wrist. Before she turned to go back to the stove, he planted a little kiss on it. "What's that for?" she wondered. Tiger just shrugged in response. He wasn't sure what that kiss was for himself.

Tiger remembered another loud conversation from a night not so very long ago. During the days leading up to it, the Martino house had been particularly unsettled. There had been lots of hollering, table-slamming and tears. One evening after Tiger was supposed to be long asleep, there was a rap on the door, followed by Poppa's low voice, then Tony's booming one. Poppa talked plainly about how Tony had been acting lately, the drinking, the fighting, and voiced his general concern about the family.

"It's none of your God-damned business," Tony told him. "And if you don't keep your fucking big nose out of it, I'll take them and move them away. You'll never see them again." Tony proceeded to slam the door in Poppa's face. Rosanna proceeded to sob herself to sleep again on the bed. Tony continued drinking bourbon at the kitchen table. He was something of a junk drinker, imbibing what happened to be around, whether he liked it or not. So long as it gave him a buzz, that's all that mattered.

After that night, Poppa never spoke to Tony about his behavior again, for his worst nightmare was Tony leaving with Rosanna and the kids. If he did, Poppa would no longer be able to weigh the severity of the shouts, standing in the darkened hallway below, silently listening, wincing, trying to judge if it were time to call Sully and Harry or just let the storm blow over. If Tony took them away then Poppa would no longer be able to protect his daughter, no matter how feebly.

Poppa told it different, why he bought the Nash. Now Tiger was absolutely certain the old man had heard his parents' argument and felt the need to explain himself. "You only live once," Poppa began. "So, I decided, why not treat myself? Why not take Grandma Bridget around in style? Why not drive Tiger McPunch around like a prince," Poppa grinned, gripping his pipe with his teeth.

But Tiger felt more like the Pauper than the Prince. His knickers were worn thin in the seat and his shoes needed cobbling. Poppa offered to lend a hand but Rosanna was proud. She wouldn't take his money. It wasn't his place to help them, she said. It was her husband's. Rosanna had managed to squirrel away a little bit of money each week without Tony knowing, except now that was almost gone, too.

But on this day, in the back seat of the Nash, Tiger felt as splendid as anyone. Especially with Poppa humming in his lovely soft, wavering style. Tiger knew the words to the song he hummed:

"Momma may have and Poppa may have
But God bless the child that's got his own..."

And now, Tiger would have his own. He was making his own money and he would hand every bit of it over to Rosanna. Between him and Kewpie, they'd get by. That's when Tiger began to hum "I'll Get By." Poppa rested his pipe in the car's ashtray and sang the song's next line, which was,

"...as long as I have you."

While Poppa might confuse the names of singers, politicians and movie actors, when it came to lyrics, no one could beat him. He cleared his throat and out came a voice that was unexpected. It was very wee and surprisingly delicate for a man of his size and stature:

"Though there be rain and darkness too
I'll not complain, I'll see it through..."

However, Poppa skipped over the next line, which Tiger knew by heart. It was:

"Poverty may come to me, that's true."

Instead, Poppa sailed right into:

"But what care I, say
I'll get by as long as I have you."

Tiger and Poppa sang the last line of the song together, very pleased with themselves. Poppa pushed his wire-rimmed glasses up on the bridge of his very fine, very distinguished Roman nose and smiled some more. Tiger settled back in the Nash's cradle of leather and looked out the window.

Poppa drove toward the Navy Yard with big sweeping movements, his hands grasping the steering wheel like a captain piloting a ship. The Nash's ride was smooth as churned butter as it hugged the streets and sailed across the cobblestones and trolley tracks. It was one hell of a car. "Mind if I take the long way?" Poppa wondered. "It's more picturesque."

In truth, Tiger didn't mind anything Poppa did. His decisions always seemed to be the right ones, in everyone's best interest. On Eighth Avenue, they passed the 14th Street Armory, with its Doughboy piercing the air with his trusty bayonet. Poppa had once told him that the building's cornerstone came from the battlefields of Gettysburg and Tiger remembered this every time they passed the foreboding fortress. He pictured Uncle John's face as the Doughboy's as he scoured the French battlefields long before Tiger was born.

From Eighth Avenue, Poppa made his way up the hill of Union Street and turned onto the Grand Army Plaza Circle. Prospect Park stood to the right, all green with promise. But today, it wasn't time to play, but to work.

To Tiger, the Grand Army Plaza Arch was even more glorious than the *Arc de Triumphe* in Paris, France, to which it was often compared and in fact, modeled after. Although he'd only seen the latter in picture books, Brooklyn's arch was that much more grand because it stood practically in his own backyard. Its official name was the Soldiers' and Sailors' Memorial Arch but no one ever called it that, for that tagline was quite a mouthful for fast-talking Brooklynites. To most, it was simply The Arch. It was built in 1892 and honored the Union troops of the Civil War.

"See it?" Poppa asked.

Tiger knew exactly what his grandfather was referring to. Poppa drove slowly enough so Tiger could scan the vast sculptures, among largest in the borough. He quickly picked out the soldier who held a pair of binoculars, a new invention in the 1860s. Several soldiers, Tiger noted, were colored.

The Arch was a busy, bustling masterpiece, it was true. However, Tiger did not share his grandfather's enthusiasm about the binoculars. Now, Tiger liked Army men as much as the next guy but his favorite part of the Arch was the winged angel blowing her trumpet at the top. If you looked hard enough, you could almost make out her tiny bronze nipples through her wind-rippled robe.

Poppa veered onto Vanderbilt Avenue. Tiger could see the spire of the Williamsburg Savings Bank Tower to the left, rising high above all else. They passed rows of brownstones with old carriage houses sandwiched between them. After Bishop Loughlin came Queen of All Saints (church and school), with its carvings of judgmental holy folk scowling upon the sidewalks below. Tiger thought these saints looked even scarier than Lon Chaney but for some reason, he still loved looking at them. These holy folk were almost life-size, looming one story above street-level, and soiled with decades of grime. Good Catholics could identify each and every one them by their saintly accessories. Tiger picked out St. Patrick's funny peaked cap, John the Baptist's stone staff, St. Francis' rope-tied rock robe and the Virgin Mary, looking somewhat disappointed that she was now living in Kings County.

On Myrtle Avenue, the old liquor sign on the corner store announced its wares in two directions, as though the proprietors wanted to make sure the drunks saw it coming and going. Vanderbilt continued downhill to the waterfront. The Brooklyn Navy Yard spanned across hundreds of acres and there were several gates both for cars and for foot traffic, since many workers lived nearby in Fort Greene and could walk to work. However, Poppa, for some reason, preferred sailing down Park Avenue and using the Cumberland Street entrance. That's the approach he and Tiger took this day.

No matter how many times his grandfather brought him to the Navy Yard, the boy's heart grew both full and light at the same time when he laid eyes on the place. To Tiger, the Brooklyn Navy Yard's big, wide, high Cumberland gate seemed like the portal to heaven. Or something like it.

15 At the Navy Yard

Despite the Cumberland Street gate's vague resemblance to the threshold of a mechanical heaven, St. Peter didn't helm it, but a kindly older gentleman named Horatio did. Horatio looked very official and ominous, that is, until he smiled. Then all ceremony and seriousness faded away. But when Tiger thought about it everyone seemed to smile at Poppa, especially when he was navigating the gleaming Nash.

The Cumberland gate wasn't pearly or golden but was colossal just the same, industrial and somewhat ominous. Beyond this entrance, the Navy Yard was alive, a busy, bustling sub-city, an entity unto itself. Poppa knew everything about the place—he'd spent most of his adult life working here—and he passed most of this knowledge on to Tiger, who sucked it up like an eager, young sponge.

As far as the boy was concerned, his own father had nothing much to give to him, no supreme scepter of wisdom to hand down like a birthright. What could Tony possibly teach him? How to open a beer bottle with his teeth? How to bully,

shove, bruise and otherwise instill terror? How to open
and close train doors? But Poppa could, and did, offer Tiger
something real, something tangible, something that mattered. A
man of simple means, Poppa didn't have much to give him in
worldly goods but he gave the child something which couldn't
be bartered or bought: he gave him pieces of himself.

Most kids Tiger's age didn't know or care about such things
as the intricacies of shipbuilding. But Tiger did. He cared and he
remembered. The official name of Poppa's workplace was the
New York Naval Shipyard but few referred to it as that. Most
called it the Brooklyn Navy Yard. Within its walled-in
boundaries, there were almost five miles of paved streets, four
dry docks ranging from 326 to 700 feet long, two steel shipways
plus six pontoons and floats for salvage work. Though Tiger had
tried to do so several times, there were too many buildings to
count: barracks, a power plant, foundries, a large radio station,
a small hospital and machine shops. There was even a railroad
spur. But Tiger didn't want to think of anything that might remind him of his father. Not today.

Poppa's official title was "shipwright." His Union book proclaimed that he was a journeyman and a member of the International Association of Machinists, but Tiger thought he pretty
much ran the place. Most often, he worked outdoors, confidently
but politely giving orders. As foreman, he sometimes supervised
a gang of men whose job it was to install guns onto the ships,
including foundations and guard rails. Sometimes Poppa worked
indoors in one of the barn-like machine shops, making templates
of complex shapes so the ironworkers could do their welding.
However, he was happiest outside, especially on fine June days
like this one.

Sure, there had been lean years at the Navy Yard, what with
pay cuts, time cuts, and all. But things were looking up. Just last
year, the Thomas Bill restored the wages of federal defense
government workers like Poppa. He celebrated by purchasing
the Nash. Without a word, he just went to the showroom one
afternoon, picked out "Betsy" and drove her home. "Life's too
short," he explained to Bridget, as he rolled up in front of the

house. And she agreed, getting in to take a spin, still in her housedress and apron. "It rides as smooth as silk," she told him.

By the second week in April this year, Poppa and his men were back to 40 hour work weeks but were paid for 48. Their sick leave and vacation days were also restored. It was a heck of a lot better than the T.W.U. but then again, the Machinists Union had been around for decades instead of just a couple of years.

As disarmament treaties unraveled around the world and both Japan and Germany began to misbehave, the American Navy was reborn. Back in 1933, the Public Works Administration declared that 32 warships would be built over the next three years and were to be divided between private and public shipyards. The Vinson-Trammel Act would create the largest peace-time Navy in American history. It took forever for approvals, red tape and what not, but between 1934 and now, the Navy Yard's workforce doubled.

One of the busiest shipyards on the eastern seaboard, the Brooklyn Navy Yard got its fair share of the pie. When Rosanna was about Kewpie's age, Poppa helped build the *Arizona*, the *New Mexico* and a slew of other battleships. Now he was busy at work on the *U.S.S. Brooklyn*. History had a habit of repeating itself, and Tiger was part of it this time.

While Tiger knew he wasn't nearly as important as a shipwright or a yard rigger, still the boy made his contribution. Mainly he did whatever Poppa asked him to do, whether it be retrieving a bucketful of bolts from the machine shop, picking up a set of blueprints from the draftsman's building, fetching binoculars or a fresh grease pencil. No matter what his task, Tiger did it cheerfully and quickly, for he belonged to something tangible and vital. Every part served its purpose, Poppa liked to say, and Tiger imagined himself a small but significant piece of the whole.

Although he had witnessed it before, Tiger always marveled at the transformation in his grandfather when he changed from street clothes to work clothes. Poppa wasn't as neatly pressed and particular as he usually was, but somewhat smudged and caked, in his no-nonsense, dingy jumpsuit and newsboy cap. Even his manner changed. Though never impolite, Poppa

became a fellow of few words, all business. But Tiger
understood this completely. In the Navy Yard, when they were
working together, Poppa was no longer his grandfather but Mike,
master machinist, gang boss, someone "most experienced at
general work," as his Union book stated.

The sheer size of the *U.S.S. Brooklyn* amazed Tiger, and the
cruiser wasn't even among the largest ships they built here.
While it would be 10,000 tons at completion, battleships could
go 45,000 tons or better. The *Brooklyn* was still laid up in the dry
dock but it had changed drastically from the last time Tiger had
seen it. Back then, it reminded him of a huge skeleton with a
mammoth exposed spine. It hadn't even remotely resembled a
sea vessel. But now, the steel bones were covered with a skin of
more steel and it was slowly taking shape. Its bow and massive
sides were being fitted together like an enormous puzzle. The
workers balanced on narrow walkways, hammered flooring into
place and scurried up wooden ladders like a team of kinetic
insects. And Poppa presided over his portion of the kingdom like
a kindly drone.

Old as he was—and Tiger wasn't really sure how old his
grandfather was—Poppa still got right in there with the boys.
He was no stranger to a blowtorch or to any of the other tools.
He knew a blueprint inside-out and upside-down. The manner
in which he viewed his work, the way he explained tasks
to his men—clearly and concisely, never talking down to them—
filled Tiger with pride. And he was proud to be associated with
him even if just by bloodline. Somehow, it made Tiger feel
worthy, too.

Although the cruiser's flooring had been bolted in securely,
Tiger still walked it gingerly, bringing cup and water from one
man to the other. He kept thinking of the *Brooklyn's* exposed
bow and raw hull the year before and how fragile it had seemed.
To a young boy of ten, it's difficult to trust in the concept that out
of absence, of nothingness, such solid matter could be built.
Tiger felt so tiny scurrying across the surface, smaller than when
his father hollered at him, more minute than when he didn't
know the answer in class. Only this was a different sort of
smallness. It was the sense of being a miniscule cog amid

vastness. But even little cogs were important. That's what Poppa always told him, anyway. "When even the smallest bolt is wrong, the whole thing is wrong," his grandfather liked to say.

The day had grown quickly hot and it wasn't yet nine in the morning. The sun was visible above the Fort Greene rooftops, the rows of graceful Victorians so different than the Navy Yard's no-nonsense brick boxes and metal warehouses. The men thanked Tiger as he offered them cool water from the bucket. No one refused it, although they were accustomed to the heat. Most came from climates much hotter than this, places where it never snowed. Their dark skin gleamed with perspiration, some the color of an eggplant and others as pale as tea with milk.

Poppa handpicked the men in his gang for their hard work and dedication, and everyone wanted Poppa as a foreman because of his fairness and his appreciation. They worked extra hard for him because he didn't work them as hard as some bosses. He gave them breaks when they needed them and always, at the end of a shift, said "Thank you," looking straight into their eyes and truly meaning it. Poppa asked about their families, remembered names of their wives and children and inquired about the health of ailing relatives. He was a true gentleman and a fair boss.

Tiger was making his rounds with the bucket, which he'd filled for the third time. He took a moment to consider the cranes, at least a dozen of them, hovering above various parts of the Navy Yard. They looked to him like the bones of dinosaurs with long bodies and spindly legs. So tall and oddly delicate, they seemed ready to topple, yet were solidly mounted to tracks. Like great beasts, they moved back and forth, sliding slowly along the rails, suspending a network of hooks and wires which effortlessly moved about hunks of steel and set them in place almost soundlessly.

It was a clear day, and Tiger could see far into Manhattan. Beyond the Williamsburg Bridge was the wedding cake spire of the Woolworth Building and the graceful gold figure on top of the Municipal Building. It was so cloudless that Tiger could almost make out the lines of the golden creature's face. Further up the skyline was his favorite building, the Empire State

Building. It stood almost directly across from the dry dock where they worked. Only five years old, Tiger admired its firm lines, so straight and strong and ballsy. He now liked it much better than the frilly Woolworth Building, his previous favorite. Plus the Empire State Building had starred in its own movie. How many buildings could boast that? Poppa had taken Tiger to see *King Kong* the first week it had come out and...

A lilting, thickly-accented voice disturbed Tiger's reverie. "I've heard of sleeping on the job, but daydreaming?"

Instead of being embarrassed, Tiger smiled. "Sorry, Manny," he said, and approached a small, muscular and dark man with his dipper and bucket.

"A fellow could die of thirst," Manny grinned back at the boy. He took the tin cup, filled it, gulped the cool contents, then took another. "How's my favorite Gunga Din?" Manny inquired.

Tiger was still impressed that Emanuel Ortez Vega was familiar with Kipling's poem, could quote it, even. And the boy still remembered the response Manny had given him all those months ago: "What, you don't think we can read back in Panama? You think all yard workers are illiterate savages? With a grandfather such as yours, how could you possibly think this?" Now Tiger knew better. Manny could dress down a coworker in at least four languages, although he was much more gentle with women and children. Since their initial encounter, Gunga Din became Manny's pet name for Tiger, a boy who was no stranger to nicknames.

"I'm fine, Manny," Tiger answered. *"E tu?"*

"Muy bien, gracias," Manny responded. "Your pronunciation is getting much better." One of Tiger's goals in life was to speak as many languages as his grandfather, but no one knew his aspiration except Manny, who was helping him achieve this quest, word by word.

Tiger and Manny were very fond of each other. Manny saw in the boy a spindly but spunky child reminiscent of himself. The wounded eyes, the drunken father (men in the Navy Yard, like men most places, gossiped like washerwomen), the determined spirit. And in Manny, Tiger saw an adult who did not treat him like a boy. Tiger longed to have muscles that glowed, though his

wouldn't be the color of Brooklyn dirt like Manny's were.
He longed to do a job that was important as well as dangerous.
Manny was one of Poppa's best workers and the men had
a mutual respect for each other that was never spoken but
simply understood.

Similarly, instead of vocalizing their affection, Manny and
Tiger danced the dance of bravado and macho. Like bucks
clashing antlers, like goats crashing horns, they constantly tested
each other. Instead of saying, "You're a good boy who will get
through this rough time," Manny demanded of Tiger, "Name
three battleships built here."

And instead of telling Manny, "I value your friendship," Tiger
told him, "*The Maine*, the *Connecticut* and the *Tennessee*. And
Robert Fulton's steam frigate, the *Fulton*, which was launched
in 1815."

Manny nodded thoughtfully. "Lucky guess. You just picked
three states and..."

But before Manny could finish, Tiger put down the bucket
and counted off on his fingers, "The *Maine*, 6,682 tons, launched
in 1890. The *Connecticut*, 16,000 tons, launched in 1904. The
Tennessee, 32,000 tons, launched in 1919."

"Your grandfather taught you well," Manny conceded. "What
about this place? How old is it?"

"Commissioned in 1801."

"How big?"

"Approximately 260 acres."

Manny wiped his glistening brow. *"Bueno."*

Tiger was on a roll now. "And did you know that it's built on
the site of Peter Caesar Alberti's tobacco plantation? He was the
first Italian to arrive in Brooklyn."

"And certainly not the last," Manny laughed. He patted the
boy on the back, feeling the knobs of his spine. Manny returned
to work and Tiger moved on to the next thirsty soul.

It was a busy day for Tiger, as most were at the Navy Yard.
Retrieving tools, delivering work orders, sweeping up the
machinist's shop. Before he knew it, lunch time rolled around.
Poppa was feeling particularly magnanimous that day. Before the
lunch whistle blew, he gave Tiger a crisp bill and told him to take

the bicycle they used for errands to the frankfurter wagon just outside the gate. Tiger managed to fit a plank of wood between the handlebars and ferried 40 hot dogs safely back to Dry Dock #3. He also suspended two paper shopping sacks of frosty Coca Cola from the handlebars, the bottles clinking with each pump of the bicycle pedals.

The men let out whoops of joy when Tiger returned with this wondrous booty and Poppa announced that lunch was being served in the main dining room. The workers thanked him profusely, shaking his hand and clapping him on the shoulder. Poppa told Tiger to keep the change even though he tried to give it back. Twice.

The hot dog vendor stationed outside the Cumberland gate was elated at his good fortune. And the immigrant men gladly set aside their lunch pails of savory pigeon peas and rice, warm potato *latkes* wrapped in newspaper now spotted with grease or sandwiches made from sausages left over from Sunday's gravy. Perhaps they would give those uneaten lunches to someone less fortunate or maybe they would eat them after quitting time. It was a day of good fortune for everyone.

Poppa's Navy Yard crew sat on the deck of the *Brooklyn*, enjoying their meal in pairs and small groups. Someone had devised a way to open the soft drink bottles on an edge of the diamond-plate stainless steel decking. This flooring had several uses. A good number of the men, Poppa included, had fashioned bracelets from unused strips of this scrap metal, etched them with circles and swirls, soldered in patterns of delicate flowers and bent the metal to fit the wrist of a wife, mother, daughter or granddaughter. The stainless steel resembled sterling silver but shone more brightly and never rusted. And this afternoon, the ship's flooring also served as a gigantic picnic bench of sorts, pleasantly radiating the heat of the sun.

Manny sat on the deck beside Poppa and Tiger. The boy tried to follow the conversation, which flicked back and forth between English and Spanish, with a smattering of Italian, which Manny also spoke. Manny's Italian was peppered with a Spanish accent and Poppa's Spanish, flecked with delicately Italian-accented Brooklynese around the edges.

Lying back on the cruiser's warm deck, Tiger closed his eyes, his belly full of frankfurters and icy Coke, and listened to their words swirling above his head. He must have dozed because the next time he opened his eyes, Manny and Poppa were smiling at him and he heard the music of hammers against metal in the distance. For a moment, he'd forgotten where he was. But even half asleep, Tiger knew that he was far from the El and that he was safe.

16 Homecoming

It was a homecoming feast worthy of two princes. Bridget truly believed that every meal every day, was worthy of celebration. You didn't have to spend a lot of money or make a big fuss. You just had to put care and a little bit of yourself into it. All it required was some onions, garlic, fresh parsley, tomatoes, a bit of chicken, and you had a mouthwatering cacciatore on your hands—and in your belly.

Kewpie didn't have to work at Kresge's that day and by some miracle, she didn't run off with her girlfriend Louise. So, it didn't take much for Bridget to convince her granddaughter to accompany her down the Avenue to pick up a few things for dinner. Kewpie didn't mind being seen with the old woman, who always dressed like she was going out on the town, even if she was just going to the Kosher butcher.

A pretty beaded sweater was draped across Bridget's shoulders (a gift from Kewpie and Tiger the previous Christmas), despite the fact that it was almost summer. She wore a simple dark blue shift, belted at the waist. The familiar carved golden cross dangled below the dress's neckline. Bridget was never without her cross, the one her father had given her when she made her First Holy Communion at ten years of age, two years later than most girls. New to the country, the Marcos simply hadn't gotten around to the sacrament until then.

The old woman's hair was pulled back into her customary bun at the nape of her neck and her right ankle was wrapped tight with an A.C.E. bandage. There was also the strong, pleasantly medicinal scent of Gentian Violet about her. It rose above the distinct fragrance of Evening in Paris. Bridget rubbed the healing tincture into her right leg to ease her painful varicose veins. It worked well but left a slight purple tint in its wake and often stained the bandage she wrapped around her ankle for extra support.

Kewpie liked the feel of her grandmother's arm linked through hers as they made their way down 47th Street. The forsythia had almost lost their bloom. Beneath the woody bushes lay the yellow bugles of their flowers, flattened underfoot. But the honeysuckles were already coming out, clinging to fences, christening the air with their sugariness. Rosanna had taught Kewpie and Tiger how to pluck off a blossom, give it a firm squeeze and suck the dewdrop of sweet nectar that this elicited. They'd both been thoroughly impressed that Rosanna knew of such a sensual delight and never forgot it.

There were kids everywhere, clinging with death grips to fire hydrants, playing "Johnny on the Pony," tossing bottle caps in games of Skully, flipping baseball cards against brick walls, shooting marbles. In the middle of the block, Kewpie and Bridget had to pause for a stickball game, which they didn't mind one bit. They had a chance to admire Mrs. Lieberwitz's roses, which were blooming early this year. Her daylilies were the color of the sun. Rumor had it that Sadie tossed coffee grounds into the dirt to make her flowers come up stronger. Others said it was dog poop. But whatever her secret, Mrs. Lieberwitz's garden was impressive.

Rosanna was inside the Lieberwitz compound, visiting with her old friend, who was under the weather with gout. She'd brought a day-old coffee cake from Ebinger's and said she'd stay

a few hours, keeping Sadie company. This was a customary way
for Rosanna to pass an afternoon when she was all caught up
with her chores, sharing neighborhood gossip, exchanging
nuggets of information about their kids. But there was no sign of
Rosanna or Sadie Lieberwitz in any of the front windows or on
the porch. Kewpie and Bridget didn't bother to stop. They were
enjoying each other's company and the peace of the day.

Kewpie also liked the feel of the delicate shift of her
grandmother's weight from foot to foot as they walked, but not
too quickly. The brush of old body against young body was sure,
safe and predictable. Bridget gave Kewpie's arm a little squeeze
when she spotted Augie on his stoop, reading a book. Kewpie
nudged Bridget back. "Hey, Kewpie, Mrs. Paradiso," Augie
acknowledged, his breath catching in his throat.

"Hey, Augie, what's shaking?" Kewpie nodded.

"Good afternoon, Augusto," Bridget said rather regally as
they passed. "Lovely weather we're having." And then to
Kewpie, "Such a nice young man." To which the girl gave her
customary eye-roll. Kewpie wasn't interested in nice young men.

As they stepped into the road at 12th Avenue, Kewpie
tugged hard on Bridget's arm, bringing her to an abrupt halt.
Billy-the-Bike-Boy sped past, practically grazing the tips of
their noses. Despite his moniker, Billy wasn't a boy but a
simple-minded man in his 30s. He screeched to a stop,
stammering, "S-s-s-s-orry, Mrs. P." Paradiso was a mouthful
he wouldn't even attempt to tackle.

"Just try and be more careful, William," Bridget told
him gently.

"I w-w-w-ill," Billy promised.

"What a shame," Bridget told Kewpie as Billy-the-Bike-Boy
rode off and they began crossing again. "You know, he wasn't
always like that, dear."

"I thought they just squeezed his head too tight with the
forceps," Kewpie laughed. "My father says he spent a little too
long in the birth canal."

Bridget's face went serious. "That's not what happened. It's a
terrible story, really" she began. "Billy was a regular kid, just
like anybody else. A lot like your brother, in fact. But then he fell

127

out of a tree, right onto his head and that was that. He was never the same again." Kewpie reddened at her own insensitivity. "But he's a kind soul, isn't he?" Bridget added. "A good, decent fellow, and that counts for something in my book." Bridget's "book" was invisible but nonetheless important and multiplying page by page at a steady pace almost daily.

From Moe the greengrocer, they bought two large heads of broccoli rabe, which looked fresher than anything else. Poppa liked it a great deal, explaining, "Slightly bitter but palatable, sort of like life." Bridget prepared broccoli rabe nicely, steamed it slightly, then sautéed it in garlic and a robust olive oil.

After Moe's it was down to the Jewish chicken market. "Kosher, smosher," Bridget said. "I just like Moskowitz because you know it's fresh."

Bridget knew Moskowitz's chickens were fresh because they were killed right in front of her. Kewpie could never understand how this mild woman could patiently wait, hands folded across her belly, as Moskowitz or one of his workers, grabbed a fat, frantic fowl, stretched its neck flat, flipped it over and slit its throat the clean, Kosher way. Bridget even watched approvingly as the blood drained into the bucket and the feathers were quickly boiled and plucked from its newly-dead body.

Soon, they were outside the shop whose overhead sign read "Moskowitz Poultry." You would be aware of this even if you didn't notice the sign because chicken feathers dusted the sidewalk and occasionally floated through the air. There was also the unmistakable odor of barnyard droppings mixed with sawdust and death. Kewpie waited outside. "I can't stand the smell of blood," she explained.

Bridget still remembered the girl's shock when, at age five, she witnessed the proverbial "chicken without a head" running madly through Moskowitz's store and hightailing it out the door before expiring on the pavement. Patrons and passersby alternately crossed themselves or spat on the sidewalk to ward off evil spirits, depending on their religious persuasion. Kewpie was understandably horrified and stood frozen on the spot. She'd refused to eat any sort of poultry ever since.

Back in Bridget's kitchen, the cacciatore sauce bubbled happily on the burner. The air was filled with a wonderful tomato perfume, far too vast for the room itself to contain, so it wafted into the hallway, up the steps, into Rosanna's apartment, out the window screens, across the alley and into Mrs. Rosenkrantz's. But even Mrs. Rosenkrantz didn't complain.

There was still plenty of time before Poppa and Tiger returned from the Navy Yard, so Kewpie offered to wash Bridget's hair. She knew the portly, old woman had trouble maneuvering this task, even in the cavernous, claw-footed bathtub. It was easier for her to bend over the kitchen sink with Rosanna or Kewpie helping. They set everything up on the drain board beforehand. Resting on a hand towel were a tortoise shell comb, hair pins, a boar's hair brush and a cake of brown soap.

Bridget changed into a floral housedress and hung her street shift in the bedroom closet. She appeared before Kewpie in the kitchen, ready. The girl was at least six inches taller than her grandmother and the old woman seemed even tinier with her head dunked in the sink. "Too hot?" Kewpie wondered.

"Just right," Bridget sighed, careful not to get water in her mouth. Her granddaughter's touch was firm yet gentle as she worked the bar of Kirkman's soap into her scalp. Bridget swore by Kirkman's. She used the soap flakes to clean the house and the brown bars to cleanse her body from head to toe. She used so much Kirkman's, in fact, that it won her a little tin match safe. It depicted a Kirkman's washerwoman whose bucket held a cluster of kitchen matches. Rosanna also had a Kirkman's washerwoman and kept it on the shelf above the kitchen sink upstairs. Except she stowed pocket change in it instead of matches. She called it her mad money but the truth was, Rosanna only did practical things with it.

Bridget's skin was very soft, Kewpie noticed. She wondered if it was the Kirkman's or just her grandmother's own tender nature seeping through. Even though her mother used Kirkman's just as much as Bridget did, Rosanna's hands felt like a fine grade of sandpaper. But maybe it was just the rough nature of her present life that toughened even her skin.

Kewpie tried not to get water down Bridget's back as she gave the final rinse, using a coffee cup. She helped Bridget straighten up, first wrapping a bathroom towel around her head like a turban. "You look just like Carmen Miranda," Kewpie laughed. Then they took their places in the kitchen chairs. Bridget unraveled the towel and Kewpie sat behind her with the comb. Graceful curves and undulating swirls were carved into the handle. "Was this really a wedding present?" Kewpie asked.

Bridget dried her hair and nodded. "Along with the brush and mirror. I don't have much but I do have a few fine things."

It always surprised Kewpie how long her grandmother's hair was. She usually kept it wrapped up in a tight, little meatball, as Poppa liked to call it, but when she let her hair down to wash it or brush it out at night, the multicolored cascade was always breathtaking. Long strands of shining chestnut, dark mahogany, glittery silver and icy white reached the base of her spine and spilled over the back of the kitchen chair. Kewpie started at the top of Bridget's scalp and worked the thick-toothed comb down to the ends of her grandmother's hair, which curled slightly.

Kewpie combed in silence, concentrating deeply on the act, working on section by section with the care and regularity of someone painting a wall or ironing a silken garment. It lulled her into a quiet place. Bridget, too. The girl could feel the woman's head grow heavy. Her grandmother's eyes were closed in contentment and there was a slight smile on her face.

"I like these," Kewpie said, cradling one of Bridget's earrings in her puckered fingertips.

"What? These old things?" Bridget smiled. "Poppa's family sent them over from Cosenza when we were still keeping company." The earrings were simple teardrops, 18 karat gold that had dulled and mellowed to resemble copper in the 40 years she'd worn them. Bridget still had the box they'd come in, although she'd long discarded the envelope they were mailed in. "Those old Gindaloons from the other side believed that wearing teardrops protected you from crying real tears in life."

Kewpie laughed. "Grandma, you're an old Gindaloon from the other side yourself!"

"Angela, don't call me old." Bridget tickled Kewpie as one might do to a child. They laughed some more, then continued with the task at hand. The girl then finished the pleasant chore of combing her grandmother's hair. The silence was comfortable and comforting. Above the hum of their breathing was the sound of the cacciatore simmering. When they checked it, the gravy had mellowed from a dull red to a well-seasoned orange.

"Can we braid your hair this time?" Kewpie wondered, already separating her grandmother's hair into sections.

"All right," Bridget told her. "But turn off the burner before you start. The sauce should be just about right." Sure enough, the gravy looked and tasted perfect. It could sit and wait until they were ready for dinner and be warmed up just before serving. Kewpie extinguished the flame and went back to her grandmother.

Braiding was a slow process with hair this long. Kewpie took her time, moving wrist over wrist, weaving the strands patiently with her fingers. Bridget noticed that Kewpie was wearing a new ring. Perhaps that's what had been hidden in Augie's sugar bowl on Dish Night a few weeks ago. Kewpie wore the pink, heart-shaped stone on her pinkie, the finger of no commitment, but she was wearing it just the same.

Bridget and Kewpie didn't speak. Not until Kewpie was finished with one braid and began on the other. "I hope he doesn't come back," she said plainly. "Ever." The girl's voice was flat and cold. Bridget knew exactly who she was referring to, even though a name was never mentioned.

"I mean it," Kewpie said for emphasis. "Never would be too soon."

"But Angela, he's your father," Bridget told her.

"He doesn't act like a father. He does things a father shouldn't do," the girl said impassively, looking down at the floor, and her grandmother immediately understood.

Suddenly, Bridget did not want to eat dinner. She didn't want to do anything but cry. Instead, she sat still as her granddaughter wrapped one braid and then the other around her head and fastened them in place with bobby pins. Kewpie brought Bridget the tortoiseshell hand mirror to admire her work and knelt in front of her grandmother, expectantly awaiting her verdict. "Better than the Queen of Sheba," Bridget declared. The girl's eyes were smiling and so were her grandmother's.

But then Bridget grew grave and sighed weightily. "Angela," she began. That's all Kewpie needed to crumbled into her grandmother's lap, sobbing. She smoothed down the girl's golden curls and let her cry, telling her, "There, there." However, she avoided murmuring things like, "It's not so bad," because she knew it was. It was unthinkable.

Bridget didn't know what to say. She didn't know what to do. She didn't want to tell the child lies. It took Kewpie several moments to stop crying, and when she did, the front of Bridget's housedress was wet and the girl's eyes were swollen slits. "I won't let him hurt you anymore," she said.

"Promise?" Kewpie asked.

"Promise."

Kewpie tried to believe her.

They hadn't even heard Rosanna return from Mrs. Lieberwitz's, but now there was the distinct tap, tap, scrub of her cleaning the woodwork in the hallway. They could detect the slap of a brush in a bucket, the sound of water streaming, the swish of her making her way up the wall as she moved slowly on hands and knees. Bridget no longer could do such chores, so Rosanna silently took them on without complaint.

Rosanna didn't mind doing the cleaning or performing other household chores. They were easy, predictable and rewarding. With Kirkman's and a little elbow grease, everything old became new again. But the thing was, dirt and dust and grime, they always kept coming back. You cooked and you needed to clean the oven. You went outside and you tracked in street smudge. You did absolutely nothing and watched dust pile onto furniture and lampshades regardless. Life was a dirty business. That was a fact.

In truth, Rosanna hadn't gone to Sadie Lieberwitz's and her friend's gout wasn't acting up at all. She'd waited until Kewpie and Bridget were busy elsewhere in the house and crept across the street to Dr. Lewis's. He was happy for the crumb cake but sorry that his neighbor hadn't been feeling well. How long had she suffered? Rosanna couldn't recall, but when her ailment became too painful and too troublesome, she called on him.

Dr. Lewis's office hadn't changed in ages. It was in dire need of a paint job and the row of squeaky brown leather chairs were cracked and patched with almost-matching tape in spots. The magazine covers on the end table were brittle with age but Rosanna didn't read. Her mind was racing. What if something was terribly wrong with her? What would happen to her children, to her parents?

Dr. Lewis took her inside immediately. It was his wife Eva, a trained nurse, who ushered Rosanna into the examination room, where everything sparkled and was neatly arranged. Rosanna sat at the edge of the table like a fragile species of bird, ready to take flight. Mrs. Lewis's efficient manner and cool dry fingertips as she checked Rosanna's blood pressure had a calming effect, but still the patient's heart beat hard in her chest, almost hurting. "It's through the roof," Mrs. Lewis whispered to her husband when he entered the examination room.

When he noticed the green and brown striped Ebinger's box on the table, instead of saying thank you, he said, "*Nu?* I'm not fat enough?" But this was just his way and after all these years, Rosanna understood. In a softer voice, he asked, "So, what's troubling you?"

Rosanna took a deep breath. "I've been bleeding," she began.

On her back, staring at the ceiling and being deftly prodded, Rosanna was reminded of her husband. She heard the El like thunder in the distance and felt a pang of bittersweet. Not love exactly, but lost love perhaps, obliterated affection mixed with fear. The fear of what might happen if he came back. *When* he came back. Because Tony always came back.

Dr. Lewis's eyes were magnified pinholes of concern behind his thick-rimmed black glasses. He removed his bloodied rubber gloves, tossed them in the metal trashcan, and seemed to move in slow motion. Rosanna quickly redressed as Dr. Lewis busied himself with his prescription pad with his back turned. When she was done, Rosanna sat back down on the table, her legs dangling. Dr. Lewis rested his hand lightly on her knee. "It doesn't look good, Roe," he told her. "I think you need a hysterectomy but I want you to see a specialist."

"A specialist?" she repeated. "But we can't afford a..."

"Dr. Schantz is an excellent doctor," Dr. Lewis stressed. "His office is only a few blocks from here. I'm sure he can see you this week at no charge as a special favor to me." Rosanna said nothing but her dark eyes implored him. "I know it's a bad time but this is important, Rosanna Maria," he added.

"I know it is, Morris."

Dr. Lewis patted Rosanna's hand in assurance. "Just bring him one of your Icebox Cakes," he told her. Rosanna looked at the doctor in disbelief, both about her diagnosis and about his generosity. "He owes me one," Dr. Lewis explained, and wouldn't let Rosanna leave his office before Eva got Dr. Schantz on the telephone and made an appointment for later in the week.

Now Rosanna knelt in the hallway on her hands and knees, scrubbing the woodwork, a piece cut from an old towel wadded between her legs. Every so often, she felt the blood drip from her body and settle there, but she ignored it and told no one, only scrubbed harder.

It wasn't long before Tiger and Poppa came home, the boy so exuberant from his day at the Navy Yard. Tiger was full of talk of cranes and pulleys, cruisers and soda pop, of how the statues around the perimeter of All Saints seemed much more beneficent on the ride home. They both liked Bridget's braids. Poppa agreed that she did resemble the Queen of Sheba and sang a few lines from "The Sheik of Araby."

> *"At night when you're asleep,*
> *Into your tent I'll creep..."*

Kewpie turned away, although it was a very joyful scene.

The entire house was fragrant with Bridget's chicken cacciatore. The men declared themselves starving, so everyone sat down as soon as the spaghetti was done. Poppa doled out generous portions of pasta heaped with chicken, and just spaghetti and sauce for Kewpie. The gravy was so orange it almost hurt the eyes, the chicken so tender and perfectly done, it slid from the bone. He made sure to give everyone a healthy dollop of broccoli rabe, glistening with olive oil, studded with little chunks of browned garlic. When he was almost sated, Poppa sopped up the delicious gravy with the heel of the Italian bread.

Somewhere across Brooklyn, on Mermaid Avenue, to be exact, Tony was coming home from the day shift. The week before, Denise had announced that her furnished room was too small for them and besides, Aunt Mimi would frown upon two unmarried people (well, unmarried to each other) living in sin, especially under her pious roof. Besides, Denise wanted to cook for Tony. So, they'd gotten an apartment in an Old Law Tenement on the corner of Mermaid and West 19th temporarily, just until they could find a better place.

Sure enough, Tony arrived that evening to a steaming grilled cheese sandwich, cut on a bias, its gooey center oozing onto the plate. He had indeed lost weight during the past few weeks, and as he undressed in the locker room, one of the other conductors remarked, "Man cannot live by pussy alone...even *primo* pussy." And it was true.

Tony sat down to eat his grilled cheese, ravenous.

17 Private Dick

John knew that everyone thought it was because of the war. "That's why he likes skulking around and spying on people so much," he'd overheard his sister-in-law Astrid telling his wife. Astrid should only know, he thought, and she would have a private dick tailing her husband. Besides, John remembered Astrid when she was still known as Margaret and ran around barefoot in the unpaved streets, picking up horseshit and throwing it with glee just like all the other neighborhood punks. She couldn't put on airs with him because he knew her when— and before the nose job, too.

John remembered his wife Camille when she was even younger. She was the ripe age of nine when he'd gone off to war at 18. A great deal had happened by the time John came back from Europe, happened to the world and to the old neighborhood. John himself returned to Borough Park a little different than before. From a distance, he watched Camille grow and change as he went on with his life.

In time, Camille blossomed into quite a lovely woman. She went from gangly to gorgeous in slow motion, before his very eyes. One day, she was in ruffles and bows and the next, decked out in silk skirts and heels. Camille traded her pigtails for a smart shoulder-length bob and was suddenly wearing lipstick. John had been around the world, and around the block, more than a couple of times, and he knew a good thing when he saw it. A good woman, too. Lord knows, he'd had plenty of the other kind, even married one. But that was when Camille was still in middle school and he was young and dumb.

"He's damaged goods," Astrid snarled to Camille one Sunday when she was paring curls of Pecorino Romano cheese onto a salad of sliced fresh zucchini.

"You should know," Camille shot back, drizzling on the olive oil. John loved, among other things, his wife's spunk and sharp wit. All of the Paradisos had it to some degree but in Camille, it was the most refined. In Astrid, the spunk had gone sour.

"What's that supposed to mean?" Astrid barked as she added a few roasted peppers to the salad as garnish. But then she noticed the tragedy of an oily pepper seed on her custom-made chartreuse suit and dashed for a talcum powder/seltzer cocktail to make everything right again. However, the suit jacket never quite recovered.

And neither did Astrid after she discovered that Sam had been cheating on her. However, she decided to give him another chance, three times now, and counting. The Paradiso Girls didn't seem to have much luck with men. It was either hit or miss with them, and when they missed, it was by a long shot.

But this was only John's opinion and he didn't force it down anyone's gullet. Besides, you know what they say about opinions. "They're like assholes. Everyone's got one," he'd told Astrid over Christmas roast last year. Poppa'd chuckled quietly over this gem but Sam enjoyed it so much that he sprayed little droplets of bourbon and soda onto Bridget's festive holiday tablecloth. Then, to Bridget, who was doing her best to mask her smirk, John said, "Pardon my French, Momma."

"He picked it up at the back of the Front," Sam tried to explain.

"Nah, Sammy Boy, that's pure Brooklyn," John said. "Born and ill bred."

Astrid left the table in a huff, which was not an unusual occurrence. But this time, it was more because Sam didn't defend her than from John's off-color remark. John worried that he'd offended Bridget, whom he loved as much as his own mother, God rest her soul. However, when he helped clear dishes from the table a few minutes later, he found Bridget in the kitchen, laughing so hard that nothing came out of her mouth. Her belly bobbed up and down and tears trickled from her eyes. John kissed her on the forehead and went back to the dining room to get more dishes.

If the truth be told, John enjoyed skulking around, as Astrid put it, for as long as he could remember. There was a lot to be seen from hiding in plain sight. As a boy, he realized that if you just stood still and kept quiet, the world would go on around you, barely noticing your presence. He could stand in Dora's Luncheonette, disappear into the woodwork, and watch kids stuff their pants pockets with Red Hots. He would see the soda jerk split the profits with his absent boss instead of putting the full price of an egg cream in the register. He would notice a neighbor duck into another neighbor's house when his wife and children were attending mass at St. Catherine's. Every Sunday, without fail, for the hour or so it took Father Dunn to drone through mass.

As a child, John did nothing with this knowledge, this knack for learning secrets. He simply did it because it was something to do. It amused him and helped passed the time, making his dull days not so dull. This realization of how handy invisibility could be also helped him later in the trenches, and it helped him in his new line of work.

Some people simply could not let go of the past. It seemed to validate them. They were always looking for a lost love or were haunted by an unresolved argument that sputtered out rather than was settled. Closure. They sought closure in a sometimes open-ended world. And that's where John came in. He provided proof, hard and fast evidence that couldn't be ignored and forced them to make the decision they knew that had to make anyhow.

Maybe they didn't want that philandering, good-for-nothing bum of a husband back, but they just wanted to know where he was. Maybe they didn't want to make up with the mother who abandoned them when they were five, but they just wanted to know why she'd done it. In the same vein, Rosanna hadn't asked him to go find Tony, but John himself was curious. He had to admit that things seemed especially peaceful at 1128 47th Street with Tony gone. Now at three weeks and counting, it was the longest he'd ever disappeared. This was clearly not his typical four-day drunk, but much more than that. Rosanna didn't seem particularly perturbed, though.

In fact, she rarely breathed a word about her husband's vanishing act to any of them. She seemed unusually at peace. Not about money, of course, but about practically everything else. Somehow, she managed to squeak by with what the kids brought in and what she took in doing ironing and laundry. What her sisters slipped into the pocket of her cobbler apron or convinced her to take by closing her work-worn hand around a small wad of bills was also a great help. Despite money problems, John often caught his sister-in-law humming as she did housework or while she chopped onions, even heard her singing once or twice.

Why, just the other day, he'd heard, *"There's a boat that's leaving soon for New York..."*

The melody spilled effortlessly from Rosanna lips and made him smile. She'd been cleaning the kitchen floor on all fours with the door open. John stood in the hallway, eavesdropping.

"You could be on Broadway," he laughed.

Rosanna shrugged and wiped her hands on her housedress. "It was on the radio last night," she said. "Just sort of stuck in my head." She kept on scrubbing.

"It's nice," John told her.

His sister-in-law worked her way to the door, crawling closer as she finished wiping down more squares, taking her pail with her. "They played almost the whole show...*Porgy and Bess*," she recalled. "Beautiful songs but awfully blue songs, too. It's such a sad story."

"Sad sells," John figured. "People are always trying to forget their own sorry tales of woe. But put someone else's sob story on the screen or on the stage and they're falling all over each other to buy tickets."

Rosanna shook her head and admitted, "I never thought of it like that." She crawled backwards across the door's sill. John leaned over and placed the bucket in the hallway as she finished swabbing the linoleum. He gave her his hand and helped her up. "Thanks," Rosanna told him. She liked her brother-in-law a great deal, even though he was a bit jagged around the edges. But John was a good egg and he had a noble heart. "My diamond in the rough," Camille liked to call him. And it was true.

Rosanna kept hold of John's hand with her scrubbing hand, which was moist and cold and slightly scratchy. In contrast, his was smooth and warm from easy work in the projectionist's booth. Being a private dick was easy on the hands, too, she figured. "Johnny, I just wanted to…I mean, Camille gave me the envelope and I wanted to…" she stammered. Rosanna was getting pink in the face.

"You don't have to thank me," he told her, patting her hand. "We're family. I just wish it could have been more."

John feared that his sister-in-law might cry and he hated it when women bawled. It happened in his second line of work more than enough and he didn't like it happening on his private time as well. Rosanna's lip started to tremble. She bit down on it hard then looked up at John with her big Basset Hound eyes, an older, more weathered version of his wife. "I think I can get a couple of tickets, Roe," he said, deftly changing the subject. "For a Broadway show, I mean. A funny one. You and Cam could have a night out on the town and I can look after Tiger. I think Kewpie can pretty much look after herself."

"Oh, I couldn't," Rosanna began.

"Yes, you could," Camille smiled, halfway up the staircase. She'd just finished making raviolis with her mother and was on her way up to visit with her sister.

Rosanna touched the ends of her hair that showed under her kerchief. "I don't have anything to wear."

"I'm sure I have a thing or two that would fit," Camille said. "You'd look swell."

"I have an old Army buddy who works security at *On Your Toes*," John told them. "I'll give Danny a ring and see what he can do."

"Think of it, *On Your Toes*! Astrid will be so jealous," Camille laughed. "Ray Bolger. Monty Woolley. 'There's a Small Hotel'..." She spun her sister around and laughed some more. Though the youngest and oldest of the Paradiso brood, Camille and Rosanna were always close. Something wonderful and mysterious bound them together and it did John's heart good to see this. He left the two alone to have a sister talk as he trotted downstairs to his in-laws' apartment, whistling "There's a Small Hotel" in spite of himself.

Little did any of them know that *On Your Toes* was the show, in a sense, that took Tony away from them and made him decide to steal Denise away from her fancy man. That creep was just the sort of fellow who could afford to sit her shapely derriere in orchestra seats and might even know Monty Woolley personally. It got right under Tony's skin. All his life, he'd been outshone by the "haves," being a "have not," and he was sick of it. Tony would let that swell know he was all business, that he could snatch his gal back from under this rich mook's nose with nothing more than an empty wallet, a well-placed fingertip and a smile.

John was on the horn with his pal Danny, leaning in the doorway beside Bridget's delicate three-footed telephone table, when she sauntered by with a big platter and announced the raviolis ready. "So get your bony behind into the dining room," Bridget smiled, and he did.

And now, a few hours later, John was standing under a dead street lamp in Coney Island outside a falling-down brick building on Mermaid Avenue, a stone's throw from the Shrine Church of Our Lady of Solace. His attention was focused on a set of windows on the second floor. The curtains were flung open and the windows themselves yawned wide in the late June evening, trying to catch what little ocean breeze there was. John still wore his suit jacket but loosened the tie and opened the first button of his collar. Camille thought he was working as a fill-in projectionist at the Minerva in Park Slope but instead, John decided to come spy on his errant brother-in-law, the rat bastard.

It didn't take much to tail Tony. He was easy pickings as most drunks usually are. They weren't especially aware of their surroundings and moved about in a dull, pickled haze. After Momma's wonderful ravioli dinner and dessert of strong dark coffee and home-made banana cream pie, John left the others to play Pinochle while he supposedly went off to work. But not before secretly slipping his nephew Tiger a quarter to see that his Aunt Cam got home safe.

John had checked Tony's schedule earlier that afternoon, giving the guy who picked up the phone in the control tower some cock and bull story about wanting to surprise his old Army buddy. John knew that Tony had a shift that day and knew when he clocked out. He timed it so he'd hop a ride on Tony's last train into Stillwell. John let a few trains go by until he saw his brother-in-law's fair-haired head pop out of the conductor's cage toward the middle of the cars. Tony was too much of a louse to be trusted in the first or last car since it was far too easy to catch a passenger in the door and drag them the length of the platform, or worse. No, it was safest to slip a conductor who liked the sauce in a middle car.

Hat pulled down over his eyes, John looked like any other working stiff in a suit. Just to make sure Tony didn't notice him, John stepped onto the car as Tony looked the other way. John tried to make himself comfortable in the wicker seat, which, in his opinion, was built too small for long-legged frames like his. He was bristling with anger at seeing his good-for-nothing brother-in-law again, even if Tony did look gaunt and hollow. That's what cheating on your wife and abandoning your kids does to a fellow—it eats you apart from the inside out. Then again, maybe it was the floozy.

In the ten or so stops it took to get to Stillwell Avenue, John had killed his brother-in-law a dozen different ways, usually using his bare hands, the most satisfactory method of all. Most people would be surprised at how easy it was to crack open a human skull. It wasn't nearly as hard and durable as folks imagined. Just the right angle at the edge of the curb, for example, and it split like an overripe pumpkin. He'd seen it happen in France loads of times. Hell, he'd even done it himself. It was difficult to believe that John, who was so tender and considerate with his young wife, had been so brutal with others. But that was during the War. This was a war of another kind.

John's favorite means of extinction was grabbing Tony by the throat, telling him off, watching the life drain from his face and his eyes roll back in his head, then bouncing his noggin off a brick wall as hard as he could and hearing it crack like DiMaggio at bat. Sometimes when John lay restless and awake at night, he thought of this. It had an oddly calming effect on him and he could finally sleep.

John could see the lights of the Wonder Wheel slowly making its circle long before he heard Tony's announcement, "Last stop Coney Island, Stillwell Avenue. Everybody off the train. This train is out of service." To John, there was something magical about Coney Island at night. You couldn't see the grime or the chipped paint. The neon drowned out the ordinariness of the streets and made them sparkle.

Swarms of people got off the train so it was easy for John to blend in. Keeping ten paces behind Tony, John tailed him from a safe distance, leaning against a girder to have a smoke while Tony slipped into the locker room to change out of his work clothes. He took no more than six minutes. Must be some piece of tail, him wanting to get home so quick, John told himself. Either that or he didn't trust her as far as he could spit. But whatever the reason, there was no dilly-dallying in the bars like Tony used to do before coming home to Roe and the kids.

And after just a five block walk, John saw what Tony was rushing home to. A buxom blonde strolled past the open window wearing nothing but a full slip, not even a brassiere and panties underneath. John could make out her breasts bouncing as she moved, her pointy nipples coming through the sheer material. He could see the dark triangle of her pubic hair, her buttocks as lively as two cats fighting in a paper sack. In the time it took for Tony to climb the stairs to their second-floor walkup, John had gotten a healthy glimpse of the dame and then some.

It was like watching a movie with the sound turned off. Not much different than working the projection booth where the dialog bounced into the theater instead of back into the booth. John was pretty good at figuring out what was going on in the booth and in real life. This doll didn't seem to be much in the kitchen but she could sure fill a glass as well as she filled out her silk petticoat. It seemed that Tony had a drinking buddy as well as a lover. Where Rosanna was a teetotaler at best, this baby she kept up with Tony drink for drink.

As far as John could tell, Tony's dinner consisted of Nathan's fries (the bright yellow and green wrappings were an easy giveaway, even from across the street) and several tumblers of scotch. No wonder Tony looked so bony. He would probably give his left nut for some *steak a pizzaiola* or *pasta e fagioli*.

So, John had found his brother-in-law. The question was what to do next. In John's estimation, Tony was no great loss. But then again, Tony wasn't his husband nor did he ever love him. Hell, he barely tolerated the asshole. Should John make Tony come home or let him die of cirrhosis of the liver in Coney? This was a great source of puzzlement to him. He'd have to ask Harry and the fellows what they thought.

John knew it was time to go when he saw two shadows wrestling on the wall in the apartment above him. Every so often, the girl's head came into view as she pounced on what he assumed was the bed. John saw her rippled back, then her bare behind as she crumpled her slip in her fists and rode Tony like a cowgirl. Instead of arousing John, this only succeeded in making him sick to his stomach. He had seen more than enough.

But John couldn't go home just yet so he wandered around Coney Island's network of midways. He needed time to decompress. To cool his head, he tried his hand at "Shoot the Star." A fair marksman, he won a stuffed turtle, much to the dismay of the barker at the booth. John gave the toy to a little girl passing by. Bringing it home to Camille would take some explaining and only complicate matters. Next he shot a chipmunk, a piano player and a raccoon at the old West saloon. At another booth, he took potshots at a real live freak. He watched someone get a tattoo of an eagle on his bicep in one of Coney's many skin art parlors. But nothing seemed to work.

It was crowded at Coney, especially for a Wednesday night. At some booths, the folks were waiting three deep and forget the long, snaking lines for the rides. John made his way past Zippy the Pinhead, past Al/Alberta, the he-she, past the Dog-Faced Boy. He was relieved to see that there was barely a line for Tirza the Wine Bath Lady. John paid his nickel and entered the worn canvas tent.

Inside, Tirza was all about the lighting, which was dim. When John was a boy, her booth had been illuminated by candles but due to fear of fire, they switched to electric lights. That was many Tirzas ago; over the years there had been several, but this Tirza was by far his favorite.

John took a seat toward the back. He didn't know what it was about Tirza, but she kept him coming back. He knew she wasn't really taking a bath in wine; it was just grape juice. He knew she wasn't really naked in that big see-through bathtub; she wore a flesh-colored body stocking, much like the ones aerialists wore. He also knew that her real name wasn't Tirza; she was a nice Irish girl named Peggy McMahon who lived in Windsor Terrace with her family. But something about this gave John a sense of hope.

So, Tirza bathed, and when she was done, John went home to his wife, his faith in humanity restored for the moment.

18 Land Without Shadows

Tiger had saved enough money to go to Coney Island on his own. This wasn't counting what Rosanna forced him to keep from his wages at the Navy Yard and the pocket change he picked up doing odd jobs. The boy wasn't too proud to make the occasional grocery delivery for Penner's or for the butcher. Liberty Meats, the Italian butcher on the Avenue, which was owned by Sal, not Moskowitz of the Kosher chickens. Moshe Moskowitz was too cheap to hire a kid to do errands and often made deliveries himself, pocketing the tips, too.

Tiger liked Sal, who'd gone to school with his Aunt Jo. The boy suspected that Sal was still sweet on his aunt even though they were both married to other people for what seemed like forever. Was it possible to love someone since you were a kid with a secret corner of your heart while you went along with your life, married someone else and even had kids with them, Tiger wondered. Yes, it was very possible, he decided. Almost anything in this life was possible, even probable.

In any case, Tiger had amassed his Coney Island savings in several ways. His aunts were known to slip him a spare quarter now and then, unbeknownst to his uncles. And his uncles likewise would sneak him a handful of change and whisper, "Mum's the word." Sully, too. Tiger put this Mum Money in a jelly jar which he wedged between his bed's mattress and sagging springs then wrapped in an old, clean sock for safekeeping. The jelly jar was almost full. Although Tiger gave most of his earnings to Rosanna, this Mum Money was a secret and it was all his.

But Tiger didn't have to dip into his private stash to go to Coney Island this time. Uncle John slipped him a fin while passing him in the hallway one muggy Friday afternoon and told Tiger to take Kewpie out there the very next day. His sister thought it was a fine idea. With five dollars, they could spend the entire day at Coney, from dawn till dusk, splurging on food, rides and the midway attractions. They arranged to take an early trolley and Kewpie promised to be ready by nine.

The next morning, Rosanna was already up and soaking wash in their big enamel bathtub by the time Tiger awoke. It wasn't their clothing but Mrs. Finn's. The old lady was feeling poorly lately, more poorly than Rosanna herself. She poured Tiger a cold glass of milk and smiled as she ruffled up his scruffy hair. "You could use a crew cut," she said.

"Good morning, Mom," Tiger responded, taking the big serrated bread knife and shearing off a hunk of leftover Italian bread to smear with butter.

"Where are you off to so bright and early?"

"Me and Kewpie are going to Coney Island," he told her. Rosanna made a face but didn't bother to ask who in her family had given him the cash. "I know we could use the money for food or something," he continued.

Rosanna cut him off, even though she had thought of it herself. But instead she told him, "What's that saying? Something about man not living by bread alone?" She forced herself to smile. "Both you and your sister have been working hard. You deserve a treat. I only wish..." Then she stopped short.

Rosanna scrubbed Molly Finn's grubby slip even harder. Did

the woman ever wash it before? Then there were her voluminous, once-upon-a-time white underdrawers to wrestle with. "Ma, you're doing a great job," Tiger began and took a deep breath. "It's much nicer here without him."

"Yeah, it is much nicer but I can't. I can't do it alone, Anthony," she said. "Times are hard, even with help." The boy chewed thoughtfully on the doughy oval of Italian bread. "Still," he said. "It's good not to get hit or yelled at."

"That it is," she agreed.

Tiger was amazed to see Kewpie up before eight. True, she was yawning and stretching and her eyes were still glued shut, but she was fumbling around the kitchen at least. She plopped into a chair and gulped down the milk her mother set before her. Without a word, Rosanna began unfastening Kewpie's pin curls. The black bobby pins went into the front pocket of Rosanna's apron, which seemed to have space for everything.

Although she and Kewpie didn't talk much these days, Tiger still knew that Rosanna loved his sister. He wondered if Kewpie knew. When his mother bent down and quickly kissed the crown of her daughter's head, the girl didn't shrink away, but briefly grabbed her mother's hand and gave it a little squeeze. "You're cold," Kewpie said. "And it's boiling hot in here."

"It's the laundry. Cold water for whites," Rosanna explained, as she went into the cupboard for cereal.

"I wish you didn't have to scrub some crusty old lady's bloomers," Kewpie sighed.

"Wishing doesn't make it so," Rosanna declared emphatically. "But thanks. Anything to help put food on the table."

"I wish you could come with us," Tiger said, however, Kewpie didn't echo his sentiments.

"Me, too," Rosanna told him, setting down the bowl and cereal in front of Kewpie. She went back into the icebox for the milk bottle.

Kewpie opened one eye and studied Tiger. He studied her back. Although his sister resembled a sleepy space creature with her hair going every which way, he had to admit that she looked pretty nice when it was all combed out. Would Augie still love her if he saw her like this, all uneven, askew, unkempt and lost in a frayed nightshirt. Yes, Tiger decided, he probably still would. Poor bastard.

Kewpie slowly chomped her Corn Flakes to which Rosanna snuck in a few slices of banana. Tiger helped himself to another buttery slice of bread. He was already dressed in knee pants and a striped short-sleeved shirt that had been his cousin Matthew's. Kewpie slipped out of the kitchen.

The next time she appeared, her hair was combed and she was wearing a simple sleeveless cotton shift with a wide skirt and espadrille sandals. The pea-green of the dress made her eyes seem greener themselves, not so gray like the gunboats at the Navy Yard, Tiger observed. He also admired the dress's alternating pattern of seahorses and fanlike coral. The big skirt swirled and whispered when she moved, much like the ocean. It showed off the little buds of her chest and Tiger knew the bigger boys would notice, too. At any rate, this seemed a very appropriate outfit for their day by the sea, even only a Brooklyn sea.

Tiger knew that Aunt Astrid had made Kewpie the dress and that it was her first time wearing it. His aunt had found the material in a dry goods store that was going out of business on Madison Avenue, discovered it under a bolts of damaged chintz, a perfect remnant to make a summer frock for Kewpie. Despite her lofty ways, constantly correcting posture, augmenting her nose and her name so she didn't have to be who she really was, Aunt Astrid had a good heart beneath all the muck. Plus she was a whiz on a Singer sewing machine. She didn't want her niece and nephew looking "less than" even if they had an S.O.B. for a father. Plenty of rich kids had drunks for dads, too.

Tiger and Kewpie didn't even have to discuss how they'd get to Coney Island. Their preferred mode of travel was the trolley whenever possible. Anything to take them further away from their father. It was almost a disgrace to him, a train man and staunch Union supporter, to have his children ride the trolley instead of the El. Kewpie and Tiger weren't above being spiteful, getting back at their father in tiny but significant ways. Even if he never knew it, they did.

Besides, with the trolley, you could open the windows and

feel the breeze, which grew stronger the closer you got to Coney.

Even with the windows down on the El, it was noisy and the air never seemed to get inside the way it did on the trolley. Plus the trolley had a pleasant bounce about it, not so jerky as the train. At this hour, they were bound to get a seat, especially so far from the end of the line.

Kewpie and Tiger were out of the house a few minutes to nine. Before long, they heard the trolley's rumble and the clang of its bell. Kewpie liked the car's elegant lines which reminded her of a flat-topped pagoda. Painted on its face were the instructions "Front Entrance" to deter the skells from trying to sneak in the back door. The Martino kids put their nickels in the slot. Tiger personally enjoyed the clinking sound the coins made as they swirled together in the fare box when the driver pushed the lever. It secretly made his heart stir.

Tiger grasped Kewpie's hand as they maneuvered along the trolley's wooden floor to empty seats in the back at the right-hand corner, the best ones on the entire trolley in their opinion. Kewpie didn't even mind that her brother's hand was sweaty. It felt like she imagined a baby bird would: brittle and tense. When Tiger wasn't looking, Kewpie wiped her palm on her dress then took his clammy hand again.

As Coney came into view, it literally took their breath away. The ocean sparkled and the massive amusement park rides, roller coasters, brightly painted rails, spinning objects, fantasy animals and indoor arcades pulsed with life. Looming above it all, a 150 foot Ferris wheel spun.

Coney Island was also the place where a half-dozen or so elevated and once-underground subway lines peeped their heads up out of the earth and snaked their way toward the same terminus. A network of parallel tracks was suspended above the streets, joined together by common platforms. There was a train yard beyond the Stillwell Avenue station where Tiger liked to imagine the spare cars sleeping away the night. His father had brought him there once to have a look see. The thick arteries of rails seemed to stretch on forever.

Back at the Stillwell Station, there was a huge control tower, locker rooms and a mess hall of sorts. It was where many train lines began and ended, and it was where their father worked, so Kewpie and Tiger avoided it like a leper colony and moved on.

The station itself was like a small village. On street-level, it contained a pub that was always dark and gritty, even in the blaring midday sun—Tiger and Kewpie both knew this because their father had taken each of them there separately as youngsters—and a tiny triangle of a candy shop called Phillips. As Kewpie and Tiger hurried past the Stillwell station, they looked into the face of a navy blue uniformed conductor with a measure of dread, holding their breath. With a gasp of relief, they found the man mustachioed, black-haired and not their father.

They didn't bring their bathing costumes on this trip, although there was a long, crowded expanse of beach and Steeplechase's big pool for swimming. Kewpie and Tiger rarely swam at Coney, not wanting to be distracted from the rides by the sun, water and sand. Once Bridget had taken Kewpie to Stahl's Bath House off the Boardwalk. It was a beautiful building, tall blonde brick with columns and arches. Kewpie liked the terra cotta figures of old King Neptune, topless mermaids and various sea creatures but had been put off by the pudgy naked bodies of immigrant women. She never let her grandmother take her back there again.

Tiger knew as much about Coney Island as he did the Brooklyn Navy Yard, possibly more. In addition to the two big amusement parks—Luna Park and Steeplechase Park—there were roughly 60 bathhouses, 70 "ball" games, 13 carousels (but B & B on Surf Avenue indisputably was the best), 11 roller coasters, five tunnel rides (which Tiger didn't like at all), three funhouses, two waxworks, six penny arcades, 20 shooting galleries, three freak shows and upwards of 200 eateries. Both he and Kewpie heartily agreed that Nathan's Famous was the only one that mattered. No trip to Coney was complete without a bite into one of their savory hot dogs which snapped when your teeth penetrated their thick skins.

For Tiger and Kewpie, this would be a day of deals, agreements and concessions. Luna Park or Steeplechase? A stationary or rolling car on the Wonder Wheel? Thunderbolt or Cyclone? ("Both!" Tiger said emphatically.) Cotton candy or jelly apples? Kewpie favored Luna Park, with its romantic recreation of the city of Baghdad, complete with towers and turrets that illuminated at night. Tiger went for the speed and violence of Steeplechase. Today, Kewpie gave in to her brother's whims, and she knew exactly which ride he would run to first: the Steeplechase Race.

"You're so predictable," she sighed, as he dragged her toward the mechanical horses. Also predictable was Tiger stopping dead in his tracks the moment he laid eyes on a large wooden sign. It depicted the scary, leering face of Steeplechase Park's unofficial ambassador, known as "Funny Face" or "Steeplechase Jack." This creepy fellow sported greased-down hair parted in the middle, big goofy teeth, scary lips and crazed eyes. Steeplechase Jack was an evil specter masquerading as someone beneficent, not unlike his father. The little boy studied the caricature of fun with his mouth somewhat ajar before his sister propelled him forward. "It's only make-believe," Kewpie assured her brother. "He can't hurt you."

Before he knew it, Tiger was walking through Steeplechase Park's wide, welcoming arch, Coney's own homage to the one at Grand Army Plaza. An entire universe of merriment was set out before him: The Pavilion of Fun, Hoop-La, the Funny Staircase, Spook-A-Rama, the Air Tower and Blow-Hole Theatre. "Don't be a gloomster...be a Steeplechaser," Kewpie sang out, mimicking the park's slogan.

"Steeplechase, the Funny Place," Tiger responded, echoing the other.

They waited on line to race the Steeplechase Race, perhaps the Park's most famous attraction. Side by side, Kewpie and Tiger rode on mechanical horses, speeding around on iron rails, first Kewpie's steed winning, then Tiger's. Hurling toward the ocean, the track climbed up, then dipped down, rising on the rails as high as 35 feet, circling around the other side of the Pavilion of Fun to the finish line. "Get ready!" Kewpie told him. "Here he comes!"

They jumped off their horses and ran as fast as they could, chased by a pint-sized clown with an electric paddle. Kewpie and Tiger were never caught but plenty people were, and some even seemed to slow down so they could get spanked on purpose.

Kewpie did her best to hold down her skirt as they ran across Blow-Hole Theatre, which shot up jets of air. Some unsuspecting ladies' petticoats went up over their heads but Kewpie knew better. She held her dress down and gave the men who parked themselves at the exit a glimpse of her knees, nothing more.

Tiger hated the Human Roulette Wheel—he once puked up his Nathan's into a trash bin immediately after coming off that ride—but Kewpie loved it. He waited at the fence outside for her to finish. She was easy to spot in her bright green dress, sitting cross-legged and smiling at him. When the humongous roulette wheel started to spin, bodies were flung left and right, skimming across the wheel's waxed surface.

The people in the center stayed put the longest. Kewpie knew this and plopped herself near the middle. She was one of the last to lose grip, laughing uncontrollably as she spun, finally landing spread-legged and revealing plenty of thigh. Rosanna would have been horrified but Kewpie still giggled. One of her espadrilles came loose—hand-me-downs from Aunt Jo—and she limped over to Tiger, the cord still fastened to her ankle. She dragged the shoe behind her "like Boris Karloff in *The Mummy*," Tiger noted.

That night, Tiger's dreams would be littered with a collage of activity: the Swinging Ship, the giant See-Saw, the sensation of blue cotton candy melting on his tongue like a Communion wafer, coming out of the pipe slide onto the Pavilion floor. Struggling up the Funny Staircase side by side, he and Kewpie kept falling down, giggling, then getting up again as the steps split in two and went in opposite directions. The Funny Staircase was a lot like life sometimes, Tiger thought, but not nearly as humorous. For when your life dissected and flung you in another direction, you usually got hurt.

Riding the Thunderbolt made Tiger feel as though he were being hurled through space, especially at twilight when everything looked a bit foggy anyway. Tiger was seated beside a fat man whose girth kept oozing onto him whenever they banked a curve. The Thunderbolt's speed was much scarier than that of the Cyclone (which he'd ridden earlier). It was a much more violent, and therefore, more satisfying ride for Tiger. However, there was nothing to compare with the Cyclone's gorgeous panoramic view of the ocean, then its terrifying first drop where you felt as though you left your heart at the top of the crest and your stomach at the bottom. Kewpie wasn't a fan of roller coasters and sat both of these out, patiently waiting for Tiger and grinning wider the more he screamed.

Lunch was a knish for a nickel and a rushed cone of delicious vanilla custard, which cost a dime. Dinner was at Nathan's. Even if the sign above Surf Avenue didn't command "Stop Here" they would have stopped anyway. They each had two franks, guzzled a shared Coke and also split a cup of fries. "I bet they haven't changed the grease since the turn of the century," Tiger joked, mimicking Poppa's words.

Kewpie smiled, "Which century?" taking up Bridget's customary retort.

Although Steeplechase Park's three-tiered El Dorado carousel was much more spectacular, for some reason, Tiger preferred the simplicity of B & B's little merry-go-round. They went there after Nathan's. The Bishoff & Brienstein Carousell was a block down on Surf, at West 10th Street. Kewpie loved carousels, but days away from turning 16, felt she was too old for them. Which was a shame because nobody's ever truly too old for a carousel, are they?

It had been a near-perfect day which was winding down to a close. The street lights were just coming on and Coney Island took on an ethereal glow, illuminated by thousands upon thousands of light bulbs. Tiger held Kewpie's hand but lightly, tiredly by now. This would be the last ride of the night, though she knew he would complain, but only halfheartedly. Tiger managed to get his favorite horse, an ivory one with green plumes and an iridescent blue sash. He once confided to Kewpie that he nicknamed the horse "Lightning," and told this to no one else. Lightning was on the outer row of the carousel, the perfect spot for grabbing the brass rings.

Kewpie waited part inside and part outside the carousel barn. She could see both the ride and the street from where she stood. The calliope started abruptly, making both Tiger and her jump. It played "Strawberry Blonde."

*"Casey would dance with a strawberry blonde
And the band played on..."*

Kewpie mouthed these words almost silently to herself.

Tiger stood in Lightning's stirrups, nabbing a brass ring on the first turn. Another clunked down in its place. Other children tried but they couldn't capture a ring for themselves. As for Tiger, he seemed to have the move patented—stand up in the stirrups, stretch as high as you can, grab the ring, slip it onto your wrist in one swift motion and on the next go-around, grab another.

Kewpie laughed with delight and admired her brother's prowess, even clapped her hands to cheer him on. Tiger beamed back at her. Then, out of the corner of her eye, Kewpie saw him and her soul froze. Her father, at the arm of a peroxide blonde. Kewpie knew her father saw her too but he just turned away wordlessly. When Kewpie heard the sound of a brass ring dropping and hitting concrete, she knew that Tiger had seen Tony as well. But their father made like he didn't even know them and just kept walking with his girlfriend. It was probably just as well that way.

Kewpie and Tiger walked to the trolley stop in silence. "Can I have just one try?" Tiger asked when they passed Uncle John's favorite booth, the shooting gallery. Kewpie had a handful of change left, enough for the trolley and then some. "Sure," she said and handed Tiger some coins. He shot at the weasels and beavers and helpless deer, just as Uncle John had done a few days earlier. Kewpie knew that Tiger had another creature in his sights, one that walked on his hind legs and liked cheap blondes. And it was all right with her.

On the ride home, the Martino kids also managed to secure the best seats on the trolley, in the right-hand corner at the very back. Tiger's head rested heavily on Kewpie's shoulder, and by the way he was breathing, she knew he was fast asleep even without seeing his face.

As the trolley pulled away from the ocean and away from the neon glow, Kewpie remembered something. Although "Coney" was an old English word for rabbit—there were apparently lots of rabbits on the island in the 1640s when the British first visited–others said that the name came from the island's shape, which was rabbit-like. The Lenape Indians called it something completely different. They knew it as "Land Without Shadows" because it was sunny on Coney Island all day long.

However, Kewpie knew this was no longer true. She knew that there were plenty of shadows in this place. Despite the electric lights and false grandeur, there were dim alleys and dark ugly corners in Coney Island, just like anywhere else.

19 Ambush

Although Rosanna didn't care much for the movies, this reminded her of a good, old-fashioned ambush. *The Last of the Mohicans* came to mind specifically. Not the serial with Harry Carey but the silent movie with Boris Karloff and Wallace Beery from many years ago. She'd heard they were remaking it and knew Tiger would love it—he wasn't even born when the first one came out. Her boy enjoyed his cinema with a touch of bows and arrows, bullets and blood, that was certain.

It had been a quiet, pleasant day. Rosanna's parents were visiting Julius, Lettie and the boys in Queens. Rosanna finished Mrs. Finn's laundry soon after Tiger and Kewpie left, hung it out to dry on the line outside the kitchen window and settled down to read *Gone With the Wind*. Astrid loaned Rosanna her copy, handsomely bound in olive green leather with fanciful blue lettering. Just recently published, the book was all the rage that summer. She sat in a comfy armchair, reading, with the metal oscillating floor fan positioned directly on her. The chair's cushions were still molded to fit her husband's body, even though he's been gone for weeks.

After reading for a while, Rosanna went for a stroll, chatted with various neighbors, enjoyed a light dinner of leftovers then sat down with Scarlett O'Hara again. But then there was a knock on the door, which usually signified trouble of some sort. Everyone who knew Rosanna knew the door was always unlocked and just came in, announcing themselves with a friendly shout. She put down the book, straightened her skirt, ran a quick hand through her hair and took a deep breath, hoping the children hadn't had a mishap on their Coney Island adventure. Then she opened the door.

Rosanna was relieved to see her brother-in-law John, who was carrying a big Manila envelope, but perplexed to see Sully standing sheepishly behind him, out of uniform. Whenever Sully stopped by, it was always on his beat and it was always with Harry. She'd grown accustomed to seeing his beefy body stuffed into his blue uniform with the shiny buttons. This afternoon, Sully was in a sport coat and slacks, with a straw hat in hand. She wished she'd looked a little neater, a little prettier.

John's necktie was undone. Rosanna rarely saw him without a necktie although this day it was close to ninety degrees. He plunked the envelope onto the kitchen table. Before she knew it, Rosanna was sitting there, flanked by Sully and John, staring down at a set of glossy black and white photographs. They were a lot like movie star glamour shots except these weren't glamorous at all. They were crude and gritty. "I had no idea you were a photographer, Johnny," Rosanna said simply. "I mean, I know you liked movies and all from working in the projection booth, but this…"

"Oh, I played around with a Brownie camera during the War," he told her. "Nothing fancy. But I sometimes take pictures for my P.I. work."

"That means Private Investigator," Sully explained.

"I know what it means, Paddy" Rosanna told him gently. "But I didn't hire one." And to her brother-in-law, just as softly, she said, "I didn't ask you to find anyone, John."

He blushed slightly and answered the oilcloth. "I know you didn't. But how long can you go on like this?"

Rosanna's eyes flashed darkly. "We're doing just fine, thank you."

Sully put his hand near Rosanna's as it rested on the tabletop. "Roe, even if you don't want him back, which I can't blame you if you don't, it's only right that he support you and the kids."

Rosanna moved her hand. "I don't want anything from him," she said, shuffling through the 8 x 10's like an oversized deck of cards. A blonde in a window. Peroxide curls. The kind of hairdo you don't get from bobby pins fastened with your own hand. The sort they give you in a fancy beauty shop while wearing a pink smock, not in a friend's bathroom with a rag wrapped around your shoulders. The woman seemed to be wearing a slip of some sort with lace around the brassiere cups. Not like Rosanna's, which were cotton and unadorned. Saks Fifth Avenue as opposed rummaging through a bin downtown on Fulton Street.

In another photograph, the woman had her arm strung through Tony's and was smiling. The woman wore a floral headpiece of fake violets, the type Astrid made. It wrapped around her skull like a crown of thorns. Her dress seemed hand-tailored instead of bought off the rack. Shoulder-length curls white as old snow. A poor man's Jean Harlow, Rosanna decided. And her husband was no rich man, that was for sure. In fact, he looked worn-out, much thinner in the photographs. That floozy probably wasn't much in the kitchen, Rosanna figured, the bedroom seemed to be her specialty.

"You developed these yourself, did you, Johnny?" Rosanna wondered aloud.

"I made a darkroom out of the spare room," he told her. "Put up black curtains, the whole works. I'm dabbling in it, you might say."

"Do you realize what this means, Roe?" Sully asked.

She didn't respond immediately, but took a deep gulp from the tumbler of seltzer in front of her. Even unexpected guests received royal treatment at the Martino house, no matter if it was just a cold cup of something or other on a hot day. She set out a tray of cookies which no one touched, though the seltzer was almost finished. Sweaty rings formed on the oilcloth due to the ice she'd chipped from the melting chunk in the icebox. "Yes," Rosanna finally answered. "Yes, Sully, I do realize what this means." Then she was silent.

Oddly enough, Rosanna didn't feel a pang of jealousy. Set him out with the trash, Astrid liked to say of Tony every chance she got, and this woman certainly looked like trash. Although Astrid had no right to say a thing like that, considering what she'd married. Sam didn't raise a hand to her sister, it was true, but he was something of a run-around. Everyone knew it, even Astrid, but she let him get away with it as long as he didn't parade it around in her face. "That one has Roman eyes," Bridget had whispered to Rosanna in confidence the first time she saw Sam.

"Momma, you mean roaming eyes, not Roman," Rosanna told her.

"Whatever. I don't trust him as far as I can throw him," her mother said, stirring the Sunday gravy. And it wasn't the fact that Sam wasn't Italian. There was something wily about Sam, his smile too wide, his compliments too ingratiating. He seemed to try too hard, which in this family, was just as bad as not trying hard enough. And Bridget had been right about him, as right as rain.

Rosanna placed the photographs on the table and slid them back into the envelope. She rewrapped the string around the little paper circle, sealing it tight. "What do you want me to do?" Rosanna asked them.

"You mean, what do you want us to do?" John responded.

Rosanna folded her hands in her lap. "Nothing."

"Nothing?" Sully asked in disbelief.

The rent her parents charged wasn't much. It basically covered a share of the house's taxes, utilities and upkeep. Plus Rosanna did her part helping them care for the place, washing down the hallway, sweeping the front walk, keeping the furnace going in the winter. The kids even helped shoveling snow. More than once, Bridget had told her, "Without you, we wouldn't be able to keep up the place." And even when he was around, Tony had been useless, grumbling about even the slightest chore like changing the porch light bulb. It was much easier for Rosanna to do things on her own. But now that she was sick, it would be more of a challenge. She could handle it, though, she was sure of it. Anything was better than having him back.

Rosanna nodded her head emphatically and said again, "Nothing. I don't want to do anything about it." And as an afterthought she added, "But thanks. Thank you for giving me the heads up."

For some reason, Rosanna thought of Haile Selassie and all of his troubles. She'd just seen a picture of him in the *Eagle* that haunted her thoughts. The poor exiled Ethiopian Emperor had stood before the League of Nations, begging them for help. Mussolini had invaded Ethiopia more than six months earlier and the country was losing its defense hold against him. But the League couldn't agree on how or if to help Ethiopia at all. Instead of coming to Emperor Selassie's aid, the League of Nations argued back and forth. So ultimately, they did nothing while the Ethiopian army succumbed to Italian tanks, aircraft and poison gas.

And here Rosanna was, offered assistance on a silver platter. All she had to do was ask for it but she was too afraid. Too scared of what Tony might do to get back at her, that he might hurt the children or her parents, even. And she was worried that she really couldn't make it on her own. After all, Rosanna knew the hell she had but not the hell that might be.

John and Sully stayed and made smalltalk about the weather and about Poppa's 4th of July barbecue coming up in a few days. Rosanna offered them both more seltzer and they sampled a few cookies. Sully tried to concentrate on the conversation but he was fuming. He wanted to go down to Coney himself and kick that fuckface's ass just for ha-ha's. As it was now, Sully would probably have to go down to the Lucky Buck for a few beers just to set himself right again, just to rid himself of the rage. But Sully never got drunk. Not the way Tony did anyway. Every now and again, he just needed the cleansing, cold, sudsy liquid to get back to normal. Whatever normal was. These days, he didn't know anymore.

The conversation ebbed then jumpstarted unnaturally again. Both men seemed to be looking to Rosanna for more. For assurance, perhaps. "We'll get by," she said emphatically, even managing a little smile. "I'll take in more laundry. I can do cleaning. Mrs. D'Angelo could use a hand and she's loaded." Sully scowled. "She's also a tightwad." Then, "There's more to a husband than just support, you know."

Rosanna took hold of Sully's hand for emphasis. And Patrick Sullivan did not shrink away, although from the corner of her eye, Rosanna thought she saw her brother-in-law start at the forwardness of her gesture. "We still get Union benefits, Paddy, if that's what you mean," she told him. "He's still my husband on paper and I can do without his other 'benefits.'" The pawing, yelling and carrying on, she meant.

Sully looked all the way up from Rosanna's wrist to where her bare arm met the sleeve of her cotton shift. It was the first time in a long time that he didn't notice purple or green bruises staining her skin, fresh as flowers or fading like awful memories. Even her face was without florid evidence of recently being backhanded. But her eyes had dark circles beneath them and she looked very tired and pale. Not pale the way the Irish get with their pasty, white skin but pale the way olive-skinned Italians like Rosanna get—greenish, hollow, with those half-moon smudges raccooning their eyes.

Rosanna Martino's skin felt alive under Sully's gaze. Even though she studied the swirls on the oilcloth, she knew Sully was studying her. "I'm not saying it's easy," Rosanna told them. "But in some ways, it's easier than having him around." She glanced from one to the other. "And I've been having...health problems on top of everything," she continued. "Female trouble. Dr. Lewis's been looking after me. He sent me to a specialist. But I should be fine, really."

In truth, Dr. Schantz had said Rosanna needed surgery after just a brief look. A hysterectomy...it sounded so ugly and medieval. And how could she have an operation with the kids home from school and her parents needing her. "It's not a good time," she'd told Dr. Schantz.

"It's never a good time," he shot back. He wanted Rosanna to
check into United Israel-Zion as soon as possible. But Poppa's
barbecue was coming up and Kewpie's birthday besides. Plus
Kelly and the family hoped to make the drive in from Arizona
for a visit before the fall set in. Rosanna couldn't go on the way
she was, though, soaking through rags like tissue-paper and
being bone-tired from the loss of blood. The iron tablets Dr.
Lewis gave her helped but it was like the small Dutch boy with
his finger plugging the dike. Or like shoveling shit against the
tide, as her father might say.

"And please," Rosanna continued, releasing Sully's hand,
"Don't tell my folks. They'd only worry. And there's nothing to
worry about."

Both John and Sully gave their word.

Kewpie and Tiger stepped off the trolley and made their way
down 47th Street. Or more closely, Kewpie carried Tiger
piggy-back. He was still gently snoring on her shoulder as the
trolley jerked to their stop. The strap of her dress under his
mouth was damp with his drool and she smiled when she
realized this. Tiger clomped across the trolley's wooden floor,
barely awake, guided and supported by his sister. He scarcely
made it down the steps without falling, punch-drunk like his dad,
but with tiredness instead of alcohol.

Without saying a word, Kewpie hoisted Tiger onto her back,
as her father used to do when they were kids. She was a sturdy
girl and could easily manage Tiger's gangly limbs flailing and
his knobby chin digging between her shoulder blades. Mr. Wong,
who was closing down the restaurant, nodded a silent hello.
Kewpie kept hoping they would meet up with Sully or even
Augie, who would no doubt help them the rest of the way home,
lifting Tiger like a sack of feathers.

She grasped the Kewpie Doll she'd bought in her free hand
and had to stop halfway down the block to boost Tiger up her
back again because he kept slipping away. Sensing this, the boy
caught his sister tighter around the neck. Kewpie took the five
steps in front of the house slowly and laboriously, much like
Bridget climbed them, avoiding the loose brick on the top step

at the left-hand corner that jangled like a loose tooth. Poppa kept saying he was going to fix it but never seemed to get around to it. "You can build battleships for strangers but you can't fix a blasted old brick for your family," Bridget liked to chide him good-naturedly.

Kewpie paused on the front porch, soaking up the warm breeze. In less than a week, she'd be 16, almost a woman. Although she wasn't having a big bash like Louise, Grandma Bridget promised to make her favorite cake—a butter sunshine pineapple upside-down cake with fresh pineapple—and that was something. She thought Tiger was asleep until she felt his breath in her ear, words too faint to hear. But then he spoke again. "Don't tell them," he sighed.

And Kewpie nodded. She knew exactly what he meant. "Don't tell them we saw him," he said again. "He'll ruin everything." Kewpie promised not to say a thing and set him down on the porch.

They clattered up the steps, laughing. The apartment door was wide open and Kewpie could see her Uncle John and Sully just standing up, their summer hats in hand. Sully wasn't even in uniform and her uncle had an envelope clutched in one fist. Something was wrong. Tiger was suddenly wide awake and standing at attention.

The kids looked startled, it was true. Kewpie's face was slightly flushed and damp, although she looked pretty in her handmade dress. Tiger was as scrawny and scrappy as ever, in his too-big hand-me-downs. Was it from his sister Irene's son, Sully wondered, or from Lettie's? He remembered something John had told him one night at the Pink Pussycat: "I never had a new suit of clothes or three meals a day until I joined the Army." Then John had downed his entire shot of scotch. Sully sincerely hoped this wouldn't be the case for Tiger. He knew the boy got three squares a day but as for the clothes, they were either too big or too snug, never just right.

"Irene sends her regards," Sully told Rosanna.

"Tell I said hi too," Rosanna nodded.

"She says she'll come by soon," he added, backing out the door. "She has some things for Tiger."

"I'd love to see her anytime, even empty-handed," Rosanna joked.

John kissed his sister-in-law on the side of the head, which smelled vaguely of Kirkman's. He did the same to the kids, who both were pleasantly sweaty, and slipped a quarter into the pocket of Tiger's droopy knickers. When Sully shook Tiger's hand, he performed a magician's sleight of hand and there was a shiny coin wedged between Tiger's fingers. Rosanna knew exactly what was going on but didn't say anything.

"See you in a couple of days," John told them.

"You, too?" Rosanna said in Sully's direction.

"I'm working on the 4th," he said.

"You can still stop by for a frank and some potato salad."

"Only if you're making it," he told her. "I can't stomach Astrid's with those little carrot hunks and gherkins."

"I'm making it," Rosanna assured him. "But beggars can't be choosers." When she realized what she'd said, her cheeks colored. If anyone was a beggar, it was she.

When their guests were gone, Rosanna sent the children off to bed. "It's late," she explained, "and you've had a big day. You can tell me all about it in the morning."

Kewpie gave her mother the little doll with the pudgy plastic face, blue bug eyes and lemon yellow ringlets. "I got it with my own money," she said, then disappeared into the bathroom to change into her nightgown.

While his mother was turning down the bedclothes, Tiger stood on his tippy-toes and slipped one of the quarters into the little tin Kirkman woman's laundry bucket. He turned to leave, but after a brief moment of consideration, turned back and added the other quarter soundlessly.

Tiger stripped down to his undershorts in the bedroom, excitedly telling Rosanna about the Human Roulette Wheel, the Thunderbolt and the carousel, leaving out the part about his father. She tucked her children in with a kiss, then retreated to the porch beyond their room. They could hear the familiar music of the old chair as it rocked. So could Sully, standing on the porch beneath her. Rosanna could feel a comforting presence but wasn't exactly sure what it was. It felt good anyway.

Sully was long gone when Poppa's Nash rounded the corner and inched its way into the narrow space between their house and Mrs. Rosenkrantz's. He steered Betsy into the backyard garage. Rosanna was startled awake by the headlights, then began to drift back asleep again, still rocking. Before she closed her eyes, she thought she heard Tiger muttering something in his sleep, only she couldn't decipher the words.

But Kewpie was wide awake and she heard exactly what her brother said. "Don't tell," he mumbled. "Don't." She wouldn't breathe a word about seeing their father to anyone, lest the spell be broken and everything would crush to bits.

20 Independence Day

Astrid clutched the jar of dwarf-sized pickles in her fist like a weapon. "What do you mean, you're not putting them in the salad?" she barked menacingly.

Rosanna hugged the bowl of sliced and peeled potatoes to her chest protectively. "Not everyone likes them is all I'm saying," she told her sister.

"Nonsense," Astrid shot back. "They do it at the 21 Club. And just the other day, there was a recipe in..."

It was hot in the crowded kitchen. Rosanna wiped her forehead with the back of her hand. "Look around you, Astrid. This ain't the 21 Club, kiddo."

But Astrid wouldn't give up. This was another of her personality flaws, not knowing when to fight and when to give up, not being able to differentiate what was important and what was not. And in the vast scheme of things, potato salad was no big deal. But Astrid pressed on, undaunted, "Who complained? Huh? I bet it was Johnny?"

Camille shot Astrid an annoyed glance but said nothing. She knew better. Camille went back to roasting a pepper over the gas burner. She skewered it with the tines of the fork, moving it back and forth in the open flame. When the pepper's bright red skin blistered and blackened, she turned it slightly to char another side.

"Your father always burns them on the grill," Bridget told Camille, ignoring Astrid's tirade. (Bridget had learned to do this back when Astrid was known as Margaret and liked to throw kicking, screaming, flailing fits as a child when she didn't get her way. Some things never changed.) While the women were responsible for all of the indoor cooking, for some unexplainable, primal, hunter-gatherer reason, the men laid claim to the outdoor cooking. This is why the ladies did as much as they could indoors.

Astrid wore a jaunty little hat festooned with red and white striped firecrackers and studded with over-ripe blueberries. It made her look all the more insane. She wore it like barbed wire, painfully and obstinately, since it was one of her most inspired creations (which Lord and Taylor had the good sense to reject). Camille turned the pepper thoughtfully and wondered if the firecrackers on her sister's head would indeed explode if someone were to set fire to Astrid's angry blonde head.

"You people are so pedestrian!" Astrid continued. On her thin, pursed lips, the word 'pedestrian' sounded like a curse. She hoped her family was too pedestrian to know what the word meant but they all did. "Honestly..." she went on.

Bridget nudged Astrid with her fleshy hip. "What does it matter who said it? It was just someone with good taste, Margaret," she told her daughter. Bridget refused to call her daughter by her store-bought name, as she referred to it. "Get off your high horse and chop a few cloves of garlic," she continued, "I hear it's all the rage in *The Fannie Farmer Cookbook*."

With a harrumph Astrid reluctantly began to chop garlic. "And don't put *alici* in the antipasto," she added.

Rosanna had just opened a can of anchovies with the container's tiny key. The strong scent of oily fish filled the kitchen. "But they're Poppa's favorite," Rosanna reminded her sister. "How about I only put *alici* on half?"

Astrid put her hand to her forehead in a manner that would rival Marion Davies. "But just the smell alone turns my stomach," she gagged, adding a weak cough for emphasis. "And those disgusting little hairs remind me of..."

"Margaret, stop being such a scootch," Bridget told her.

That was all it took for Astrid to set the paring knife down on the table and leave in a tizzy. "I thought she'd never go," said Jo, who was just getting back her sense of humor three months after losing the baby. "She's always trying to complicate everything."

Even Julius's wife, Lettie, whose real name was Letecia, knew better than to make a fuss about things as insignificant as this. From Czech peasant stock, Lettie had wavy, wheat-colored hair (her natural shade, a constant source of annoyance to Astrid, whose unnatural hair color came from a bottle, and was straight as an arrow besides) and startling green eyes. She stood apart physically from most of the Paradiso Girls—blonde, petite and lean rather than dark, tall and wide-hipped. But as Bridget liked to put it, "Lettie comes from the same place." And that was a simple, warm, uncomplicated place.

Lettie and Julius's youngest son, Carl, who was barely two, hung onto Lettie's skirts and followed her wherever she went like an extra appendage. He also sucked his thumb. However, Carl was treated like an additional piece of Lettie—an extra finger or toe, for example—rather than a curiosity, as though having a toddler clutching your hem was the most natural thing in the world. When his aunts patted his head and tickled him on the neck, Carl rarely looked at them, and never let go of his mother's leg, except briefly to switch thumbs.

Lettie and Julius's older son Matthew played with Tiger under the kitchen table. Though he was a year younger than Tiger, Mattie was bigger and more solid, thus the source of numerous, fine hand-me-downs for Tiger. Lettie had an eye for bargains as well as quality. The boys giggled quietly about their aunt's antics, which often were more entertaining than Fibber McGee on the radio. "She's gonna bust a blood vessel," Tiger observed, because Aunt Astrid had stormed out of the room, beet-red in the face.

"Let's hope so," Mattie said, then knocked down Tiger's fortress of dominoes with his soldier's bayonet.

"You boys playing nice down there?" Bridget wondered.

"They are, Grandma," Kewpie noted, taking a peek.

"Nicer than you girls are playing up there," Tiger told his grandmother. He could tell by the way her legs and lower body shook that Bridget was laughing.

A barbecue to an Italian family like the Paradisos meant that they pretty much ate the same foods outdoors as they ate indoors. For example, there was always an antipasto. It was simply carried into the backyard on the same floral patterned, big-as-a-manhole cover platter as it was served on in the dining room. And there was always Italian bread. You needed it for the sausage and peppers, which were cooked inside in a cast iron skillet. The only real differences were that they ate on a long makeshift table squeezed into the cement and grass backyard and that the other meats were cooked—or charred—by the men on the grill.

It was time for the exodus where everyone grabbed a dish or bowl, carefully toted it down the back steps into the yard and set it on the table, which was actually a four by eight sheet of plywood balanced on a pair of sawhorses and covered with a festive tablecloth. No one was the wiser. A small army of folding chairs were propped up against the house's back wall. There were chairs of all varieties, some found on the street good as new, others passed along from friends who no longer needed them and still others that were borrowed for the occasion. Some people came and went all day like the tide, sampling the incredible array of food, staying for a drink or two, then moving on, while others didn't budge from their seats until dark.

Most of the Paradisos' friends and neighbors adhered to the same belief they did: "If you can't knock on the door with your elbows, don't bother coming at all." It was an adage that was widely practiced, accepted but never said aloud. People with less always seemed to be the most giving, if not with material goods, then at least in spirit. And this sort of generous nature was precious and dear, something that couldn't be procured or bought. It existed within you.

After all, what did it take to boil up a box of elbow macaroni, toss in a few spices and stir in a dill dressing concocted by your maternal grandmother's aunt in Warsaw three generations ago? Not much in effort or in money but it spoke volumes about the kind of person you were. The very act of cooking and sharing food with others was nurturing and charitable plus delicious. You were sharing a piece of your family history, a hunk of where you came from in the form of offering a handed-down recipe. In Bridget's view, nothing counted more than generosity of spirit. And if the Paradisos had nothing else, at least they had this.

One look at their improvised table served as evidence. A platter of sausages and peppers glistened in the sunlight beside a creamy mountain of Rosanna's potato salad, sans carrots and gherkins but with a splash of pickle juice in the mayonnaise-mustard dressing (her secret ingredient). There was a separate platter of roasted peppers which Camille had lovingly hand-roasted one by one on the burner then delicately peeled and seasoned, a medley of olives including the shriveled black ones which reminded Tiger of nanny goat pellets, marinated mushrooms, cheese wedges (a collection of ends which Bridget economically asked Sal the butcher to save for her and she bought at a cut-rate), marinated cauliflower salad (courtesy of Mrs. DePalma's wonderful recipe) and green beans which Rosanna had pickled the week before when they'd been on sale, dirt cheap. The cabbage, both red and green, was grated by hand, as were the carrots, and tossed lightly in an oil and vinegar dressing. Lettie contributed the fresh beet salad, dotted with raw onions and liberally salted, her grandmother's recipe from the Old Country. It was carted in a deep dish covered with tin foil and set on the car floor beneath Carl's feet (which didn't reach the mat) on their pilgrimage from Sunnyside.

From Mrs. Rosenkrantz, there were crunchy golden brown potato *latkes*, which she claimed went with everything, even an "American" barbecue. She also supplied the sour cream and applesauce garnish. Mixing meat and dairy wasn't a concern for her today since this was a non-Kosher meal fraught with *goyim* anyway. Although Mrs. Rosenkrantz was often not the most neighborly neighbor, the Paradisos felt it was in their best interest to invite her rather than risk having their celebration doused with buckets of water if it grew too rowdy. And, as Poppa pointed out, Bertha loosened up after a glass or two of wine, which he kept handy. Despite her protests that her son was a classically trained musician, they could usually persuade Ti-Tu to trade in his violin for a ukulele and strum a few tunes for sing-alongs.

Independence Day was Poppa's favorite holiday. For him, it was a bigger deal than even Christmas. It was the day he got to honor his adopted country, to celebrate it, to rejoice. He'd done all right for himself here and so had his children, well most of them. While Bridget had come to America from *Fiorenze* up north as a young girl with her family, Poppa came by himself when he was a teenager, from the boot tip of Italy, San Vincenzo to be exact, with money he'd saved himself for the fare.

If Poppa thought hard enough, he could still remember his passage on the steamship, the *Giuseppe Verdi*. He could recall the tapestry of sounds and the odor that constantly lingered in the tight, close air. In fact, he still had the photograph he'd bought upon landing in the United States. It depicted a full moon over the modest New York City skyline. He kept it in a silver frame in the dining room. Poppa had arrived with just a few dollars in his pocket, a strong back and the desire to succeed. And that he did.

Fifty years later, he had a nice house and a new car, a fine family and good friends. There's no telling where he might be if he were still back in Cosenza. Probably in sad shape, just squeaking by like his relatives, poor rural folks he sent money to as often as he could. Yes, Michael Archangel Paradiso was a very fortunate man.

Poppa puffed on his pipe and thought of this as he burned the hamburgers. Pitiful as he was at the grill, he rarely handed it over to anyone else. To him, manning the charcoal was like being the captain at the helm of a ship—you never relinquished control, except when you had to go to the bathroom. So what if the burgers were a little crusty or the hot dogs were slightly rubbery? He'd never killed anyone, at least not yet.

Wearing a polo shirt with a bandana tied around his neck, Poppa took a sip from the glass of beer he stowed on the ground near the grill. He contentedly surveyed his surroundings. Everyone seemed to be having a good time. And they were all there, all the important ones in his life. All except for Kelly and his family. But the rest could just about make up for the hollowness he sometimes felt from missing his son, Sophie and the grandkids. Well, almost.

Smoke billowed up from the grill. Poppa swatted it away. "You got a license for that thing?" boomed a big voice behind him. Poppa wheeled around. It was Sully, in uniform, with Harry close behind him. Harry gave Jo a quick peck on the cheek and a squeeze on the bottom which he didn't think anyone noticed. But Tiger gave Mattie a shove and they giggled. Their aunt blushed.

"I got better than a license," Poppa laughed. "I got low friends in high places in the police department." Poppa put down the spatula and grabbed Sully's hand, chucking him on the chin and laughing. "Welcome, welcome…grab a seat, boys."

Chairs magically unfolded and found their way to the patrolmen. "This yours?" Sully asked Rosanna in a loud whisper as he heaped his plate with potato salad, knowing full well the answer. Astrid rolled her eyes dramatically. Of course, she wouldn't touch the stuff but Sam complimented his sister-in-law's potato salad prowess profusely, taking a second helping and even licking the back of his fork when he was done. Astrid folded her arms across her chest and shook her head.

"Nice hat, Maggie," Harry told Astrid, reveling in the ruffled feathers the use of her old name caused.

"It's Astrid, Harold," she huffed.

"Ah, you'll always be Maggie to me," Harry joked. "I knew you when." He took a bite of his hamburger, dwarfed in his ham-hock fist. "I knew you when you were a brunette."

Astrid stuck her artfully-chiseled nose in the air and adjusted a firecracker or two on her head. Sam suppressed a chuckle and with a stern glance, warned Tiger and Mattie not to laugh. Then he busted out with a loud guffaw himself. Even Mrs. Rosenkrantz, who had no sense of humor, couldn't help a chuckle. "Ha!" Astrid huffed and shoved a cigarette into a rhinestone-encrusted holder. She lit the cigarette with a shaky hand.

A grubby paw suddenly appeared on the table, feeling its way around the salt and pepper shakers, the ice bucket and finally alighting upon a potato *latke*. Both the hand and the *latke* disappeared under the table. The greasy fingertips soon resurfaced and attached themselves to a charred chicken leg which promptly levitated and was lost beneath the tablecloth.

Bridget lifted the edge of the cloth, smiling, and unveiled not Tiger or Matthew but Jimmy Burns crouched on the concrete like a dog, furtively gnawing on the now-bare chicken bone. She rested a plump hand on Jimmy's shoulder and told him, "Why don't you come up and join us?" But the boy was alarmed at being revealed. He sprung into a sprint, banging his filthy cast against a bowl of macaroni salad as he ran down the alley and back to the street.

As Jimmy Burns fled, he nearly collided with two small, dark people hesitantly making their way into the backyard. At first, Tiger thought he didn't know either of them but when he looked more closely, he recognized Manny's compact, sinewy form and flashing black eyes. It was the first time Tiger had seen him in a suit and outside the Navy Yard, and he had never met Mrs. Ortez Vega before. She was pretty, with skin the color of the milky coffee his mother occasionally let him have. Her waist was tiny, accentuated by the full skirt of her dress, and she wore a small straw hat that would fit one of the Pomeranians.

Manny seemed nervous, shaking hands, and introducing his wife Consuelo around, who was even more self-conscious than he. Manny had carried a big cast iron pot all the way from Fort Greene, on the sizeable walk from their apartment to the train station and on two trains themselves. When the Ortez Vegas set the pot onto the table and uncovered it, steam rose from the savory pigeon peas and rice inside, which were still warm. Sam, Harry and Sully delved into the pot with a renewed intensity. After all, they hadn't eaten for ten minutes or so.

Tiger introduced his cousin to his friend from the Navy Yard like a grown-up. "*Mucho gusto, Matteo*," Manny said with a hearty handshake.

"That means 'Pleased to meet you, Matthew,'" Tiger translated for his cousin's benefit.

Tiger even permitted Consuelo to kiss him on the cheek. "I've heard so much about you, Anthony," she said, grinning and using his real name. No doubt, Manny told her stories about the boy when he came home from work and they'd delighted her.

Anthony Martino, Jr. didn't know what to say. "You can call me 'Tiger," he told her. "All my friends do." And she did. But Consuelo said it daintily, barely pronouncing the 'g,' with an exotic roll of the 'r.' Tiger liked the way it sounded.

It wasn't long before the Ortez Vegas were swept up into the vortex of the Paradiso Family's warmth. Although Consuelo couldn't pronounce the word *latke*, she took a liking to them, especially with sour cream. "Like a good Jew," Bertha Rosenkrantz noted, raising her glass of burgundy in a mini toast. The burgundy was made in the basement of Poppa's good friend Enrico Serano and was very potent indeed. "And Kosher," Bertha proclaimed.

Plates were filled, emptied and filled again. Sadie Lieberwitz and her husband Heshie arrived from down the street, contributing her wonderful cucumber-onion salad. Although everyone said they couldn't eat another bite, somehow they always managed to sample each new dish, nibble on an olive or have another hamburger or hot dog. There was always room for just a little bit more, always space at the crowded table for another body or two.

In spite of herself, Rosanna was having a good time. The children were behaving—Tiger was off playing jacks with Mattie near the garage and Kewpie was getting a ukulele lesson from Ti-Tu under the watchful eye of his mother. Rosanna could flit about, filling glasses with fresh lemonade, urging Sam to try a new salad or laugh at a joke Manny told without fear of being rebuked for it by her husband later. She was also without concern that someone would look at Tony with what his drunken logic might perceive as being "the wrong way." Before you knew it, he'd be taking a swing at an unsuspecting guest, grabbing Astrid's behind or making a rude comment to a dear friend. And even if he didn't, Rosanna always worried that he might and the anxiety would ruin her party mood anyway.

Today was different, though. It marked Rosanna's own private Independence Day in a sense. If they were rich and if she were 20 years younger, it might have been a coming out party of sorts. To mark the occasion, she rubbed a dash of rouge into her cheeks and put a swipe of Camille's Secret Blush lipstick on her mouth. Rosanna even let Kewpie pull back her hair with ivory combs and twist the strands into an elegant French braid. It was the first time she was wearing the shift she'd secretly made with a few yards of remnants material Astrid had given her. The hem could have been straighter but she liked the luxurious shade of blue, which reminded her of a peacock's feathers. To say something would have been inappropriate, but Rosanna knew that Sully noticed her dress and her joyful spirit.

Inside the house, the telephone rang. Bridget began a rushed shuffle toward the back door, favoring her bum leg. She knew who was calling because practically everyone else in their lives was there. Like a deft running back, Tiger sped and danced in front of his grandmother, flung the screen door wide so it wouldn't slam on her and managed to answer the telephone on the third ring. "It's Uncle Kelly," he screamed so everyone else could hear. "Long distance!" as if no one knew. Poppa handed the spatula to John, who was temporarily entrusted with the grill.

The conversation was largely about the weather and the activities of Kelly and Sophie Veronica's four kids. It barely touched upon how much they missed each other. Yet this was so present and so palatable between their words you could almost taste it. Bridget beamed as she spoke, a little too loudly than necessary, and she could hear the smile in her son's voice on the other end of the line as well.

"How could anyone leave a good job at Consolidated Edison, pack their family into a truck and move them across the country into the desert?" Astrid addressed the barbecuers rhetorically. Although Kelly's old truck had broken down on the Jersey side of the Holland Tunnel, they somehow made it all the way to Tucson without a problem after its initial repair.

A handful knew the answer to Astrid's rude rhetorical question but most didn't. However, no one bothered responding. Both John and Sam—and Dr. Lewis, who'd just arrived—knew that Kelly had done such a brave, brazen thing because he was sick. It was thought that the sun and dry heat of Arizona would help his "condition." But in truth, his condition was leukemia, and nothing would help. He would be dead within a year, leaving Sophie alone to fend for herself and their brood, plus make a go of their catering business which they'd called "Brooklyn Made." Sophie Veronica would grieve in private but put on a stoic front in public and for her children's sake. In the end, she would come through it all right because she was of strong Brooklyn stock by way of Romania.

Every once in a while Bridget said, "This must be costing you a fortune," but continued to talk nonetheless. It was Poppa's turn next.

"They're all doing fine," Bridget informed her guests after she rejoined the barbecue. She then regaled them with the story of how Sophie adapted an old washing machine with canoe paddles to mix the potato salad which Brooklyn Made sold to area stores. Arizonians had never tasted anything like it. It was a variation on Rosanna's recipe and she was glad her sister-in-law and brother had found success with it.

Bridget couldn't resist turning to Astrid and interjecting, "Without pickles and carrots, imagine that." This comment set Astrid off anew but everyone else laughed, including Eva Lewis, who'd recently crossed the street to join the festivities with a bowl of her cole slaw.

Tiger and Mattie were itching to light "those damned firecracks" as Bridget called them. She'd been blinded in the right eye as a child and understandably hated them ever since. The boys were kept at bay and told to wait until dark.

Guests sifted in and out through the alleyway as natural as the waves at Coney Island lapped at the beach. The conversation was always animated and there was always laughter, no matter who was there, whether the guests knew each other or not. They knew the Paradisos, that's all that mattered. Plus they were all thought special enough to be invited into their ebullient backyard, to eat their food, drink their booze and be treated like the cherished friends they were. It was the one thing all these strangers had in common—the Paradisos—and that was really saying something.

Soon after dark, the coffee percolator could be heard gurgling in the kitchen, and on the great jerry-rigged table, salads and crispy meats were substituted for desserts. There was a bowl of red Jello beside Mrs. Lieberwitz's masterpiece—a cake frosted with homemade butter cream icing and studded with blueberries and strawberries in the shape of an American flag. There was a freshly baked stollen from Mrs. Rosenkrantz and powdered donuts, which were Jo's specialty. No one could resist those sweet dollops of dough gently lowered into boiling oil, cooked to a light gold, fished out with a wire scoop, cooled, then dusted with confectioner's sugar.

When Rosanna brushed past Dr. Lewis, en route to the kitchen, he asked in a low voice so no one else could hear, "How are you feeling?"

"A little better," she lied. "I think it's clearing up."

But despite the makeup, Rosanna still looked tired and pale. "I spoke to Dr. Schantz," he told her. "He agreed that you should go into United Israel as soon as possible. He said he could work out a payment plan and…"

Astrid, who was always suspicious of something or someone, drew near. "It's not a good time," Rosanna whispered. "What with Kewpie's birthday and my brother Julius moving the family down to Mexico…" She left for the kitchen in mid-sentence.

Just after Poppa switched on the brightly-colored tropical fruit lights, Rosanna carried out Kewpie's birthday cake, ablaze with 16 candles plus one for good luck. Although her birthday was on the 13th, they never forgot her with a cake at the 4th of July barbecue. Kewpie would have to wait until her actual birthday for Bridget's butter sunshine pineapple upside-down cake.

Another guest arrived in the semi-darkness. A slender man dressed in blue, carrying a cap in hand, almost apologetically. He seemed to be wearing a uniform of some sort but was too small for Sully or Harry, who were still there. The man's polished buttons caught what little light there was and glowed. The figure reeled slightly, then lurched forward again. No one could quite place him until he stepped into the light of Kewpie's birthday-cake candles.

It was Tony.

21 | Happy Birthday, Kewpie

"Happy birthday, Kewpie," Tony said, even though he didn't carry a present. All he brought was himself in his rumpled work clothes, dressed the way he'd been when he'd left almost a month earlier. But no one said a word, not even Kewpie.

Luckily, Jo was standing beside Rosanna and was able to grab the birthday cake from her hands. The platter was from the set Bridget was building from Dish Night at the Loews 46th and it would have been a shame to lose, not to mention the cake. Rosanna's jaw hung slightly ajar as she stared at her estranged husband. Candle wax dripped onto the white icing but no one started to sing. Kewpie seemed frozen to the spot. Even Tiger was speechless.

Harry was the first to speak. He stepped forward in his burly, imposing manner, blue uniform to blue uniform. "What brings you here, Tony?" he asked.

"What brings me here?" Tony growled. At this point, Harry and everyone else within a few feet of Tony were treated to the sickly-sweet aroma of whiskey on Tony's breath. In the humidity of the summer night, it seemed to ooze from his skin. "What brings me here?" he repeated. "I live here. Remember?"

Kewpie approached the table, closed her eyes and silently blew out the candles. If she dared to make a birthday wish at all, it would have been that her father would disappear. But when she opened her eyes again, there he was right in front of her, in the dim glow of Poppa's festive fruit lights, leering at her.

Tony pitched forward and gave Kewpie a sloppy bear hug. She dangled against his body like a rag doll, her own arms limp at her sides. Finally, he released her and she receded into the poorly-lit banana and pineapple twilight.

Nobody knew what to do or say. To make a fuss in front of friends and neighbors at a happy gathering like this just wouldn't be polite and besides, it would only make things worse for Rosanna behind closed doors. But to let him back into their lives without question wouldn't be right either. Everyone looked to Rosanna for a sign but she gave none. She just stared blankly at the tablecloth and wrung her hands. To Sully, this was a signal, loud and clear in its silent suffering, but no one else seemed to recognize it. And he wasn't technically family, so what could he do?

Rosanna had hand-frosted "Happy Birthday, Kewpie" with chocolate icing onto the vanilla surface of the cake. As was the tradition, Kewpie schmeared her name for good luck. However, at that moment, Kewpie felt extremely luckless. She could feel her father watching her, could smell him, even. She wished she'd worn something looser, not so form fitting, so she could disappear into the material. Instead, Kewpie had chosen to wear a flouncy off-white dress with cap sleeves made from some left-over fabric Aunt Jo had. The two made a vow never to wear the dresses, which also were cut from the same pattern, at the same time. But they both looked lovely in them, as lovely as sisters.

With a shaky hand, Rosanna cut thick hunks of birthday cake for the remaining guests. "No Aunt Bea pieces," Harry joked.

Bridget gasped in mock drama. "God rest her soul. But she was chintzy with a piece of cake," Bridget admitted. Even though Bridget's sister Beatrice was long gone, her legacy of cutting wafer-thin cake slices lived on. She could have fed at least 100 from Kewpie's modest sheet cake.

Rosanna smiled at Sully as she handed him an especially generous slice. But her jocularity soon faded when she remembered that Tony was hovering in the shadows. The former buoyant mood of the barbecue deflated upon Tony's arrival. Though some of the guests had never met him, all knew of him and it was easy to see that he was trouble.

Manny told Consuelo in Spanish that Tony had the eyes of the Devil. And she responded, looking straight at the evil man, *"Si, e un corazón negro tambien."* Translation: Yes, and also a black heart. They left soon after making this observation. Manny squeezed Tiger's shoulder, wishing there was something he could do or say to make the remainder of the evening less painful for him but knew full well there wasn't.

Everyone agreed that the cake was indeed moist. Moist as well as delicious, quite an achievement in this weather. And that it was refreshing. The icing was a perfect consistency and not too sweet. Compliments went all around the Paradiso backyard in several configurations, all of them forced and awkward. Tony even managed to choke down a slice of cake, although assisted by swigs from his almost-empty flask. In his absence, he had graduated from a medicine bottle filled with liquor to a fancy engraved silver flask. Every so often, he'd duck into the darkness and take a healthy gulp, thinking no one noticed, except everyone but little Carl did.

Undaunted by the party's shift in spirit, which was as profound as a change in the wind, Matthew and Tiger persisted in lobbying for fireworks. No one could dispute the fact that it was undeniably evening. The sky was pitch black, the vibrant pink and blue baby blanket colored sunset long faded. Sully and Harry were back on the beat, no doubt busy with complaints of noise, second-story porches on fire and half blown off fingers. John was the bearer of the punk stick whose tip eternally shone red and would light the ends of countless fireworks of varying intensities. Tony was too far gone to even suggest that he be the one to do the honors. He knew better. He might have been a drunk but he wasn't stupid.

John took the boys to the front of the house to light the firecrackers by the curb. This way the next day, the street sweeper could easily gather the small, colorful curls of paper from the gutter with his broom, into the dustbin then into his great wheeled trash can. Under their uncle's close supervision, Matthew and Tiger graduated from little firecrackers like the ones that decorated Astrid's hat to cherry bombs and screechers that ricocheted along the ground and popped, chasing anyone in sight. When they were ready to shoot the pretty fireworks like Roman candles, they called Bridget, who watched from the safety of the front porch, nervously fingering her eyebrows, oohing and aahing appropriately at the bursts of brightness and the sparkling stars left in their wake.

Julius sat alone in the backyard, contentedly listening to the bustle in the kitchen as the women washed dishes and put things away. The decision of whether to toss or save and who would take what home (for there wasn't room for everything in Bridget's icebox) was a Herculean task that required finesse and fine negotiating skills, among other things. "Harry likes peach cobbler so much and he was already gone by the time Carmella came with it..." Or, "Sam really enjoyed those butter beans, so please..." And, "It's too much for your father and me. Besides, it would be a shame to..." The exchange of foodstuff also couldn't smack of charity; it had to sound as though you were truly doing Bridget a favor by taking something off her hands. Julius smiled quietly to himself, listening to the give and take in the dance of the leftovers.

He looked up at the sky, its surface indigo. The moon was full and heavy, its shadows and valleys prominent since the air was cloudless and clear. It resembled a wise but jovial old man's face, a rotund soul who knew many secrets but wasn't telling them. The stars were chunks of broken glass. It was a bona-fide van Gogh night. "van whoosis?" Julius' sisters, all except for Astrid, might ask. But Lettie knew who van Gogh was and she didn't put on airs about it either.

Would the sky look the same in Mexico? Was he making a big mistake taking this job? His brother Kelly had moved his family halfway across the country but Julius would soon be dragging his to another country entirely. Although the position was only temporary, it offered him the unique opportunity of painting, teaching and studying in Mexico City. There was also talk that Diego Rivera himself might make an appearance. Lettie had given Julius her vote of confidence. She said that her home, that the boys' home, was wherever Julius was. Then she hugged him for a long time.

Ever since he was a young boy, Julius had been different. It wasn't just his aristocratic name, which, believe it or not, was a common one in the Paradiso Family. He had three other cousins named Julius. But this Julius was unique. Even as a kid, Julius had "gentle hands" as Harry so aptly phrased it, and meant it in the most charitable way. When other boys were making spit balls, Julius was trekking all the way to the library at Grand Army Plaza to copy the great paintings he saw in its reference books. When he rode the El, Julius didn't doze or read like most people, but drew quick sketches of his fellow riders, Hasidism and harlots and derelicts alike.

It was true, Julius was unlike any of his other siblings. He was soft and wary and thoughtful. He was refined and didn't smack of Brooklyn in the least. Unlike Astrid, Julius's demeanor wasn't affected, acquired or studied, it was simply the way he was. Julius sometimes stammered when he was nervous, which was often, especially when he spoke on the telephone. But perhaps this is what made his brother and sisters love him all the more, because Julius was so different than they were.

The young painter was fully occupied looking at the stars that evening, listening to the women bustling about the kitchen, concentrating on the laughter and fireworks coming from the front sidewalk. Julius was startled when he saw a movement in the yard, not ten feet from where he sat. The flick of a match, an unsteady hand bringing that match to a thin, drawn mouth, then taking a long drag on a cigarette. The face was briefly lit like a Halloween goblin's, burned deep orange, then went dark. "Cat got your tongue, Julius?" Tony asked.

"Nnnnn-no," he stuttered.

Although the hot day had cooled nicely and an occasional breeze made it all the more pleasant, Julius felt warm. He felt as though he were gently boiling, simmering from someplace beneath his skin's surface. A thin layer of perspiration rose on his forehead, which he quickly wiped away with a checkered handkerchief. "Do I make you nervous?" Tony wondered, picking up on the fact that he did immediately.

Julius forced himself to carefully form the words in his head first before he released them into the air, defenseless. "Hardly," he told his rogue brother-in-law, without faltering this time.

Growing up, his brothers and sisters rarely remembered seeing Julius angry. He hardly ever raised his voice, even as an adult. Julius's boiling point was set on high, unlike Kelly's, which could flare suddenly like a summer storm. But it had been extremely frightening the two times they saw Julius lose his temper. He'd been little more than a child then. The first was the result of months of taunting by a bully. It escalated to the usually placid Julius beating the boy to a pulp in the street. Without any recollection of how it happened, Julius found himself straddling the kid and noticed that his own fists were bloody. By the time he realized where he was and what he'd done, Rosanna was screaming and Sully was trying to pull Julius from the boy's prone body. But Julius clung to the brat like an alley cat on a meat scrap and it took two other fellows besides Sully to drag him off.

The other time, Julius had chased another street tough down 13th Avenue with a butcher knife in hand. He had no idea how he got there, only that the boy had shoved him over the edge after taking his charcoal pencils and snapping them like twigs. For months, Julius had saved the pennies he earned shining shoes to buy those pencils. A kindly cop escorted Julius home after they pried Bridget's kitchen knife from his fist. It was the last time anyone fussed with "that crazy Paradiso kid" as he became known throughout Borough Park.

But this night, Tony set off something in Julius which frightened the docile artist. Julius could not think rationally. His mind kept flipping and skipping like a damaged gramophone record, skipping and flipping to the same sore spot. This man was robbing his sister's life from her. He was stealing her joy, stealing the joy from her children. If only he would just drink

himself to death, pass out on the trolley tracks or disappear for
good instead of torturing them like this. If only he would get into
a bar brawl with the wrong person or bed down with the wrong
husband's wife, someone who would end his wicked days with a
machete in the skull or a bullet in his brain. It would be much
better for everyone concerned if he did.

These sorts of thoughts horrified Julius. He rose abruptly and
straightened his suit pants. Tony stood shakily and straightened
his own rumpled uniform, mimicking his brother-in-law. Julius
brushed past the drunken man, drawn to the front of the house by
his son Matthew's happy giggles. Julius was almost there, almost
protected from his own paralyzing rage but then it grabbed him
by the collar and took him by the throat. Julius had no choice but
to grab Tony by his own shirt collar. He pulled Tony close, so
close that he could count the man's whiskey-oozing pores, even
in the weak light. Julius was a slight man, a full head shorter than
Tony and was outweighed by him besides, but his anger was so
extreme, so palatable that it made even Tony stop and listen.

Julius didn't raise his voice. He spoke in barely a whisper
through gritted teeth. "If you hurt them…" he said. "If you hurt
them," he began again. "So help me God, I will kill you. I will
kill you with my bare hands."

With that, Julius let go of the blue lapels that smelled of
perspiration, cigarette smoke, cheap perfume and alcohol. He let
go of them with an abruptness, as though they were on fire. But
Julius wasn't finished. He snarled quietly into Tony's face, "And
believe me, no one will be sorry that you're gone." Julius turned
on his heels and disappeared into the alley, toward the fireworks.

Tony gave a little laugh and shook his head. Julius might be a
little twerp but Tony knew he wasn't joking.

Bridget stood at the sink, washing a deep pot, gazing out
the back window. She saw Julius go and saw Tony looking
bewildered in the moonlight. She rinsed the suds from the pot
and handed it to Kewpie, who was helping the women dry,
armed with a damp dishtowel. "Run upstairs and get some
things," Bridget told her. "Just enough for tonight. Make like
you've been sleeping downstairs with me and Poppa all along."

At first, it took a moment for what Bridget was saying to

register. Kewpie stood there stunned. "A nightgown, some bloomers, a change of clothes," Bridget continued. "Go!"

Kewpie put down the pot. She handed her dishrag to Rosanna, who immediately understood. "We can get the rest of your things tomorrow when he's sleeping," Bridget added. She kissed her granddaughter on the side of the head. "I won't let him hurt you again," she murmured.

Kewpie grabbed Bridget's hand and kissed it, tasting garlic and cinnamon and hope on her delicate parchment paper skin.

22 Strangers on the Stairs

'It's like being beaten,' Rosanna thought. 'Except these scars, these bruises you can't see.' True, her children, her family, her neighbors couldn't detect them, yet she herself would know they were there, nagging away at her like a pebble in the heel of a shoe. Rosanna would wear these silent scars sheepishly on the inside like all the others and they would have plenty of company.

Lying on her back, staring up at the ceiling, tears seeped out from the corners of her eyes, wetting the pillow beneath her head. Rosanna cried silently, effortlessly. Even after so many weeks of blessed ordinariness and almost-happiness, it amazed her that sobbing came as easily and naturally to her as breathing. Soon, the tears changed their course and ran into her ears. Although they burned, Rosanna didn't brush them away. She dared not move. The hair framing her face became tangled and soaked as her body became drier and resisted him more. But still, her husband pumped, undaunted.

Tony didn't notice at first. He was consumed in the pounding, as emotionless and persistent as a jackhammer. Each movement was like a punch, each plunge like a punishment. He knew she hated it and he hated her for hating it. He knew she despised him. He had succeeded in turning her devotion into disgust through each evil act, through every indiscretion and gesture of thoughtlessness. But that was really something, wasn't it? Turning an emotion as potent as love into hate. It was quite an achievement, if not a good one.

Tony asked himself why he had come back. Was it because he missed the children? Was it because of Kewpie? Was it the vague terror in his kids' eyes when they spotted him at Coney Island? Or was it because he missed Rosanna's cooking? Like the guys at Stillwell said, 'Man cannot live by pussy alone.' Or grilled cheese, take-out and franks and beans, straight from the can. Even hobos ate better. But then there was Denise's primed, perfumed body, tiny and plump beneath her knickers, exquisite as a wrapped candy morsel. That's what kept calling him back to her unkempt apartment.

'I can't do this...I can't do this...' Rosanna told herself over and over again. 'I can't let him back in.' Yet she was doing it. And there Tony was, worming his way in—into her body and into their lives, as though he'd never left. But what choice did she have? She was afraid of what he might do if she stood up to him. Do to her and to the kids. For herself, she didn't mind so much. She could endure the beatings. And if he killed her, at least her pain would be over, but where would that leave her children?

She wouldn't put anything past her husband. He hated to lose, lose anything, even things he didn't want. Tony could sweet-talk any judge to get hold of the kids. He could say Rosanna was crazy and steal them away from her. Not because he wanted them, but because he knew how much she loved them and how much she didn't want him to have them. Him having them would destroy her and he would be glad.

Or else he could go on a drunken tear, wipe out everyone in the house, her parents included, and not even remember the next day, the dripping, blood-stained walls his only reminder. It happened all the time, not in the scrubbed Queen Annes of Borough Park but in the tenements of the Lower East Side and in Hell's Kitchen. It could happen anywhere, given the right circumstances. And it could happen right here in a heartbeat.

Should Rosanna make a run for it? Take Kewpie and Tiger and hide out at Jo's place. No, he would find her no matter where she went, he would seek her out and wreak his wrath on her, on her family, and even Harry would be unable to stop him. Should she and the kids hop a bus to Arizona? What would that say to them? That it's okay to just run whenever life went sour? No, she would tough it out; she would have to. Besides, Rosanna was so defeated, so deflated, so utterly crushed that she couldn't think straight.

She glanced at the clock on the nightstand and could barely decipher the numbers through her blurry eyes. She couldn't believe how long he kept at her. How he could keep going, drunk as he was, with no encouragement. Turning her head to the side, Rosanna avoided brushes with his mouth. She tried not to gag as Tony sweated alcohol onto her, the droplets searing onto her skin where her upturned nightgown revealed pale flesh. He didn't even care when she lied and told him that she had her monthly. He merely told her to put a towel on the bed and proceeded to go about his business.

Finally, Tony just gave up. He rolled off Rosanna's body, sat on the edge of the bed, shriveled and red, licking his wounds like a dog.

For a moment, Rosanna thought she'd won. But then she felt his open palm strike the left side of her face and tasted blood. She checked her teeth with her tongue. They were all still there. None were loose as far as she could tell, although there was a ragged cut on the inside of her mouth. She swallowed her own salty blood then pulled down her nightgown and covered her body. "Cunt," he said. "You're nothing but a dried-up, old cunt."

'Yes,' she thought, rolling onto her side, but not the side where he'd struck her. 'Thank God for small favors. And St. Jude, too.'

It didn't take much begging for Tiger to convince Rosanna to let him sleep on the front porch that night. It was a lovely, balmy evening as the full moon watched over him. Tiger sleeping on the porch also meant that he was one more room away from hers. With the throb of the summer streets, the cars and the firecrackers, her son wouldn't be able to hear anything that went on in Rosanna's bedroom. No curse words, no smacks, no headboard rhythmically pounding.

Instead of sleeping on the ground this time, Tiger built his bed on a layer of blankets piled onto a lounge chair opened out flat. He covered himself with a thin sheet and pulled it up to his chin to deter vampires. Tiger lay on his side, facing 47th Street. Every so often, there was a series of pops, then an explosion of colorful flashes and thrilled voices. Laughter and lights: shining blue, royal purple neon, valiant red. The greens were Tiger's favorite, like broken glass only prettier. He only wished Kewpie was there to see it with him, to talk with at least, but he knew she was in a good place.

Downstairs in Poppa and Bridget's apartment, as Kewpie unfolded the small square bed that masqueraded as an ottoman and listened to Poppa talk about Bernard Castro, an Italian immigrant like himself, who borrowed $300 to start his convertible-bed business, she felt tired. Her limbs felt almost too heavy to move as she heaved herself into the Castro. Bridget covered her with a light linen blanket and kissed her on the forehead. "Thank you, Grandma," she said just before the old woman turned and left.

Bridget said nothing in return, so Kewpie thought that perhaps she didn't hear. But she did. She just didn't know how to respond. To say, "You're welcome" would be admitting too much, acknowledging all the times her father's unforgivable behavior went ignored, leaving Kewpie helpless and defenseless in its wake. To answer was to accept what had been going on and how all of them had left her unprotected. And Bridget couldn't do that, so she didn't answer at all.

As Bridget listened to her granddaughter softly snoring in the alcove, she smiled in the darkness. Poppa squeezed her hand, kissed her goodnight and was soon buzzing away himself. Bridget lay awake, listening to the house settling and creaking, noting the sound of the wooden beams, plaster and lathe drifting off to sleep themselves.

Even on the lumpy Castro convertible, Kewpie slept better than she slept upstairs. All the while he was gone, in the back of her mind, even when she dreamed, she worried that her father might come back unexpectedly in the early morning hours. She even had nightmares about it. And now it had happened.

In the morning, Rosanna's pink bruise shone like a beacon in the bathroom mirror. The bottom left side of her face was swollen as well. There was a crust of dried blood in one corner of her mouth. She felt a stab of pain when she touched her teeth on that half of her face with her tongue. It also hurt to smile but she doubted that she'd be doing much smiling with Tony back. But at least it wasn't Tiger who got hit. At least it wasn't Kewpie who got worse.

As she made coffee, Rosanna looked out the side window at the punching bag Poppa kept hanging in the garage. She felt an odd camaraderie with the inanimate object, swollen and heavy as a big leather teardrop. 'That's me,' she thought. 'That's what I am.' She was a human sponge, a martyr. Except they didn't canonize you for what Rosanna suffered through. Being abused by a drunk was minute compared with getting your breasts hacked off like Saint Agatha or having your eyeballs popped out like Saint Lucy. Rosanna's penance was her little deaths, each day learning to abide by a touch more sadness, a bit more grief until all semblance of happiness was gone.

What could she do? Should she talk to Sully? He'd made it clear that he wanted to help. So did John and Harry. All she needed to do was say the word. But Rosanna couldn't take that step. She knew what she had now. She knew what her life was now, but she didn't know what it would be if she took a leap off the ledge. Her husband's rage frightened her, the fury of an alcoholic, the wrath of someone with nothing left to lose. There's no telling what he would do.

Should she approach John? Though quiet on the outside, she could only guess what simmered in this man's core. He didn't speak much about the War but Rosanna didn't doubt that he'd probably killed, and not just once. One word to John and it was likely that Tony would never be seen again, and that no trace of him would ever be found. But then Rosanna would be forced to exist in a limbo between guilt and relief, knowing that perhaps she had not taken a life herself yet she was instrumental in the loss of one. And being a moral Catholic woman, this would be too much for her to bear. It would be even more terrible for her to endure than a miserable existence.

One overcast Saturday afternoon, Rosanna had taken her dilemma to Saint Catherine's. She waited patiently in line along the church's wall, hands folded, for her stint in the confessional box. Once inside, the wooden panel slid open and it was her turn to unburden her soul. Although there was a thick screen between them, Rosanna could tell Father Dunn was on the other side of the mesh wall and she was certain he recognized her voice as well. Father Dunn was gentle, kindly and concerned but Rosanna doubted he'd ever had a girlfriend, let alone knew much about relationships besides the sanctimonious one he shared with God.

The dizzying smell of incense gave her a dull headache. Rosanna listened patiently as Father Dunn told her to try her best to be a dedicated and supportive wife, to stand by her husband no matter what. And to pray, always to pray. To put it in God's hands. But Rosanna didn't dare tell Father Dunn that she thought God had abandoned her. 'What about when he hits me for no reason,' she wanted to ask, 'or when he disappears for weeks at a time.' It was too shameful to mention anything to the priest about Kewpie. In the end, Rosanna left the confessional feeling worse than when she'd gone in.

So, she prayed. That's what Catholics were taught. She prayed to Saint Jude, patron saint of the hopeless. There was a prayer card hidden in her nightstand drawer that was creased and worn with faith and held together with cellophane tape that had yellowed and curled around the edges. Rosanna took it out after everyone was fast asleep and worried it through her fingers, rubbing it like a magic amulet as she murmured its prayer, which she knew by heart, even in the dark:

> *O most holy apostle, St. Jude, faithful servant and friend of Jesus, the church honors and invokes you universally, as the patron of hopeless cases, of things almost despaired of. Pray for me, I am so helpless and alone.*

*Make use, I implore you, of that particular privilege
given to you, to bring visible and speedy help where help
is almost despaired of. ...Come to my assistance in this
great need that I may receive the consolation and
help of heaven in all my necessities, tribulations,
and sufferings...*

So far, Rosanna heard nothing from this beloved saint,
received no sign, no comfort from this green and white robed,
staff-bearing holy man who bore a slight resemblance to a
bearded, stone-faced Charlie Chaplin. But perhaps St. Jude was
just busy with other causes more hopeless than her own.

Rosanna watched the coffee bubble in the percolator's little
glass window like brown lava. She peeled Tiger's arms from
around her waist as he begged to have some. "Just a drop,"
she told him, warming up a pan of milk. "Or else it'll stunt
your growth."

"Aw, Ma," he said.

"Don't 'Aw, Ma' me," Rosanna scolded, then smiled in spite
of herself. Her mouth stung.

"What happened?" Tiger asked, reaching up to explore the
mark on her face.

Rosanna sidestepped his touch. "Stop," she whispered. And
Tiger did. He was a good boy.

Rosanna thought for a moment, pouring the warm milk into
her son's coffee cup. "I bumped into the wall in the middle
of the night," she lied to Tiger. "Tripped on one of your toy
soldiers, I think."

"Sorry," Tiger told her, although he knew this wasn't
the truth.

"That's okay," she answered. "It wasn't your fault, not really."

Following his mother's lead, Tiger dipped the ends of his
toast in his caffe latte. Two rooms back, Tony snored loudly, like
an evil ogre in a fairy tale. Except this was no fairy tale. This
was their life.

Tiger talked excitedly of his night on the porch, of the
fireworks, of the moon that looked so big and heavy that he
feared it might fall from the sky and onto the tracks of the El,

rolling along the rails like a big luminous pinball. "The things you think of," Rosanna said, shaking her head.

She emptied more frothy milk into Tiger's cup and added two teaspoons of coffee. He stirred the mixture vigorously, took a sip and grinned. Then he went serious and he looked more like a worried old man than a ten-year-old child. "Make him go away, Momma," he said quietly. "Please, make him go away."

Rosanna looked at her son helplessly, her eyes shining like two sad coffee beans. "I wish I could, Tiger. I..." she stammered, just like her brother Julius.

"He'll ruin everything," the boy said. Rosanna rubbed Tiger's back as he put his head on the kitchen table and cried. "I thought a mother's job was to make sure nothing bad happened to her children. I thought you said..." Everything else came out garbled. Rosanna stroked Tiger's hair, which was standing on end in sweaty peaks. He needed a summer crew cut. To save money, she would take the electric razor into the backyard and do it herself, maybe that afternoon.

"Who's this crying like a girl?" Tony's voice boomed. "Kewpie, is that you?"

Tiger didn't even look up. He just made a beeline for the front door and barreled down the stairs. Tony stumbled into the bathroom. Rosanna could hear him retching behind the closed door as he tried to brush his teeth. She turned on the radio and Ruth Etting sang "Mean to Me," drowning out the awful gagging. Hearing the chanteuse's jaunty voice offered Rosanna a twisted consolation in the thought that Ms. Etting, who married the mobster Moe "The Gimp" Snyder, might actually be having a tougher time than even Rosanna herself.

Outside, Tiger wiped his snotty nose on the back of his arm. He then smeared it on the brick wall of Mrs. Rosenkrantz's house. No one saw. He found Poppa in the garage with the wooden doors flung open, vigorously pounding his punching bag. Poppa did this when he was angry or when he was particularly health-minded. This morning, Tiger guessed that Poppa was mad, judging by his firmly set jaw, steady gaze and the strength behind each wallop.

Poppa was in decent shape for an old fellow. Though thick

around the middle and barrel-chested, he was still strong as a bull. It came from working hard at the Navy Yard. The punching bag moved stubbornly with each slug. Tiger watched the muscles in his grandfather's arms ripple and soften, like the surface of water as the waves changed its face. Poppa was wearing a cotton under vest which Grandma Bridget had bleached and scrubbed bright, and white summer slacks.

Although Poppa didn't look, he knew exactly who was standing behind him. "You doing all right, Tiger McPunch?" he asked the boy.

"Yes, Poppa," Tiger answered. "So far, so good."

"And you'll keep me apprised of the situation?" his grandfather asked, although it was more of a gentle command.

"Yes, Poppa," Tiger answered.

Poppa stepped aside to give Tiger a turn at the punching bag. Lean as he was, Poppa was impressed with the boy's force and determination. Tiger gritted his teeth and grunted like Joe Louis, who'd recently got the crap beaten out of him by that Nazi Max Schmeling. In spite of the fact that the punching bag probably outweighed Tiger, he succeeded in moving it. Poppa attributed this to anger more than anything else.

Tiger flung his arms forward in rapid succession, closing his eyes. His hair stuck to the sides of his face in sweaty clumps as more liquid seeped out of his head. After a while, Tiger decided that he was done and simply stopped. "I guess I licked him," the boy said firmly.

"I guess you did," Poppa told him.

Though it was only noon and Rosanna knew Tony's shift didn't begin for hours, she was glad to see him go. His uniform needed pressing and his shirt collar was grimy but she wasn't about to clean it. He didn't eat a bite or even accept a cup of tea for his delicate stomach. Brushing past Rosanna without a word, he put his hand on the doorknob. She took a deep breath. "Tony," she sighed. "You can't just come and go the way you please."

He wheeled around to face her, a smug half-grin on his face. "And why can't I? It's my fucking house," he informed her.

"It's my parents' house," she told him politely with her eyes downcast. "They're too old for this."

"Too old for what?" But try as she might, Rosanna couldn't find the words to stand up to him. "This has nothing to do with them," he said obstinately.

Rosanna looked at Tony, then glanced away. "It's hard on the children," she offered. "They don't know what to…"

"And how about you?" he snorted. "Is it hard on you?"

"I don't care about me," she told him.

With an abrupt movement, Tony grabbed Rosanna's chin, so quickly she didn't have time to flinch. He surveyed the damage on her cheek. The bruise was blossoming from pink to purple. "And put some makeup on that thing, will you?"

"Like it's my fault," she muttered.

Tony pinched his wife's chin harshly between his fingers then pushed her face away. "Don't you get it? It's always your fucking fault."

Tony stomped out of the apartment, slamming the door behind him. In her kitchen downstairs, Bridget twisted a lemon half into a strainer. She shuddered at the sound of Tony's voice and the slam of the upstairs door, for she knew that Kewpie was probably halfway up the hallway steps by now and the girl couldn't avoid an encounter with her father. They had both thought Tony was still in a cockeyed coma and that it was safe for Kewpie to venture upstairs to get more clothes.

Upon seeing her father, Kewpie stopped in mid-step and tried to retreat. But Tony was quick on his feet, even hung over. He pressed his body against Kewpie's and pinned her to the wall. "You gonna treat me like a stranger?" he asked, low and between his teeth. "I'm your fucking father." His breath was as rancid as day-old trash.

"Pop," Tiger said at the foot of the stairs, and Tony backed off. Kewpie ran back down the steps and disappeared like a mouse into the shadows, kicking into the metal milk box in the corner as she ran.

"What is it, kid?" Tony asked his son.

"I want to show you my new cap gun. Uncle Harry…"

"That's nice, Tiger," his father told him. He patted the boy's head as though he were an obedient puppy, then rushed past without even looking at the silver-plated weapon in the boy's hand. For a second, Tiger wished the gun were real. Then the next moment, he knew he would have to confess this wanton thought to Father Dunn in the stuffy wooden box this coming Saturday.

But then again, maybe not.

23 Basic Training

'If the new guy opened his bug eyes any wider, they might pop right out of his fucking head,' Tony thought. His uniform was crisp and new and creaseless. It was the first time the kid had ever worn it. Tony's was getting white around the sleeve cuffs and if you looked close, you could see that it was dotted with greasy stains. All obtained after he stopped going home to Rosanna and set up house with Denise. It's amazing what could happen in less than four weeks' time.

The conductor-in-training hung onto Tony's every word as though it was scripture, and Tony reveled in it. To him, the element of power and control was almost as good as sex, but not quite.

"There's not much more to it than this," Tony began, pausing dramatically until the kid actually held his breath in anticipation. "You listening?" The kid nodded enthusiastically. "You open the doors and you close the doors," Tony said. "Open, close. Got it?" Another hearty nod. "And don't drag anybody. That's all you need to know. Listen to me and you'll be good to go."

Tony was dying for a drink but he couldn't get a reading on the trainee yet. Was he one of the guys or a beakie? Did he yearn for acceptance from his coworkers or from his bosses? Tony's flask weighed heavily in his right pants pocket like an extra testicle and he was painfully aware of it.

He was also painfully aware of his desire for Denise. He knew that she probably craved him too, but would she take him back into her bed, their bed, after he skipped out on her for a few nights? She hadn't been to work three days in a row. Was she pining away for him like a B-movie queen, sobbing into damp, fragrant sheets, her slip dramatically draped across her creamy thighs? Or was she just taking the Sea Beach instead of the West End to and from work to avoid seeing him? Tony preferred to think it was the former, but with a girl like Denise you never could tell. Tough as rock candy on the outside but sugary and soft as nougat within.

Tony had the knack of getting the best of Denise, as she so delicately phrased it. While other men were put off, even paralyzed, by her beauty, Tony was fueled by it. When other guys had already shot and fired, he was just loading his gun, and taking his sweet time about it. He knew how to unravel her, make her whimper like a newly-weaned pup, get her to tremble with a deft crook of his finger so that she begged and pleaded for him to finish her off. In that begging, she promised all sorts of indelicacies, and usually followed through with them. Things his wife could never even imagine.

And then there was his mouth. Perfecting what most men avoided, even taking pride in the act. "It's not so different than this," he tried to explain to his cronies over a platter of raw clams at Ruby's on the Riegelmann Boardwalk. "Only warm, silkier and much more succulent." They just didn't get it, no matter how he attempted to enlighten them. But this was okay with Tony, all the more for him.

Although he wasn't supposed to on the first go-around, Tony let the new guy work the doors on his own so Tony could retreat between cars with his flask, his skin itching for a drink. His fingers trembled as he unscrewed the top. The warm liquid oozed down his throat and made him shudder. Immediately, it calmed his belly and his nerves. The world, and the El itself, seemed a better place.

The kid did fine and was more fastidious than Tony ever was in his ten or so years riding the snake. The trainee gave the motorman the all clear signal with a firm ring of the bell like a pro. Tony drank more than his share, leaning against the swaying chains, balancing one foot on the moving metal platform of each car. He fancied himself a tightrope walker, a gymnast on a balance beam of steel. He could keep his footing even as the train jerked and shrieked along the curve which led from Bensonhurst past the train yard to Stillwell.

Tony was a gladiator, riding the riveted steel shells of Cars 484 and 239, which were painted a dark, industrial green like all the others. "The City of New York" was stenciled on their sides in gold, giving them a rather swanky look. Straddling the cars, Tony felt like a king. Alcohol had a habit of doing that to him, of feeding the grand illusion of things.

With whiskey in his belly, Tony made a litany of silent resolutions to himself. He would be a good husband, a doting father, a model employee. He would quit hitting, quit cheating, quit drinking, quit square-rooting, quit pawing, but not today, of course. Then in the next breath, he convinced himself that he was godlike, that he could do anything. He could live two separate lives, with Denise and Rosanna, and excel at both. It was all a matter of balance, like keeping his footing on a moving train.

Denise would be happy with sex; Rosanna would be pleased as punch without it. He would be content with simple, delicious meals in his belly at 47th Street and the pungent taste of blonde on his lips at Mermaid Avenue. In his drunken bravado, Tony convinced himself that neither woman would mind, because after all, they would have the gift of him the way they wanted him.

But Tony didn't take into consideration reality: jealousy, logistics, finances, and his own inability to follow through with anything.

There were a few things he couldn't live with, and wouldn't. For instance, the wounded way his children looked at him, or refused to look at him at all. He didn't know which was worse. Kewpie, for one, always avoided his gaze, except when he forced her to confront him. And the sad, disappointed way his in-laws looked at him also got to him when he let it. They had been nothing but generous and good to him, better than his own blood family, and he rewarded them with disrespect and spite. Tony couldn't bear to focus for long on what he'd done to his wife. How he took Rosanna's blind, stupid, honest love and twisted it into loathing. He managed to bury his tiny pangs of guilt beneath a sea of booze so that he barely felt anything at all, not even remorse.

But Tony's wave of repentance shifted when the flask was empty and he crossed the line from pleasantly tipsy to a belligerent drunk. His future instantly went from rosy to hazy. His outlook, from hopeful to hopeless in a few drops of scotch.

The train crawled into the Stillwell Avenue station like a slug, a slug that screeched and rasped against metal. Already there was a dull pounding in the back of Tony's brain and his shift wasn't even half over. Luckily it was break time. Tony figured that if he didn't eat dinner, there would be just enough minutes to get to the liquor store near Sea Gate (he couldn't risk going to the one under the El and being spotted by a foreman) and back.

But then he saw her sauntering along the concrete catwalk that connected the train platforms to each other. Denise wore a flimsy summer dress, stiff with crinolines, bright with sunflowers. Tony directed the kid to the canteen so he could have his brown-bagged grub on his dinner break, then Tony flew up the metal-trimmed steps to Denise. When she saw him, her face brightened then immediately darkened. She didn't turn away when he took her by the shoulders and kissed her hard on the mouth, not caring who saw. "I have to talk to you," he told her. "But not here."

Tony led Denise down the steps and to the very end of the platform. There was a darkened, out of service Culver Line train on Track 6. Tony used his pass key and shuttled Denise inside, closing the door behind them. He ushered her through car after car until they were safely out of sight and he was confident that no one from the station or the control tower could see them. They were also well out of view from the tenement windows that overlooked the Stillwell station.

Tony released Denise's arm and turned to her. She smacked him across the face so hard that his head wheeled to the side. Then she smacked him again. She lifted her hand to whack him a third time but then started bawling. Tony grabbed Denise by the wrists and backed her against a sealed door. He pressed against her pelvis, leaving an indelible imprint, and kissed her mouth again, this time biting her lower lip. He felt Denise's resistance drain as her knees buckled. "You fuck...you bastard..." she cried.

"Ah, D, it was only three nights," he told her.

"It was four, you cocksucker," she informed him. "And you didn't call. Not one word from you at all. Nothing. For all I know, you could have been dead."

"You would have read about it in the papers," he told her, walking his fingers up her leg. Tony crinkled up his eyes in a way he imagined made him look irresistible. "Come on, it was my daughter's birthday," he lied. (Actually, Kewpie's real birthday was in a few days, and it would pass with little fanfare, at her insistence, since her father was home.) "And what was I supposed to say anyway? You would have given me a hard time, just like you are now."

Tony worked his hand under Denise's skirts, feeling the crunchy squares of her stiff slip, the tops of her garter belt then, quite unexpectedly, the moist folds of her. No obstruction, no resistance. "No bloomers?" he wondered.

"It's so hot..." Denise began. Deftly, Tony kneaded her wet, slick flesh, working the lips between his fingers, seeking the bud at the top, pronounced and prominent with longing. He sunk his teeth into her shoulder, which was bare since her sleeve had slid down her arm in the tussle. Denise fumbled with Tony's regulation belt buckle, then his zipper. "Bastard," she crooned, like it was a compliment. Tony liked the way it sounded in her breathy, heated voice.

He twiddled and twisted and gently coaxed to Denise's pleas of harder, then softer, then there, there, right there. Denise shuddered and stammered around his fingers, collapsing onto him, still grasping his shaft like a billy club. "I'm so fucking mad at you," she moaned, then, "Again...please...more."

In recent years, his wife was always visibly relieved when the act was over, but not his Denise. But then again, Denise hadn't been battered, brutalized and beaten down on the battleground of marriage as Rosanna had. And it was a dry, desolate place.

Tony tried to maneuver Denise onto a wicker seat but knew it wouldn't work. Too narrow, too shallow, and he could just picture the dappled basketwork pattern etched into the backs of her ass and thighs. Fucking her on the seat would mean he'd have to kneel on the red rubberized flooring just to get inside her or else squat like a quarterback. And given his current state, the last one wasn't an option. However, he gave it the old college try, Denise's legs akimbo and spider-like on his shoulders, her spiked heels dangerously near his skull, a cramp already blossoming in his thigh. Then she said, "Honey, my stockings," breaking the spell entirely.

Well, not entirely. Always a resourceful girl, Denise reached up and grabbed hold of the porcelain straps overhead and suspended herself from them. He hiked her onto his hips, impaling her in one swift motion. Holding Denise fast, Tony moved like a pitching sea while she pumped herself up and down, still hanging from the triangular porcelain straps. Crinolines like a cloud, Tony pierced her soft, moist, rainy center. With Tony's pants cast like a net down around his ankles, Denise rode him like a wave, spikes puncturing his buttocks as he punctured her. When she came this time, she was crumpled and crying. He followed a beat after. The notion that he could demolish, destroy and conquer using only his cock as a weapon was his personal point of vanquish.

The metal fan blades overhead were frozen and still. Most of the windows were shut tight. Denise and Tony were bathed in sweat. The green and wicker woven seat beneath him felt damp. Like a gentleman, Tony offered Denise his handkerchief, then shoved it back into his pocket. Her makeup was splotchy. She tried in vain to repair it with the aid of a compact mirror. Tony noticed that the compact bore her name and had something else etched into its silver surface—an inscription, a dedication of sorts. Probably a gift from one fancy man or another. It looked expensive, just like Denise did. But looks often were deceiving, especially in her case.

And so began Tony's crusade to convince Denise to go along with, or at least try, his scheme. Two women, a double life, the best of both worlds, for him at least. Denise listened carefully as she powdered her nose. "You knew I was married when you met me," he pointed out. "Besides, it's not her, it's the kids. It's for the kids' sake."

Denise thoughtfully uncapped a tube of lipstick. "My old man run out on us before I could remember him," she told Tony. "I know what it's like to grow up without a dad." She dragged the blood-red cake of color across her mouth. "You sure you ain't gonna fuck her?" Tony shook his head, dead serious. "Then I suppose we could give it a whirl, then."

Tony's mood brightened. He would have kissed her but her lipstick was fresh and he knew it would cause a row. "But I ain't gonna sleep alone every night," Denise told him. "And I ain't gonna play second fiddle to no one, not even your kids." Tony couldn't imagine Denise's sleek, curvy, fiddle-like physique being second-best to anyone or anything.

According to his wristwatch, Tony's break was over ten minutes ago and he was already five minutes late getting the seven o'clock West End out of Stillwell. Denise carefully made her way along Track 6 and out of the station with Tony following close behind.

When he arrived at his train, the newbie was nervously shuffling on the platform and the stationmaster was glaring at his pocket watch. Tony gave his best and brightest Jimmy Cagney smile, chucked the stationmaster on the arm and said, "Oh, that greasy Guinea food. I been in the can my whole freaking break. Sorry, chief."

McBride, the stationmaster, who was Irish through and through, took a particular evil thrill in Italian slanders. He grinned and patted Tony on the back. "Stick to meat and potatoes, my boy," McBride suggested, in a brogue as smooth as bourbon. "And Guinness. It's as mild as mother's milk, you know."

"Try telling that to my wife, Mr. McBride," Tony shot back. And they both laughed like old friends sharing a secret joke.

"You're seven minutes late out of the gate," McBride told him. "Try making it up as you go."

"Will do, boss. Will do." Tony practically shoved the trainee into the box and slammed the doors on McBride's big, stupid donkey face with a grin. "Shanty Irish Mick bastard," he added under his breath as the train peeled out of the station. "Cocksucker from County Cork. You Gaelic jerkoff from Galway."

The new guy looked at Tony with horror. "You'll see," he told the kid. "Just you wait and see." And with that, the El made its way toward Bensonhurst, Borough Park and beyond, dragging Tony along with it.

24 At Farrell's Bar & Grill

Sam shook his head in slow sadness. "Like a little whooped dog," he said again. "That's what she reminds me of. A little whooped dog. All the happiness beaten out of her." He shook his head again and drained his cold, amber-colored glass of beer.

Sam, John, Harry and Sully were conferring at Farrell's Bar and Grill "in the ass-end of Park Slope," as Harry so delicately phrased it, rather than the Pink Pussycat, which was in their own backyard. They chose to meet here to avoid seeing anyone they knew. People had the habit of listening to everything that went on in bars, even things that weren't any of their own damned business.

Farrell's was a good spot for the four men to jaw. It was a fine drinking establishment, dimly lit and anonymous, with dark, polished wood and even darker mirrors lining the walls. There was no jukebox and no barstools—if you couldn't stand, you could no longer drink there, that was Old Man Farrell's credo. The men knew that Tony had been thrown out of Farrell's more than once and that he had been unofficially banned from the premises by Houlie, a bartender whose real name was Kevin Houlihan. So there was no chance of running into Tony either.

Sully liked Farrell's no-nonsense ballsiness. It had opened three years earlier, as soon as Prohibition was repealed. A few miles from Borough Park, Farrell's was worlds away, separated by the rolling hills of Green-Wood Cemetery and the graves of Alice Roosevelt and "Boss" Tweed, and perched near the edge of Prospect Park.

The beer was arguably the coldest in the borough. Nothing fancy, only Ruppert's, Budweiser and Ballantine Ale on tap, which flowed up from kegs in the basement, winding their way through ice-encrusted pipes. The bar backs were often seen wielding baseball bats, not to swat unruly patrons, but to pack the melting ice around the brass pipes. Sully enjoyed watching someone's face when Houlie, who was a particularly brawny fellow, opened the brass hatch in the long bar's center, grabbed a baseball club and plunged it into the icy depths between the pipes. The beer was frosty and cheap, sold by the pitcher, by the six ounce glass or in cardboard "to go" cups. A half-finished pitcher sat in front of the quartet. It was going to be a long night.

They had secured one of the few tables to be found at Farrell's, which was situated toward the middle of the large, deep room. The grill was dormant as it was long past the pub's food-serving hours. The back section featured low tables and chairs, and was the only place where ladies were permitted to drink. No woman was ever served at Farrell's bar itself, and though never shuttered out, only a certain kind of woman drank at the establishment in the first place. Lace-curtain Irish ladies like Eileen Daly and prim Italians mommas like Bridget wouldn't even think of setting foot in the joint. In fact, there was only one woman, ancient, sunken-jawed and wizened by rum, at a back table this evening, drinking alone.

From their vantage point in the corner, Sully and Harry's cop instincts were satisfied. They could survey the entire expanse of the bar and inspect who came in the front door besides. Although dressed in street clothes, just one look at the pair silently screamed "copper," what with their wide shoulders shoved into not-wide-enough suit jackets, straw hats not quite big enough for their fat Irish heads and their puffy pugilist features. Sully and Harry were different bookends on the same library shelf.

Unlike the Pink Pussycat, which was an alcoholic's paradise, Farrell's was the sort of place regular Joes went to unwind after work, shoot the breeze with their pals and catch up on neighborhood gossip. While their wives did this very same thing in kitchens over pots of weak tea or on front stoops watching their kids play, husbands did this as reflected in the dark mirrors of Farrell's. Jobs were secured here. Plumbers and painters were found. Reasonable apartments in houses owned by an uncle's cousin once removed were united with neat, dependable tenants. Births were celebrated. And after being waked at Smith's across Prospect Park West (otherwise known as Ninth Avenue to the locals), deaths were mourned.

At Farrell's, you found the fanciful tapestry that made Brooklyn great, stretched across the polished, wooden expanse of the bar. Here was a beautiful melody of plain and ugly faces, noses broken in brawls, scars earned in street scuffles, cropped crew cuts and greasy curls, where five o'clock shadows met with plump jowls doused with citrus aftershave. You could tell the dock workers from the transit workers and the office grunts from the linemen at the Ansonia Clock Factory a few blocks away.

Sam was still immersed in his tragic Southern melodrama, which became even more sorrowful with every glass of Bud he drained. Harry was surprised that his brother-in-law didn't start crying, "Woe is Roe." Instead, Sam shook his head again and simply said, "Whooped dog."

"Would you lay off the whooped dog crap?" John asked. "And besides, you're one to talk about how to treat a wife, Sammy. At least I left my first one."

"And your daughter, too, from what I hear," Sam shot back with intensity.

John visibly bristled and inched towards Sam, not like a whooped dog but more like a pissed off junkyard dog. Harry inserted himself between them, placing a meaty palm flat on each chest. "Now, boys..."

Sam backed off and slammed an open hand on the table. "I resent that remark, John. My indiscretions, though few and far between, are very discreet. And who isn't guilty of a little hanky-panky now and then."

"Discreet indiscretions...maybe that's the way they do it in Georgia but not in Brooklyn," John told him, sipping a Coca Cola. "I've never run around on Camille. Not in the seven years we've been a couple."

"Me neither. No need to with Jo," Harry said.

Sam affected the air of a wounded Southern belle. He placed his manicured hand on his chest for emphasis then ran the other through his Brilliantined hair. In a certain light, Sam might be said to resemble William Powell, without the pencil mustache. Tiger would dispute this claim, Kewpie would swoon and Poppa would mistakenly refer to the movie actor as William Cooper, and dispute it as well, while Astrid would revel in her husband's remote likeness to the moving picture actor as though it truly meant something of significance.

"Gentlemen," Sam began, "You all know my wife. Do I need to? Just to maintain a little sanity?" And they busted up laughing, seeing Sam's point.

Only Sully remained stone-faced; he didn't see the humor in it. "He's killing Roe," Sully blurted out. "He's killing everything we love about her." The other three stared at the big cop in disbelief. Sully had practically declared his silent adoration for Rosanna outright, something Harry had always suspected but never dared ask.

Sully reddened so deeply that the tips of his ears stained purple. He tried to cover his tracks, to redeem himself, but it was too late. Everything he said dug a more cavernous trench of devotion. "I mean, her spirit. Her... For Christ's sake, just look at her eyes. Not to mention the bruises. And what about the ones we can't see?"

Even Harry was surprised at his friend's declaration. Sully was the one with the tough, crusty heart, the one who never believed the grieving widow's story, who always thought suspects thieves, liars and low-lives until they'd proven to him otherwise. But Harry did his best to cover for his buddy, just like he'd do on the job. "Sully's right," he told the rest of them. "The eyes have it."

John chomped thoughtfully on a mouthful of ice then swallowed. "We've got to do something."

"But what?" Sam said. "She's never asked for help."

"She turned me down when I offered." John shrugged. "Maybe she's scared."

"Don't you see?" Sully told them cautiously. "She's asking for help all the time. Maybe not in words but..."

"Oh, right. It's in those dreamy Paradiso peepers," Sam said, fluttering his lashes, which revealed eyes that were Savannah blue instead of puppy dog brown.

"This is serious," Sully announced. "Dead serious." He studied the floor tiles. There were thousands of them, six-sided chips, wedged one against the other like people on the El. The tiles were mostly white but interspersed with black, green, rust and yellow to form smooth floral shapes. Big, cold, Black-eyed Susans.

Sully heard that Italians had done most of the mosaic work in the city. He wondered if this were true. Poppa Mike would probably know. The old fellow knew practically everything there was to know about Italians. Sully would have to ask the next time he saw him.

The intricate lobby of the Woolworth Building, with its caricature of the architect Cass Gilbert and old Woolworth himself filling a piggy bank... Even the tiled subway murals: the tall masted ships at Fulton Street, the beavers at Astor Place (the block's namesake Jacob Astor had made his fortune in beaver skin hats), the terra cotta wreaths and Greek coffee cup pattern at Borough Hall and even Court Street, which was Sully's personal favorite. He loved the vivid tiled patchwork quilt around the subway station's name and along the inside of Brooklyn's own regal cupola atop the Borough Hall Building.

Each and every one had supposedly been crafted by Italians, more artful, more colorful and more impressive than even Bridget's most elaborate antipasto. Sully smiled slightly as he pictured the men with their hairy arms and backs, wearing sweaty sleeveless undershirts or thick sweaters and fingerless gloves as they worked, for the subways were burrows of extremes, boiling hot in the summer and icy in the winter. He imagined tough fellows with a delicate touch, recreating a vibrant subterranean world with squares of fired ceramics that was more beautiful than the real world above.

Just past Farrell's door saddles, the tiled pattern was angular and geometric, like something you'd see on an urn at Pompeii. Then it burst into a flower garden as you approached the bar. Sully tried to count the tiles but his eyes teared up and his head fogged from the effort. Harry nudged him. "You okay, pal?" he asked.

"Yeah," Sully told him, draining the glass easily, as if it were a thimble. Already, Harry was refilling it. "But I'd like to rip that bastard a new asshole."

"How about making it official, involving the cops?" John proposed. He had already emptied another bottle of Coke and was busy chewing on the ice again.

"Not unless she lodges a formal complaint," Harry informed them. "And she won't. Downright refuses to. I've already talked to her about it."

Someone at the bar ordered a Gimlet. Houlie laughed and bounced a coin on the wood, suggesting, "Here's a nickel for the subway. Take it to Manhattan and get your fancy-pants drink there." Everyone else lining the bar laughed while Mr. Gimlet sheepishly requested Ruppert's.

"I think we ought to talk to him," Harry announced.

"There's no talking to that mook," John said. "Believe me, Sammy and I have tried." Sam managed to nod forlornly without mentioning whips or mongrels.

At the bar, Houlie worked the chipped, slightly-warped baseball bat through the ice around the taps, much like a milkmaid heartily churning butter. "Only makes it harder on her," Sam added.

"I'm saying just one of us should go," Harry pressed. "Not to gang up on him. Not to threaten him or anything. Just one of us should go and have a polite discussion with him. Man-to-man."

"He ain't a man," Sully growled. Then in the next beat, he said, "I'll do it."

"Nah, I will," Harry offered.

"Why? Cause I ain't blood? Cause I ain't family?" Sully snapped back.

"I ain't blood either," Harry said gently. "And you are family. But I think...I think you're too close. I think this hits a nerve."

Sully pushed his full glass of beer away. A small wave of liquid spilled over the side. "It does but I'll do it anyway. I know where he lives when he's not with her. Mermaid and 19th, right, John?"

"Second floor walkup," John said. "Crummy brick building on the corner."

The other three men considered Sully warily. Already, his giant, Irish heart was on his sleeve. "I can do this," Sully assured them. "I can do it right."

The crowd at Farrell's was beginning to thin out. Only the hardcore drinkers remained, or people with nowhere else to go. Sully, Harry, John and Sam didn't fit into either category. They were ready to take their empty glasses and spent pitcher up to the bar when Houlie deposited a shot of whiskey in front of each of them. Then he gestured to a small man sitting at the bar in a rumpled suit. His porkpie was clutched tightly in his fist and he looked like he'd had a hard day, a hard life, in fact.

The man cleared his throat but his voice cracked anyway. He seemed unaccustomed to speaking loudly and unused to addressing more than one or two people at a time. He raised his glass. "This is for Jack," he said, "My nephew. A good boy. A brave boy. I just came from Methodist Episcopal. He died there tonight."

Everyone else in the bar hoisted their shot glasses high above their heads, even Houlie, who rarely drank. Some bit their lips. Mr. Gimlet sniffled and choked back a sob. "To Jack," they said, as one. "To Jack."

Sully looked at The Three Musketeers surrounding him. "To Roe," he said.

Even John drank and he hadn't touched the stuff since he got back from the War, when he'd drunk enough for an entire lifetime. The liquor was warm and bitter as bile in his stomach, but not bad, not bad at all.

The Three Musketeers went home to their wives, with John behind the wheel of Sully's car. Sully didn't feel like driving or being cooped up in his car either. So, he tossed John the keys and headed home alone to his furnished room on foot. Sully needed to calm his thoughts, opting for the long walk around the perimeter of Green-Wood Cemetery. He went along McDonald Avenue and turned down Fort Hamilton Parkway, the tall, green spire of St. Catherine of Alexandria Church beckoning him. The grotto on the church's 41st Street side was darkened so he couldn't see the sharp, pointed rocks that composed its cave, although he knew they were there. He also knew by heart the lines of the Virgin Mary's pure white robe, the sky blue of her sash and the words in the donut above her head: "I am the immaculate conception." Her pained expression reminded him of Rosanna's sometimes.

In this manner, Sully returned to Borough Park, passing beneath the tall girders of the El on his way.

25 Million Dollar Baby

S.S. Kresge Company's "5 and 10" was prominent among the other stores on 13th Avenue. It was distinct amid the hodgepodge of Kosher butchers, dry goods shops and fruit stands that were patched together to make the fabric of the street. Mainly because Kresge's took up the space of five or six stores and its sign, instead of being hand-painted or in Hebrew, was made of raised wooden Roman-style letters that were gilded and stood out against the sign's rich, red background.

Inside, Kresge's hammered tin ceilings were high and the displays were inviting. The luncheon counter along the store's left-hand wall gleamed and the food you ate there was hardy and delicious. The savory chow mein sandwich was Kewpie's favorite. It was cooked by a kindly Polish woman named Harriet Kaminski, rather than by a Chinaman. The other workers liked to tease Harriet that everything she made tasted like *kielbasa*, but even she knew they were just ribbing her. Like a culinary chameleon, Harriet's dishes took on the flavor of each given land, and it was surprising to discover that a slender Warsaw refugee was behind each one.

In addition to the wonderful food Kresge's served, the prices throughout the store were reasonable, and the products they sold dependable. It was a plain fact that the country was in the throes of the Great Depression, and Kresge shoppers felt they were valued, even revered. Kewpie was proud to work there. It was a good job, especially for a sixteen-year-old, and she was a conscientious worker. She always clocked in a few minutes early, making certain her post at the cookie and candy counter was clean and tidy. Her bosses appreciated Kewpie's diligence and treated her fairly, like an adult. Kewpie had worked there almost seven months already and if she played her cards right, she might even make junior assistant manager.

Kewpie's bright white smock was always spotless and meticulously pressed. She took particular pride in this, hand-scrubbing it, even when she was tired and came home late, carefully placing a thick towel over the oilcloth-covered kitchen table and smoothing out the smock's wrinkles with a steam iron. The name on the uniform's upper-right hand breast pocket proclaimed "Angela" in fancy burgundy script instead of Kewpie. Angela was a grown-up's name, a different person entirely than Kewpie. She even permitted her coworkers and some of her favorite customers to call her "Angie."

Whenever Kewpie breezed by, the store's manager, a tall, strapping Norwegian fellow with corn silk blonde hair by the name of Olie Olsen, would hum, sing or whistle a few bars of Billy Rose's "Million Dollar Baby." Especially the lines that went:

> *"I found a million dollar baby*
> *In a five and ten cent store..."*

This would always make Kewpie smile and Olie, whose red blazer bore a name tag that announced "Olaf," would grin his big-toothed Oslo farm boy grin. "Forget Fanny Brice," Olie would tell Kewpie, "that song was written for you, Miss Angela."

Olie rode the B-16 bus all the way from Bay Ridge to Borough Park each morning. Many Norwegians had settled in the Ridge like Brooklyn-bound Vikings. You could get *fiskbullar* (codfish balls) in sealed tins, freshly made herrings in either cream or wine sauce, and visit the offices of the *Norske Tiden* (Norwegian Newspaper) on Fifth Avenue, down in the 70s. Kewpie had been to Bay Ridge with Bridget a few times, to Leske's Bakery with its magnificent black and white cookies, swirled with creamy frosting, and to a little hole in the wall delicatessen there to buy *kumpa*, luscious potato dumplings. Not only was the *kumpa* cheap at Marit's shop but the complicated, time-consuming dish was even better than Bridget could make herself from the recipe shared with her by Olie's wife Tomina.

At Kresge's, it was one big happy family. Most of the workers came from different corners of the world. Besides Norway and Poland, the waitress Katie Sweeney hailed from Limerick and their porter Pietro came from Cosenza, not far from Poppa's village of San Vincenzo. "Yah, we're a regular League of Nations, yah," Olie liked to say. And it was true. Between all of the employees, they could speak any language their diverse customer base spoke, even Brooklynese like Kewpie and Julia, the buxom assistant manager.

With her blemish-free skin and her slim-hipped body, Kewpie certainly wasn't one of those teenagers who "ate the profits," her managers noticed. Although she loved sweets, Kewpie wouldn't think of sneaking tastes behind anyone's back; it would have been dishonest. And she was extremely patient, her bosses also noted, especially with youngsters and old folks. She had a caring touch which was most appreciated. When a kid came in with a nickel that he found in the gutter pressed in his fist and stood hypnotized in front of the swirling rainbow display of penny candy, Kewpie offered helpful suggestions about gumdrops, Red Hots and nonpareils (her personal favorite) but never pressured or rushed them, sometimes taking other customers before a decision was finally made and she weighed her young patron's careful selection, then pried the hot coin from their sweaty palm.

Take Mr. Taylor. Everyone in the neighborhood called him "The Birdman" behind his back, some laughingly to his face. He was a slightly hunchbacked ancient gentleman who wore a stained black trench coat even in the summer, his unkempt snowy hair spilling over its collar. Most people thought him a bum but he was merely eccentric. Mr. Taylor had a great deal of cash stashed in the Williamsburg Savings Bank and owned a ramshackle house on Fort Hamilton Parkway besides, but he watched every penny like the proprietor of a poorhouse.

Every Tuesday and Thursday, Mr. Taylor bought a pound of broken cookies from Kewpie at half-price, not for himself but for the birds in McKinley Park, which he enjoyed a leisurely walk to and from twice a week, to help strengthen his heart, he informed her. Kewpie always smiled politely at Mr. Taylor when he came in and never called him "The Birdman," even behind his back. There was something gentle about him that she liked.

"You look as pretty as a summer's day, Angela," Mr. Taylor told Kewpie as he painstakingly counted his pocketful of change onto the glass counter.

"Thank you," she responded, blushing slightly.

"That's from Shakespeare," he added, "Paraphrased, of course," in an accent that was slightly reminiscent of Albania or Lithuania or one of the other "ania's." Mr. Taylor sounded a lot like her neighbor Mrs. Lieberwitz, who originally came from Romania.

Kewpie nodded, remembering "Shall I compare thee to a summer's day?" from English class at P.S. 131, and colored an even deeper shade of crimson. But Mr. Taylor was perfectly respectful, not wolfish in any way like boys were when they whistled at her on the street or leered at her like grown men did, suggesting nasty things under their breath which she pretended not to hear. Mr. Taylor was merely making an honest observation as one might remark on a brilliant sunset or a handsome painting of Uncle Julius's. "Thank you," Kewpie said again, in an even quieter voice this time.

Mr. Taylor nodded and gathered the paper sack in his fist. He slowly turned to go as another customer hurriedly stepped up to the counter, almost knocking Mr. Taylor to the ground. "Kewpie..." the slurred voice said. It was Tony. Not quite eleven in the morning and he was already hammered.

"Not here, Dad," she pleaded. "I'm trying to work."

"Not here? If not here, then where?" Tony said, a bit louder.

"At home?" she wondered.

"I never see you at home," he informed her, leaning in close. His teeth were yellowed, his breath sour. He reached over the countertop and grabbed hold of her arm. Although he pulled Kewpie onto the tips of her toes, she still refused to look him in the eye. She tried to wriggle out of his grip but he only held on tighter.

Mr. Taylor stepped up like a ragamuffin knight in his worn overcoat. "Sir...please unhand the young lady," he began.

Tony looked at the old man and cocked his head defiantly to the side. "And who the fuck are you?" he asked. "I'm her father."

"I'm just a customer," Mr. Taylor told him, still clutching the sack of broken cookies in his hands. "But I can see you're upsetting her."

"And you're upsetting me!" Tony bellowed. He let go of Kewpie and took a swipe at poor Mr. Taylor. His bag of cookies went flying across the Notions aisle. Mr. Taylor fell back against a bin of needles and bobbins that were on sale this week but at least he managed to keep his footing. Kewpie put her hand to her mouth and ran out from behind the counter to help him. His cookie fragments were crushed to a powder, too small for even the hungry birds to eat.

"I'm so sorry...so, so sorry," Kewpie muttered, kneeling on the polished linoleum, trying to gather up the mess in her hands. Tony fell to his knees beside her. "What are you doing here?" she asked the floor's speckled pattern. "I thought you were working the day shift."

"They gave me a week on the street," Tony told her. "It's a long story." Then he took her hard by the wrist again. "We need to talk."

"Let go of me, Pop...please," Kewpie gasped, her eyes flickering up to meet his. "You're making a mess of things."

Tony sparked with anger. "That's just like me, ain't it? Always screwing something up, huh?" He held fast to his daughter's bony wrist and tried to yank her to her feet. "You sound just like your fucking mother."

Kewpie began to cry and let her father pull her up from the floor like a heap of laundry. Julia came rushing out from behind the perfume counter. The assistant manager was a full-sized gal but quick on her feet. She had five kids of her own and liked Kewpie a great deal, treated her like another daughter. Julia wouldn't allow anyone to disrespect her Angie, not another manager, not a surly customer, not anybody.

"Sir, please let go of my girl," Julia said. As the only daughter in a scrappy family of ten sons, hers was a poor, hardscrabble life, but Julia wouldn't take guff from anybody, especially not a rummy. Through her embarrassment, Kewpie felt a flicker of delight that Julia would stand up for her like this. She reminded Kewpie of a gutsy, dark-haired Alice Faye with weight as she went head-to-head with Tony.

"She's my girl," Tony growled, pawing Julia to the side.

"You mean, she's your beau?" Julia responded in disbelief. "Angie's barely sixteen."

Kewpie bowed her head. "I'm his daughter," she told her boss. And as if the first statement were too impossible to believe, she added, "He's my father."

"I don't care who he is," said Julia, planting her feet firmly on the ground and wrapping her hand around Kewpie's trembling one. "No one gets treated with disrespect in my store. Not my customers, not my workers, no one."

Kewpie became the gooey center of a human taffy pull with Julia firmly grasping one hand and Tony tightening his hold on her arm. Julia started to walk away and tried to take Kewpie with her but Tony wouldn't be deterred. He released Kewpie's wrist only to clutch onto her shoulder. He began pulling her toward the front door. Although Kewpie didn't budge, her work smock did.

The sound of ripping material seemed to fill the whole of Kresge's. The thin strap of the cotton sundress Kewpie wore beneath her smock tore also. Her hands shot up to her chest to prevent herself from being exposed. Kewpie's pale shoulder looked thin and vulnerable in the store's harsh lighting, like the flesh of a newly-plucked goose. She doubled over in horror and sunk to the floor, mortified and sobbing.

Kewpie's wailing immediately brought Olie to the Sweets counter. He lumbered like a tow-headed polar bear toward the sound of strife. Tony didn't wait to be escorted out or even to be asked to leave. He knew Olie could make a mess of him even if the square-head weren't infuriated, which he clearly was. Judging by the manager's flushed face and clenched fists, it was a plain fact that Olie could lick him but good. The towering Norwegian looked as though he might just burst from his blazer, a Nordic volcano ready to blow. Tony had been on the losing end of far too many bar fights to ignore the fact that he would easily get his ass kicked by this palooka whose physique was muscular from his soccer-filled Sunday afternoons at Leif Ericson Field, after attending services at Zion Lutheran Church, of course.

So, Tony left his daughter a pathetic crying heap on the linoleum. Julia fell to her chubby knees beside Kewpie to console the child, brushing her neat pin curls away from her blotchy face, cooing gentlenesses to her that no one else could hear. Mr. Taylor couldn't care less about his cookies—Olie gave him a new bag along with profuse apologies. The old man felt like crying himself, so profound was the girl's embarrassment. And Olie was so enraged that he had to keep reminding himself to breathe. He unclenched his fists as he sucked air in and out of his massive lungs, and soon his breathing was back to normal. Olie wanted to call the cops on the bum for what he'd done, but Kewpie wouldn't hear of it.

Luckily, Kresge's wasn't yet crowded, so no one but Mr. Taylor and Kewpie's coworkers stood watching the fracas. Pietro appeared from the stockroom with a broom and dustbin. He swept up the pulverized crumbs without a word or a fuss. Kewpie and Julia moved to one side and then another so he could whisk it all away. When the girl glanced at Pietro sorrowfully, he assured her in his singsong Italian accent, "It's okay, *signorina*, it's okay." But it wasn't okay.

Julia helped Kewpie into a spare smock she had stashed in her locker. It was voluminous but freshly laundered. The name on the front read "Loretta" from a long-gone employee no one remembered, but it would do for now. Behind the luncheon counter, Katie wrung her hands and Harriet watched briefly before turning back to the grill. "Sonomonbitch," Harriet muttered, as she flipped a hamburger, "Sonomonbitch."

After a few minutes, Julia was able to coax Kewpie to stand but she still couldn't bear to look at anyone. Julia ushered Kewpie to a silver-stemmed stool at the far end of the food counter, away from the other customers, and eased her onto the red leather cushion. Katie slid a utensils setup on a napkin in front of Kewpie, then deposited a chocolate egg cream in a tall glass beside it. Harriet placed a lovely chow mein sandwich between Kewpie's neatly folded hands. "You likee," Harriet said, nodding, knowing it was the girl's favorite item on the menu.

Katie added, "Eat, honey. There's no charge. It's on old Sebastian Kresge."

Julia kissed Kewpie on the forehead before she left her, noticing that her hair smelled of baby shampoo. "My old man was a drunk too," Julia whispered. "You'll do okay. I know you will, Angie."

Kewpie chewed thoughtfully and took alternate sips of the egg cream in between the bites. Another Brooklyn illusion, there was no egg and no cream in egg creams, just milk, seltzer and a generous splash of Fox's U-Bet chocolate syrup. However, egg creams were was still delicious, despite the misnomer. Kewpie sniffled and wished she could get to the lace-trimmed hankie that festooned the breast pocket of her own uniform. But the paper napkin at the counter would do just fine. After today, she would never come back to Kresge's again, not even to shop. She could never bear to show her face there again. It would have to be Woolworth's from now on.

Olie waited patiently until Kewpie finished her chow mein on a bun. He waited until she slurped the last bit of egg cream through the striped straw. Kewpie stopped sipping when she heard the sound of air gurgling, then she neatly blotted the corners of her mouth and fished around in her side pocket (not Loretta's) for a coin. "Don't you dare leave a tip," Katie told her in a brogue that meant business. Kewpie put the nickel back into her smock.

The stool beside her creaked as Olie lowered himself onto it as lightly as possible. He was a formidable man and was as precariously perched on the small round seat as a rhino on a lily pad. His knees practically touched his shoulders. "Why don't you take the rest of the day off, Angela?" he suggested.

Kewpie shook her head violently. "Oh, I couldn't."

And then Olie realized that this was because she didn't want to run into her father, either on the Avenue or at home. At least at Kresge's, she was protected, because he wouldn't dare return. Kewpie sniffled and wiped her nose on her hand. Olie handed her his enormous cloth handkerchief. It was embroidered with the letters OO in a bright, hopeful blue by his wife Tomina. Kewpie blew her nose heartily then balled up the handkerchief in her fist. It was the size of a small tablecloth. "Angie," Olie began.

'He's going to fire me,' Kewpie said to herself. 'I know he's going to fire me. I'll just leave. I'll just walk out.' Kewpie made her way to her feet. Standing up, she was as tall as Olie was sitting.

"Please sit," Olie told her. Even though he'd been in America since he was a little boy, in times of strong emotion—like with a rude customer or a ruined order—Olie found it difficult to find the proper words in English. Kewpie waited patiently until he located them. "You're a fine girl, Angela. A fine young woman," he corrected. "And a fine worker, too. We're a family here, a happy family." He stammered and turned his blue eyes toward the tin ceiling as if hoping for divine intervention. "What I'm trying to say is that we need you. I hope you will stay. I hope you won't feel too badly about what happened here today. And please, please don't blame yourself. It's not your fault."

Olie looked so pained, sincere and earnest that Kewpie just couldn't leave. At least not today. She thanked Olie for his kindness and for the free meal, thanked all of her coworkers for being so understanding, especially Julia.

After Kewpie handed Olie back his tainted handkerchief, she went to the restroom to wash her face and hands. The cold water felt soothing on her burning skin. When she returned to her post behind the Sweets counter, she noticed that Pietro had done an excellent job cleaning the floor. There wasn't a crumb left on the linoleum, not one tiny reminder of what had happened. Except perhaps the mark that was etched inside of her.

26 Brief Encounters

By mid-afternoon, no one could tell what had happened to Kewpie at Kresge's. By then, her work smock had been expertly repaired by Sandra, a woman who worked in Notions. Sandra was a fine seamstress, renowned in the Playa Mariano district of Havana for her sewing skills. Back in Cuba, she had made elaborate costumes of feathers, mesh and beads for showgirls but now Sandra was happy as could be at Kresge's for she was finally free from Fulgencio Batista's iron hand. On Kewpie's next break, she and Sandra slipped into the storage room so Sandra could also mend the shoulder strap of Kewpie's dress with just a few skillful stitches. Right then and there, Kewpie decided not to tell anyone at home what her father had done that day.

Kewpie didn't tell Rosanna, who was busy cleaning the hallway steps with a carpet sweeper, doing her best to ignore the gnawing pain that burrowed deep into her belly like a sharp-clawed rodent. The pain had worsened since her secret visits to doctors Lewis and Schantz but she refused to admit this to herself. However, sometimes, late at night, the aching was so bad that she curled up on her empty mattress and cried. The doctors warned her that she needed to have the surgery as soon as possible, but for the life of her, Rosanna couldn't see how she could manage it. It was expensive, and besides, too many people depended on her.

Kewpie didn't tell Poppa and Tiger, who were both still at the Navy Yard, enjoying Bridget's meatball sandwiches during their lunch break. She'd packed a spare hero and they decided to give it to the new guy, Herve, who had nothing to eat and no money to buy anything with until his first paycheck. There was always someone hungry and someone in need, so Bridget usually had enough leftovers from the night before to make an extra sandwich or two. Besides, the ice in the old Sears and Roebuck melted so quickly in the summer, sometimes more quickly than Willie, the iceman's man, could bring it. And it was better to feed another hungry soul than to have food spoil.

Kewpie didn't tell Bridget either, who was busy in the front yard, trimming red, yellow and pink roses from the wiry bushes that snaked up the trellises on either side of the front stairs. The bushes grew so frantically that their arms threatened to twirl around the banisters and the porch railings themselves, and like beneficent monsters, they often did. Bridget's roses thrived in the stark humidity of city summers and were a source of pride to her. The armful she'd just cut would look wonderful on the dining room table and would probably last at least until Sunday dinner, especially with an orange-flavored St. Joseph's aspirin in the water. (That kindly carpenter worked miracles on all sorts of things, even flowers.) The roses' heads were slightly bowed, the buds half closed but they held the promise of spreading their wings into something magnificent.

And though Kewpie seriously considered confiding in her Aunt Jo, she ultimately decided against it. So Jo, who sat on her bed with her sewing basket beside her, letting out the waists of three of her best dresses yet again, had no clue what had gone on in Kresge's either. The radio played a live broadcast of Ray Noble's Orchestra from the Brooklyn Paramount which had been recorded a few weeks earlier. Jo's bare foot tapped in time with a

Glenn Miller solo as she snipped and then drew out a long white thread.

Harry watched his wife from the deep pocket of his favorite armchair in the living room. He studied her as he pretended to read the *Brooklyn Daily Eagle*. Jo never was never happier than when she was pregnant. He sure hoped and prayed this baby would take. Harry didn't even care whether it was a boy or a girl. He just wanted a baby in Josephina's arms at the end of nine months. And Harry, in his easy chair, looking at his wife with adoration and maybe a slice of pity, had no idea of his niece Kewpie's ordeal at the "5 and 10" either.

Nor did Sully, who waited patiently for Tony to arrive at 1901 Mermaid Avenue. The sky was beginning to go all peachy over Nortons Point, way out in Sea Gate. Plenty of suspicious-looking characters, which Coney Island was famous for, came and went, but Tony wasn't among the legion of slugs who passed. For instance, there were stock boys seeking cheap thrills in sideshow booths, places where women propelled peeled hard-boiled eggs from their tender bodies, even ping pong balls. There were also sordid street girls who'd gladly slip under the Riegelmann Boardwalk to earn the month's rent with a quick grope or two. A tug and a rub and they'd be gone. No harm done. Although the very thought of putting a price tag on what others did in moments of love turned Sully's stomach, he had to agree that it was better than robbery. Yet this was a robbery of another sort— thievery of self.

The sky went indigo and still no sign of Tony. Maybe he was already inside the second-floor walkup, sleeping one off. Perhaps Sully had missed him coming in somehow, but Sully rarely missed the lowlife he was tailing.

The truth was that Tony was holed up in Ruby's Bar on the Boardwalk, methodically downing one beer and then another, doing a shot of Four Roses after every second one. He'd arrived at Ruby's about half past noon, jumping a West End train soon after the uproar at Kresge's. The beachside bar wasn't crowded at that hour and he'd managed to secure his favorite barstool facing the sea. This way he could drink, watch the waves and ogle the girls as they passed, their bare feet sizzling against the hot wooden planks of the Boardwalk, their damp bathing suits sticking to their even damper crevices. Perhaps he'd even get a glimpse of a dusky nipple from the top of a bathing costume or a tuft of strawberry blonde fluff from the crotch of a swimsuit. Or spy a filly who couldn't make it to the restroom line stealing off to a hidden corner and relieving herself with a furious splat on the scorching sand between her feet, thinking nobody could see. Tony cherished moments like these.

Though he was only a few blocks from Denise, he still didn't want to go home to her. He didn't want to see or talk to anyone he knew, especially not a dame. Tony told himself time and time again that what happened that morning didn't matter but it did. Regardless of how many quarts of watery suds he swallowed or how much cheap liquor he swilled, he still couldn't get Kewpie's wounded look out of his head. It was worse than the way she glared at him late at night. At least the darkness shielded him from the full strength of her ire. But he could still feel her steel gray eyes seething and bubbling over, even in the dark.

Seeing his daughter crumpled up on the floor so despondent and defeated made Tony feel like a total piece of shit. Which, of course, he was. Even Tony himself knew this. So, why not reform? Why not quit drinking? Why not vow to become a better person? Why not be kind to the people you claimed to love? What would it get him, Tony asked himself? Probably not much more than he had now. You work hard and you break your nut, for what? Just to squeak by? No, thanks. Tony would much rather drink, and drink hard. At least it was something he was good at.

About people didn't drink, his friend Bobby Callahan used to say: "Imagine waking up in the morning and realizing that this is as good as it's gonna get." Meaning, that Bobby couldn't even fathom a day without a drink—there was nothing to look forward to. Tony tried to imagine waking up with his mouth not tasting like the bottom of an unclean birdcage, without his head throbbing or his belly flipping. But he couldn't. Like old Bobby C., he simply couldn't picture not drinking. Tony had always been a drinker and he couldn't remember not being one, not even as a kid.

Bobby Callahan also liked to brag that his liver was the hardest part of his body. And you know where Bobby was now? Green-Wood. Dead at 35 of cirrhosis. Some punk found his body stretched out on a bench in Prospect Park, soiled in his own stink. His mutt Dingo by his side, barking and snarling frantically, not even letting the cops near to check his master's pulse. But Bobby was long gone by that time, cold as a stone angel's ass in Green-Wood. They had to muzzle Dingo just so they could take Bobby's body to the morgue at Kings County. Dog so mean, no one else wanted him, so they had to put him down. Kind of like Bobby. Maybe even like Tony if he wasn't careful.

Tony took another shot, winced and shuddered. It was smooth as fire going down. Fuck Bobby. Fuck everybody. Tony wasn't going to die alone. And he wasn't going to kick off anytime soon. Besides, he had not one woman but two. And he had a family, kids, a nice place to live. Two nice places to live. And neither of them a shit hole furnished room like Bobby Callahan's, perched above a Chinese takeout place across from the El, always rumbling, stinking of grease and dog piss. True, Denise wasn't much in the housekeeping department but housekeeping wasn't everything.

It was getting dark and Tony had been at Ruby's almost eight hours. Maybe it was about time to go home. If he could walk.

Sully, massive as he was, was bashful when it came to one-on-one encounters, especially with someone he didn't know all that well. He took a deep breath, straightened his uniform jacket (he'd worn his work clothes to seem more official and foreboding) and pushed the apartment house's chipped red outer door. It was unlocked and yielded easily. The second door, full of rectangular windowpanes and covered with a grimy lace curtain, was also unlocked. Sully closed the door softly behind him and made his way up the warped staircase to the second landing. The hallway smelled of ammonia trying to mask an even worse odor. The stairs creaked with every step, the old linoleum squares of red and used-to-be-white curled at the corners.

Sully already knew where the apartment was situated from John's photographs. He made a left at the top of the staircase

since the flat's unwashed, uncurtained windows bordered
Mermaid. He paused and sucked in another lungful of air, more
to calm his nerves than anything else. The walls on this level
were painted light brown, which didn't match anything else in
the building. The paint had probably been lifted from a jobsite
was Sully's best guess. If it's free, it's for me.

Patrick Sullivan easily found the door upon which 2A was
stenciled in black. He closed his fist and knocked. The sound
seemed louder than it ought to be, but maybe that was from
nerves, too. Sully heard the feathery step of female feet, the click
of a light switch, saw a burst of yellow-white under the door,
followed by an expectant, sing-songy, "Just a minute!" Then the
door pulled open without the scrape of a peephole or the benefit
of a security chain protecting the inhabitant.

Just as Sully had expected, he wasn't confronted by Tony
but face-to-face with his woman. Diane? Donna? Dolores? No,
Sully remembered that John had said her name was Denise.
Denise Walters.

At first, the Walters woman's expression faded, but just for a
moment. Although Sully wasn't the gentleman caller she'd
expected, her face perked up with the prospect of what could be.
You just never know, Denise was fond of telling her friends, and
you never can tell. Denise Walters was many things, among
them, a risk-taker. But was she ready to trade one blue uniform
for another? Well, maybe this one wasn't a drinker.

"My, my," Denise said with a mischievous grin, "they're sure
making them awful big these days." Then, "What can I do for
you, officer? And please excuse the way I'm dressed. I was
expecting my beau."

Denise wore a pink chemise over which a light matching robe
was draped but she made no attempt to cover herself. She also
wore fuzzy pink high-heeled slippers. Sully could see that she
was the kind of woman who might appeal to some men, most
men, in fact. But not him. Sully saw the broad as cheap and fake,
from the brown roots of her bleached hair to the tips of her
chipped, lacquered toenails. Denise was the sort of dame who
wouldn't age well. Already her belly was slightly rounded, and
he would guess that she didn't have any kids yet, at least not any

that she kept. Sully preferred the diamond in the rough type of gal, the woman whose best qualities weren't visible to the naked eye. And Denise clearly wasn't this type.

Sully took off his cap and held it against his bulky chest. "My name is Officer Patrick Sullivan," he told her, making no move to extend his hand, clarifying that this was not a social visit. "I'm here to see Anthony Martino."

"Well, he ain't here," Denise sighed, swinging the door open wider. "I ain't seen him all day. And when I do…"

Sully's eyes strayed from the woman's barely-masked curves into the apartment. He could see the disheveled bed with its grubby-looking sheets and coverlet partially on the floor. There were beer and liquor bottles decorating practically every surface, chairs and sofas as well as tabletops. Plus the kitchen table was littered with dirty dishes and takeout cartons, the sink piled high with the same.

Denise couldn't believe that this schmo would rather look at a mess than at her. She ran her hand through her straw-stiff hair, which crested in unkempt waves. "I was just resting," she tried to explain. "I been feeling a bit under the weather lately."

But Sully wasn't interested. He put his cap back on his head and made sure it was straight. "Any idea where Mr. Martino might be?" he wondered.

"With his wife and kids, for all I know," she snapped.

"So, you know about them?"

"Sure," Denise said. "Like it's any of my business?" Then she realized how she sounded and thought better of it, softening her tone. "Why?" she prodded. "He in some kind of trouble?"

"Not yet," the big cop told her. "I just want a word with him."

As if on cue, the lopsided staircase creaked. Sully turned and Denise raised her gaze to see Tony weaving his way up the steps, leaning against the sticky banister. He shifted to the stability of the wall, rising along its length, pulling himself up step by step, and by some miracle, mounting the top step. For a moment, he teetered precariously at the apex as if gravity might have its way with him and send him crashing back down, ass over teakettle. But Tony steadied himself and used the handrail to propel his body toward the open door of the apartment, bouncing from wall to banister like an intoxicated pinball. Finally, Tony stood in front of Sully, still wobbling, examining him from head to toe as if the towering cop were an amusing apparition.

Denise gathered her sheer robe around her, knowing Tony would disapprove of the way she was dressed—or undressed—in front of a stranger and faded into the apartment. Sully loomed above Tony, who slumped against the wall. He seemed much scrappier than Sully remembered. He wondered what Rosanna ever saw in the man.

In a strange way, Sully felt sorry for the little man, for the rummy he was, for the shipwreck he'd become. Tony's breath was reminiscent of something that might have been scraped from the bottom of a beer keg. He looked up at Sully and laughed, laughed uncontrollably holding his middle until tears rolled down his cheeks. "Look who it is," Tony bellowed. "Look who the fuck it is. Little Paddy Sullivan. My, how you've grown." And he laughed some more.

Sully didn't even crack a smile. "I want to talk to you, Tony. About this," he added, gesturing to the partially-open apartment door.

Tony reeled backwards, trying to stand on his own two rubbery feet, and failed. He felt for the wall behind him then stood his ground with its assistance. "This or anything else about my life is none of your fucking Mick business," he slurred.

When Sully reached past Tony to close the door, smashed as he was, Tony flinched then balled up his fists instinctively to fight. But Sully just wanted the door shut so they could speak more privately. "Is there somewhere we could go? I don't want the neighbors…"

"Anything you got to say to me, you can say right here. I don't give a shit about the neighbors. They're all a bunch of cunt whore, reefer smoking sons of bitches. And I hope they hear me!" he shouted.

Inside the kitchen, Denise held a gritty glass tumbler to the wall and pressed her ear against it. However, she didn't really need to do this to hear. The more Tony drank, the louder he got, and judging by the decibel level, he'd probably been drinking a very long time.

Sully had rehearsed this part of the encounter over and over again in his head. Sometimes he couldn't sleep because he practiced the speech so much in his mind late at night, staring up at the ceiling. But even so, he still didn't know where to begin. It was odd for such a large man to be so intimidated by such an insignificant one but it was more than Tony's size that worried Sully. It was his predicament. Tony was so low, so base, so potted, that he had reached rock bottom. And those hopeless sorts were the worst to go up against, especially on the job. The guy who'd just shot his wife and kids in a blind rage, the worn-out chorine who'd just slit the throat of the crooked promoter who'd pushed her too far, they were the ones who were so far gone that turning on a cop would be the least of their problems. And this is what concerned Sully about Tony. This and what he might do to Roe afterwards.

"We talked it over, all four of us," Sully began, "Me, Harry, Sam and John. We see what it's doing to your wife, to the kids. You not being there and all…" Sully looked at Tony's defiant expression, his shit-eating grin and knew that he would get absolutely nowhere with him. It filled Sully with rage. His face colored from collar to cap. His mind went blank with anger and then he just exploded. "But you know what?" Sully shouted, "Maybe it's worse for them when you're there."

"What the hell is that supposed to mean, Officer Donkey?" Tony challenged. He bucked against the big man's chest like a bumper car down at Steeplechase.

Instead of backing away, Sully butted Tony in return, but with such force that it flopped Tony against the wall as though his spine had softened. "It means just what it sounds like, you rotten, no good drunken bastard," Sully told him. "I seen the looks in their eyes. I seen the bruises. And it's got to stop. So, be a man and just disappear. Believe me, they'll get on without you. They'll do just fine and dandy."

Tony wiped the spittle from the corner of his mouth. "Look at the set of balls on you. Who the fuck do you think you are? You banging my wife?"

"Your wife deserves more respect than that," Sully said. "I'm just a friend, a friend with good advice." Sully poked his finger into Tony's chest for emphasis, feeling bone and ribs and hard edges. "I'm warning you, for your own sake. You better change your ways or get out."

Tony struggled to keep his eyes focused on Sully's wide, furious mug, "Or else what, cop?"

"Or you'll have hell to pay," Sully told him. "And me to deal with."

Tony started laughing again. He laughed so hard that he slid down the wall with the weight of his own guffaws. Sully grabbed two handfuls of Tony's shirt and pulled him up to meet his face. Tony's feet dangled inches above the ground. Sully smelled sweat and dirt and swill. He gagged slightly yet yanked the sod closer.

"Drunks have accidents all the time," Sully informed him in a calm voice, shaking him hard with each sentence. "They go off rooftops. They fall across trolley tracks. They crack their thick fucking skulls on the curb and their heads break open like watermelons. I seen it happen. And the worst part is, no one's sad to see them gone. No one cares. It's kind of a relief. Know what I'm saying?"

Sully let go of Tony's shirt with one final bounce against the wall. Then he wiped his hands on his trousers, straightened his uniform and his hat, and turned to leave. Sully was almost at the staircase when Tony let out a roar and charged down the hallway after him. Just a few more steps and Sully could have moved aside, leaving Tony to sail past him and thump his way to the bottom of the landing. But instead of falling, Tony was on Sully's broad back like they were playing "Johnny-on-the-Pony." Sully shook him off just as easily as if he were a kid. Unable to stand any longer, Tony slid to the filthy linoleum with his head lolling. "Do me a favor," Sully instructed. "Don't mess with me."

He took Tony by the hair, which felt unwashed, and lifted him to his feet so that Tony was now leaning against the chipped, ancient wainscoting. Sully's massive hand crashed into the wall beside the drunk's face, raining plaster and paint chips onto Tony's shoulders and the already litter-filled ground. So forceful was Sully's punch that his fist stuck in the wall. He had to work his hand out of the plaster before he could leave.

But Sully paid no mind to his bloodied knuckles and broken skin. He'd had worse. He'd done worse. He didn't even look back as he made his way down the steps, hearing Denise open the apartment door, screech in horror and clatter to Tony's side in her high-heeled slippers.

27 Call It Sleep

Kewpie couldn't remember a time when she had slept so soundly. At least not since she was a child. Instead of waking with a start, she eased into consciousness, vaguely aware of the tapestry of sound around her, the familiar pattern of noise that wove through her world. The soft patter of Bridget banging about the kitchen, running tap water for the percolator, retrieving the (now three) coffee cups from their hooks on the wall above the sink, shuffling about in comfortably-worn house slippers and humming softly as she did so. Tiger and Poppa were already dressed and up and in the alleyway beside the room where Kewpie slept, polishing the Nash to a gleam before the sun grew too strong.

And then there were the voices of the birds. People might not think of birds when they thought of Brooklyn, but in truth, it was something of a haven. Prospect Park nearby was in the midst of a migratory path, a vast swatch of green with an inviting lake, much more welcoming than the verdant stripe down Manhattan's middle known as Central Park. Kewpie liked to think of Prospect

Park as Central Park's prettier, littler but much more approachable younger sister, a Cinderella of sorts. Prospect Park served as the entire borough's backyard, not three miles from Kewpie's own little square of garden as the crow flies.

And speaking of crows, Kewpie was familiar with them as well. Even with her eyelids still closed against the morning light, she could distinguish between the deep-throated caw of a crow and the hollow screech of a blue jay, the chatter of a mosaic-feathered starling and the melodic song of the cardinal. Uncle John had taught her the subtle differences. A city boy, he had done a good deal of traveling overseas and had all sorts of useless tidbits to share. Kewpie figured he'd seen some terrible things in the War, but never dared ask, so to balance things out, he took on gentle hobbies like bird-watching and stargazing.

Bridget's sewing room, which now doubled as Kewpie's bedroom, was directly below the one she usually shared with Tiger. When it became clear that Tony intended to come and go as he pleased, Kewpie and her grandmother wheeled the Castro from the alcove into Bridget's sanctuary, squeezing it through two doorways, pushing the sewing table into a corner and clearing a few drawers for Kewpie in the dresser Bridget used to store fabrics. Late at night, Kewpie liked to imagine that she heard Tiger breathing, his mouth slightly open, lost in a deep slumber. But in reality, she couldn't hear him at all. However, the thought was a reassurance to her.

Bridget and Poppa's room lay beneath her mother and father's. Although she could occasionally hear a weighty, clumsy footfall, Kewpie couldn't discern much more. Sometimes her father's voice, harsh and slightly raised, sifted down through the floorboards. He hadn't been home for two nights running which meant he would probably return tonight. There was a lazy pattern to his appearances which Kewpie had begun to notice and dread, and probably the rest of the family took note as well.

Slipping on her robe, Kewpie decided that she would ask Tiger to accompany her to the Garden tonight. Her treat. Maybe she could convince him to forego his and Poppa's nightly Pinochle game.

The Garden was an open-air movie theatre which she and Tiger both loved. It occupied a usually-empty lot briefly in the summer months, disappearing suddenly like a mirage come September and resurfacing just as abruptly come July. There was a certain novelty to sitting on a long, wooden bench, waiting for the sky to fully darken and watching a movie al fresco with your neighbors. Women would go there with baby buggies, grab a seat at the end of a plank and pray the child wouldn't wake, jiggling the carriage furiously whenever Errol Flynn or Cary Grant came onscreen. But invariably, an infant would wail and then another. There would be a sea of shushes, then laughter. You were bound to miss large chunks of dialogue but then again that was part of the Garden's charm.

Wherever they went, Kewpie knew she would see Augie, who had the habit of appearing out of thin air and mooning at her no matter where she was. But even seeing Augie was better than seeing him. Him being her father.

Kewpie joined her grandmother in the kitchen. Rosanna was sitting at the table, looking gloomy and grave as usual. The girl greeted her mother, but not warmly. She still blamed Rosanna for most of what had happened, for what her mother no doubt suspected but never acted upon, for what she didn't do or couldn't do. But Kewpie was softening, especially at seeing Rosanna's worried, furrowed brow. The girl kissed her mother and grandmother good morning and smiled. They both smelled the same, like years of cooking and Kirkman's soap.

Bridget was at the stove, her usual post, stirring something sweet and savory in a pot. The pleasant scent permeated the air. "It's still warm, I think," she said, grabbing the coffee pot. Bridget poured only a half cup into Kewpie's beige earthenware mug.

"Aw, Grandma…" Kewpie began protesting.

"Tut-tut-tut," Bridget responded. "A *caffe latte* for you. Only half coffee. You're still growing."

"Your grandmother's right," Rosanna added, topping off the thick, brown liquid with white foam from the pot of milk simmering on the stove. Kewpie reached for Dish Night's white genie's slipper sugar bowl. "And not too much sugar," Rosanna reminded her. Kewpie rolled her eyes but only heaped one teaspoonful into the cup.

From all their years of cooking together, her grandmother and mother's movements in the kitchen were perfectly synchronized and wordless. It was lovely to watch the way they wove in and out of each other's path, handing off an implement one might need, locating a spice or finishing chopping up the garlic the moment the other's recipe called for it. They moved like poetry. Kewpie wondered if she and her own mother might someday work together so effortlessly and somehow doubted it.

Kewpie took a sip of her milky coffee. Rosanna placed a clean dishtowel on the table and lined up eight Pyrex cups. Bridget turned from the stove, carrying the heavy, battered pot—her favorite pudding-making pot—with both hands. She ladled a generous scoopful of rice pudding into the glass cups. Kewpie could see each small bowl dotted with raisins, fresh chopped apples and speckled with cinnamon. "The milk was ready to turn," Bridget explained, as though making rice pudding needed an explanation. She was going to add more pudding to each cup when she noticed Kewpie's wide, hungry gaze upon her. Bridget smiled as she handed Kewpie the pot and the wooden spoon. "Careful," she said. "It's very hot."

This was Kewpie's favorite breakfast. Well, actually, it was a toss-up between warm rice pudding and a plump, steamy meatball fished from a Sunday gravy simmering on the stove. But today, rice pudding was her favorite since it was there. She blew on the spoon before licking it then let the pudding ooze down her throat without even chewing. Sweet, textured, thick and satisfying, it was even better than the cardboard goodness of a Communion wafer slipping into an empty belly.

The cups had to cool on the kitchen table before they went into the icebox. Rice pudding was to be tonight's dessert, if it lasted that long. Harry might slip in from his beat, peer into the depths of the icebox, and that would be that. When the Pyrex cups stopped steaming, Bridget jigsawed them into the Sears and Roebuck. She hid them behind a carton of eggs so they'd be safe until suppertime. Bridget often had to chase her son-in-law away with a spatula if he discovered the puddings beforehand, but always in good-humored jest. That's another thing that made Bridget laugh so hard she'd stop dead in her tracks and hold her belly until the waves of hysterics subsided.

The rice pudding done and the pot soaking in the sink, Bridget brought Poppa and Tiger two tall glasses of lemonade. They welcomed the cool drink, and her. From the side window, the two remaining women in the kitchen watched Bridget O'Flynn get a hug around the waist from Poppa. They heard her praise Tiger's car-waxing technique and his rippling muscles.

Both Kewpie and Rosanna smiled as they listened to the exchange, then gazed at each other, their grins slowly fading. They sipped coffee in silence until Rosanna broke it. "I'm sorry," she said simply.

"For what?" Kewpie asked. She wasn't going to make this easy.

"You know what for," Rosanna said to a cup of rice pudding. Then after some consideration, she added, "About him. About everything."

Kewpie shrugged. She wasn't going to say it was all right because it wasn't. Not hardly. But she didn't want her mother to fester with regret either. "There isn't much you can do," the girl finally admitted.

"Sure there is," Rosanna told her daughter, looking up. Kewpie always thought her mother's eyes were a deep, inky brown but when you examined them up close, they were reddish, tinged with bronze, the shade of milk chocolate in the sunlight. They would have been nice eyes if they weren't so weary. "A mother is supposed to protect her children, no matter what," Rosanna said. "Your brother told me that."

Kewpie shook her head. "Oh, Ma. You can't even protect yourself from him. How can you protect us?"

Rosanna opened her mouth to respond but nothing would come out. "Besides," her daughter added. "Women are trapped. They have to depend on a man for everything. But not me. I'll be different."

"I hope so," Rosanna said quietly.

Tiger ran into the kitchen, smelling lemony and waxy, showing off a shiny, new quarter. "Pa..." Rosanna began to complain as her father appeared in the doorway.

"He earned it," Poppa told her. "He earned it fair and square."

Bridget insisted that she had more than enough for the Martinos to join the Paradisos for supper downstairs. It was an indoor picnic, with fried chicken made earlier in the day, velvety macaroni salad and another salad of tomatoes from Mrs. Lieberwitz's garden, tossed with olive oil, a splash of vinegar, sliced black olives and fresh basil, also from the Lieberwitz plot. Kewpie refrained from the fried chicken but enjoyed everything else.

Afterwards, Poppa leaned back in his chair, patting his full belly with satisfaction, and Bridget noted this with pride. Miraculously, all eight rice puddings survived till suppertime and after a breather, the five diners heartily enjoyed them. The remaining three would wait patiently for Harry and Sully, who, as if possessing a sixth sense, would magically appear an hour later and unexplainably gravitate toward the icebox. Then they would arm-wrestle to see who'd get the last one.

Stuffed as they were, it still wouldn't prevent Tiger and Kewpie from sharing a tub of buttery popcorn at the Garden. There was no need for Rosanna to send them off with a packed lunch as she did for an afternoon matinee at the Elton, which consisted of two cartoons, a serial, a newsreel and a movie. The sun was already setting so the children hurried along, anxious to get good seats as far away from baby buggies as possible. "Come on," Kewpie told Tiger, towing him. "I hear it's a good one."

As most girls did, Kewpie liked Shirley Temple, or Shirley Pimple, as Poppa called her. It probably had something to do with her amazing profusion of curls. But Tiger had little appreciation for the child star or her namby-pamby movies, their neatly sewn-up plots with infinitely happy endings. Even at ten and a half now, Tiger knew life wasn't like that. It wasn't always neat or happy. Orphans, no matter how adorable or cheerful, didn't always get rescued by clandestine relatives. Butlers and stable boys didn't ever sing and dance with their young charges. Gangsters weren't always kindly when they won a kid in a bet.

You couldn't always teach crippled cousins how to walk, no matter how earnest your intentions—Tiger heard that Shirley Pimple was currently filming *Heidi*. But still, a free movie was a free movie.

Kewpie held Tiger's hand as they made their way down the street and he didn't mind one bit. He missed his sister even though she was just living downstairs. He missed their sleepy nighttime conversations, their tired words flung out into the safe darkness of their once-shared room. He missed the comfort of hearing her breathing a few feet across the room, of seeing the yellow moonlight slashed across her face, making it even prettier. Prettier even than Carole Lombard, he thought. But Tiger didn't miss Kewpie's pouty sadness or her stubborn silence, which seemed to have passed with the move to Poppa and Grandma Bridget's. And he figured it was better that way.

Tiger didn't even wipe away Kewpie's kiss, when, for no reason at all, she gave him a peck on the cheek as they paused to cross the street. His hand tightened around hers of its own accord when they passed the haunted house belonging to Jeremy Flynn on the corner of 47th Street. It was said that Old Man Flynn had a big cauldron boiling away in the basement even in the summer. Half of his windows were boarded up and tattered curtains streamed from the other half. His front steps were broken and there was always a chained mastiff behind his pitted wrought iron fence. Even the postman didn't set foot beyond it, just slipped letters between the fence's slats so that the mail piled up on the brown lawn.

Jeremy Flynn didn't like kids; he didn't like anyone, especially Italians. Tiger felt a chill as he and Kewpie rushed past and Evil Eye Flynn took him apart with his one good eye. The other was clouded with a blue film. The teeth in his awful mouth were either missing or broken. "Summer teeth," the kids called them—as in, "Some are here, some are there." Frankenstein Flynn's voice, like a rusty gate, creaked out, "Skinny Guineas with ravioli eyes." Raven the dog barked furiously, threatening to snap his chain in two. Kewpie and Tiger broke into a rushed canter, narrowly escaping the scalding cauldron in the Flynn Chamber of Horrors and were soon safely across the street.

People were already starting to fill the benches of the Garden. It was really just a vacant lot in the daylight. But nighttime transformed it into something delightful. Colored Christmas lights were strung from pole to pole. Uniformed ushers helped you to your seat with lanterns and flashlights. So far, the ever industrious Augie, who worked at both the Loews 46th and the Garden, was nowhere to be seen but Kewpie expected him to materialize at any moment.

Kewpie permitted Tiger to buy them a small popcorn to share with part of the quarter Poppa had given him earlier. He surprised her by slipping a box of nonpareils into her hand as well. She smiled in the dim light, thanking him. "I'm putting the rest into the Kirkman's lady," he whispered to Kewpie. She nodded in approval.

A few blocks away, Rosanna sat at the kitchen table, a cup of tea steaming beside her. (She was of the staunch belief that boiling liquids consumed in hot weather kept you cool.) Halfway through *Gone with the Wind*, she turned the pages as quickly as she could. She read:

"Then, sudden terror struck her and her rage melted..."

Rosanna thought she heard something, a soft creak on the stairs, but it was probably just a combination of the old house settling and the suspense of the book, which Rosanna liked a great deal, and not just because Scarlett O'Hara was having a tougher time than she. Rosanna turned the page.

"She closed the door and leaned against it and she was very frightened. More frightened even than she had been that day when Sherman's army was in the house. That day the worst she could fear was..."

The door burst open. Rosanna jumped. The kids home early from the movies? Her heart dropped when she saw that it was Tony. He lurched in the doorway then shut the door quietly behind him and turned the latch, locking it.

"You scare easy," he told her. "Always did."

"I wasn't expecting anyone," Rosanna said, closing the book and laying it on the table.

"Where are the kids?" he asked.

"Should be home any minute," she lied.

"I thought you said you weren't expecting anyone," Tony reminded her. He took a few steps closer until he was at the edge of the kitchen table. "They're at the movies. I saw them go into the Garden."

Rosanna pushed the book an inch along the oilcloth. "You can't just keep coming and going as you please. You didn't come home for two nights and now..."

"Why can't I do whatever the fuck I want?" Tony challenged.

Rosanna folded her hands in her lap and held onto them so that he couldn't see them shaking. "And what do you want, Tony?" she wondered. She tried to control the tremble in her voice but it was no use.

Tony's head jerked to the side at a jaunty angle that told Rosanna she was in trouble. He assumed this posture whenever he was extremely agitated. She tried to brace herself for the worst. "What do I want?" he snarled. "To come and go as I please, for one thing. It's my fucking house."

Tony came a step closer to Rosanna so that their feet were almost touching. Not knowing what else to do, Rosanna stood up. To flee or fight, she wasn't sure which. She studied the linoleum and noticed a few crumbs over by the stove. She'd have to do a quick sweep later. Rosanna knew that she couldn't avoid looking at Tony forever and finally raised her eyes to meet his, which were narrow slits and without one shred of kindness in them. They sparked with something dangerous. The glowing green orbs flecked with gold that she'd lately come to fear and hate, yet once loved, were much like her son's, but lacking Tiger's innocence. Tony's were bloodshot, the whites sewn with painful threads of red.

Tony and Rosanna stared at each other. In another time, another place, they might have appeared, to an unknowing observer, to be a couple on a polished wooden dance floor, on the verge of taking a swirl to "Pennies from Heaven" or even "Secondhand Rose." But instead of grasping his wife lightly in his arms and moving as one, Tony punched Rosanna. Hard. In the gut. Rosanna held her stomach and doubled over. She fell to the kitchen floor. Astrid's copy of *Gone with the Wind* teetered off the edge of the table and fell beside her. Sitting in the backyard, enjoying the mild evening, Bridget and Poppa heard nothing.

At first, Tony observed his wife with no remorse but then he saw the blood pooling beneath her body. It stained her cotton housedress and seemed to be coming from between her legs. Did he really punch her that hard? His drunken mind reeled. He unlocked the door then ran down the stairs, calling for her parents.

At the Garden, Shirley Temple had just been rescued from a storm at sea by Guy Kibbee. Though the lovable moppet had lost her parents, she still managed to hang onto her curl. Tiger didn't like Guy Kibbee. The old rummy had made an appearance at the Loews 46th a few years back. The management had to escort him from the bar on the corner to the stage to wave shakily at the audience. Tiger remembered this clearly even though he was quite young at the time. He remembered because Tony had staggered home that night, bragging about who he'd been drinking with the entire afternoon. Tony figured he was one hell of a drunk if he could drink a famous Hollywood actor under the table, and was extremely proud of this fact.

A flashlight blinded Kewpie and Tiger for a moment, settling on their faces then going dark. "Kewpie," Augie's voice said with an urgency. "You and Tiger have to come with me. There's been an accident."

Although they never did see the end of *Captain January*, Tiger could just imagine how it ended. Happy.

28 Lucky

"All I can say is that she's very lucky," Dr. Schantz told them. "She's lucky you came in and found her when you did, Mr. Martino," he added, gesturing toward Tony, whose eyes were puffed with crocodile tears.

Dr. Lewis stood at the specialist's side, looking ominous and concerned. "I told her it needed to be taken care of, and soon," he said, his voice tinged with Yiddish drama. "We were very fortunate that Dr. Schantz was already here delivering a baby, or there's no telling what might have happened."

"Rosanna is a strong, young woman. She should bounce back in no time," Dr. Schantz added. "It's a shame we had to do a hysterectomy at her age, but it was our only option. She lost a lot of blood but..."

Dr. Schantz looked out into the sea of Paradisos before him and noticed that two of the sisters and all of the brothers-in-law, plus that big cop, had bandages on their arms to mark where they'd given blood. This way, Rosanna wouldn't be charged for the pints she required. That very thought—the fact that they could help her in this crucial situation—consoled each of them, even Astrid.

Bridget and Poppa were too old to donate. Tony didn't even step forward; it was obvious he was inebriated. And after Jo went into a small room and spoke briefly with the nurse, it was announced that she couldn't give blood because she was anemic. "Low iron, my foot," was Astrid's response. Astrid herself had fainted with quiet hysterics after they took the needle from her arm. But at least they'd gotten a full pint out of her before her performance and they were able to use her blood just the same.

Rosanna could hear a smattering of conversation from the hallway outside her room as she drifted in and out of a delicious haze. She was in a ward of four beds at United Israel-Zion Hospital on 10th Avenue and 48th Street, which was a only few blocks away from the house. "A good Jew hospital," Tony liked to say. "Them Jews insist on the best of everything. After all, they're God's chosen people, and we're just pieces of Christian shit."

Rosanna lay between two crisp white bed sheets, like a slice of luncheon meat in a sandwich, she imagined. Picturing the bed as Wonder Bread and herself as a thick slice of liverwurst, she chuckled. When was the last time she had giggled like a schoolgirl? Possibly the last time she'd been zooted up on morphine. When Anthony, Jr. was born. Different place, different decade. At Methodist Episcopal, they'd yanked him out with forceps and he had two black eyes to show for it. When her daughter first laid eyes on Junior, Kewpie cried and locked herself in the bathroom because he wasn't the fluffy, pink baby sister she'd been wishing for. Tiger came out scowling, looking like a losing prizefighter instead of a newborn, a chip on his shoulder and mad at the world from Day One. At least his attitude had changed since then but his life hadn't.

Rosanna didn't remember much about what had happened earlier, just Tony surprising her in the kitchen then waking up in the iron hospital bed. Her belly still hurt but it hurt in a different way. Dr. Schantz explained to her why. He said the emergency surgery had been a success and that she was very fortunate indeed. There was a tube of amber liquid going into one arm and another that disappeared between her legs. A bag of dark, cloudy pee was strapped to the bedrail. Hers. She didn't want the children to see her like this but then again, she knew they'd probably seen worse.

Watching the fans whirl around on the ceiling made her tired, made her eyes feel weighted from the very effort of keeping them open. But she wasn't sleeping, only thinking in a half-dream. What would happen to her now? To all of them?

When her sister Jo peeked in, Rosanna's eyes were shut and she seemed to be resting, so Jo left. The Paradiso coalition stayed out in the hall but elected Jo to go and rescue the children. Earlier, John had been sent to the waiting room to let them know that everything was all right and he was still there, no doubt regaling them with horrific stories from his childhood. But in some strange way, Tiger found his uncle's tales of woe reassuring, for the man's past was far more terrible than his own present. And Uncle John turned out okay, didn't he?

When Jo rounded the corner and caught a glimpse of her niece and nephew's glazed expressions, she knew John was up to his old tricks. "...and in the winter," he said, "we didn't even have gloves, that's how poor we were. We had to wear socks on our hands."

"Dirty ones or clean ones?" Tiger wondered.

"Clean if we had 'em but usually not," John answered. "We never missed a day of school in the cold weather. At least the classrooms were warm, warmer than our apartment. We lived in a cold-water flat, you know."

"We know, we know," Kewpie and Tiger said in unison.

Jo stood behind them, trying to get her brother-in-law's attention but John kept talking, undaunted. "If the lunch lady liked you and knew you lived nearby, she'd tell you to run home and get a pot with a cover," he continued. "She'd fill it with the leftover soup so at least you'd have dinner that night."

"But how could you eat soup with socks on your hands?" Tiger worried. "How could you even hold a spoon?"

John sighed. "We'd take off the socks once we got to school, kid."

Jo tried to break in but John had regained momentum. "And did I ever tell you that I never had three meals a day until I joined the Army?"

"You did," Kewpie said. "Or a new suit of clothes. We remember."

Jo put her hand lightly on John's shoulder. "You kids are lucky. You have it pretty good," he told them. Kewpie glanced at her aunt briefly, as if to say, he has no idea, and neither do you. Then the girl turned away.

At last their uncle released the children from his sad stories. John went back to the others while Jo sat on a hard chair beside Tiger. It was past two in the morning and the poor child was beat. Tiger put his head on his aunt's shoulder. "You two should go home," she said once again.

"Not until we see her," Kewpie told her aunt firmly.

Jo reached for Kewpie's hand across the space that separated them and squeezed it reassuringly. "She's fine, I swear. She's weak and woozy but she's fine."

"We still want to see her," the girl insisted. "We'll just wait until we can." Kewpie was concerned for her mother but she was also afraid to go home. Her father might insist she spend the night upstairs considering the circumstances and her grandparents might be too exhausted or upset to argue.

Augie returned with a stack of comic books for Tiger and some movie magazines for Kewpie. "Sorry I took so long," he said. "Nobody was open. I had to go way down to 36th Street."

"You didn't have to," Kewpie said, accepting the magazines with gratitude.

"I know I didn't," Augie told her. "But I did."

His hand lightly brushed hers then hung useless at his side. Tiger thanked Augie then dove into *New Fun Comics*. He flipped the pages until he found "Doctor Occult." Kewpie added, "You really didn't have to leave work either."

Augie shrugged. "Mr. Acerno said I should make sure you both got here safe."

"Well, we're here all right," Kewpie said sharply, then smiled.

"He said he'd pay me till 11, if that's what's worrying you," Augie told her.

"But it's after two," Kewpie pointed out.

"I can tell time, thanks," Augie reminded Kewpie.

Jo and Tiger watched the repartee like a tennis match or a snappy "Nick and Nora" dialogue, except with Brooklynese accents instead of the screen couple's stylish tones. Although Tiger preferred William Powell and Myrna Loy, this was entertaining just the same. Jo tried to suppress a grin but failed. She thought that any love, especially young love, was grand.

Augie finally took a seat beside Kewpie, who pretended to be immersed in an article about Frances Farmer, "The New Garbo." Kewpie smirked as her would-be beau carefully positioned his arm across the back of her chair, mindful not to touch her. Augie smiled, too. Kewpie liked the way he stood up to her, not in a mean way but holding his own. And Augie, he liked her spicy yet sweet manner as well. There was something special about a girl who could whistle through her teeth and was a champ at stoop ball.

So, Kewpie dug into her movie magazines and Tiger paged through *Tip Top Comics*, catching up on "Terry and the Pirates."

Jo noted that the kids clearly wouldn't budge. She stood and smoothed down her skirt, which was tighter than Tiger ever remembered it. "I'll see what I can do," she told them before she disappeared toward Rosanna's ward.

Five minutes later, the children were standing outside their mother's hospital room. Dr. Lewis was counting off a list of do's and don'ts on his stubby fingers. "Don't talk too much," he began. "Don't cry. Don't say anything to upset her. Tell her something nice then leave. *Nu*? She's been through a lot and she's very tired. Two minutes, not a second more." Then he gave them each a pat on the bottom and sent them on their way. "You know, Dr. Lewis brought you into this world," the good physician reminded them, much like Uncle John liked to remind them about his sock-mittens from time to time. It seemed to offer him solace of some sort.

The children weren't prepared for what they saw in the fourth bed of the long, narrow hospital ward. First, it smelled odd. Clean and sterile, yet dirty at the same time. Like illness, murky fluids and fear. Aunt Jo led them to a small, pale woman swaddled under the sheets, hooked to bottles and tubes. It took both of them a moment to realize that this woman, as colorless and substanceless as wax, was their mother. There was a large bruise on the side of her face where she had fallen. Her hair was feathered against the pillow, a tired brown mixed with wires of gray. She looked old and not really alive.

Tiger began to sniffle. Kewpie gave him a tiny nudge and emphatically told him, "No," between her clenched teeth. Immediately, he stopped. "Brave soldiers don't cry," she whispered. Tiger wiped his nose on the back of his hand and swallowed down his bitter tears.

Their mother's eyes were closed but when she sensed a presence, the lids fluttered open for a moment, then drifted shut again. It seemed a difficult chore to keep them unglued but she managed. "Ma," was all Kewpie could think to say. Then she took hold of Rosanna's fingers, the ones in the hand without all the tubes. The hand was cold.

"Angela," she said through dry lips. "Where's Anthony?"

"Here, Ma," Tiger said, stepping up. He squeezed himself between the bed rail and his sister.

"I'm okay," she assured them. "I'm really okay." She licked her parched lips. "Must look worse than *The Bride of Frankenstein*, though."

Tiger considered his mother for a moment and then concluded, "You're hair's not as scary." Kewpie gave him another nudge but he ignored her. "And no electrodes."

Rosanna managed a weak smile. "I'm all right so you can go home now and try to get some sleep." They obeyed. First, Kewpie leaned down to kiss her mother on the forehead. Tiger couldn't reach. He began to climb up the bed rails but Rosanna winced, so Kewpie lifted him. He was skin and bones but wiry and alive. Rosanna's cracked lips curled into a half smile.

"See you tomorrow," Jo said, squeezing her sister's shoulder. She turned to follow the children but Rosanna's hand shot up and latched onto her wrist. She pulled Jo closer so that her ear was level with Rosanna's mouth.

"Don't," Rosanna's voice crackled.

"Don't what?" Jo asked.

Rosanna took a deep breath. "Don't let him get his hooks in them." A lone tear slid down the crease of one eye.

Jo was startled. "What do you mean?"

"Don't leave them alone with him," she heaved. "I'm afraid I might never see them again. I'm afraid..."

Jo smoothed down Rosanna's hair. Minute electrical sparks met her hand and the thin strands stood up to meet it. "I don't want you to be afraid of anything," Jo told her favorite sister. "I just want you to get well."

Rosanna bit down on her lower lip. Her body began to heave with silent weeping. It hurt to cry but she just didn't have the strength to hold back the tears anymore. "Harry and I will take care of them," Jo assured her. "We'll take care of them until you come home. Promise."

The small, gray woman nodded, comforted for the moment. Jo brushed her sister's hair with her fingertips until her breathing became deep and regular, like a slumbering child's. Only then did she go out to join the others.

By the time Jo reached the waiting area, Tony was belligerent, insisting that he see his wife. The liquor was wearing off and he was beginning to feel poorly. "No," Jo told him firmly, so firmly that it startled even her husband. She puffed out her chest slightly, like a brazen pigeon. "And the kids are coming home with us," she added. "It'll be easier that way. You won't have to worry about them with work and all."

Tony grimaced, wondering if she knew he still had three days left on his suspension and was just being a smart aleck. But he didn't say anything more, didn't even put up a fight. With bravado of booze fading, Tony knew how lucky he'd already been that night and he didn't want to press his good fortune. He was also concerned that Rosanna might have said something to Jo about how he'd delivered that devastating punch, but didn't think his wife would dare.

The night nurse, passing by with an empty enamel bed pan, noticed that something was amiss in this family encounter. Tony stood on one side of the wide hallway while everyone else was on the other. He was clearly the outsider, clearly not one of them.

Tony saw the nurse's disapproving glance and scowled. It had been that way his whole life. Us and them. The haves and have nots. Even with his own people, blood relatives, wherever the hell they were now. If any of them were still alive. And who really gave a damn about them anyhow. He sure didn't, except for his brother Tommy. But that's only because Tommy was half a retard, and he worked in a bar, which was handy.

As the rest of the Paradiso Family convened to take the short walk home together and then disburse like seeds to the wind, Tony headed toward the El at 45th Street and Fort Hamilton Parkway.

Alone.

29 *Chachkas*

Aunt Jo's home was different than Tiger's in many ways. The first, most obvious to the boy was the presence of *chachkas*. Doodads, knick-knacks, as they were called in less-ethnic households. In other words, there was a lot of stuff here and there and all over the furniture. For example, there were crocheted doilies on end tables and under plants. The fact that there were plants to begin with was another striking difference. Aunt Jo had a way of making things thrive, all except for babies.

While Bridget prided herself on her green thumb and had ivy pouring out of flower pots suspended from wall hooks, plus snake plants reaching ceiling-ward from heavy ceramic tubs on the floor, all of her daughters except for Josephina possessed what she liked to call a black thumb. Camille worked full-time so she didn't have time or patience for such flimsy things as flowers. Astrid didn't have patience for anything but herself. And whenever Bridget gave Rosanna a rooted clipping from her strongest, best stock, it died within days. 'Must be the alcohol in the air,' Bridget thought to herself. 'Must be the poison atmosphere,' Rosanna muttered under her breath, tossing yet another brown, withered stem into the dustbin.

As for the *chachkas*, they were everywhere, on practically every available surface in Aunt Jo's home: a ceramic flamingo from Florida, a shimmering crystal cascade from Niagara Falls, a cut-glass lighter and matching ashtray—a classy wedding gift from Tiffany's, an Arizonan burro from Kelly and Co. that held a temperamental cactus. And photographs. Picture frames a myriad of sizes of various family members, even those they didn't like, including Astrid, who, of course, complained about the quality of the print and the sternness of her expression. She hated it because it was B.N.J.—Before Nose Job. But Tiger thought it was a pretty good likeness, despite the old *schnozzola*. It captured her birdlike intensity to a T.

There was also a piano in the apartment, even though neither Aunt Jo nor Uncle Harry played. But he'd gotten it cheap when the Finkelsteins were moving to Massapequa and both he and Aunt Jo hoped their child, if they ever had one, would someday learn to play. Tiger pecked out "My Mother Went to Germany" on the black keys with the pointer fingers of each hand. He sang along with each note:

> *"My mother went to Germany.*
> *My father went to France.*
> *My sister went to Macy's*
> *To buy a pair of pants..."*

"Didn't know you could play," Aunt Jo said to her nephew, smiling. She had two glasses of milk and a plate of cookies on a tray.

"My father taught me on a bar piano one day," Tiger told her.

"You shouldn't be hanging around in bars, Anthony," she reminded him.

"I had to use the bathroom," he insisted. "I had a ginger ale and he had a glass of beer. Just one. I swear."

"No need to swear. I believe you," she said, then put the tray on the coffee table.

It was the first time they'd mentioned his father in a week. The man hadn't tried to visit Tiger or Kewpie once, which was fine with Jo but she could see that it bothered the boy. (Tony hadn't been to visit his wife one single time either.) Jo did her best to make the kids comfortable. They were set up in the baby's room on two thick-mattressed cots borrowed from the Lieberwitzs. The crib had been hastily dismantled and stowed behind a large bureau before Jo got out of the hospital after losing the child that spring. Harry had taken it apart, angry and sobbing, the second he'd come home, empty-handed and broken-hearted, on the night their little girl was born dead.

Tiger claimed he didn't mind the childish yellow paint on the walls or the teddy-bear stencils, which Aunt Jo had done herself. He thought the pretty room even smelled of baby, smelled clean and sweet, but he didn't tell his aunt because he didn't want to upset her. She was looking so rosy-cheeked and jolly these days.

When Aunt Astrid told her how big her caboose was getting, Aunt Jo grinned evilly and said that no matter how big it got, it still wouldn't be bigger than Aunt Astrid's trap, which she should kindly keep shut, please. Tiger recalled this terse conversation, which was almost as animated as Fibber McGee and Molly on the radio, and smiled. Aunt Astrid was a fine version of the braggart Fibber and Aunt Jo was the sympathetic, patient Molly McGee.

Tiger was now playing with his lead soldiers atop the girly-colored rag rug on the floor in the nursery, the fighters' worn black and gray bodies contrasting nicely against the carpet's pastel swirls. The night of his mother's accident, his aunt and uncle had Tiger and Kewpie each pack a suitcase of clothing. They also let Tiger take as many toys as he wanted. He just took a bat, a ball, his weathered baseball mitt and the soldiers. That's all he needed.

The O'Leary apartment was in a regal two-story limestone down 44th Street. It wasn't a railroad flat like the Martinos'. Only three blocks from the El, you couldn't hear its call, even in the pin-drop silence of midnight. To reach their digs, first you had to climb a tall, stone staircase of a dozen steps which led to wide, wood and glass double doors covered with lace curtains that came all the way from Ireland. Until just recently, the house had been owned by a relative of Harry's from Dublin, an unmarried stonemason who was a bit stone-faced himself. Cousin Dermot missed the Mother Country and abruptly decided to move back, selling Harry and Jo the house at a fair price.

Jo kept the place spic and span. Cousin Dermot's mother, God rest her soul, had sent the lacy curtains years ago, as well as a few fancy tablecloths, which she found locked in a cupboard after Dermot moved back to Ireland. Jo promptly hung up the curtains and used the tablecloths every day, scrubbing out stains vigorously by hand with a spritz of seltzer. "What's the point of having nice things if you never use them?" she reasoned. A churchgoer but not much of a Bible quoter, as many Catholics are, Jo added, "Besides, remember what the Good Book says about not hiding your light under a bushel basket?" And she was right, there was no point in keeping those lovely linens sealed in a breakfront drawer at all.

Harry and Jo rented out the ground floor apartment to a radiologist and his wife. The O'Learys had the top floor to themselves, which was up another set of stairs. The rooms were large and airy with high ceilings. The floors were of polished oak and there was ornate woodwork framing the doorways. Between the living room and dining room were a set of pocket doors, which Jo always kept flung open wide to let in the flood of sunlight. But when shut, the glass displayed a stunning pattern of rosettes and tulips, a beautiful surprise on the rare occasions they were closed.

Chachkas. There were even chachkas in Jo's the kitchen—an Aunt Jemima salt and pepper shaker, the Kirkman's soap washerwoman and a Kirkman's Chinaman, too. (They named him Mr. Wong.) The kitchen floor itself was tiled, not covered with linoleum. Tiger loved its complicated checkerboard pattern of small black and white squares. He often thought of trying to play checkers on it, and told Aunt Jo, who laughed as she stirred a tremendous pot of corned beef, cabbage, potatoes and carrots. To Tiger, their dinner smelled like a humongous fart but he didn't say this out loud. And anyway, it tasted delicious, especially with the tender meat cushioned between two squishy slices of fresh rye bread, slathered with mustard and a crunchy half sour pickle on the side. Earlier that day, Aunt Jo had sent Tiger to the pickleman on his own to get a tub of half sours and another container of dills. He returned in one piece and with a handful of change, which she let him keep.

His aunt and uncle's apartment was midway between the United Israel and Poppa and Grandma Bridget's place. Tiger visited his grandparents every day, sometimes twice. It took some convincing to get Aunt Jo's permission to let him go there alone, crossing the busy two-way streets without her by his side and clutching his hand for dear life, but she finally relented. He promised to be cautious and to look both ways, even when crossing one-way streets. When Tiger first arrived, Aunt Jo tended to mollycoddle him but with his gentle guidance, she was coming along nicely. She didn't know what it was like to have kids, big or little. The boy gave her some time to get her sea legs for when her own children came along and she was doing swell.

Tiger didn't go out to play much. He didn't like to leave Aunt Jo alone, though she didn't seem to mind. However, when Uncle Harry worked nights and was around during the day, Tiger would go off adventuring. His uncle didn't sleep nearly as much as his dad did and was far more cheerful. He sensed that his aunt and uncle actually enjoyed being alone together, even relished it, so Tiger would go off to see what Jimmy Burns was up to or play stickball with the guys in the schoolyard when Uncle Harry was home.

Aunt Jo didn't like Tiger playing ball between manhole covers in the street, though. It was dangerous, she said. Uncle Harry agreed, telling them an awful story about a kid in Sunset Park who was running backwards to catch a high pop and was mowed down by a bread truck. They had to scrape him off the asphalt and off the truck's front fender. The very thought made Tiger shudder, so he had no problem complying with his aunt and uncle's very reasonable request. That's why he only played stickball in empty lots or in the schoolyard.

When he worked nights, Uncle Harry often came to visit and this always seemed to delight Aunt Jo, seeing him unexpectedly, even if just for a minute or two. It was good to hear his key in the door and to hear his happy whistling in the hall as he bounded up the steps. This was a far cry from the fear and blind sense of dread that went with Tiger's father's arrival, expected or not. And Tony didn't whistle. Not even when he was sober.

Tiger lay awake in the baby's room. Kewpie was out with her friends, at a movie without him. But it was okay. He had no interest in seeing *My Man Godfrey*, even if Carole Lombard was in it. Tiger wondered if Kewpie was at the Loews 46th, the Minerva or someplace else. He hadn't been to the movies since they were yanked out of *Captain January* at the Garden by Augie. Picture shows had lost their charm. Even the allure of Dish Night wasn't enough to bring Tiger there. Although perhaps with a bit of prodding and the promise of popcorn he might reconsider.

A soothing breeze roused the yellow gingham curtains, which Rosanna had made for her sister a year or two earlier. Jo took them down, washed them, ironed them and put them back up again every six months or so. She wanted the room to be ready for the child that wasn't yet ready to come. The cheerful, pleated material fluttered gently and looked nice against the walls that were painted the color of butter. Even though it was dark and Tiger couldn't make it out, he had memorized the pleasant shade. He decided that yellow was a good color for a baby. The kind of color that made you feel warm and safe, even in the dead of winter with snow piling up outside the windowpanes and frost scratching patterns along the glass.

But in the middle of August, shimmering piles of snow would be a welcome change. During the day, the heat seemed to radiate up from the concrete and slate sidewalks. Tiger wondered if you could indeed cook an egg there as people often commented. Sometimes the steam of a Brooklyn summer felt exactly like the blast of heat that came when you opened an oven door to check on a cake. During the hottest parts of the day, Tiger would play indoors with his soldiers. Aunt Jo would let him chomp on chips of ice, which she coaxed from the melting block with a pick. She had to change the pan several times an afternoon, that's how fast it disappeared.

Willie, the iceman's helper, seemed to sense when the chunk had faded to almost nothing, because there he'd be, ringing the doorbell with his right hand while a fresh block of ice was slung over his left shoulder, held fast with a steel clamp, dripping despite the damp towel wrapped around it, pincers burrowing into the frozen surface like crab claws.

Willie wasn't a big man but he was all muscle and looked tough, even though his eyes were blue as robin's eggs and always smiling. Uncle Harry said that Willie boxed at the Police Athletic League down on 9th Street and that he was pretty good. But it was hard for Tiger to picture this because the iceman was always so polite and seemed so good-natured, even when he took a moment to shadowbox with Tiger after he'd safely sealed the ice into the Sears and Roebuck. But you never could tell about people. They often weren't what they seemed.

Lying in the quiet room, Tiger watched the branches of the ginkgo tree outside the bedroom window paint ever-changing shadows on the walls and ceiling. They were like fans opening and closing, shifting and sifting back and forth, from ceiling to wall, from wall to ceiling, like dreams. It reminded him of watching a silent picture show. Ginkgos were the best leaves of all, he thought, so delicate and Oriental and out of place here. But then again, in Brooklyn, everything seemed to fit and work well together somehow. Tiger loved how thin and soft the ginkgo's fallen leaves were, as diaphanous as Cinderella's lost fan at the ball. But the tree itself was deceptive, massive, gnarled and hardy. It didn't seem to match the leaves at all.

The one thing Tiger didn't like about ginkgo trees were the nuts that dropped from their branches in the autumn. They were yellow-brown and gushy and sometimes burst open into smears that stuck to the sidewalk. And worst of all, they smelled like a combination of dog poop and puke. The neighborhood kids called them "stinkos" because, let's face it, the fallen seeds stunk.

But undaunted by the putrid odor, Chinese folk came from far and wide, perhaps even from China itself, seeking out the finest specimens of ginkgo nuts, bearing paper sacks which they filled with the most choice, unbroken seeds. While Irish and Italian kids ran about with polly-noses on their own snouts—the fallen seeds of maple trees, which resembled wings, when split in two, could be split once more and fastened to one's nose with the gummy maple glue—Asian children dutifully bent beside their parents and grandparents, gathering up their rancid treasures.

Ginkgo seeds made a delicious soup, which was an autumnal delicacy due to the seasonal nature of the main ingredient. Tiger highly doubted this fact until Mr. Wong showed up on their doorstep the October before last with a covered, steaming ceramic bowl of the stuff for Poppa and Grandma Bridget to sample. And Tiger, because he happened to be downstairs, had no choice but to taste it too because he didn't want to hurt Mr. Wong's feelings. He had to try it, they all did, with Mr. Wong looking on expectantly, then nodding with approval when they declared the savory soup delicious, and easily drained their bowls in front of him. After Mr. Wong left, Poppa looked at Tiger and proclaimed, "It's not every day that you get the opportunity to try poop soup." He missed his grandparents.

As the shapes of the ginkgo's triangular leaves teased their way across the bedroom ceiling, Tiger's eyes grew heavy but he still could not sleep. His mind was racing from Kewpie to the movies to Carole Lombard to his father and his own cheap Lombard imitation to his mother lying all alone, pale and colorless in her steel-edged bed. Tiger pictured his own bedroom a few blocks away lying vacant.

Tiger could hear the radio two rooms away as Aunt Jo listened to the Lux Radio Theater and knitted yet another pair of booties. He could even hear the needles clicking together if he concentrated hard enough. Tiger thought about his dead baby cousin Hope. He wondered where they put her and if she had any idea how much her parents loved her and how Aunt Jo still cried for her, some six months later. Jamming a hankie into her mouth to quiet the sound, the boy would hear his aunt weeping softly late at night. But only on the nights Uncle Harry was at work. Sometimes Tiger would see the handkerchief balled up on the floor the next morning, its lace trim still damp.

Did anyone love Tiger so fierce? His mother, maybe. Grandma Bridget, definitely. Aunt Jo, sure. And Poppa, too.

Kewpie, it went without saying, though she would never admit it to his face. But his father? No. Tiger guessed that his father didn't truly love anybody. Not even The Floozy, as Aunt Astrid called her, with a theatrical eye-roll. Tiger figured that his father probably didn't even like himself. Hate was more like it. Maybe that's why he acted the way he did.

The leaf patterns on the ceiling seemed to be waving to Tiger. Hello or good-bye, depending on your point of view. Tiger missed his own bed and his cramped room with low ceilings. The crown molding around the door frames here were nice. So were the plaster floral garlands around the ceiling light fixtures but still, they weren't his. And he missed his mom, too.

Other than that first night, when Tiger had a special dispensation to visit Rosanna in the hospital, they wouldn't let the boy into her room anymore. "No children allowed" was United Israel-Zion's policy. So, he had to make do with waving to his mother from 48th Street while she stood weakly in front of the third floor window and pumped her hand forlornly in return. Tiger didn't know how she ached to cradle his scruffy head against her belly and kiss the top of his overgrown crew cut, smelling the pleasant, sweaty boy smell of him.

Was that even her hunched before the window some 30 feet above, framed in red brick and bright clinical light? Tiger couldn't know for certain. Perhaps it was some other wan, hollow shape, but surely not his mother. Rosanna's skin was always warm to the touch, her hands dry from too much scrubbing. He longed for her comforting Kirkman's meets onions-and-garlic scent, and would have it soon enough. But until then, with one of his aunts or Kewpie holding his hand, Tiger always waved back at the woman in the window, no matter who she was, waved furiously and undaunted.

On the doorstep of sleep, Tiger's mind kept going back to the ginkgos. He thought they were beautiful but most people simply couldn't get past the smell. And what was beauty anyhow? It wasn't just how something looked but how it made you feel inside, Tiger figured. Looking at a ginkgo leaf made him feel strong and hopeful: the frail triangle of the leaf transected by sturdy veins, the knotty tree trunk and roots that went deep into the earth, far below the concrete. This was a tree that could survive, and in fact, flourish, in the tainted city air, in the muggy summers and the bone-chilling winters. No matter what you threw at a ginkgo, it was okay. It could take it and not merely exist but thrive. Kind of like Brooklyn folk.

Tiger knew a lot of people like that, and like the ginkgo, he thought they were beautiful, too. Not in the traditional way. Not like his father's girlfriend, with her unearthly white hair, her ghostly sallow skin and painted-on features. He thought Bridget beautiful, though he was aware that she was a solid woman, perhaps even portly. But to Tiger, the permanent crinkle of too much smiling around her eyes (and he was partly to blame for that), the twists of steel gray, white, silver and black that wound through the tapestry of her hair, her beneficent eyes—even the blind one—was a picture of loveliness.

And Aunt Jo was beautiful, by any definition: smart figure, Cupid's bow lips, glittering green eyes. But to Tiger, it was her kindness that made her so. Something that Aunt Astrid didn't have, never would. The two sisters were of a different heart. Uncle Harry liked to quip, "That broad doesn't have a heart," but Tiger knew it wasn't so. Aunt Astrid's was just encased in a tough wrapper.

Sometimes Tiger's mom was so gruff and harried and disheartened, he didn't think she liked him, let alone loved him. But then there were times when she read to him, or when she slipped him a bag of cookies for no reason at all or when he caught her looking at him with moist eyes as he played with his wooden train on the kitchen windowsill. Those times, he was certain that she loved him, maybe loved him too much.

There were other times when she'd go into his room and he'd pretend to be asleep. It wasn't anything like his father and Kewpie, though. This was clean and kind and tender. Rosanna would watch Tiger sleeping with a vague smile on her face. Then she would cover his hair, his neck, his eyelids with kisses and he would try not to flinch. He wouldn't even wipe the kisses off. And his mother's face, in the moonlight, framed by the shadows of ginkgo leaves (for there was also a staunch ginkgo outside the house on 47th Street) was the most beautiful thing Tiger had ever seen in his life. Yes, there were tired lines around her mouth, dark circles cradling her eyes and an unfathomable sadness within them. But there was also love which was so evident Tiger could almost taste it.

Finally, the boy drifted off to sleep in his dead cousin's room, thinking of his women, hardy urban flowers, and pungent spices and of ginkgos. But they were all one in the same. And in the stillness of the summer night, for the first time in the week he'd been at Aunt Jo and Uncle Harry's place, Tiger heard the El call to him like a lost friend, as if in a dream. Then he was asleep.

30 Down at Coney Isle

Tony's head hurt so bad he couldn't stand to open even one eye, and when he finally managed to, it was only a sliver. It didn't seem possible, but the place was more a wreck than it had been the last time he was conscious of it. And it got worse every day. The bed sheets smelled stale. When was the last time she'd changed them? There was a Chinks laundry down the block, but Denise still couldn't manage to strip the bed and haul her lard ass down there.

They had long since run out of clean towels. A damp, moldy pile could be found on the sullied bathroom floor. There were articles of clothing strewn everywhere like fallen flower petals. Draped over the furniture, thrown on the tables, even in the kitchen. Tony had tried separating them into piles of not so dirty and filthy but soon gave up. There wasn't a clean work shirt among the mess. As a matter of fact, he doubted if you could find a fragment of anything clean in the entire place. He tried talking to Denise about it in their rare sober moments but she always became rambunctious, declaring, "I ain't your fucking maid!" then burst into tears. It was a lose-lose situation.

What few dishes they had were already used, piled in and around the sink, threatening to totter over like a leaning tower of crud. The cockroaches scuttled about brazenly in the daylight, not even bothering to run when a light switch was flipped on. Just the other day, Tony smashed the skull of an unsuspecting mouse with a cast iron frying pan, scattering bacon grease and rodent brains all over the kitchen. He gagged while he wiped it up as Denise shrieked hysterically and supervised.

Tony surveyed the bump in the bed beside him and couldn't believe the awful transformation in Denise. Her chest rose and fell with effort as she slept, snoring audibly. 'The only person I know with breath worse than mine,' he thought, then sat up, wincing at the throbbing that caught him between the eyes like a bullet. He scratched his balls then studied the dirt under his fingernails and wondered where the cat went—the cat that shit in his mouth.

The breasts that stood like perky stone hillocks beneath Denise's clothing rested on her belly when she removed her brassiere. Both slung to one side, they slept peacefully on the concave mattress beside her. From between Denise's legs emanated a stale ammonia odor—he couldn't recall the last time she'd bathed. Farmer's baths with a frayed washrag just weren't cutting it any longer.

As the boys in the locker room liked to say, "The curtains don't match the rug." And Denise's dark tuft of hair down below was unkempt and indeed, didn't match the curls on her head. Her coiffeur was the only thing Denise was meticulous about. Tony figured that would soon change, too. But no matter what, every Thursday night, Denise painted her scalp with a noxious peroxide cream. Her hair was crackly to the touch, like dry grass, even without hair spray.

Though they lived only blocks from the ocean, Denise's skin was ashen and rarely saw the sun. "Bad for the complexion," she told him, like a bleached-blonde vampire. What some might call alabaster was in truth an unhealthy shade drained of life. Tony could see thin blue veins trailing along the entire length of her body. Tony studied his girlfriend's curves not with love or desire but with criticism. He surveyed Denise's form from toe to head to left arm and down to the tips of her partially-painted fingernails. His eyes traced the road map of her body, snaking up to Albany, going up past Lake George then made a beeline west to Niagara Falls (where he and Rosanna had spent their honeymoon 17 years earlier) then south to Jamestown before he lost interest in the game.

Denise used to paint her fingernails cherry red but had now taken a fancy to a shade which was closer to the color of dried blood. However, the lacquer was chipped and the nails themselves were flea-bitten, chewed down to the raw cuticles. Tony had never been fond of that color but now he hated it all the more. It reminded him of the growing pool beneath his wife's prone body after he'd slugged her.

Tony couldn't bring himself to visit Rosanna at United Israel-Zion. Oh, he went there several times, made it as far as the starched hallway outside her ward, but he couldn't manage to step inside her room. Even if she never told anyone what had happened that night, he worried that someone would figure it out. And even if no one did, there were Rosanna's eyes to contend with. Somber at the happiest of times and silently accusing at the worst of them.

Once, as Tony lingered amongst the dark folds of 10th Avenue, he saw Tiger clasping his sister-in-law Camille's hand and waving wildly at a high window. The boy broke loose from Camille's caring grasp to jump up and down, flailing his arms crisscross overhead as one might do to flag down a rescue plane. Tony didn't step forward, just watched from the cover of gloom, one moment thinking it should be him holding his son's hand and the next minute, not giving a flying fuck. He didn't approach them after Tiger hung his head and they turned to go. Tony just took a deep gulp from his flask and caught the West End back to Coney.

Tony was amazed at how slovenly Denise had become in such a short time. It took most married women years to slowly slip into neglect, but that was usually after having a half-dozen kids, being sick or dirt poor. And none of those applied to Denise.

Maybe it was the drinking. Some people just couldn't handle the drink like he could.

Tony made sure to keep enough in his pocket for the sauce and was tight with what he gave Rosanna to run the house. But she always did the best with what she had. The place was always spotless and his wife always looked dowdy yet presentable. There were new dresses made from extra material Astrid had procured plus damaged lipsticks and pots of rouge that Kresge's couldn't sell. Kewpie brought them home for her mom like treasures, rescued before they hit the trash.

It had gotten so that Tony's Coney Island Baby could barely drag herself to work each day. She claimed ill health and indeed her constant drinking to keep up with Tony was taking its toll on her usually-robust constitution. So Smith & Associates cut her hours to part-time and brought in another girl to pick up the slack. It was probably Denise's good looks which kept her around so long, for despite her lack of office skills, she was easy on the eyes. So what if she could barely type? She was their own private, living, breathing, big-breasted Petty Girl teetering about in high heels and skintight skirts revealing long legs and generous thighs, a pin-up in their very midst.

But when Denise's marginal talents in the workplace began slipping further into oblivion and she began calling in sick more regularly than she came in, declaring she was "under the weather" every other day—when in reality she was merely hung over—they had no choice but to can her. It didn't matter how voluptuous the gams or how clingy the sweaters, Smith & Associates simply needed a warm body, even a plain-faced warm body, to answer the telephones and type, even if it was hunt-and-peck. Erma Gaunt, with her broomstick physique and long-faced visage vaguely reminiscent of Buster Keaton, was prompt, punctual and a crackerjack secretary besides. Miss Gaunt was quickly signed on to work full-time after Miss Walters' curvaceous derrière was given the boot.

This meant that Denise had even more time to accompany Tony to Ruby's or to the Terminal Pub. She would plop her ever-widening bottom onto the barstool beside him, not budging for hours, except to use the little girls' room. This meant that

Tony didn't have a spare moment to himself, only when he was riding the rails, but then he was working, so it didn't really count as free time.

With a touch of healthy fear in his heart and a slight sneer on his lips, Tony went back to opening and closing doors on the West End line after his one-week suspension. He needed this job, and monotonous as it was, it paid okay and had good benefits. Only a blooming idiot would fuck it up, and with Rosanna stuck in the hospital, Tony needed the gig all the more.

Not that he was giving his family any money. He truly felt like a piece of shit about that. Denise was sucking him dry, and not in a good way. Even that had dwindled to almost nothing. She was either drunk, hung over or in a bad humor, and not much fun under the covers any more. Those fuck-me pumps were gathering dust under the bed, no doubt the shiny, red patent-leather straps gnawed by mice, even rats, which Tony had caught glimpses of skulking about in the corners. He had noticed the black pellets they left in their wake, about the size of pill capsules, for a week now but had yet to see one of the furtive rodents full on. Once or twice he spied a flash in the corner of his eye of a creature that seemed to be the size of a small cat. He didn't tell Denise though; he simply couldn't take the carrying on.

Tony had to get out of that stinking apartment and escape for at least a little bit. So while Denise was in the can, he tiptoed out the door. The back streets of Coney Island a few blocks from the Boardwalk were without glitter and unlit by the million light bulbs that supposedly illuminated Luna Park alone. Many of the streetlamps here were dead, shielding the back-alley activities that went on. If you wanted a hand job from the he-she who worked the freak show, a marijuana cigarette or a whorehouse, you could find all three within steps of each other.

Tony's shirt stuck to his back with sweat as he walked with purpose, yet had no idea where he was headed. He'd grown used to the lighter fluid scent that emanated from under his arms and it became his signature cologne of sorts. He passed by a number of atrocities, not taking full note of them until they obstructed his path, forcing themselves upon him.

"Loose joints, loose joints..."

"Suckie, suckie. Come on, mister. I suckie good." A tiny, wizened Asian woman gave him a gumless grin. She was probably not yet thirty but her opium habit made her look twice that age. Tony detected its acrid smoke clinging to her kimono, which she fumbled to open. "Lookie, lookie. It true what they say. Crack go side to side, not up down." Tony kept going.

A pimple-faced teenager stepped in front of him, hands jammed into his pockets. "I got girls. Young girls. Virgins. Pretty, young girls. Never been cracked." Tony paused only briefly and saw a small figure cowering in a doorway. He pushed the boy aside without losing step.

Tony glanced up at the windows of a fourth-floor walk up halfway up the next block curtained with a thin gossamer fabric. He could also make out the glow of red light bulbs coloring the night. Curls of heavy opium smoke sifted out the open window, wafting their way up to the indigo sky.

There was an after-hours bar Tony knew of, holed up in a basement on West 17th. The walls were incessantly damp and dripping. The cement floors were constantly sticky. The room itself was always thick with cigarette smoke and there was a chill in the air even in the summer. And you could hear the bells from Our Lady of Solace every hour on the hour. Tony felt his sagging back pocket. His flask was still half full so he didn't even hesitate before moving on.

Not far from the after-hours was an alley that bordered a sagging wooden fence. Carved into the fence were holes of varying sizes and different heights for men of all statures. Suck holes, they were known as, in crude street talk. And this was by definition a crude street. As for what lurked behind the fence, you simply took your chances. Sure, it could have been a blonde cupcake like Thelma Todd, before she met her untimely end, but most likely, it was someone with the lanky, rubber-band frame of ZaSu Pitts. That is, if it was even a woman behind the fence at all. You never could be too sure. The one time Tony was inebriated enough to poke his business through the opening, he swore he felt razor stubble. And that was enough for him. He yanked himself out, buttoned his fly and was gone in a flash.

As he hit the high road, Tony noticed two men at opposite ends of the partition, their slacks around their ankles, their white asses pumping in opposing rhythm. August nights, the suck hole was busy. It wasn't unusual for a fellow to leave his good-girl on the Boardwalk, say he was going for ice cream, drop his drawers at the West 18th Street alley, then be back with a creamy vanilla cone in each fist. Or for a guy to set up his wife and kids at Nathan's, take a load off by way of the fence and return before the family finished their dogs. Now, that was low in Tony's book.

But Tony's book bore a different bunch of rules for others than the statutes he had for himself. He was lawless and went by the moment, went by what he needed right then and there. Tony did what suited him and to hell with anyone else. It had been that way since he was a kid. If he didn't look out for himself, who else would? And although his circumstances had changed for the better as he grew older, his attitude didn't. Even after his mercenary mother was dead and buried, even after he'd been embraced by the caring Paradisos and was touched by the love of a good woman, a sweet-natured virgin who married him and bore his children, he still didn't change. Tony was the same guttersnipe scrounging for his next meal, conniving for his next dime as he had been at Tiger's age. And he'd started drinking around then, too.

When Tony reached the corner of Mermaid and West 19th and glanced up at his current residence, he still couldn't bear to go home to Denise. He lingered beneath the dead streetlamp across the pavement, noticing that the window was open and the lights were on in their place. Denise was probably fuming, wondering where he'd run off to and cursing the very day she stepped onto his train. Already in Tony's nostrils was the apartment's rancid stench that would greet him, the unpleasant odor he would soon get used to after just a few minutes and then not even notice. But he carried it around with him everywhere. It stuck to his clothes, to his skin.

Tony could almost hear Denise's high-pitched yelling that would begin the moment he walked through the door. He turned his back on the tenement, stepped into the road and headed toward the ocean. It was two short blocks to the Riegelmann

Boardwalk. Near midnight, the wooden walkway was almost as crowded as it was in broad daylight. Going against the grain, Tony was bobbled about like a little fish fighting the tide but he just kept moving steadily. Fighting the tide...that was the story of his life.

He found a place on an almost-empty bench facing the water. There was a young couple pitching woo at the other end. Tony's stomach tightened as they whispered into each other's ears, giggled, squeezed and cuddled. It was sickening but he didn't feel like moving. He lifted one butt cheek off the seat and farted quite audibly in their direction. The breeze was coming from the south, so if they didn't hear it, they certainly smelled it, for it was carried to their very laps as if on a silver platter. "Geez," said the guy. "Keep that to yourself, why don't you?"

The fellow and his honey, who possessed the pushed-in face of a Pekingese, were already getting up off the bench when Tony prepared to fire again. "Check your shorts," the Pekingese snapped as they strolled past, arm in arm. "I'd see a doctor if I were you."

"And I'd see a vet if I were you," Tony said under his bitter breath, fumbling for his flask with his left hand. He molded the thumb and pointer finger of his right hand into a fleshy gun of sorts, pulled the trigger and fired off another fart at the parting couple, more pungent than the first.

It made Tony remember happier times back at 47th Street. He had an odd before-work ritual where he'd summon Bridget out into the hallway under false pretenses. And she'd fall for it every time. "Ma," he'd call downstairs, leaning over the banister.

"What is it, Tony?" she'd wonder, ducking her head out her door.

Tony wouldn't say another word but would rip loose with a champion fart. Instead of being upset, his mother-in-law would stand there laughing, laughing so hard that nothing came out of her mouth. Five minutes later, he'd leave for work and she'd still be standing there, silently guffawing and holding onto her gut. Tony had to choke back the tears recollecting, then got pissed off at himself immediately after. He was growing wistful for a fart. What a sick, hopeless fuck he was.

The horizon in front of Tony was pitch black now. He couldn't discern the line between sky and sea. There were no ships out on the waters of the Atlantic and even the stars were hiding. The moon was a luminescent sliver, a shining curl of lemon peel in a blanket of black satin. From one of the concession stands behind him came the crackly strains of a song Tony remembered from when he was a kid:

> *"There's the Bow'ry boys with Nellie,*
> *And the East Side girls in style*
> *The girls from up in Harlem, too,*
> *And Johnny with his smile*
> *The merry-go-round and coasters*
> *Are crowded all the while*
> *With future wives and husbands*
> *Down at Coney Isle."*

It could have been written today instead of near the turn of the century. All of those people were still here now and Tony hated each and every one of them. Every guy with a gal he loved who loved him back. Every Johnny with his smile and Nellie, too. Future wives and husbands and future ex-wives. They were all there, strolling the Boardwalk, hand in hand, arm in arm, taunting him with their happiness.

'I really made a mess of things,' Tony thought to himself and immediately began to cry. Not a quiet sniffle or two, mind you, but a big, drunken, blubbering boo-hoo. Two cops patrolling the Boardwalk paused to observe him for a moment or two but then went on their way. Neither knew how to deal with a crying man or wanted to. 'I got nowhere to go,' he muttered into his damp chest, fat tears running down his face, dripping from his eyes, snotting up his nose. He'd loused up the one true home he ever knew in favor of a whore in a shit hole. But things had been screwed up long before Denise. And now, he couldn't even get himself to visit his wife or his kids either. He couldn't look Roe, the children or anyone in her family in the eye, and if Denise squawked about money or the mice one more fucking time, he just might throttle her.

So, Tony sobbed into his flask, wishing he could cry into a beer, but barely able to walk, not knowing what to do or where to go. People stared at him as they passed and then quickly turned away, busy with their stalks of cotton candy, munching on frozen bananas and admiring their Kewpie dolls. One or two children pointed at him and were yanked into politeness by their parents. But Tony didn't care, he kept right on blubbering.

And less than three blocks away, on Mermaid Avenue, Denise Walters crouched on her dirty bathroom floor, vomiting into her skuzzy toilet and wondering where the son of a bitch was now.

31 Where the Heart Is

Once again, Uncle Harry pulled some sizeable strings and United Israel-Zion let Tiger inside, this time to see his mother home. Not only did they let him in but they also permitted him to man the oak-handled wheelchair to cart Rosanna away. En route to her ward, Tiger sped it down the hallway, careful not to bump walls, ignoring any impulse to pop wheelies. He also took care to apply the brake liberally. "Easy does it," warned Uncle Harry, "or I'll have to issue you a summons, bub."

It was the first time Rosanna had laid eyes on her son up close in two weeks and Tiger looked so happy, so joyful, so luminescent that she wanted to cry. He also looked as though he'd filled out, no doubt from the constant shoveling in of food from her mother and sisters descending upon the skinny child, stuffing him to the brim with food and with love. It didn't quite make up for the fact that his momma was ill but it sure helped. After all, who could refuse bowls of creamy chocolate pudding and Lobster Claw pastries with their delicate, flaky crust? Certainly not Tiger.

Rosanna chucked him on the chin. "How's my little *faccia lada*?" she asked.

"Ma, quit calling me a funny face," her son grinned.

Rosanna tried to put on a brave front as she eased herself out of the hospital bed and into the wheelchair. Earlier, one of the nurses helped her get dressed and even put a splash of rouge on her cheeks. Another nurse applied a swab of lipstick to Rosanna's mouth. After they left, Rosanna rubbed off both, fearing she might resemble Lon Chaney in *The Phantom of the Opera*.

Tiger looked worried as his mother winced and stood with Harry gripping her elbow to steady her. Rosanna supported her incision and forced a smile, which Tiger returned with a 100-watt one. "Park your carcass," Harry told her as Tiger gently edged the wheelchair seat against her bottom. She dropped lightly into it, grimacing again but this time with her back turned so they couldn't see. Tiger was suddenly serious, pushing Rosanna in the chair, mindful not to jostle her unnecessarily, making certain to go slowly and steadily, so as not to hurt her. "Just like Old Queen Vickie," Harry said, trying to make her feel better. And he did.

John had borrowed Poppa's Nash and was waiting by the curb for them. Poppa and Tiger had shined it up special for Rosanna's homecoming and it gleamed both inside and out. The burgundy paint shone brightly and the black leather interior had been rubbed to a dull gloss. "People must think we're picking up someone important," Tiger noted, rolling the wheelchair to the edge of the sidewalk.

"We are," Uncle John told him. He opened the car door with a flourish and bowed. Rosanna gave him a queenly nod of the head. Tiger and Harry each took hold of an arm and helped her to her feet. It was becoming easier for Rosanna to stand, but walking still pained her. To get into the Nash, all she had to do was take a step, turn and slide a few inches along the Nash's slippery seat, which she managed well enough without their help.

It was only a few blocks to the house. John did his best to avoid potholes, swerving slightly to and fro as though piloting a fishing boat through Sheepshead Bay. Rosanna was glad to see United Israel shrink in the rearview mirror. They had treated her with a professional brand of compassion, but she longed to be home, and in less than five minutes, she was.

Poppa and Bridget were sitting in their Adirondack chairs on the porch, awaiting their daughter's arrival. Sully stood beside them, turning his policeman's cap nervously in his hands. John sailed the car into a parking spot in front of 1128 instead of into the driveway because it was a shorter distance for Rosanna to walk.

When she stood, Rosanna saw stars but waited until they dissolved before she took thoughtful baby steps with one arm slung across Tiger's shoulder for support. His thin arm cradled her waist. The small boy acted as his mother's crutch, gladly and skillfully ferrying her to the base of the stoop. Her parents were immediately on their feet and down the brick steps, flanking her. Though Poppa and Bridget had visited her once a day, sometimes twice, while she was in the hospital they missed her terribly and it showed.

"The doctor said you weren't supposed to climb stairs," Harry reminded Rosanna.

"Bah," was her response. But when she raised her foot to mount the first step, knives pierced her stomach and she immediately put her foot back down on the ground. She knew she couldn't do it.

"I made up Kewpie's bed for you nice," Bridget said.

"Thanks, Ma," Rosanna told her. "But I just want to be in my own place. You understand, don't you?" Bridget did, but then there was the matter of the staircase. Besides the five front steps, there were more than a dozen in the hall.

"We could put her in a kitchen chair and carry her up in it," Harry suggested, as though Rosanna weren't even there.

"No," Rosanna said succinctly. "I can do it. Little by little, I can."

Sully, who had been standing silently on the outskirts of the conference without saying a word still didn't speak. He simply scooped Rosanna gently into his arms and started up the stairs. "She's light as a feather," he assured them.

Tiger ran ahead of Sully, throwing open first the house's outer door, then the inner one. The others followed behind Sully as swiftly as they could. He was careful not to bang Rosanna's legs into the banister, deftly side-stepping it with the grace of Ray Bolger playing the role of a big bruiser of a cop. But instead of the memorable solo Rosanna had seen in the picture *The Great Ziegfeld*, this was a *pas de deux* in which only one was dancing.

Rosanna permitted herself to burrow her face into Sully's broad chest. She took a deep breath of him. Not at all unpleasant, but musky and distinct, the saltiness of healthy perspiration mixed with liberal parts of Burma Shave Cream and bay rum cologne. When she tilted her head to look into Sully's face, her cheek brushed his, which was cleanly shaven and soft, slightly pink from being meticulously scraped with a single-edged razor that very morning. Rosanna closed her eyes and breathed again, feeling for the first time in a long time, cradled and protected.

The door to the Martino apartment was unlocked. Tiger pushed it open and ran inside, greeted by Aunt Jo, who started slightly. His other aunts were working but would surely stop by that night. Instead of a dusty mess, Rosanna was met by rooms which gleamed from top to bottom, much like Poppa's Nash. She looked around in awe, as if it were someone else's place, not hers. "We gave it a good cleaning," Tiger said proudly. "Me, Kewpie and Aunt Jo."

When Sully gently set Rosanna down on the shining linoleum, she was a little sorry to leave his arms. He pulled out a kitchen chair with an air of chivalry. Rosanna bent her knees and sat, smoothing her dress across her lap. "He's quite the scrubber," Jo told her sister, ruffling up Tiger's hair then kissing her sister on the forehead. "And he needs another haircut."

There were roses on the table, not store-bought, but from Bridget's garden. Short-stemmed red, pink and yellow blossoms set out in a Mason jar. There was a plate of home-made sugar cookies and a big pitcher of iced tea sweating onto the neatly-ironed tablecloth. "You baked in this weather?" Rosanna said to no one in particular.

After a sip of cool, lemony tea, she wondered, "Where's my girl?"

"They've been giving Kewpie extra hours at Kresge's while you were in the hospital," Bridget explained. "You know, to help with expenses and all. She wanted to take off but then figured the extra money would be a help. But she'll be home for dinner and we'll all take turns coming up here during the day so you can rest and get strong." Rosanna was too exhausted to argue.

After tea and cookies, the men were heartily thanked by Poppa for their help. Rosanna was tired from her homecoming and gladly laid down in her freshly-made bed. The sheets smelled of lilacs, which she truly appreciated, as she shut her eyes. Tiger hung the keys to the Nash on their designated hook upon the kitchen wall downstairs, right outside the back door, then retreated to the cozy dimness of the parlor to stage a lead soldier battle. Poppa pretended to read the *Eagle*, then promptly fell asleep. Bridget busied herself with dinner preparations, humming melodiously in the kitchen.

The days that followed were a delicious smorgasbord, marked not by squares on the calendar but by dishes. The day we had Mrs. Dietrich's *sauerbraten* and home-made *sauerkraut*. The day Mr. Wong brought a covered platter filled with fluffy fried rice and topped with savory beef and broccoli. (He insisted that Rosanna keep the beautiful plate, painted with cherry blossoms, as a get-well-soon gift.) The day Eileen Daly toted over her wonderful meat loaf, flanked by bright orange carrots and lovely potatoes, not to mention Irish soda bread stuffed with plenty of raisins. The day Mrs. Lieberwitz brought the chocolate *babka* and matzo ball soup or Mrs. Lopez dropped off her famed *flan*.

This fine array of food in no way overshadowed the plentiful platters which Bridget carried upstairs. Crispy dishes of chicken cutlets, golden piles of eggplant, and for lunch, hearty bowls of rice and potato soup. (Bridget had gotten the recipe from Vincenza DePalma, who came from the same region in Italy near *Fiorenze* as she.) Not to mention peas and pasta and *pasta e fagioli*, Rosanna's favorite since she was a girl.

In addition, Rosanna's sisters came by with their own delicacies. Camille with her refreshing Waldorf chicken salad complete with grapes and walnuts, Jo with her cheese blintzes (Mrs. Lieberwitz taught her how to make them) and Astrid with her cardboard take-out boxes, for as everyone knew, Astrid was a horrid cook and lazy to boot. Jo sat with Rosanna most of the day, plumping up pillows, boiling pots of chamomile tea and otherwise doting on her big sister.

Mr. Salerno, their old landlord from Chester Avenue, where the Martinos had lived as newlyweds, heard the news of Rosanna's convalescence and brought a tray of *spadini* which he'd made himself. (Sicilian men are noted for their cooking talents.) Who would think that a sausage-fingered car mechanic could make such delicate, garlicky delights? Mr. Salerno pounded milk-fed veal cutlets wafer thin and rolled them around a finely-chopped mixture of hard-boiled egg, minced garlic, bread crumbs, and freshly-grated Pecorino Romano cheese so thick it looked like flecks of coconut. Fastened with toothpicks, drizzled with a good olive oil then baked until they melted in your mouth. Tiger loved veal but it was so dear that he rarely tasted it. However, Mr. Salerno said nothing was too good for his Rosanna. (P.S. his son-in-law Rossi was a butcher so he got the veal wholesale.)

Mr. Acerno from the Loews 46th sent Augie over with a plate of honey cakes made by his wife Gloria. This was traditionally a Christmas dish but Gloria knew how much Rosanna loved them, and reasoned that the profuse amounts of honey in it would ensure sweetness in the coming year. (This was a Barese belief and Gloria's people were indeed from Bari, and highly superstitious, knock on wood.) Besides, everyone in the neighborhood knew that Mrs. Martino could use a little more sweetness in her life. Plus the muscatel wine in the batter couldn't hurt.

All the way from Bay Ridge, Olie brought his wife's specialties: *kumpa* and *fiskbullar*, simple, yet delicious Norwegian peasant fare. Tomina knew that the codfish *fiskbullar* contained was very healthful and perfect for convalescence. Olie insisted that Kewpie go home to bring this meal to her mother and gave the girl extra time (off the clock) to enjoy the lunch with her. There was no telling what might befall the food in the storage room and one could only shudder to think what might be running around back there when the lights were out, he reasoned. But Kewpie knew that Olie sent her home with the *kumpa* and *fiskbullar* (which were still warm) because he had a sympathetic heart and missed his own mother back in Oslo.

There was a constant procession of caring friends who came by with covered dishes, coordinating it so that at least one visited with Rosanna each day. She was especially glad to chat with Sully's sister Irene, whom she hadn't seen since Old Man Sullivan's funeral a handful of years earlier. Little Red, as Sully liked to call her, could always make Rosanna smile, and indeed, Irene often got her in trouble for giggling in class. Her flaming hair hadn't faded at all, though now she wore it in a short bob rather than in a ponytail, and her dancing blue eyes still glittered like they did when she was a girl. Three sons between the ages of five and fifteen hadn't dampened Irene's enthusiasm for life. "But I'm always tired," she laughed musically.

Irene brought a home-baked angel food cake all the way on the train from Queens. She picked up some fresh strawberries from the greengrocer and a small carton of heavy cream, which she hand-whipped with a bit of sugar at the kitchen table. Rosanna was slightly embarrassed that the kitchen looked so tatty even though she knew that Irene wasn't one to judge. She'd had humble beginnings herself and both parents were heavy drinkers until their deaths. Irene married a cop who became a lawyer and they had an impressive home in Jackson Heights. "But we both come from the same place, Roe," Irene liked to remind her, borrowing one of Bridget's famous phrases.

Irene bustled around Rosanna's kitchen as though it were her own, filling the tea kettle, putting it on to boil, knowing exactly where Rosanna kept the tea ball by intuition. They each spoke of their children lovingly and proudly without bragging. Like the good friend she was, Irene avoided mentioning Tony or even asking about him, and she didn't speak of her own Raymond too much. "How we've changed since we were girls," Irene smiled, blowing into her cup of tea.

"We would spend hours brushing each other's hair and talking," Rosanna recalled.

"I loved being in this house," Irene said after a sip. "All of those brothers and sisters running about. It was hard to keep track of who was where."

Rosanna took a forkful of cake, which was light as a summer cloud. The berries were ripe and bursting, lost in swirls of cream. "Still is."

"I was so jealous of you, Roe!" her friend admitted. "I mean, you had sisters."

"And plenty of them."

"Meanwhile, it was just Paddy and me. And our folks. I don't remember them being around much. But when they were..."

The sound of Irene's spoon knocking against the china cup as she stirred filled the small room. The thin porcelain was still too warm for Rosanna to put to her lips, so she pulled back. "It's over and done with," she said quietly. "They're dead and buried. Just let it go, honey."

Irene looked into the cup. "I wish I could. But it's always there. It's a part of me, of Paddy and me." She gathered the nerve to look into Rosanna's sad puppy dog eyes. "Roe," she said after a deep sigh, "I try not to say anything about other people's marriages. Sometimes folks fight all the time yet it works somehow. Sometimes a relationship looks like a wreck but it's like steel. But this...," Irene continued, "with this man...Tony's tearing you to pieces. I'm afraid there'll be nothing left of you."

Irene's strong voice cracked. She forced herself to take a mouthful of tea then fit the cup into the saucer, her hand trembling. "Maybe I shouldn't tell you," she added. "Maybe you already know. Oh, heck, even a blind man could see. But my brother's sweet on you. Paddy's in love with you. Has been since we were kids." Rosanna was dumbfounded.

Little Red stood up abruptly and started clearing the table, even though there was still plenty of tea left in their cups and cake on their plates. "I'm sorry," she said with her back to Rosanna, washing dishes. "I swore I'd never tell you. I guess I've said too much but I thought you should know."

Without thinking, Irene dried her hands on her pretty summer dress, store bought, probably from Gimbels without waiting for it to go on sale. She grabbed her purse from the ladder-back chair. "You've got such a long ride ahead of you," Rosanna said.

"Not so bad," Irene told her. "Paddy's getting off his shift soon. He's going to drive me back home, and I convinced him to stay for dinner. The boys are crazy about him. Raymond, too."

Rosanna smiled. "It probably didn't take much convincing for him to come for supper. You're a great cook."

"For an Irish girl," Irene smiled back. "You're not so bad yourself."

"I really miss not being able to cook," Rosanna admitted.

"You'll be back in the saddle soon enough."

The girlhood friends embraced as grown women, holding and rocking each other, not really wanting to let go just yet. But eventually, before she started crying, Rosanna pulled away. She squeezed Irene's shoulders and looked at her. "And thanks for coming, really. The cake was wonderful. The kids will love it."

In the days that followed, Rosanna did a little more. She could stand for longer periods of time without feeling exhausted. She could walk with little pain and even move from sitting to standing without wincing. When no one else was home, she began to do small chores, like sweeping, careful not to make noise and send Bridget dashing up the stairs to chide her. In truth, Rosanna found it difficult to do nothing. She'd finished *Gone with the Wind* in the hospital and was now reading *The Good Earth*, which she'd taken five years to get around to. (Astrid might not have good taste in anything else but she certainly had a flair for choosing fine reading material.) Lying idle was bad enough at United Israel but back at home it was almost unbearable and impossible besides.

So day by day, Rosanna felt a more renewed. She attributed this partly to rest and partly to the help her children were giving around the apartment. She didn't have to wash so much as a plate herself. But Rosanna also liked to think that her swift recovery was due largely to the healing food that was brought to her. Besides being delicious and filled with strengthening broths, hearty root vegetables and such, it was also filled with the love of her family, friends and neighbors. She could taste it in every spoonful, could detect it in every bite, as sweet and thick as honey on her tongue.

32 Wild in the Streets

With Tony nowhere to be found, Kewpie was back to sleeping upstairs again. She shared Rosanna's bed, just in case her mother should need something in the middle of the night during her convalescence. With her children safely within arm's reach and her errant husband who knows where, Rosanna now needed nothing. The pain in her belly, this time from the incision, was subsiding with each passing day.

Kewpie was at Kresge's and Tiger was presumably running wild in the streets the day Dr. Lewis stopped by to remove Rosanna's stitches. Though she insisted that she could manage the stairs for an office appointment, Dr. Schantz permitted his attending physician (that would be Morris Lewis) to make a house call to save his neighbor a trip. With the steady parade of desserts that were no doubt still arriving at the Martino house, Dr. Lewis was only too happy to visit.

Indeed, he had his pick of Mrs. Lieberwitz's leftover chocolate *babka*, apple streusel from Helen Pateau or Mrs. DePalma's moist and delicious, all-occasion layer cake. A difficult decision, Dr. Lewis finally chose the *babka* and streusel to accompany his cup of tea before he set to work.

The coarse black thread of the stitches contrasted with the skin of Rosanna's stomach, which was pale as a length of cotton. She looked away as Dr. Lewis gently snipped, faintly droning an unrecognizable melody. "I look like a gutted carp," Rosanna said to the ceiling.

"Better a gutted carp than a dead one," he said matter-of-factly. "Rosanna, you came very close…"

"I know, I know," she sighed.

"How are the children?" he inquired. "Now that Angela's belly no longer aches and her head no longer hurts, I hardly see her." After a pause, he said in a lower voice. "And just so you know, when I examined her, she was fine. Still intact. A virgin, I mean."

Rosanna blushed at the plaster ceiling. "I figured. She's a good girl."

"Yes," Dr. Lewis agreed. "But some boys, some men aren't so good." Rosanna jumped slightly despite the fact that Dr. Lewis had been very careful with the scissors. "Did I hurt you?" he wondered.

She shook her head. "Thank you for telling me."

"*Nu?* You're her mother. You should know. And Anthony, Jr.?"

Rosanna smiled. "He's fine. Running around. Exploring."

Dr. Lewis set down the scissors. "Keeping out of trouble?"

"Well, Harry hasn't told me otherwise," she said.

As his mother had her stitches deftly removed, Tiger ran rampant through Borough Park. He crossed the streets carefully and looked both ways, but with change jangling in his pocket and Jimmy Burns at his side. The sliver of Brooklyn transected by the El, was his oyster. And he meant to crack it open. Poppa didn't take him to the Navy Yard every day and on the occasions he didn't, Rosanna reluctantly left Tiger to his own devices. "A boy needs to roam," Harry had told Rosanna after Tiger enlisted his uncle's manly intervention. "Needs to figure out right and wrong for himself," he added. "He's a sharp cookie, he'll do okay." And in private, Uncle Harry flashed Tiger a mock sneer and shook his fist at the boy, the silent message being, 'You'd better!'

It was another hot day. Tiger soon tired of stickball and street games. The deciding moment came when he and Jimmy Burns, two of the smallest kids on the block, were mercilessly crushed in a game of "Johnny-on-the-Pony." It was an especially violent, sadistic urban pastime. To play, one kid clung to the Johnny pump, or fire hydrant, while another came running toward them at breakneck speed, leapt into the air and landed on them. You had to hang on for dear life, under backbreaking weight, as child after child plunged toward you and plopped on top.

Tiger and Jimmy Burns had drawn the shortest sticks and were the first two to be waylaid. They put up a valiant effort but were toppled by only five children, one of them Fat James DeBiasi. Tiger and Jimmy slunk off together shamed, and with badly-skinned knees and Jimmy rubbing his bum arm, having recently been liberated from its cast.

As friends went, Jimmy Burns was all right, even for a Dodgers fan. He wasn't mean spirited, even when the Dodgers won, and he had calmed down considerably since the Superman incident. But he would be forever remembered as the nutty kid who jumped from Mrs. Rosenkrantz's garage roof wearing a cape, at least until the Burnses moved to Midwood.

Jimmy was a wild-haired, wild-eyed boy. Rosanna didn't like him very much. He'd had lice twice that she'd known of and not one but both of his parents were drinkers. To Tiger, this was a plus. Although he didn't feel superior to Jimmy, at least Tiger didn't feel "less-than" as he often did with other kids. Besides, Jimmy knew what it was like to be roughed up by a cranky lush, to scrape his dad up off the parlor floor and help him into bed, to have the cops escort his old man home. Between the two boys, this was understood, so they shared no embarrassment, no stuttering explanations, no fiery-faced moments.

But unlike Tiger, nobody looked out for Jimmy Burns, except maybe Sully, who took a shine to the boy after breathing him back to life. Maybe Sully saw himself in Jimmy Burns or maybe he saw a potential delinquent he could keep on the straight and narrow with a little guidance. Nobody went out looking for Jimmy if he didn't come home for supper, and often, there was no supper in the Burns household. And nobody came after him if he tarried outside after the streetlights came on.

Some nights, strange vagrants and down-on-their-luck sods his parents brought home from the Pink Pussycat were found in Jimmy's cot, snoring off a good drunk, leaving the boy to sleep on the fire escape in summer or curled up on the floor near the clicking steam radiator in winter months. Next to Jimmy Burns, Tiger knew he was lucky. The sob stories Jimmy told often mirrored tales from his own father's childhood. Tiger sure hoped his friend didn't turn out like his dad did.

From the coins his aunts and uncles slipped him on the sly, Tiger's pockets were heavy that afternoon. Though his mother would worry and surely scold him, Tiger decided not to go home for lunch but instead, eat his way through the neighborhood with Jimmy in tow. Although Tiger was a rangy child, you could count each and every one of his friend's ribs and even make out his clavicle, vaguely lily-shaped, at the top of his emaciated chest. But boy, could Jimmy pack in the grub.

Their first stop was the pizzeria under the El. The stern and severe lady behind the counter always wore black, black dusted with semolina flour. "Someone in the Old Country probably died 50 years ago and she's been in mourning ever since," Tiger quipped to Jimmy, who laughed a bit too hilariously for such a small joke. They nicknamed the humorless pizza lady Seraphina and often contemplated what she kept hidden in the sizable bun she wore at the nape of her neck. Her hair was pulled so tight that it kept her in an eternally bad mood.

Seraphina knew little English, just words like, "Nickel!" and "You pay now!" which she barked in perfect Brooklynese. Words like "Please," "Thank you" and "Come again" never found their way into her limited vocabulary. And Seraphina was especially cranky to Mario, her rotund, jovial husband who always had a big grin on his face, perhaps just to annoy her. She often called him things like *"Discraciata"* in a condescending growl, which was just about the worst thing you could call someone in Italian. It meant that you were worse than a disgrace.

Tiger and Jimmy surmised that there was something deep and serious behind Mario's wide smiles. Perhaps one day, they would come for their customary slice and find Seraphina "gone back to *Italia*" and all the pizzas mysteriously decorated with sausage meat after Mario went off the deep end and put Seraphina through the grinder. One could only hope.

Mario's Pizza only served square slices, Sicilian style, for the couple was from Palermo. Besides, everyone there knew that Sicilian pizza was the only kind that mattered, and once you took a bite, you couldn't help but agree. Even a shanty Irish kid like Jimmy Burns knew this was true. Crunchy on the bottom, doughy on the top, smothered with Seraphina's sweet marinara sauce and Mario's home-made mozzarella, it was like your first taste of the Eucharist. It was that holy. Perhaps it was sacrilegious to say so but Tiger suspected that even Pope Pius XI would agree, even though he wasn't from Palermo.

Tiger went to the pizzeria window that opened onto New Utrecht Avenue and waited for the El to finish passing overhead before he ordered. But before he could, Seraphina snapped over the din, "What!"

"A slice, please," Tiger practically begged.

"Justa one?" she inquired, eyeing the two boys with contempt. Tiger nodded. They wanted to save room for other local specialties. Seraphina sighed, shook her head and grabbed the scissors. Instead of plunging them into Tiger's skull, she cut the thin wafery slice of pizza in half and wouldn't hand the pieces over until Tiger produced a nickel. He let Jimmy have the slightly larger one with the edging of crust intact since Jimmy liked the crust and he didn't. They wouldn't dare ask for napkins and instead, wiped their faces on the backs of their hands and licked the sauce off their fingers.

The pizza went down easy enough but there was an urgent need to follow it with something wet and sweet. Next stop, Dora's Luncheonette and Candy Store. Tiger was strictly forbidden to eat anything unwrapped from Dora's. Usually, he obeyed Rosanna's sanction, only selecting Baby Ruths and Bonomo Turkish Taffy, but today was different. Wax lips, candy buttons on paper tape and Black Crows, he would sample them all, and more. But first there was the matter of a drink. Today, a simple fountain soda, even a Lime Rickey, wouldn't suffice.

Once inside Dora's Luncheonette, Tiger and Jimmy Burns chose a pair of empty stools side by side. Dora approached them in a dirty housedress and moldy slippers. There was an open sore on the back of her left hand. Dora was truly a sight to behold, but the thing Tiger couldn't stop staring at was the giant mole that had settled on Dora's cheek like a dead waterbug. The bad-tempered shopkeeper couldn't abide by being stared at so Tiger forced himself to look away as he ordered a chocolate egg cream with two straws from the comely Chesterfield Girls on the yellowed, grease-spattered sign above Dora's hairy mole.

"I love eggs. Haven't had them in a dog's age," Jimmy told Tiger as he kicked his feet against the base of the counter. Jimmy was so thrilled that he would have spun on the tattered stool had it not been frozen in place with decades of rust.

"There are no eggs in egg creams," Tiger told him knowingly. "Watch."

They both observed as Dora deftly mixed a splash of milk, a liberal pump of Fox's U-Bet and a spritz of seltzer with an unwashed spoon until it foamed. She was as skilled as an alchemist, adding the straws and not one salted pretzel rod from the ancient canister on the countertop, but two. Although she might have been slovenly and ugly as original sin, at least Dora had a heart. She placed her creation on the sticky counter between both boys and watched with pride as they sucked down the whole thing in practically one slurp then began working on the pretzels. Tiger thanked her and left the money on the counter, including a generous gratuity.

And for dessert, there was Piccolo's. To Tiger's amazement, Jimmy Burns had never sampled a Charlotte Russe, which in Brooklyn, was pronounced "Charlarusse" with no space between the words. The dessert so good that its name was a breathless utterance, almost prayer-like.

"Never had a Charlarusse? Where'd you grow up? Jersey or someplace?" Tiger snapped, but then felt immediately repentant when he realized that Jimmy had probably never tasted a fancy sweet that was store-bought. There probably wasn't much dough-re-mi around the Burns house for such treats. Jimmy's face flushed all the way to his prominent ears. Instead of apologizing, Tiger put his arm around Jimmy's shoulder and said, "Come on," ushering him toward the bakery.

The boys sat on the sidewalk outside Piccolo's as Tiger eagerly peeled the cardboard casing from the base of the pastry, undressing the dessert in broad daylight. Jimmy studied the Charlotte Russe's layer of spongy cake topped with whipped cream, chocolate sprinkles and a maraschino cherry. He'd often seen them lined up like velvety chorus girls in Piccolo's front window but had no idea what they were. "Prepare to taste heaven," Tiger told him dramatically.

Jimmy closed his eyes and bit, attempting to take a layer of each sugary substance in one mouthful. It was the most delicious thing he had ever tasted. He decided right then and there that he would marry a woman named Charlotte or perhaps name his daughter Charlotte if the first were not possible.

Tiger took a bite, then Jimmy, and back and forth until all that remained was the candied cherry. Tiger let Jimmy have it since he remembered hearing that maraschino cherries stayed in your stomach for three years before they were digested. Tiger was beginning to feel a bit queasy anyway as they headed toward Kresge's. Jimmy, who was on a culinary roll, hoped Kewpie might be able to slip them some penny candies on the sly, or at the very least, maybe they had enough money left to share one of Harriet's legendary chow mein sandwiches.

Tiger caught a glimpse of himself in the window of a drinking establishment called The Stumble Inn. He didn't look too good. His face was smeared with evidence of what he'd eaten that afternoon. There was red sauce on his chin, chocolate ringing his lips, a dot of whipped cream on his nose. He was a mess.

From deep inside the dark folds of The Stumble Inn emerged a familiar face. Tiger's father approached the other side of the glass and waved at him. The bile rose in the boy's throat, and before Tiger could run, Tony was out of the bar and squinting in the daylight, a rogue father embracing his unwilling son. The next second, Tony was leading both boys into the cavernous blackness of The Stumble Inn like the Devil himself, smilingly ushering them into hell.

33 The Stumble Inn

Tiger had only been inside a bar perhaps twice in his life but Jimmy Burns had practically grown up in them. In fact, he'd spent much of his infancy in beer halls up and down the Avenue, strapped into a baby buggy while his parents drank more than their fill. If his older sister Maureen hadn't found an old pram put out with someone's trash, Jimmy wouldn't have even had a carriage. Sometimes he slept the whole night in it.

Jimmy was a good baby, quiet, although his demeanor was probably more from the paregoric (an opium derivative) added to his bottle or from a measure of rum rubbed on his gums to ease his teething pain rather than from a mild temperament. A fair portion of Jimmy's youth was passed being bounced up and down on a drunken knee, occasionally dropped, once burned by an uncle who'd forgotten that he had a cigar butt wedged into his cheek when he bent to kiss the child.

So, while Jimmy felt quite at home at The Stumble Inn, Tiger felt uncomfortable there. Yet, Tiger never recalled seeing his father so cheerful and downright magnanimous. "This here's my son Anthony, Jr., Teddy," Tony howled proudly to the barkeep. To which Teddy Long responded with a disdainful look. Not anything against the boy, who seemed nice enough, but the salty old suds slinger didn't believe children had any place in bars, and rightfully so. Tony was too far gone to realize Teddy's disapproval. He deposited his son on a barstool, then planted Jimmy Burns on the seat beside him. "Set these fine young men up with a bit of ale, would you, Teddy?" Tony bellowed. Then to the boys, "Ginger ale okay with you fellas?"

It was a joke which Teddy had heard far too many times for his liking. The barkeep slid two glasses of bubbly soda in front of the boys, who thanked him politely. Jimmy eyed the cherry at the bottom of Tiger's cup lustfully after he chomped down his own. Tiger speared it with a swizzle stick and offered it to his friend.

Bars meant one thing to Jimmy: free food. A bowl of salted peanuts stood an arm's length away. Keeping plates of brackish snacks like nuts, potato chips or dried chickpeas on the bar was a wise move for one simple reason—they made patrons thirsty and ensured that they drank more booze. Jimmy had managed to make a dinner of pub offerings more than once in his young life. Plus where there were peanuts, pretzel twists were soon to follow. He hoped that maybe Mr. Martino had tied on a good enough drunk to offer him a pickled egg or a pig's knuckle or two from the congealed jar at the end of the bar near the cash register.

Although Tony was at a loss at where to begin with his son, he sensed that Jimmy Burns would be an easy mark. Tony knew his folks, who were assholes, so he also knew that the kid was starved for attention as well as for grub. And he might be able to get to his own son through Jimmy, who chewed hungrily on the edge of his cherry stem. "Wanna see something?" Tony asked Jimmy, who nodded eagerly in response.

With that, Tony flipped a quarter onto the bar. It landed in front of a faded lady with heavily-rouged cheeks and vermillion clown lips. Her hand covered the coin, which disappeared into her fist, then her purse. "Show 'em, Colleen," Tony ordered. The bar girl fished the cherry out of her cordial glass and popped it onto her mouth, stem and all. She worked her frightening lips around the way a cow might, concentrating and rolling her eyes as she chewed her cud. In a few seconds, Colleen opened her mouth slightly and stuck out her tongue as one might do to receive a Communion host. It was coated with a white film and tinged with crimson dots. Tiger saw that Colleen was missing more than a few teeth. The stubs remaining in her mouth were brown and wobbly with decay.

However, on Colleen's tongue lay the most amazing thing. The cherry stem had been neatly worked into a tiny knot. She spit the stem into her hand then laid it on the bar, grinning close-mouthed with satisfaction. Tony wedged his way between both boys and deposited a friendly hand on each of their shoulders. "When you're a little older, I'll show you what else she can do with her mouth," Tony said, then winked.

His father's hot, foul breath made the fine fuzz on the inside of Tiger's ears stand on end. A wave of nausea passed over him as distinctly as a surge at Coney Island. Tiger doused it with numerous gulps of ginger ale.

Tony saw that Jimmy Burns' glass was almost empty. With a glimmer in his eye, he emptied his shot of bourbon into the tumbler without anyone else, not even Teddy, noticing. When Jimmy took a slug of his drink, his eyes bugged out and the bourbon sprayed from his mouth like a garden sprinkler. Teddy was there in a flash, damp bar rag in hand. "Take it easy, kid," Tony warned, patting the Burns boy on the back. "Musta went down the wrong pipe," he told Teddy, who didn't believe him for a second. It was an old prank but a good one in Tony's blurry eyes.

Through the bar's thick curtain of cigarette smoke, Tiger studied a blonde-headed woman tucked into the shadows who didn't find Tony's little hoax very funny. She looked a lot like the lady Tiger had seen with her arm linked through his father's as the boy rode B & B's carousel except this one was heavier and not so pretty anymore. Her Harlow hair had a dark stripe along the scalp. When the woman saw Tiger staring, she backed further into her corner and cloaked herself in the dim light.

Tony nudged Tiger in the ribs. "Come on. You remember the song. I taught it to you when you were knee-high to a tadpole."

"Which song, Pop?"

"Why, 'Kitty and the Baby,'" Tony said, nodding around to his friends.

Tiger wasn't about to sing in front of a bunch of strangers, even if they were three sheets to the wind. "Aw, Pop, I ain't no trained seal," he whispered, hanging his head. "Please don't make me."

This was just the opportunity Jimmy Burns was waiting for, to be accepted, to be one of the gang, even if it was just a gang of lushes. He had no qualms about being a circus animal; they were well-fed, steadily rewarded for their performances with bits of dead fish and crackers. "What song?" Jimmy wondered. "I know lots of songs. My folks used to be in vaudeville."

"Vaudeville my ass," Tony quipped to the others. Then to Jimmy, he said sweetly, "'Kitty and the Baby.' It's an old standard."

"Sure, I know it," Jimmy said. He cleared his throat and warbled in a voice as pretty as a choirboy's:

> *"I went downtown to see my lady.*
> *Nobody home but Kitty and the baby.*
> *Kitty was drunk and I was sober.*
> *Kitty laid a fart and knocked me over."*

The place went wild. Even Teddy Long cracked a smile. Jimmy slid off his barstool, took a dramatic bow then hopped back up on the seat, beaming. Tiger was disgusted with the entire spectacle, namely with his friend. But there was no stopping Jimmy Burns now, especially after that yellowish pickled egg he gulped in two bites.

"Oh, oh!" Jimmy said, wiping the bits of yolk from his lips, "I got something better. A poem. My Da taught it to me. It came all the way from Ireland."

Even Tony didn't understand at first. "A limerick, you mean? That's not from Limerick, Ireland, that's...oh, never mind. Go on, then."

Young Mr. Burns was on a roll. He made a squeaky half turn on the barstool to face his audience and began:

> *"My name is John Johnson.*
> *I live in Wisconsin.*
> *I make five dollars a day.*
> *And then I meet Nellie.*
> *I jump on her belly.*
> *She takes my five dollars away."*

For this, Jimmy Burns was rewarded with a shiny pickled pig's knuckle.

There were a few chuckles in response but none from Colleen and certainly not from the Shadow Lady. Tiger was still trying to get his head around Jimmy's rhyme. Why would that man give Nellie so much money? For trampolining on her stomach? It didn't seem like a fair deal. But still, the words to that ditty made Tiger feel uncomfortable in the knickers.

While Jimmy entertained the crowd, Tony sidled up close to his son. He tried to get on Tiger's good side but the boy didn't seem to have a good side where his father was concerned. Perhaps Tiger's cockiness came from so many weeks of not living a fearful existence. There had been no fear of Tony's volatile, drunken temperament, no fear of being spanked for even the smallest infraction, no fear of being shouted up one side of the block and down another for dropping a spoon. Not to mention, no late night fights with Rosanna and the business with Kewpie. Now Tiger's fear had returned anew and was, in fact, perched on the barstool beside him.

After being swaddled in the Paradiso women's tenderness and being left to his own devices, perhaps Tiger was a bit too sure of himself. Perhaps he had gotten soft from not walking hand in hand with terror and not tucking it into bed with him each night. But the old dread crept into his heart again as brazen as you please, as though it had never left.

Still, Tony tried to win over his son nonetheless. If Tony was nothing else, he was charming. Even his brother-in-law Harry had to admit, "That man could charm the stripes off a zebra then eat it for lunch. Raw."

Tony put his hand on Tiger's shoulder then moved it to the back of his neck. It was such a vulnerable spot. Spine thin as a stickball bat, ringed with tense, catlike muscles. Tony could snap it like a broom handle in a heartbeat but instead he worked his fingers up to the boy's hairline and down his back again. Tiger's belly was so full and the bar was so dim, he could have been lulled to sleep right there. "How's the family?" Tony crooned in a soft, seductive voice.

"Okay," Tiger told him.

"Your Ma feeling better?"

"Yeah," Tiger admitted. "I guess."

"And that old battleaxe Astrid...did Gentleman Sammy kill her yet?"

Tiger cracked a sleepy smile. "Not yet."

"Your sister still at Kresge's?"

Tiger nodded, his eyelids heavy. "They gave her a raise, I think."

Tony cupped the back of Tiger's head with his palm. The boy seemed so small and vulnerable. "And your grandparents?"

"Haven't seen them for a few days. They went on a vacation."

"They take the Nash?"

"Nah," Tiger said. "They went somewhere with Aunt Lettie, Uncle Jul and the boys. Niagara Falls, I think. I wanted to go but Ma said 'no.' They're supposed to come back tomorrow."

Tony's hand abruptly stopped caressing his son and flickered up to his own chin, which he rubbed in thought. Then he tried to smooth away the slight grin that had formed in the corner of his mouth. "You boys better get going," Tony told Tiger and Jimmy suddenly. "It's near suppertime and your Ma will be worried, son."

Tiger had the odd sense that he'd done or said something wrong but he wasn't sure what it was. A sense of dread rose in the back of his throat and tasted as sour as bile.

Jimmy Burns was working on a bowl of pretzels. A pile of crumbs had gathered on the polished wood beneath his chewing face. He was on his second cup of ginger ale and was good for another, but Tony was clearly through with them. He plucked Jimmy off the barstool in mid-gulp and placed him on the ground. Tiger climbed down on his own. Jimmy didn't move until he'd finished the soda standing up and placed the glass back on the bar with a resounding clunk. "Thanks, Mr. M.," Jimmy belched.

"See ya, Pop," Tiger said, then turned to leave.

He felt his father's heavy hand on his arm, his strong fingers piercing him. "What, no kiss for your dear old dad?" Tony wondered. "Not even a hearty handshake?" Dutifully, Tiger stood on his toes and kissed his father's unshaven cheek. Tony held him there fast, grasping both shoulders as though he might shake the boy violently. Instead, Tony whispered in a harsh voice. "Don't tell anyone you seen me, okay?" he said. "It will be our little secret. All right?"

Tiger stared into his father's sea-green eyes that did not blink or look away. It didn't seem that Tony would let go until he said something. "All right," Tiger told his father. "Okay."

Tony released his son's shirt and smoothed it down. "Good," he said. "Good."

The fading afternoon light was harsh after being Shanghai-ed in the black hole that was The Stumble Inn. Tiger and Jimmy discussed the spots they saw in front of their eyes, which were startled into dilation after the bar's drunken darkness. The sounds of the street engulfed them: the metallic clang of "Kick the Can," the bell on the knife man's wagon, the wail of a baby alone is a carriage outside the dry goods store, the singsong of Moe, the greengrocer, trying to unload a bushel of overripe tomatoes.

Jimmy Burns knew that he had no dinner waiting for him at home. Tiger's stomach was still tender and rebellious from all the junk he'd piled into it, but Jimmy's belly was as tough as a pot-bellied stove and even stood out like one. The pretzels, hard-cooked egg, pig's knuckle and finally, the lupini beans, only served to whet Jimmy's appetite and he was jonesing for more. Tiger, conversely, was trying to forget how the Charlotte Russe's whipped cream was curdled by the pizza's tomato sauce and how they all sloshed together in a tepid sea of ginger ale and chocolate egg cream. "Let's see if the bagels are hot," Jimmy suggested.

Tiger thought a bland, boiled circle of bread might do his sour stomach good and might possibly absorb some of its awful acid. They headed down toward 39th Street, dodging stray dogs and bigger boys seeking little kids with chump change in their pockets. The blind man was selling pencils on his customary corner and Moskowitz, the chickenman, was chasing him from the front of his store. Jimmy paused to observe the necks of one and then two unfortunate fowls wrung, slit and then drained of blood.

Tiger couldn't watch. He stood in the doorway, looking down, making small piles of sawdust with his shoes, spreading the piles flat then piling up the fine wood powder again. Through the corner of his eye, he saw Jimmy Burns grab a handful of feathers and Moskowitz catch him by the worn shirt collar. "To look is for free," Moskowitz told him. "But I sell chicken feathers two cents." Jimmy emptied his hand and wiped it clean on his pants leg. "Get out of her you snot-nosed kid," Moskowitz added, giving Jimmy a small shove. "A boy of the streets." He noticed Tiger. "You not so bad kid. Get home to your Momma."

The bagels were indeed hot, too hot to hold, in fact. Jimmy trotted down the steps of the basement where they were boiled then baked then dumped into big, wire bins. Jimmy convinced one of the workers to give him two for a penny. Paulie, who was a friend of Jimmy's brother Duncan, pocketed the money so the boss wouldn't see. It was common knowledge among street urchins that Paulie often did this, sometimes so often that he had to move slowly so that the pennies in his pocket didn't jingle. Jimmy Burns was well-schooled in all the ins and outs of the street and Tiger often marveled in his sordid wealth of knowledge

Tossing the onion bagel from hand to hand until it cooled enough to sink his teeth into, Tiger noticed that the sun was getting low in the sky. He had to admit that the first crunch of the bagel was heavenly, crust and blackened onion bits giving way to a warm, downy interior. But the charred onion was too much for his belly to bear with all of the sweetness already in his gut. Tiger couldn't manage more than two more forced bites. The bread stuck in his throat like a chunk of cement. He spit it out into the gutter. When Jimmy asked if he could finish the rest of Tiger's bagel, he handed it over.

With onion bits clinging to the corners of his mouth, Jimmy Burns declared, "Pickles!" The pickleman wasn't far, with his wooden barrels of vinegary concoctions set out on the sidewalk. Tiger was partial half-sours, but not today. Jimmy could hardly wait for Herb the pickleman to stick his hairy arm deep into the bowels of the barrel and in fact, made Herb go in twice before he found a pickle to his liking. "Not big enough," Jimmy kept saying.

They sat on the curb, side by side with Jimmy slobbering and chewing and biting and slurping. Pickle juice dripped from his chin as he chomped merrily. Tiger tried not to look, tried to ignore the garlicky odor which rose from Jimmy's face and hands. Even after he wiped his mitts on his shirt and smeared his mouth on his sleeve, Tiger still smelled it. His stomach roiled and boiled and the more he fought it, the more powerless he became.

Then it happened: Tiger's least favorite bodily function. He spread his feet as wide as he could and puked between his knees.

Tiger vomited everything he'd eaten that day and possibly the entire week before. In addition to disgusting him, it amazed Tiger how much had been in his stomach, which is supposedly only the size of your fist. The mozzarella from the pizza floated on top of it all and looked barely digested. An orange pool had gathered between his soiled shoes and began running down toward the sewer. "Yuck," was all Jimmy Burns had to say, picking a bit of dill from between his front teeth.

Tiger hung his head, mortified, too weak to move. A hefty paw descended upon him, too large for his father's, not bony enough for Moskowitz. Tiger looked up to see Uncle Harry, pulling him to his feet. "Tiger," he said without a hint of a smile in his usually-laughing Irish eyes, "it's about time you came home."

34 The Long Way Home

Uncle Harry didn't say much on the way home from 13th Avenue. The walk seemed a lot longer than usual. Jimmy Burns had disappeared as soon as the towering cop materialized, leaving his friend Tiger alone. But it was all right. Uncle Harry, the big lug, though he cut a formidable figure, was kind and especially soft-handed with his nephew.

Without asking anything about the puddle of puke that was solidifying between Tiger's feet in the gutter, his uncle whipped out his handkerchief and wiped the corners of the kid's mouth. "You look like hell, Tiger McPunch," he said as he did so. The handkerchief smelled clean, like fresh-squeezed lemons, and had been ironed into a neat square by Aunt Jo, a neat square that was now specked with vomit.

No one paid much attention to the large policeman walking stoically beside the grubby boy. Instead of leading him home with a weighty fist on the shoulder like a truant might, Uncle Harry held Tiger's hand, a scrappy chicken's claw lost in a meaty ham hock. The hulking man looked straight ahead, taking large steps which Tiger had to practically skip to keep up with, but the boy didn't complain. Tiger liked how protected he felt with his uncle even though he knew he was in trouble.

It seemed to take forever to get to 47ᵗʰ Street, but then again, the longer it took, the further he was from getting his hide tanned. Only a few blocks away, Tiger could see the sparks from the El's wheels as it screamed around a turn. Then the fireworks faded and the air was quiet.

"You poor Ma's been sick with worry," Uncle Harry said about a half-block from the house. "But at least you're safe." Tiger was too scared to say anything but his uncle gave his hand a little squeeze to let him know that everything was truly all right. From an alleyway, Jimmy Burns watched them pass, then ducked into the gloom again.

Uncle Harry led Tiger up the stairs. The door to Poppa and Grandma Bridget's place was uncustomarily closed since they were still away. Tiger took a deep breath as he stepped into his own apartment. Uncle Harry stood behind him, letting Tiger go in first and gave him a gentle push to set him moving.

Rosanna sat at the kitchen table with her parents' jumpy Pomeranians circling her feet. Her eyes looked swollen and half-dead. Butchie and Ted ran to Tiger before his mother could even get to her feet. They tripped up the boy and his uncle until Rosanna snapped, "Get over here, you mangy mutts." And they did, cowering behind the spindly table legs.

Rosanna stood and hugged Tiger around the head and neck, clutching him to her chest. "Thank God you're okay," she gasped. "I was afraid he had you with him." Then Rosanna began to cry. There was no dressing down, no spanking, no flogging with the wooden spoon he'd made in shop class (a punishment which was his father's favorite humiliating act). Instead, Tiger had to contend with something worse than being beaten: his mother's tears. "I was so scared," she muttered, holding him tight, then, "Where the hell have you been?"

It was unusual for Tiger to hear his mother curse, even this mildly. "I was just running around the neighborhood," he said into her shoulder. "I didn't mean to worry you, Ma. I was just doing boy stuff." Rosanna loosened her grip. Tiger wiped his runny nose on his arm and she didn't even reprimand him. "What happened?" he asked.

Rosanna lowered herself back into the chair. "Your father... he..." and she started crying again, head in hand, elbow on the table.

Uncle Harry stepped in. "It seems your father took off with Poppa's car," he said. "Reached in the back door, took the keys right off the hook and drove it away. Cracked it up but good."

"The Nash?"

Uncle Harry nodded. "It's totaled. He managed to wrap it around a telephone pole in Bay Ridge."

Tiger's knees went weak. He edged himself into his mother's lap, despite the fact he was way too big for such things. Tiger was mindful of Rosanna's mysterious tender spot, wherever she'd had her "women's surgery." He was still a bit unclear about what or where it was but was still very careful. Rosanna's arms wrapped around Tiger's waist, holding him fast. "Is he all right?" the boy wondered.

"He's pretty banged up but it looks like he'll make it," Uncle Harry conceded. "Wish I could say the same for the Nash. How your grandfather loved that car."

Now it was Tony's turn to lie in a hospital bed and Rosanna's turn not to visit him. He'd loused things up worse than he could ever imagine. His right leg was in a cast and his ribs were badly bruised. But worst of all, he couldn't shake that big, dumb cop, Paddy Sullivan. What a fucking asshole. Tony vaguely remembered the flatfoot as a kid, a lanky, scabby-kneed guttersnipe much like himself, only a Mick instead of a Guinea, but with a no good drunken father just the same. His mom had a taste for the sauce, too. Tony remembered that Sully used to get real nervous in grade school when the teacher called on him. He never seemed to know the right answer. The schmo must have done all right, though, being a cop and all, which was more than Tony could say for himself.

Tony took a deep breath then cursed. It hurt to even breathe but it was probably just what he deserved, 'Probably better than I deserve,' Tony thought. He felt sick to his stomach when he thought of how his father-in-law's prize car looked hugging that pole on Gelston Avenue. How did he ever end up in Bay Ridge anyway? Oh, right, Denise was hungry and there was this little *pierogi* place he'd been trying to find.

"Your wife is fine," Tony remembered the doctor telling him, with that jerk-off Sully within earshot, "she's very upset..." And indeed, Tony could hear Denise in another room, cursing a blue streak so harsh it would make a nun say the rosary. The doctor cleaned his glasses on his lab coat. "...which is understandable," he continued. "She's got a few bumps and bruises but she's all right. The baby seems fine, too."

Upon hearing this, Sully gave Tony the hard eyes, a look so disdainful that Tony had to turn away. At least he was at Brooklyn Doctors Hospital and not United Israel-Zion under the prying gaze of Dr. Lewis. Thank God, or the devil, for small favors. But as Tony's hard luck would have it, Sully had picked up some overtime that very night and was hoofing it in the Ridge when the telephone pole got in the way of the Nash. Though his shift was long over, Sully refused to leave Tony's side. And not for the right reasons. Not because he cared about Tony's well-being but because he wanted to see him behind bars.

It did Sully's heart good to see the rotten bastard flat on his back with a black eye to boot. Sully only wished he'd been the one to give him the shiner. He hoped the Paradisos would have the gumption to press criminal charges against their son-in-law for stealing their car, but he highly doubted that they would. Sully had seen it way too many times before, a sick sense of familial pride, a warped sense of duty.

Nearing the end of their road trip, no one knew exactly where Poppa and Bridget and the other Paradisos were. Somewhere between Schenectady and Kingston was Sully's best guess. They'd be home tomorrow and would hear the bad tidings soon enough. No sense in ruining their last night away. Sully didn't want to be anywhere near 47th Street to see the collapsed look on Poppa's face when Harry broke the unfortunate news to him.

"Seemed like a good idea at the time," Tony had told the other officer regarding the "borrowing" of his in-laws' vehicle.

"People get all sorts of good ideas when they've tipped back a few," Officer DiCaro admitted. Sully had witnessed it before, "that Italian thing," he liked to call it. An overly-friendly tone people adopt with strangers when their ancestors come from the same boot-shaped peninsula. Sully didn't like his temporary partner to begin with—he'd heard DiCaro was a crooked cop from more than one reliable source. Even wincing in pain, Tony's charisma shone through and worked its magic on Anthony DiCaro. They shared not only the same name but many of the same bad personality traits.

Sully pulled the other cop off to the side. "Look, I know this guy from Borough Park," Sully told DiCaro. "He's bad news."

DiCaro ran his hand through his slicked-back black hair and fit his cap back down on top of it. "You Mick cops are always saying that about us Italians," DiCaro smiled through his mismatched teeth. "Cut the guy some slack. He's hurt."

Sully and DiCaro had been first on the scene. They'd been walking along Fifth Avenue near 92nd Street when they heard the impact of the crash and ran down 92nd, following the screams. Sure enough, there was a pretty good collision at the intersection of Gelston between a car and a telephone pole. The moment Sully saw Tony behind the wheel of the Nash, he stopped running. "Come on," DiCaro shouted. But Sully still couldn't move. Poppa's beautiful machine was a mass of twisted metal and crushed glass. And that whore had her fat ass in Bridget's seat, squawking to rival every seagull in the Narrows.

Sully sat on the edge of the curb, scratching his head. He felt as though he'd lost something that belonged to him. In a sense, he had. In many ways, the Paradisos were more a family to him than his own flesh and blood. Not counting Irene, Ray and the kids, of course. Losing the Nash would probably kill the poor old guy.

Tony tried to figure out how long it had been since he'd felt fresh bed linens against his skin. Quite possibly since he'd left Rosanna's household. Everything Denise touched had a gritty feel to it, even new things. She was one of those dirty girls who still seemed unclean immediately following a bath, whereas

Rosanna always had a fresh, scrubbed scent to her skin, even in the height of summer. Maybe it was the Kirkman's but maybe it was just something virtuous in his wife.

The injection the nurse gave him helped with Tony's pain but seemed to make the sting of guilt even worse. But eventually, as always, Tony managed to convince himself that nothing was his fault, not the accident, not anything. It was Denise's, for turning into such a pig, for losing her job, for luring him away, for making them lose the apartment, for craving pierogies. Nothing was ever Tony's fault. Not in his bloodshot eyes.

"*Nu?* Where's the rent, Mr. Martino?" Tony could still hear the crackling voice of his landlord startling him in the hallway. The piece of shit crept out of the shadows like a cockroach, a prowling rat-faced creature himself.

"Next week, Mr. Weiss. I promise," Tony told him, then tried to move on.

But Isaac Weiss blocked the entire landing with his corpulence. His yarmulke was askew but never fell off his head — perhaps it was nailed into place. The filthy strands of his prayer belt were visible hanging beneath his shirt and he fiddled with the ends as he spoke. "That's what you said last week and the week before that," Mr. Weiss wheezed. The very act of talking seemed to be a monumental effort for Tony's landlord. Mr. Weiss wiped his sweaty brow with the edge of his prayer belt.

"Just until next payday," Tony said with a squinty smile, then tried to move past his landlord again, but the roadblock of flesh still didn't budge.

"Payday was yesterday," Mr. Weiss reminded him, resting his folded arms on his vast belly.

"It was a little short this week," Tony lied. Actually, he'd been paid for a shift of overtime which he'd already transformed into scotch and pissed away.

"It's always something, isn't it, Mr. Martino?" his slovenly landlord said.

"Ain't that the damndest thing?" Tony laughed.

But Mr. Weiss didn't. "Mr. Martino, your rent's more than two weeks late."

Tony's foot toyed with a piece of stained linoleum that curled away from the wall. Trash was piled up in the corner and paper circulars were scattered across the floor like lily pads. "I've been holding back on the rent because toilet box leaks. I told your wife about that a week ago," Tony offered, grasping at straws now.

Mr. Weiss fondled the strands of his *gartel*, although he didn't appear to be praying. He stroked it like he would the thick ropes of a woman's hair, though Tony knew for a fact that Mrs. Weiss' pate was shaved bald according to Orthodox Jewish tradition. The rule stated that a married woman was only to appear attractive to her husband, quite a stretch even for a pious man when Beryl Weiss was the wife in question. She wore a *sheitel*, or wig, in public, or else a ratty kerchief around her head in the apartment. "*Nu?* I'll see to it that the toilet is fixed," Mr. Weiss conceded. "But what about that hole in the wall right next to your apartment door?"

"I have no idea how it got there," Tony lied. "You might as well fix that too while you're at it."

"It looks like someone punched it," Mr. Weiss persisted.

Tony shrugged in response. "No clue. But someone really made a wreck of it, huh?"

Mr. Weiss wasn't about to give an inch. "Speaking of wrecks, I've gotten a glimpse of your place. It wouldn't hurt for your ladyfriend to clean once in a while. She's not from the cleaners, is she?"

"I could say the same thing to you," Tony said, kicking a stray can of baked beans that had escaped from a pile of garbage.

Mr. Weiss' face reddened and his jowls shook with anger. "It's my house. I can keep it any way I choose," he said. "And if you don't like it, then move! But only after you pay me what you owe me!"

"I might just ditch this rat trap," Tony nodded.

"We didn't have rats before you got here," Mr. Weiss shouted. "Mice, maybe but not rats. Not before your kind got here."

Tony's rage hardened like a fist in his gut, a hardened fist that ached for another drink. With all his might, Tony shoved the big man up against the wall and pinned him there. The round fellow could have easily pushed Tony aside but Izzy Weiss didn't even put up a struggle. 'Everyone knows sheenies don't fight back,' Tony thought with sick pleasure. Then to Mr. Weiss: "My kind! My kind, you fat-fucking-kike-Jesus-H.-Christ-killing bastard! What do you know about my kind?" Tony bellowed.

There was the sound of doors being locked, of peepholes scraping open, then scratching closed. Tony felt Mr. Weiss tremble beneath the arm he had pressed into his landlord's thickly wattled neck. Even the generous folds of flesh under Mr. Weiss' chin shook. There was the rattle of a door chain, a creak of rusted hinges, the squeak of a door opening, then dim light cast into the darkened hallway, followed by, "Izzy...Isaac?"

Beryl Weiss rivaled her husband in enormity as well as in stridence. Her voluminous caftan hung down to her hose, which were rolled onto her fat ankles. Upon her head was a greasy turban as crookedly placed as Mr. Weiss' yarmulke. Gray stubs of her short shorn hair peeked from beneath her headdress. Tony could see that like her husband, Beryl was also balding. When Mrs. Weiss spotted Tony with her husband tacked to the wall, she flew into a tizzy and spat forth a litany of Yiddish to which Mr. Weiss responded in English. "No. Don't. I'm handling this," he told her, gasping.

"Ha! I see how you're handling it," his wife spat.

"Beryl, get back inside. Mind your business," he heaved.

"This is my business!" she shouted. "Pay up, you dago drunk!"

Tony didn't respond at first, just pressed his forearm further into Mr. Weiss' windpipe. The man was now purple as an eggplant and flopping like a flounder. "*Oy! Oy!* You're killing him!" Beryl Weiss yelled.

Another door opened. "You want I should call the cops, Beryl," Mrs. Tavelich from 2D wondered. For once in her life, Beryl Weiss was speechless.

When Mr. Weiss' body grew limp, Tony could no longer hold up his considerable girth, so he let the man thud to the soiled floor. Though still not conscious, Izzy Weiss' unpleasant face slowly went from plum to pink to pale. Tony took a handful of bills and change from his pocket and rained it onto the still mound. Only after Tony began to walk away did Mrs. Weiss approach her husband's body, and instead of coming to the fallen man's aid, she gathered up the money. "Touching filthy lucre on the Sabbath?" Tony said with contempt. "What a rotten Jew you are."

Tony lunged at the fat, kneeling woman and tore at the turban, revealing her ragged, bare head. He threw the cloth to the ground and spat on it, leaving Beryl Weiss wailing into the pile of cash she clutched as she hunched over on the ground on her hands and knees.

Tony had Denise pack two hasty suitcases. They made an exodus from the Weiss Wasteland in a hurry, left their battered second-hand furniture, left the leaky toilet, left the rats big as small alley cats. But before they did, Tony pissed in the kitchen, aiming his putrid stream of urine into a corner behind the stove. It would be hard to clean, hard to find even, and the place would stink more than it already did.

When Tony was sure his landlords were simpering in their apartment, arguing about what to do, he and Denise made a break for it. She didn't ask many questions because she'd been eaves-dropping on the argument. No need for a glass pressed to the wall this time. She knew enough about her boyfriend's ill temper not to open the door and cause even more of a commotion. When he was drunk enough or pissed off enough, Tony could turn on you like a mongrel. It had happened before, more than once.

Denise and Tony jumped the next West End train out of Coney. He flashed his T.W.U. badge at the man in the booth and got a free ride for the both of them. Once in Borough Park, they holed up at The Stumble Inn, with Tony wondering what the hell his next move should be. Denise pressed into a corner, trying to make herself disappear while he pondered. 'What happened to my nice life?' she wondered, 'My nice clothes, my furs and pretty baubles?' All hocked, all gone, until just this boozing bum remained. No more Broadway shows or fine restaurant meals or dancing till closing time at Roseland. It had come down to this, being homeless, knocked up and broke besides.

Tony thought and drank for two solid hours. He still didn't know what to do or where to go. But when he caught a glimpse of Tiger roaming the Avenue with that no-good Burns kid, it suddenly came to him. It came to him like a news flash.

35 Empty Space

They knew something was wrong before they even stepped out of the car. First, Rosanna had made the trip downstairs and was waiting for them on the porch, nervously rocking in the old wooden rocker. Harry leaned against one of the starched, white columns nearby, puffing on a Camel. Tiger was perched on the top porch step. Rosanna always forbade him to sit on the ledge, for fear he would topple off, but that's exactly where Kewpie sat, with her back against a post, taking her turn at reading *Gone with the Wind*. They all seemed to be waiting for something.

With her heart beating hard, Bridget finessed her sleeping grandson's head from her shoulder and onto Lettie's so she could work her way out of Julius's Ford. Bridget's pleasantly-lined face shone with the prospect of seeing the rest of her family, all of whom she'd pined for, although it had only been a week, and a wonderful car trip at that. But looking at these expectant faces, she couldn't help but speculate about who was gravely ill or who had died.

Poppa and Julius were already out of the Ford, which the kids nicknamed "Flossie," like a dependable, old milk cow. The men wrestled the elder Paradisos' two suitcases from the packed trunk, doing their best not to upset the bushels and pints of fresh fruits and vegetables that were skillfully wedged between the satchels. "Don't forget the souvenirs," Bridget reminded them. They had. 'Those two would forget the very heads on their shoulders if they weren't screwed down,' she thought and smiled. It was just then, when Poppa turned to look at his wife, that he noticed the Nash was gone. First, he thought Sam might have taken it out for a spin but somehow he knew that wasn't the case. His family's dire expressions told him so.

Bridget waddled under the weight of the paper shopping bag. The Niagara Lakes region had been bountiful with gifts: a porcelain horse for Tiger, some tortoise shell hair combs for Kewpie, orange blossom cologne for Rosanna, a hunk of summer sausage for Harry, a delicate carved rose for Jo's *chachka* collection, a lovely tablecloth from Provence for Astrid and a peeing boy in an outhouse for Sam, who liked such things, much to his wife's chagrin. There was also a decorative plate depicting the Falls for John and Camille, whose kitchen wall was lined with collector's items like these.

Bridget stopped dead in her tracks when she finally realized that the car was gone. But she didn't say anything, just resumed walking, a bit more slowly and unsteadily this time. Tiger rushed up to help her with the bag. "What did you get for me?" he asked excitedly, because he knew she always brought something good. The promise of a toy had momentarily overridden his sense of dread at his grandparents learning the sad saga of the Nash's fate.

"Tiger..." Rosanna began.

Bridget put the bag down on the sidewalk. "That's it? No hug? No kiss? No, 'I missed you, Grandma?'"

Tiger jumped up and gave her a quick peck on the cheek. "I missed you like crazy, Grandma Bridget," he told her.

Tiger lifted the bag, which was heavy and unevenly packed, alternately soft, lumpy, sharp-edged, sturdy and delicate, depending on where you poked it. "I did miss you," Tiger assured his grandmother again. "Now, what'd you get me?" Julius and Poppa came up behind them with the suitcases.

It wasn't until Bridget reached the top of the stoop when she asked, "Who died? You look like you're ready for a funeral."

"Where's the Nash?" Poppa wondered, after he said hello and set down the suitcase.

Harry didn't know where to begin. He cleared his throat and tried weakly. "I'm sorry to have to tell you this," he sighed. "But it was in an accident. He took the keys and..."

Bridget fingered the cross around her neck and leaned against a porch column. Poppa sunk into an empty Adirondack chair near Rosanna. "Who took the keys?" the old man gasped.

Rosanna burst into tears. "My no-good husband," she said, masking her face with her hands and dropping her head into her lap. "I'm so sorry, Pop."

Poppa's hand drifted absentmindedly to his daughter's head and rested there. Her hair was softer than he imagined it might be, and fine, like a child's. He still couldn't believe what Harry's words. "How bad is it?"

"Bad," Harry said. "Totaled."

"I want to see it," Poppa told him.

"I could take you," Harry nodded. "It's all the way out in the ass end of Bay Ridge. Excuse my French," he said to Tiger and the women.

Rosanna lifted her head to get a reading on her father. He couldn't sit still any longer. Poppa struggled to his feet and gave her his handkerchief. Rosanna's nose was running and her eyes were puffed, but beyond the puffiness was the expression of exasperation and utter defeat. "And Tony?" her father wondered.

"He's at Brooklyn Doctors," Harry told him. "Busted his leg and bruised a few ribs. His story is that you let him borrow it."

Poppa adjusted the collar of his sports shirt. "But we weren't even home."

"I know that and you know that," Harry said to him. "Maybe the authorities should know that, too. Robbery is a felony. He committed a crime and should be punished for it. He destroyed more than just a car, Pop."

"But he's family," the old man responded quietly.

As for the Martinos, they showed no emotion except perhaps relief at the thought of their oppressor being locked behind bars.

Poppa shook his head. "I've got to think about it," he said, making his way into the house, still shaking his head.

Bridget eased herself into the chair her husband had just vacated and took hold of Rosanna's hand. The salmon-colored dress with the pearl buttons that had looked so pretty moments ago now just exaggerated Bridget's ashen skin. "Son of a bitch," was all she could manage.

"I know," Rosanna said. "I know."

Kewpie threw down the hefty thousand page novel with a thud. "He should go straight to hell for what he's done," she told them angrily. "All of it." The girl possessed her father's stoic emotionlessness and was down the steps, moving along 47th Street without so much as a tear or a trembling lip. They didn't see her again until suppertime.

Although it was a beautiful, temperate end of summer day, Tiger didn't venture outside. The start of school was little more than a week away and there wouldn't be many days left like this. His mother kept prodding him to at least go out on the porch to play. It wasn't healthy for a ten-year-old boy to be brooding inside when the sun was shining. But Tiger still didn't go out, not even when Jimmy Burns gathered up the courage to come call for him. Jimmy nervously rang the doorbell, standing in the vestibule at the bottom of the steps, shifting from foot to foot as he awaited his friend's verdict. Finally, Tiger showed his face at the top of the landing and simply said, "No," sending Jimmy on his way. The boy had been witness to his father's shiftiness and Tiger hoped the kid had the sense to button his lip.

In some small way, Tiger felt responsible for what had happened. He should have known, should have suspected that his father had been up to something. Was this a sin of omission? But he truly had no idea that his father might do such a thing. With all the bar smoke, sugar and gluttony of the afternoon, Tiger reasoned that his judgment had been impaired. Would he be considered an accessory to the crime? Nick and Nora were always blabbing away about that. Should he tell someone? Uncle Harry, Sully or even Father Dunn, who was paid to keep his yap shut and just listen. After all, the priest had taken a vow of silence. But the boy was too scared to tell anybody, even a priest.

Tiger didn't see his grandfather all afternoon, although he kept trying to run into him. When he went downstairs to their apartment, Bridget said Poppa had gone for a walk. A long one. Bridget herself was doing what she did best: cooking away her sorrow. She didn't necessarily eat what she cooked—and today she was too heartsick to have much of an appetite—but the very act of cooking was a consolation in itself. To feed others, to make something tangible, nourishing and delicious out of raw flour, runny eggs and dead meat was truly an accomplishment in her eyes.

"Come on," Bridget told Tiger. "The eggs came all the way from a farm in Kingston. I picked them from the chicken's behind myself." Thus, she convinced Tiger to have a pepper and eggs sandwich even though he protested that he wasn't hungry. As he chewed the doughy delight, with its delicate sprinkling of grated cheese on top and symphony of red and green peppers steamed just so, Tiger told his grandmother about how he'd busied himself while she was gone. He carefully avoided the part about chancing upon his father at The Stumble Inn but did tell her about the egg creams and even the pukefest. "Could you imagine? The kid didn't even know that egg creams had no eggs in them," he said.

Tiger managed to make his grandmother smile several times, even laugh a few, but it was with a sadness behind the rich sound.

When Astrid and Sam came by, it was clear that she had already worked herself into a frenzy. But Tiger heard Sam instruct her on the porch before they went inside, "Don't even start. I'm warning you." And it came with such intensity, the threat of violence laced behind his words, that for once, the stubborn, headstrong woman listened to her husband. Astrid was especially kind and consoling. She managed to sample everything her mother put in front of her with great relish and no mention of chopped carrots or the 21 Club. Sam was full of hugs and flattery for Bridget, which she eagerly gobbled up with as much vigor as he did her no-bake blueberry tart. They'd brought home a quart of blueberries from upstate and Bridget set to work transforming them into wondrous dishes immediately. Indeed tomorrow, there'd be blueberry pancakes for breakfast and she'd call Tiger downstairs to sample some.

John and Camille came by too, Cam full of her usual sweetness, even more so, but John was livid. He didn't say much but looked like hell. His hat was pushed back on his head and underneath, his hair was explosive. His necktie was loosened and his shirt rumpled, as though he'd been up all night, plotting something wicked. Tiger caught snippets of his conversation with Sam, Harry and Sully, who'd briefly stopped by while walking the beat. Things like, "During the war...machete...never get away with...garrote..." and "gut him like a dog." Aunt Jo strolled over from 44th Street.

It occurred to the boy that this was very much like a wake. People stopping by, offering their condolences, speaking in hushed tones, anger, stark sorrow, wistfulness, swollen eyelids and a even few tears. The Nash had been part of the family, in a sense. True, it was just a machine, but Poppa loved it. He respected it, as he did most machines, from the giant turbines at the Navy Yard to the electric can opener in the kitchen. And now Betsy was gone. It wasn't so much *that* she was gone but *how* she was gone. Although the Nash was a car and not a person, it was a terrible loss just the same.

Word hadn't gotten to the neighbors yet but they seemed to know something was awry. Mrs. Rosenkrantz—who spent so much time looking out the window that she took to placing a pillow on the sill to spare the skin on her elbows—would later remark that she saw "dat bastid" driving away with the Nash in the late afternoon the day before but thought nothing of it. She tormented herself with a healthy dose of Jewish guilt which she'd managed to perfect over the years.

Bridget was glad for all the company. It eased the ache in her heart somehow. It gave her day some purpose as she busied herself feeding her family, talking, tisking, sighing, all while stirring a big, creamy pot of *polenta*. Though usually a cold-weather dish, the hearty mush of corn meal and sharp, grated cheese was always comforting for the soul, especially with a healthy dollop of marinara sauce. The tomatoes were especially savory this year, the bushel she'd brought from the

Mohawk Valley, even moreso than the ones from Pete Acerno's backyard garden.

Bridget's daughters skirted around the issue, not mentioning Tony and his crack-up outright, yet offering the proper dose of sympathy, embraces and indirect criticism. Everyone loved their little presents, which also made Bridget feel better. "You always get the perfect gift, Ma," Jo said with a squeeze, admiring her finely-crafted blossom. Bridget gave a modest shrug at the compliment, still stirring.

"And a tablecloth from France, no less," said Astrid, who never liked anything anyone gave her. "It must have cost you a fortune."

"The exchange rate was good in Canada," Bridget explained, giving the *polenta* one final flourish with the spoon.

Rosanna lined up a row of Pyrex pudding cups on the enamel drain board so her mother could plop a generous spoonful into each. She sidled up close to her mother, whose absence she sorely felt the past few days. "Thanks for the perfume," Rosanna said. "But do I smell bad, or something?"

Bridget smiled and kissed her daughter on the side of the head, smelling oranges. "I figured you could use something to make you feel pretty," she whispered, then moved on to fill the next small bowl. Kewpie, who already wore the hair combs, was close behind her grandmother with the marinara sauce and a tablespoon. Tiger, who'd washed his hands under strict supervision, followed with a teaspoon and the Pecorino Romano, which he'd helped grate without grazing his knuckles once.

Sully and Harry had long gone back on patrol. John and Sam remained on the porch, smoking and talking quietly, coming inside to sample each new dish, then disappearing outdoors again. It was made clear to Tiger that although he technically was a man, that he was too young to be included. He was sent to summon his uncles for *polenta* and left-over peppers and eggs and finally, strong dark coffee served with fresh blueberries and cream. Tiger lingered in the vestibule before making himself known and heard more strange snippets of their talk like "...something's got to be done...I know this guy in the Bronx...five hundred clams between us...worth every penny..." and so on.

Although Tiger didn't know what it all meant, he also had the sense not to ask.

Poppa arrived after the steady stream of visitors stopped and had already made their way back to their own homes again. He seemed to know when the coast was clear. Perhaps he'd been watching.

Tiger heard Poppa before he saw him. Through the upstairs kitchen window, the boy heard the dull thud of gloved fists against the punching bag that hung in the garage. Poppa often worked out in this manner—"It's good for the constitution," he explained—so Tiger was used to the sound. But this was different somehow, heavier, with purpose, more resounding. Tiger watched for a few moments, trying to gather the courage to go downstairs.

His grandfather looked crestfallen and suddenly old when Tiger first laid eyes on him. Poppa didn't seem surprised to see his grandson magically materialize and hold the bag for him. He seemed to expect the boy. Tiger flinched under the punches but held the bag fast. His grandfather packed an impressive wallop for such an ancient man but Tiger was also strong for a kid who looked so scrappy. After a few moments of silence, Poppa asked, "How about those Yankees?"

It was something men said when they didn't know what else to say. This was safe talk, guarded talk, protected talk. They talked sports instead of saying things like: "I think my heart is broken" or "I can't take it anymore." It began when they were very young and continued until they were very old. This was a predictable, comfortable, reliable dance. And people in Brooklyn during this time lived vicariously through the actions of the Yankees or the Dodgers, so the relationship worked out well.

The Paradisos were staunch Yankees fans. Poppa was known to say that he didn't care if his daughters wed Irishmen, Germans or even Chinamen, just so long as they didn't marry Dodgers fans. It was no accident that Tiger had never set foot inside Ebbets Field, even though it was just on the other side of Prospect Park and not tucked away in the Bronx like Yankee Stadium was. Poppa had never been to Ebbets Field either and he aimed to keep it that way.

"There's no stopping Lou Gehrig," Tiger said.

"Well, now that the Babe's retired, Gehrig's got a chance to really show his stuff," Poppa told him, throwing another punch. He'd taken off his sports shirt and neatly draped it over the banister. Tiger noticed that Poppa's t-shirt was ringed with perspiration about the collar and under the arms, but all Tiger smelled was lemons. Poppa used the same aftershave as Uncle Harry did. "And don't overlook The Yankee Clipper."

"Joe DiMaggio? He's nothing but a skinny kid," said Tiger.

"And an Italian," Poppa added proudly, as though they were related. "Mark my words...never underestimate a skinny kid," he said, with a twinkle in his eye directed at Tiger. Poppa took an especially hard punch. Tiger winced but held on. Poppa took a few more swipes at the bag then stopped abruptly. Signaling that he'd had enough, Poppa took his handkerchief out of his back pocket and swabbed his forehead. Poppa pinched Tiger's cheek. "So there's hope for you, Tiger McPunch," his grandfather said.

There was a long silence. "We're not poor, Pop, are we?" Tiger wondered.

"Where did that come from?" Poppa asked. Tiger shrugged in response. Poppa thought for a few seconds, then said, "No, Tiger. No, we're not poor. There's plenty with more but more with less." He put his arm around Tiger's shoulders and gave him a squeeze. It was almost dark outside now.

Poppa inquired, "Did you listen to the Tigers game last night?"

"Sure I did," Tiger told him. "You?"

"It wasn't the same in the hotel room with your uncle," Poppa admitted. "Julius doesn't give a rat's behind about baseball."

They began walking toward the back steps. Poppa grabbed his shirt from the railing and together, they climbed the stairs. Tiger stopped before they reached the door, overtaken with guilt. "Pop," he said seriously. "It's all my fault."

"What is?"

The boy spoke quickly, nervously. "The Nash. I saw him. My father. He asked all kinds of questions. I should have known."

Poppa hooked his thumb under Tiger's chin. His eyes were beneficent and filled with love for the tortured child. "You couldn't have known," Poppa told him. "Your mind doesn't work that way."

The moon was bright but waning, a hump-backed man buckling under the pressure of the universe. The stars were bright slits above which old man and young boy paused to silently observe. The rumble of the El brought them back to reality.

"I think the Yankees will go all the way this year," Tiger said.

"I think you're probably right," Poppa agreed.

36 Insult to Injury

Harry O'Leary was one of those happy-go-lucky fellows who rarely got angry. Moments of his past had been so dire that practically everything else was sunny in comparison. In the ten or so years he'd known Michael Archangel Paradiso, he'd never once raised his voice to his father-in-law. He couldn't recall a time the thought had ever crossed his mind, until now. But in the parlor that afternoon, Harry simply blew his top. "That man's a criminal! A bum!" Harry said excitedly.

Poppa was steadfast and stoic. "Maybe so, but he's family."

"Family schamly," Sully said. It was the first and last thing he would say during the encounter since Sully wasn't family, by marriage or by blood. Sully wedged himself into a cushy armchair in the corner, folded his hands neatly in his lap and willed himself into silence.

"He's a thief! He shouldn't be running around in polite society," Harry shouted. "And it's your civic duty, for cripe's sake. That man should be behind bars before he really hurts somebody."

Irate as he was, Harry would never take the name of the Lord your God in vain. Breaking any Commandment, let alone a lightweight statute like the Third, was out of the question. He would only break the Sixth in the line of duty, and only then if forced to a crisis. But these days, he was considering it more and more. It might be a question for Father Shine, the only priest worth his weight in Holy Water, in Harry's opinion. Shine worked out of Holy Name of Jesus parish in Windsor Terrace and might very well warrant a visit.

Bridget could be heard noisily trying to occupy herself in the kitchen. She refused to be drawn into the conversation. Through the corner of her good eye, she could see her son-in-law and husband standing toe-to-toe in the parlor, practically touching. The image of Poppa calmly puffing on his pipe initially appeared aloof and unmoved, yet his tensed body said otherwise. "I have a responsibility to my family first," Poppa said.

Harry flung up his arms in frustration. "But that man's the lowest of the low! I've scraped better things off the bottom of my shoe!"

Poppa's pipe had gone out. He struck a match, held it to the bowl and sucked the stem until the tobacco glowed red. "It's not him I'm concerned about," Poppa informed his son-in-law.

"Is that it?" Harry asked. "Are you afraid he's going to hurt you? Hurt Roe and the kids if you press charges?" Harry didn't wait for a response. "I swear on my life, I'd never let anything happen to any of you. You have my word on that."

And truly, Poppa was also concerned about how Tiger and Kewpie would be affected by having a father in jail and knowing that Poppa helped put him there. Also, Poppa did worry about his daughter's safety. If a man would be so reckless as to steal a car from his father-in-law, there's no telling what else he might do. Someone who'd sunk to such depths could very easily take a life, torch a house or both. But Poppa couldn't tell Harry this. Harry was so angry, he might beat the guy to a pulp, or worse. So instead of voicing his depth of concern, Poppa decided to try and make light of it. "Besides," Poppa added. "He promised to pay me back."

"With what? He hasn't got a pot to piss in." Harry's eyes were narrowed in rage. His bulky body was stiff as a stone. Poppa knew he needed to break the tension but wasn't sure how. So, he reached up and cupped his hands around Harry's broad shoulders, looking into the cop's big, Irish face with compassion. Instead of swatting him away, Harry melted. "Aw, Pop...," was all he could manage.

"Yes," Poppa said. "I know."

To add insult to injury, Tony had no place to go when Brooklyn Doctors was ready to release him. Denise moved in with her old landlady, Aunt Mimi, who was only too glad to take back the fallen angel. To give shelter to a pregnant whore was one thing, very Old Testament—maybe even a mitzvah—but to also put up the adulterer who'd caused her downfall, that was quite another.

Rosanna felt backed against a wall when the hospital phoned and asked if Tony could stay there at least until the cast came off. He couldn't get around well enough to care for himself and he was homeless besides. Rosanna could picture Tony turning on the charm and pressuring a plain-faced, shy nurse to make the awkward telephone call. She could almost hear the horror stories he invented to get the gal to do so, weaving a tale of unabashed lies and half-truths until he wore the woman down. And what could Rosanna say? Besides, he was the father of her children, and she couldn't even put a dog out on the street.

"But he's lower than a dog," Kewpie said as she snapped a clean bed sheet into the air. "I still can't believe you said 'yes,' Ma."

"What choice did I have?" Rosanna told her. "He has no place to go. Besides, you've been sleeping with me anyway. He'll share your room with Tiger. It'll be fine, I swear, and it'll be over before you know it," Rosanna assured her and tucked the corners of the crisp, white bed linens under the mattress. "It's just until he gets on his feet. I promise. And then he'll be out of our lives forever, I swear."

Disbelief and disappointment crossed Kewpie's face. She pulled the edge of the light bedspread from her mother. "Your promises aren't worth much," she said quietly.

Rosanna smoothed down the covers until not a crease showed. "You can go back downstairs with you grandparents if you want. Just until he's gone."

But Kewpie shook her head. "I don't want to leave you alone with him."

As much as he hated to admit it, Tiger was mildly excited at the prospect of bunking with his father. The plain fact was that young boys still loved their dads, no matter what their fathers did or how terrible they were, and they constantly sought their approval. They lived in the constant hope that things would magically improve, that the old man would treat them more kindly, love them back, if only the kids tried harder or were better sons. It was always something they did—or didn't do— that made their Pop the way he was. If they were the type of son a dad could be proud of, if they could hit the ball two sewers away in stickball, if they didn't fail math, if they could memorize "The Charge of the Light Brigade," then things might change. Those boys thought it was something they were or weren't that made their fathers so evil. They figured it must be something lacking in them. And that's precisely what Tiger thought.

But in truth, Tony was the one who was lacking. "That man's bad to the bone," Bridget had to admit to Jo, and Bridget never breathed a bad word about anybody.

Jo didn't respond, just silently stirred the simmering pot of blueberries with the wooden spoon Tiger had made in shop class the year before, one of many. She felt the sugary mixture thickening slightly but it would take a bit more time and patience before it became jam. Jo was afraid of what Harry might do if Tony stepped out of line. He had a service revolver and a nasty temper where that man was concerned. Besides, there were all of those late-night phone calls to John, speaking in hushed tones with his rough mitt cupped over the receiver so Jo couldn't hear. "You better not do something stupid to someone stupid," she warned him one morning.

"What?" Harry said in mock innocence. But Jo knew that he knew what she was talking about.

On the day Tony was to come home from Brooklyn Doctors, Sully was so bold as to visit Rosanna at the apartment. He knew it might be his last chance to see her for a long time. But what he'd say to her, he had not a clue. There were many things he'd wanted to tell her since they were kids but the words choked in his throat like day-old pumpernickel. However, Sully did know one thing—that he needed to see Rosanna, that he had to see her, and alone at that.

It was one of those humid, lazy, late summer days, the first day of September, to be exact. Rosanna scrubbed the kitchen sink, looking out the window. She could smell the honeysuckle vine that attached itself to the fence between their yard and the Rosenkrantz's, a stubborn city blossom that only got more lush and wild, with each passing summer.

Rosanna had introduced both of her children to the gift of the honeysuckles, taught them how to coax out the sugary nectar that gave the plant its name. And there Tiger was, baseball glove tucked into the crook of his arm, taking a delicate, bugled flower from the vine, tearing off the piece at the base, then sucking the sweetness out of the end. He grinned, licked his lips, then reached for another. Rosanna would have to try that again herself. It had been years since she'd had honeysuckle.

She was startled by the sound of Sully's knock on the door as she quickly dried her hands on a dishtowel. At first, she thought it might be Tony but her husband wouldn't knock, he'd simply barge in as though it were still his place, as though he'd never left. But Sully had manners. Hat in hand, he even carried a little box from Piccolo's and held it daintily by the red-and-white candy cane striped string. "Seven-Layer Cookies. I know Tiger likes 'em," he explained, but refused a cup of tea.

"Well, sit down at least," Rosanna smiled. Sully always got her to smile, even on the worst of days. He gave her a gentle sort of joy and made her feel comfortable in her own skin, maybe because he was so uncomfortable in his.

But Sully didn't sit. He handed Rosanna the cookies then stood there in the middle of her kitchen, balling up his newsboy cap in his hands. She put the cookies on the table and didn't take a seat either. Sully contemplated the linoleum, which Rosanna was glad was clean. "To what do I owe this pleasure?" she asked.

Sully finally glanced up, avoiding her eyes at first, those honest, chocolate-brown eyes that tore him to pieces. Then he swallowed hard and looked into her face. "I just wanted to talk to you," he said.

"So, talk," she coaxed him.

But Sully couldn't. The words gargled up in ragged fragments then went back down his throat again. The poor man looked pained. Rosanna laid her hand on his arm. "Just say it, Patrick."

This time, he looked her straight in the eyes and her tender gaze held his. "You know I only want the best for you and the children," Sully began.

"Of course, Patrick, you're a good friend," she told him.

"But that man," he said, through gritted teeth, "that man is not the best. Even though he's their father, even though he's your husband. You can't let him back in here."

"It's only for a little while," she assured him. "He has nowhere else to go. It'll be okay, you'll see."

"No," Sully said. "You'll see. Roe, I've been around a lot of bad people. Thieves, murders, liars, cheaters, all kinds of scum. And that man frightens me."

"How do you mean?" she wondered.

"There's something in his eyes..." Sully stammered. "I'm afraid he'll hurt you."

"He's already hurt me," Rosanna told him sharply. "There isn't much more he can do to me. Besides, I made up my mind I'm not going to let him hurt me anymore. The kids neither."

"Sometimes it's not always up to us," Sully explained. "I've walked into apartments and I've seen things, things you wouldn't believe. Things people do in the name of love."

Rosanna shook her head. "He's on crutches, for God's sake. He's practically helpless."

"His sort is never helpless, believe me."

Rosanna studied Sully's worried face. "What was I supposed to do? Put him out on the street? He's my kids' father, for God's sake."

"I don't think they'd mind one bit. Your parents either."

"Leave my folks out of it."

Sully had struck a nerve and was going with it. "Besides, Tony will always land on his feet. There's always someone left to scam, always some card left to turn or some floozy to welcome him into her bed."

"Stop it, Sully!" Rosanna found her way to a kitchen chair and sunk into it. "You don't know him. He's not that awful. Why, he's...a good..." But Rosanna couldn't think of one thing Tony was good at, not his job, not being a father, not being a husband. Just drinking. He did a fine job at that. At a loss, she shouted, "It's not his fault. He had a bad childhood!"

That was it for Sully. "A bad childhood! I had a bad childhood! And I don't go around whoring and stealing and God knows what else. Bad childhood? My folks run out on me and Irene when I was twelve and we were on our own since then. I'll show you a bad childhood."

With that, Patrick Sullivan simply fell apart. Rosanna had never seen a man cry in her life. A mountain was crumbling in her kitchen, weeping without shame, with abandon and in profound, ugly pain. He swayed with the effort and didn't even try to cover his face. Sully's tears spattered on the linoleum, spattered his shirtfront, soaked the hat he twisted in his fist.

Without thinking, Rosanna sprung to her feet, feeling a tiny pang where her belly had been sewn up, but it quickly passed. She wrapped her arms around Sully and his arms easily went around her much smaller, slighter body. At first, she had the sensation of hugging a tree trunk, that's how big and wide and broad he was. But Sully was different than a tree; he was warm and alive in her arms. She rocked him and cooed to him as she would to one of her children, as she might do to a man she loved in bed. And slowly, gradually, he stopped crying. Rosanna and Sully kept on holding each other long after the tears subsided and the sobs stopped wracking his body.

"I don't even know why I'm here," Sully told her.

"Sure you do," Rosanna said.

Suddenly, the door crashed open, pushed by the tip of a wooden crutch.

37 Walking on Eggshells

Tony's homecoming wasn't greeted with fanfare like Rosanna's was. No one met him at the hospital, despite the fact that he was tottering around on crutches. He couldn't expect any of his brothers-in-law to pick him up, could he? And certainly not Poppa, who, thanks to Tony, didn't even have a car. There was no one to welcome Tony with open arms, but with the way he'd screwed things up, he was lucky the whole lot of them weren't waiting for him with closed fists, poised to strike.

Then again, Tony, with that monumental chip on his shoulder, didn't think he was lucky about anything. His girlfriend was pregnant. He'd been suspended from work again, this time for driving drunk in a vehicle which may or may not have been stolen, with criminal charges pending. Tony was returning to 1128 47th Street the prodigal son-in-law, and because he was a betting man, he laid dollars to doughnuts that no one would greet him with a fattened calf on a spit. The nurse unceremoniously handed him a taxi voucher and sent him on his way. He didn't even have an overnight bag of belongings—his suitcase had been confiscated with the car—perhaps because he belonged nowhere.

It had been three days since Tony had a drink and he was going to have one now, damn it. The hollow knot in the pit of his stomach couldn't be ignored. Although he didn't have the shakes, he was certainly shaky. And not because of the crutches either. Tony had been practicing on his sticks in the hallways of Brooklyn Doctors, going up and down, back and forth, until he was actually pretty good on them. But his entire body needed a drink, ached for it.

A few blocks from the hospital, there was a little hole in the wall called Tilly's Tavern. These sorts of places had a habit of finding Tony, or vice versa. Situated near a concrete triangle of a park between 4th and 5th Avenues, near 94th Street, Tilly's had two doors, one that opened onto each avenue, making for an easy escape from the wife, girlfriend or jealous suitor. Tony liked the place. It was dark and anonymous and easy to exchange his taxi voucher with an old rummy on the barstool beside him for some filthy lucre.

'I'll only throw back one or two, just to set myself right,' Tony promised himself. 'Just to get rid of that cold, gnawing feeling in my gut.' But one or two led to two or three more. After that, Tony forced himself to head for the trolley. Whether it was his crutches or his work pass, he managed to board for free. It was a sizable ride to Borough Park from Bay Ridge, and Tony convinced himself that he'd sober up on the way. He did to a certain extent, but didn't take into account the bucket of blood bar under the El, a place so run-down and forgotten that it didn't even have a name.

By the time Tony was ready to hobble home, he could barely maneuver his crutches. A stranger might have thought he was still awkward on them and even pitied him but Tony's neighbors knew better. They had the sense to steer clear of Mr. Martino when he'd tipped back a few because there was no way of telling whether he was a happy drunk or a mean one, pissed off at the world. It was usually the latter.

None of the passersby said a word when Tony stopped to take a leak in the side kitchen doorway of Mr. Wong's place. The fetid, beer-induced stream of piss flowed all the way down to Piccolo's. After he buttoned his trousers, Tony turned quickly and surprised Billy-the-Bike-Boy, who almost fell off his squeaky Schwinn. "Watch where you're going, you fucking retard!" Tony shouted.

It was true that Billy-the-Bike-Boy wasn't right in the head but despite this shortcoming, he was well thought of in Borough Park. Billy couldn't help the way he was after the accident but he tried to make up for it by being a good sort of Joe. He was harmless and kindhearted, always doing errands for old folks who needed a hand, making deliveries for Moskowitz when he was too busy to do so himself. It was said that Billy had pedaled down every street in Brooklyn at least once, probably twice. Folks were well aware of the fact that after his mishap, Billy was retarded but no one said it out loud. At least not the way Tony did. Poor Billy didn't have a mean bone in his body and was gentle as an unweaned pup.

Billy-the-Bike-Boy stopped dead in his tracks upon hearing Tony's comment. Billy knew he wasn't like everyone else. He couldn't read or write but no one had ever called him that name, not even the mean kids in the neighborhood. Billy stared at Tony open-mouthed. "What's the matter? Don't you know you're a retard?" Tony snapped and staggered on. For good measure, Tony stopped, turned and brought his crutch down on Billy-the-Bike-Boy's rusted front fender.

"Hey!" was all Billy could muster, looking down at the crooked aluminum.

"Hey yourself," Tony told him, raising the crutch again as if he meant to bash in Billy's skull. But tipsy as he was, Tony lost his balance and fell backwards into Violetta and Nunzi DeMeo's white picket fence, scratching himself on their rose bush, which was in full bloom. Billy-the-Bike-Boy snickered quietly into his fist but Tony didn't see. He was too busy extracting himself from the roses.

Mrs. DeMeo, who was perched on her front porch like a curious whooping crane, had been staring at Tony unabashedly up to this point. But she put her considerable nose back into the peas she'd been shucking as soon as his eyes met hers. "What are you looking at?" Tony prodded, wiping a thin ribbon of blood from his neck where a thorn had gotten him. She didn't dare answer but thought to herself, 'Nothing much.' Then Tony limped along his way.

Billy-the-Bike-Boy walked his Schwinn under the El, a scraping sound following him where rubber met metal. 'Maybe Moskowitz can help me unbend it,' he hoped.

It was close to suppertime and mostly everyone on 47th Street seemed to be home. Activity crackled behind open windows. Doors were propped wide to let in the breeze. Yet as Tony passed, sashes creaked shut, kids gathered up their jacks and retreated into alleyways, gossiping women stopped talking and pretended not to see him. Bertha Rosenkrantz left her padded post at the windowsill and went to check on her potted meat. Even Tiger, although he heard the rhythmic snap of his father's crutches hitting concrete, didn't run out to greet him. Bored of honeysuckles, the boy was now intently studying a dragonfly's flight among Poppa's backyard hostas.

Tony had to admit that the old house looked good, ablaze with roses of all shades, purple hydrangea big as a baby's head and daylilies the color of the sun. But Tony couldn't say he was glad to be back. He took a swipe at a lily and snapped its neck. It bowed as if in prayer then fell to the dirt.

The five brick steps out front weren't difficult to master, even inebriated. Tony put both crutches in his left hand, put pressure on his good foot, using his right hand to grip a porch column for extra support. Tiger listened closely, half hoping for a crash and the sound of cracking wood, then immediately felt guilty. When Tiger forced himself to make his way to the front porch, his father was already gone.

The glass doors were unlocked. But Tony told himself that if those damn Paradisos had any sense, all doors and perhaps even the windows would be double-bolted against his entry. Tony could hear movement inside his in-laws' apartment, the scraping of pots, the buzz of a radio serial, and he was certain that they could hear him clunking through the hallway, but no one came out to say hello. 'Fuck them,' Tony thought, 'fuck them all. Who needs them?' Then, in the next breath, he answered, 'You do, you homeless, good for nothing, crippled prick, you do. And if they weren't such decent people, your sorry ass would be in jail.'

Tony counted the carpeted steps. Fifteen of them, and steep as hell. He took a deep breath and tackled them one by one, the way a toddler just learning the intricacies of stair-climbing might. Tony rested on each step, leaning on the banister, then heaved himself up onto the next. The flowered carpet muffled his ascent and would hopefully cushion his fall. Wouldn't they all love to see him laying there, a shattered heap, lying in a puddle of his own blood. He could picture them clustered around his twisted, broken body like a bunch of jackals. Sure they would, but he'd be damned if he'd give them the satisfaction. Tony grasped the wooden railing even tighter as he slowly made his way to the top step.

He hugged the newel post like an old friend and caught his breath. He was sweating from the effort or maybe from the beers. Tony didn't expect a handmade "Welcome Home" sign but figured maybe there would be something good on the stove. But there was nothing of the sort. The door was partly ajar as was Rosanna's custom, so she could call down to Mom and Pop and they could call up to her. Tony kicked the door all the way open with the foot of his crutch. A little too hard because it slammed against the cupboard behind it and bounced back again.

It was too fast to figure out what was happening. All Tony knew was that he saw his wife in Sully's arms. What they'd been doing, he couldn't tell. They broke apart too quickly. The cop was gone without a word and down the stairs before Tony knew it.

Rosanna was flustered and didn't seem to know what to do with her hands. "You're home," she said in a voice that was fluttery and high-pitched.

"A little too soon, it looks like," Tony told her.

"I put you in with Tiger," Rosanna continued. "I moved some of your things into his dresser. Bottom two drawers." She moved through the narrow rooms that were connected to each other like railroad cars and Tony followed. Rosanna didn't even stop at what used to be their bedroom, just kept going to the one at the end that adjoined the porch. "Kewpie's been sleeping with me since I had the surgery," she explained, "just in case I need something in the middle of the night."

"First your folks, now you," Tony said. "She's always helping out someone or another."

Rosanna's eyes did a quick study of her husband. More slight than when she last saw him, not so handsome even though his black eye was fading, tired-looking and yes, probably drunk. He wobbled on the crutches. "Kewpie's a good girl," she commented.

"More than I can say for some," he told her.

"Look, you're probably beat. I'll let you get some rest. I'm making a marinara sauce for supper. Pete Acerno gave us some fresh tomatoes from his garden. I better get started."

When she turned to go, Tony had already lowered himself onto the single bed with a sigh. "Roe," he called." And she turned back to face him, bracing herself for some sort of rabid utterance but there was none. "Thanks," he told her. Lying there with his bound leg still on the floor, Tony looked so helpless. His toes were pinched and pale white. He frowned at the effort of drawing his plaster-sheathed leg to the mattress but Rosanna didn't rush forward to help. She wasn't going to fall for it, for the charm, for the cloaked kindness, again.

"Thank my parents," she said without emotion.

"I will," he admitted. "I plan to."

"And it's only till you can get around better," she reminded him. "Till you find a place to stay."

"Sure," he said. "I know."

It was so good to wake to the fragrance of a fresh tomato sauce simmering on the burner, or to the smell of any food cooking, for that matter. Tony had no idea what time it was but the light was different now, muted, gentler, only it wasn't anywhere near dark. The shadows of the old ginkgo danced on the walls like hula girls teasing him. He heard Rosanna's voice in the other room. "Go see if your father's awake but don't wake him if he isn't," she said.

Tony hoped she was sending in Kewpie but it was Tiger who lurked shyly in the doorway, not springing to Tony's side until he saw his father's eyelids flicker open. "Ma says dinner's ready," Tiger told him, then disappeared.

The boy seemed glad to have Tony home. During supper, he talked about batting averages and the Spanish Civil War, Lefty Gomez and Franco taking power. "And how about what's happening in Greece, Pop?" Tiger wondered, then went on about the Baseball Hall of Fame, which was due to make its first inductees at the end of the year. "Do you think the Babe will make it? How about the Iron Horse?"

"Not for a very long time," Tony said. "There are quite a few who deserve to get in before Ruth and Gehrig get their due. Shoeless Joe Jackson doesn't have a chance because of that scandal but then there's George Kelly. Now when I was a boy..."

Rosanna listened to Tiger talk in a way he couldn't, or wouldn't, talk to her. In a way he seldom even spoke to Tony, who seemed to have sobered up with his nap. In one sense, it warmed her heart but in another, it broke it. There weren't many conversations like this in the past, and there would be very few like this in the future. At least not in her house.

"Where's Kewpie?" Tony asked, pulling Rosanna from her reverie.

"Working late," she told him, without even looking at him.

"Well, she's missing a great meal," he said, smiling at her. Rosanna thanked him but would not smile back.

After weeks of sleeping like a log, Kewpie found herself tossing and turning in the bed—her parents' bed—beside her mother. The sheets had rough, fumbling fingertips buried in them and made her skin itch. She swore she smelled his foul breath emanating from the pillow. Kewpie simply couldn't rest with that man under the same roof. He'd taken something from the girl, although it wasn't her virginity. He had stolen her trust. Night after night, he made off with her innocence and replaced it with fear. And now that fear closely resembled hate.

So Kewpie didn't sleep.

Neither did Tiger. He couldn't abide by Tony's snoring. Plus bunking with his father wasn't anything like rooming with Kewpie. For one thing, his father didn't like to talk about things large and small when the lights were out like his sister did. One second Tiger was telling his father about Jumbo Brown's strike-out record and the next, Tony was snoring in sleep.

The boy grabbed his light coverlet and his pillow and went out onto the porch. He curled up in the old green rocker with the sagging, wicker seat, drawing his legs up beneath him. Tiger set the chair in motion, closing his eyes, feeling the fading breath of summer whispering on his face, listening to the distant sound of the trolley's bell until the clack of the El overpowered it.

Tiger was long asleep when a heavy step approached the house, paused, then continued on its way. A nightstick twirled at the end of its leather rope, flipped from end to end, finally landing in an oversized hand, then was tossed into the air again. But even that sound faded until all that was left was the familiar creak of the old rocking chair. Nothing more.

38 Before the Fall

An air of melancholy draped over the house on 47th Street like a shroud. No one could put their finger upon it or pin a name to it, yet it was there just the same. None of the residents mentioned this unfortunate phenomenon to any of the others but still, the wicked pall was acknowledged, understood, and reluctantly accepted among them.

Even Poppa seemed different now—silent, sad, less like himself. Tiger couldn't explain it exactly but it was noticeable, even to a young child such as himself. Poppa finished out the remainder of his vacation quietly, taking lengthy walks alone, spending hours at the punching bag in the garage. While Tiger's appetite for movies eventually returned, for the first time since the boy could remember, Poppa skipped Dish Night at the Loews 46th.

In contrast, Bridget needed to surround herself with people during this difficult time, but Poppa was just the opposite. He needed to be by himself. Oftentimes, Tiger thought his grandfather might be out shopping for a new car but Bridget knew that her husband was simply walking away his sorrow. She'd been married to him long enough to know his pattern of healing.

One afternoon, Tiger spotted Poppa talking to Mr. Wong outside his chop suey house. The boy wondered why his grandfather preferred speaking with someone who was almost a stranger, rather than someone in his own family. But perhaps Poppa needed to be away from the house and things familial just like Kewpie did. Poppa always doffed his hat when he passed the Chinese restaurant's open kitchen door. Sometimes Mr. Wong came out to chat if he had a moment, giving Poppa a chance to practice his rusty Cantonese. It was comical to see the two men who were so different yet so much the same, standing belly to belly, each smoking a pipe, smiling and talking, nodding and puffing.

Another time, Poppa took Tiger with him to the foot of Pierrepont Street near the Brooklyn Bridge. There, they strolled side by side without saying a word to each other. The only brief conversation they shared was when Poppa stopped at the railing to tell the boy about the Woolworth Building across the East River. Tiger knew all about it but let his grandfather talk regardless.

It was busy at the Navy Yard but no matter how busy it was, Poppa insisted on taking his vacation, the same two weeks every year—last week in August, first week in September. The light cruiser they were working on, the *U.S.S. Brooklyn*, was behind schedule and due to be launched at the end of November. But Poppa still didn't let it get to him. Ships got finished no matter how much the bosses yelled, carried on and fretted, he said, and usually on schedule.

But what did get to Poppa was his son-in-law.

Although Poppa was cordial to Tony when he happened upon him in the hallway and asked after his leg, in truth, he had no use for the man. It wasn't just what Tony had done to the Nash; it was what he'd done to the family. However, Poppa was polite to Tony as he would have been to a stranger on the street. That's just the sort of fellow Poppa was. But in truth, he couldn't wait for Tony's cast to come off, for the good for nothing to get on his own two feet—literally—and leave. And in all the times Poppa had run into him, Tony never once apologized for what had happened. Not once.

"That man is evil personified," Bridget told Poppa late one night as they lay wide-eyed in their weathered, old bed. Like Kewpie, it was as though neither could get any rest knowing Tony was in their midst. Bridget had felt her husband's wakefulness and just started talking. Now, she was the sort who could find a positive word to say about even the most disagreeable person, so for Bridget to utter something like this about Tony spoke volumes.

"He's just a bad egg," Poppa said.

"No, he's worse than that," she disagreed. "Sometimes I think he's the Devil himself."

Upstairs, Kewpie and Rosanna lay restless beneath the cotton sheet they shared. At first, Kewpie thought it was the slumbering "Innocents" captured in the picture frame above the bed that robbed her of rest. (Like Tiger, she wasn't fond of the roly-poly, snoozing Campbell's Kids either.) Rosanna thought the cause of her own sleeplessness was that she still wasn't used to having someone in her bed again. Sometimes she and Kewpie would lay still and others, they would talk softly about the events of the day. When Tiger heard their voices, he would join them, snuggling his spindly body between his mother and sister to be a part of something, anything, and to get away from that terrible snoring. A buzz saw without a soul was in the bed next to his.

But this night, it was silent in Tiger's room except for the sound of an occasional cricket outside. The cicadas were especially loud and insistent this year, as they typically were in unusually warm summers such as this. But Tiger found strange comfort in the cicadas' high-pitched clicking that started off slow then sped up and was so loud and fast that you felt like you were going to scream. Then it abruptly stopped. He found solace in the insects' noise as well as in the silence that followed. It was sure better than drunken snuffling.

However, the women in the adjoining room took comfort in nothing for they knew that sooner or later, Tony would return. They lay under the covers like dogs dreading their cruel master's return, waiting expectantly for the sound of his heavy foot on the stair with a sense of unease and foreboding. Where Tony got the money to drink, neither of them knew, but small things began vanishing: an inconsequential trinket, a slender silver bracelet, a fancy book. Rosanna and Kewpie next expected bigger things to begin disappearing from the apartment. And soon enough, they did.

When Tony moved back in, it became commonplace for the telephone to ring, then for the caller to hang up when someone answered. This happened at all hours of the day and night. While Rosanna suspected it was the blonde woman, Kewpie thought it was someone Tony owed money to. Sometimes the hang-up call to Gedney 8-5840 was a signal for Tony to get up and go. Sometimes he returned soon after a call like this. He'd only been there a few days but it seemed like months, years, even.

Then odd things began happening throughout Borough Park. Pete Acerno's entire garden was stomped to the ground. The imprints of a left foot and a round pointed object, like the end of a broom handle, were found in the moist soil. Eva Lewis's cat went missing and was never found. "Ask the Chinaman," Tony said when Tiger told him the news at breakfast. "Wong, Wang, whatever his name is. Chances are the roast pork on the menu is roast cat." And someone put Billy-the-Bike-Boy's Schwinn on the trolley tracks, where it was smashed to bits. No one was injured, at least, but poor Billy's beloved Schwinn was bashed to smithereens. Poppa tried to make up for it by giving him a squeaky, old bicycle that had sat dormant in their basement for years and Moskowitz swore he could get it in good working order, but Billy was still crestfallen.

While Harry and Sully strongly suspected that Tony Martino was behind these incidents, they had no concrete evidence. To them, Rosanna's drooping countenance and the joyful gleam stolen from Poppa's eyes were proof enough but they needed more, something tangible, something that would hold up in court.

The Paradisos' annual Labor Day barbecue was only days away and Bridget still couldn't decide what to serve. While the 4th of July get-together was Poppa's baby, he let his wife make all the decisions on the Labor Day bash. "But my mind's a sieve,"

Bridget complained to Jo, "I can't seem to concentrate on a thing. Burgers and dogs? Chicken? Sausage? And what should I serve on the side?"

"Ma, just do what you did last year," Jo told her, rubbing her mother's stooped shoulders.

"Who can remember what I did last year?" Bridget snapped.

"Everybody loves whatever you make," Jo said. But it was of little consolation to Bridget. Jo suspected that her mother's dilemma was a small thing masquerading as a large thing to mask an even larger thing. In spite of Bridget's bleak mood, Jo coaxed her to scribble out a menu and a list. They arranged to go shopping on the Avenue the very next day. As she sipped a glass of iced tea and nibbled on a *pignoli* cookie, Jo had the courage to ask her mother, "So, how is he really?"

"I don't know what you mean," Bridget told her. "He who?"

"Any yelling? Fighting? You know, like before?" Bridget was silent. "Just say the word, Momma. Please, just let me know and..."

"And what?" Bridget wondered. Jo didn't know what to say. "He doesn't have to do anything, Josephina. He just is. He's here. And that's more than enough." Bridget pushed away the plate of cookies, her favorite vice, and got up from the table.

Similarly, Harry couldn't squeeze anything from Tiger or Kewpie. He made sure to run into them "by chance" away from the house so they could speak more frankly. For example, in the candy aisle of Kresge's or as Tiger clacked down a faraway street on the outskirts of Sunset Park in Mattie's hand-me-down roller skates. "Everything's fine," Kewpie assured him, avoiding her uncle's gaze as she handed him a white paper sack of caramels. "But I just wish he wasn't there," she continued, then went to help another customer. Tiger admitted as he paused to tighten his skate with his key, "It's sort of nice having him around but it's easier when he's not."

Up on 13th Avenue, Sully was picking up a few things at Moe the Greengrocer's after his shift one day. At first he didn't realize that the gloomy-eyed, rumpled woman two people ahead of him in line was Rosanna. After she paid for a bagful of oranges, she turned to go without noticing him. Sully put down his things and followed Rosanna out the door. It was half a block before he mustered the nerve to reach out and tap her on the shoulder. Rosanna dropped the sack of oranges. "Patrick!" she gasped.

"I'm sorry," Sully said. He rescued the fruit that rolled toward the curb then studied her as he handed back the oranges. Rosanna's eyes were ringed with dark circles again just as they'd been when she was sick. At first, he worried for her health but immediately knew the cause of her deflated demeanor. Her hair looked freshly washed but uncombed. Her dress looked clean but uncared for. Her smile was nonexistent. The spark in her eyes that he relished was gone.

To have someone look at her with such care and concern was too much for Rosanna to bear. "I've got to go," she told him and started walking again.

Sully followed. "He's tearing you apart, Roe."

Sully was much taller and his legs were much longer but he still had to struggle to keep up. "Does he put his hand to you?" Sully asked. Rosanna refused to answer, just kept moving. So determined was her step that people had to move out of her way and did. "Because if he lays a hand on you..." Sully continued.

Rosanna stopped and spun around sharply. "You'll what? Huh, Sully? What will you do? What can anybody do?"

Sully took a deep breath. "I'd fucking kill him, Rosanna. I'd kill him with my bare hands, love every minute of it and get away with it, too."

Sully thought he saw a smile flicker across Rosanna's lips, just for a second, but then her mouth became a straight, harsh line, not resembling flesh at all. "Shame on you, Patrick Sullivan," Rosanna told him. "Shame on you."

And as she turned to walk away, Rosanna caught a glimpse of a man on crutches disappearing into the swell of shoppers.

The Kirkman's Soap washerwoman was empty. Rosanna ran her fingers around the inside of the cool tin and was certain of it. She didn't even have to take it down from the shelf above the sink. Lord knows how much change she'd stashed there, in addition to what Tiger snuck in when he thought she wasn't looking. Probably enough to tie one on and then some.

This was one of those painfully calm nights when you could hear the insects rising above the urban music. Rosanna could even pick out the soft breathing of her son in the room next to hers. The downstairs doors were unlocked until Tony came in at night. He couldn't be trusted with a key. These days, there was never a time the house was left empty. Someone was always home upstairs or downstairs. It had to be that way, for safety. Otherwise, he might rob them blind, clear out the place of radios and such, anything he might be able to hock for a brew or two.

Rosanna fell into a fitful slumber with Kewpie curled beside her and awoke to the sound of birds, no snoring. It was the first time he'd been out all night since the accident, and she dreaded the hung-over bear who'd return to the apartment.

At breakfast, Tiger went on about Jesse Owens and the Olympics in between bites of day-old Italian bread. He'd bought a copy of *Life Magazine* with what was left of his Mum Money and folded a dog-ear into the story about Owens' gold medals at the Berlin Olympics a month earlier. Tiger alternated between talking about this and the Labor Day barbecue the following day. "Do you think Manny will come, Ma?" he wondered. "I haven't seen him for weeks." Then, "I'm glad a colored guy whooped those Nazis. That will show 'em, huh?" And so on.

Rosanna was happy for the quiet when Tiger went to call for Jimmy Burns with his skates slung over his shoulder. But no sooner did he trot down the steps than she heard his frantic "Mom!" Rosanna went into the hallway, hugging her robe close, to see Tony sprawled out at the bottom of the steps, snoring to beat the band. She ran down the stairs and immediately shooshed Tiger. "I don't want your grandparents to know," she explained. "Hopefully, Poppa didn't go out for the paper yet."

Tony was lying in a pool of piss that Rosanna would have to scrub out of the carpet later. She and Tiger managed to haul Tony upstairs by slinging one of his arms around each of their shoulders and dragging him up the steps one by one, careful not to crash the cast on his right leg into the steps. Tiger, God bless him, took most of the burden so Rosanna wouldn't do damage to her tender belly.

Tony was half awake and muttering nonsense, so at least he wasn't dead weight. When they came through the door, Kewpie was sitting at the kitchen table eating a bowl of Corn Flakes. She rolled her eyes and disappeared into the bathroom. Rosanna wouldn't have let her help anyway for fear that Tony might get cross and grabby. She worried that it might be damaging for a little boy to see his father like this, but she couldn't have done it without Tiger's help.

"You get his pants and I'll take off his shoes," Rosanna told the boy once inside the bedroom. She wanted to keep as far away from her husband's sex organ as possible. They laid him on the bed, on top of an old towel Rosanna had the foresight to put down first.

As Tiger peeled the putrid clothing from his father's body, Rosanna pulled clean under drawers from the dresser. An acrid stench rose from the trousers Tiger removed and from the soiled shorts within them. Tiger held the skivvies lightly between two pinched fingers and started to gag. "Just throw them in the dustbin," his mother instructed, and he did.

As Rosanna unbuttoned Tony's shirt, he pawed her robe, digging roughly beneath her nightgown. "Come on, honey," Tony mumbled, exposing one of her breasts. "Why do you have to be this way, baby?" Rosanna smacked his hands away and tried in vain to cover her chest. Tiger came back into the room before she could. The boy reddened and turned away.

"Get me a wet, soapy washcloth, would you?" Rosanna asked him next. Off Tiger scampered again, glad to be useful. "And a towel," she added. "Oh, and take his crutches from the hallway so your grandparents don't see."

When Tiger came back with what Rosanna needed, she sent him away again, this time to fetch a bucket from the broom closet. This would keep him occupied a bit longer, banging around in the clutter.

Rosanna set to work, gritting her teeth as she sponged Tony between the legs. She roughly turned him onto one side, digging into the hairy crack of his ass with the washrag. It sickened her to tend to her husband like an infant. Rosanna didn't feel one shred of affection or devotion as she did swabbing down a baby.

There was just a twisted sense of duty, nothing more.

Tony moaned with pleasure as his wife toweled him down. "That's it...that's right," he sighed. Rosanna completed the task as quickly and deftly as possible, lingering only briefly over his sad, shrunken member. It was wan, hooded and flaccid, resembling something Moskowitz might toss into the trash bin. Tony tried to pull Rosanna's head into his lap but she managed to wrestle out of his grip. "Cold fucking cunt..." he muttered.

Tiger returned with the barf bucket in hand. "Set it on the side of the bed, just in case," his mother told him.

"I don't need no fucking..." Tony slurred, then hurled the entire contents of his stomach, mostly liquid, violently into the pail. Rosanna handed Tony a clean edge of the towel she was holding to wipe his mouth. He took it, then threw it back at her.

"You're welcome," she said.

"I don't have to thank you," he sneered. "It's your wifely duty."

"Wifely duty!" Rosanna shot back at him. "We'll see about wifely duty when the cast comes off."

Tony took a sodden swipe at Rosanna. He tried to get up off the bed and go after her but didn't have the strength. "You and your fucking holier than thou attitude," Tony began. "Somebody's going to knock you off your high horse but soon," he shouted. "You think your shit doesn't smell?"

Rosanna flashed Tiger a mischievous glance and noticed that the boy looked scared. "At least I don't shit in my drawers," she told him. "Now, calm down and sleep it off." Tiger relished a small, wicked grin without his father seeing.

"Don't tell me to calm down," Tony screamed. "You're a rotten, fucking wife. Don't think I don't know what you're up to. I'm onto you. And you're a rotten, fucking mother besides."

Rosanna put her arm around Tiger's shoulder. "Come on," she told him, leading him out of the room and closing the door behind her. Tony could still be heard yelling behind it until the snoring began as abruptly as the shouting had.

Hours later, Rosanna sat at the kitchen table, chopping celery. First, she peeled the thick threads from its spine with a long, sharp knife. Then she minced it fine, the gleaming blade drawing water from the tiny pieces. She chopped the celery so fine that it was almost translucent.

Then Rosanna thought she heard Tiger calling her from the street. Wearing his skates, he couldn't clomp up the stairs for every little thing, so he often summoned her from the sidewalk in front of the house if he needed her. Sometimes she tossed down an apple, an orange or a handkerchief knotted around a few coins if the lemon ice man came around. She got up from the kitchen table to see what Tiger wanted. Her intention was to call down to her son from one of the windows in his room, but she never made it there.

The next thing Rosanna knew, she was standing over Tony's slumbering body, watching him. Drool glistened in one corner of his mouth, his face porcine and bloated with drink. The celery knife weighed heavy in Rosanna's hand as she noticed how Tony's hair lay in greasy clumps on her nice, clean pillowcase. Dirt was clotted behind his ears and his neck was ringed with gunk. Rosanna lifted the knife. She held the handle in one fist and tested its heft. When she raised it above her head, it was light, practically weightless.

Tony woke with a start. Rosanna quickly hid the knife behind her back. "Lunch ready?" he wondered.

"Almost," she told him.

Perhaps Tony had felt her eyes upon him as he slept. Perhaps he had seen the knife. But Tony didn't rest again until he heard Rosanna back at the kitchen table, earnestly chopping.

39 The Coal Cellar

Kewpie had wisely made her escape while her mother and brother were wrestling with her father in the bedroom. She quickly washed, dressed and was out the door before they were done. Although her shift at Kresge's started at noon, Kewpie ran off to her friend Louise's house and holed up there until five to twelve.

It was barely past breakfast time, but Rosanna let Tiger have the last slab of Icebox Cake as a reward—but only after he scrubbed his hands vigorously with Kirkman's. Tiger ate the cake with relish and even licked the spoon. Rosanna figured he'd earned it, just for disposing of his father's dirty drawers alone. She unceremoniously dumped the contents of the slop bucket into the toilet and pulled the overhead chain to send it out to sea then rinsed the pail in the lion-footed bathtub.

Tiger put his plate in the sink and grabbed his roller skates again to meet up with Jimmy Burns. But before he left, Tiger stopped, turned to Rosanna and told her, "And don't pay no mind to what he said, Ma."

"He said a lot of ugly things," she admitted.

"But he doesn't mean them and they're not true anyhow" Tiger said sagely. "Besides, he'll forget all about it when he wakes up."

"But I won't," Rosanna told him.

Tiger kept trying to make his mother feel better. "Heck, he won't even remember how he got home."

It pained Rosanna that her young child knew so much about the ways of drunkards and it was her fault that he did. "I suppose you're right," she admitted reluctantly.

Tiger put down his skates with a soft clunk. "But don't listen to him. Really."

"I stopped listening to him long ago," she shrugged and began washing Tiger's dish and teaspoon.

"But how can you not?" Tiger wondered. "Especially the really awful stuff. Like about you being a bad mother."

"A rotten mother," she corrected.

Tiger hugged Rosanna around the waist and squeezed but not too tight. "You're a great mother," he told her. "The best."

Rosanna dried her hand on her robe and smoothed down Tiger's hair. "I think you're pretty grand, too," she told him, kissing him on the crown. When Tiger smiled up at her, all emerald eyes, crooked teeth and brown, summer freckles dusting the bridge of his nose, Rosanna thought him the most wonderful boy in all of Brooklyn.

The house was silent. Bridget had gone out shopping with Jo for the barbecue goods and Poppa was nowhere to be found, probably on one of his cleansing walks. For good measure, Rosanna called, "Pop? Momma?" No response. She ducked her head into her parents' kitchen, taking in the empty table, empty chairs and empty stovetop. When she saw the empty key ring by the back door, her heart sunk.

Rosanna peered out into the yard. The sawhorses and the four-by-eight were leaned against the back steps. She guessed that Sully and Harry had stopped by earlier to haul them up from the basement through the cellar door but noticed that the chairs hadn't been taken up yet. She figured she could handle them herself, one at a time, without doing any harm.

The truth was that Rosanna couldn't bear to be in the apartment alone with Tony, who was still sleeping heavily last time she checked. Rosanna didn't need anything on the Avenue. She thought about dropping in on Mrs. Lieberwitz but couldn't bring herself to; Rosanna had a difficult time facing her friends now that Tony was back. Even though his presence was just temporary, she felt like sucker for taking him in. She didn't want their pity. She didn't want their distain. She only wanted peace.

And so the coal cellar wasn't a banishment but a haven, someplace silent, pensive, dank and cool, even on a smoldering September day. Tiger, however, couldn't bear to go down to the basement by himself. When forced to retrieve a huge can of cling peaches or an old box of photos, he did little to mask his horror. Bela Lugosi was surely lurking behind the furnace, poised to engulf the boy in his sleek cape. And Boris Karloff was certainly waiting patiently in a darkened corner, green arms extended, electrodes protruding from his neck, his flat head filled with thoughts of squeezing the life from young guttersnipes like him.

Then there was that fearful life-sized cardboard cutout of Father Carmine, Poppa's brother, that was stowed in the depths of the house. It was made on the occasion of the beloved Jesuit priest's 50th birthday by his devoted parishioners. Tiger, and even Kewpie, swore its eyes followed you wherever you went in the basement.

And indeed, Tiger always whistled or hummed loudly when sent to the dreaded cellar. He turned on every light as if to banish these boogiemen. But if he really thought about it, he'd been living with a boogieman since the day he was born. Dracula and the Frankenstein Monster were nothing compared to an abusive alcoholic.

Rosanna thought of her son, who was still very much a child, as she climbed down the worn wooden steps from the hallway to the basement, taking care to leave the door slightly ajar as Tiger might. Just in case what he feared was true.

But instead of demons, there were pieces of their lives hiding at every turn: a big red tricycle, now rusted, which had been Kewpie's, then Tiger's; a white enamel crib that her children and Lettie's children had used; a small pram with a wicker basket that still held Kewpie's favorite doll with its ghostly, blue, glass eyes; piles of books belonging to Margaret and others to Astrid; a basinet covered with plastic; a doggie bed; boxes of clothing; a skateboard Kelly had made as a boy; crates of empty seltzer bottles; a dusty model train set; furniture too good to throw out, too decrepit to use.

The family's past was haphazardly arranged in the basement, placed neatly in cartons or else exposed to the elements and laced with spider webs. It made Rosanna feel at once wistful and hopeful. It was a life cycle of sorts: the old things here would eventually be replaced by newer things which had lately become useless.

A slanted metal cellar door separated the basement from the backyard. "Cellar door..." Edgar Allen Poe had once written that these were the loveliest, most melodic words in the English language. But Rosanna didn't agree. "Love," maybe. Or perhaps "baby," "daffodil" or "laughter." You couldn't help but smile when you uttered these words, but the same could not be said for "cellar door."

Rosanna mounted the handful of cement steps that led to the backyard and pressed her shoulder against the heavy wedge of diamond-plate. Pushing up firmly and favoring her belly, Rosanna heaved open the door. Slanted lines of sunlight painted the basement floor. She could hear Tiger's skates ringing through the street and Ti-Tu's mournful violin wailing two stories above.

The chairs Rosanna sought were stacked against the coal cellar's far wall, a few steps from the furnace. In the winter, coal was delivered a few times a month. It came crashing down a chute and tumbled into the wooden coal bin below. Some chunks rained onto the hard-packed dirt ground and a few fragments were still there now.

It was Rosanna's job to shovel the coal into the furnace. Actually, it was Tony's job and one of the things that brought them to live at 1128 47th Street—to help Rosanna's parents, who were not as spry as they once were, with the many chores it took to run a house. But between working most nights, drinking and generally not giving a damn, Tony was usually in no shape to do the job, so it fell upon Rosanna's able shoulders.

And she didn't mind, even though many considered it "men's work." There was a certain poetry and rhythm to shoveling coal, a certain music to the crunch of a shovel against the shining, black lumps, a certain song to the solid splat of the rocks landing in the inferno, willingly giving up their souls to heat the house, for that was what coal was born to do. Rosanna even liked the clean, dry smell of it.

Her shovel was propped against the wall where last she'd left it in early April when Poppa proclaimed it time to turn off the furnace. It was usually the same day he ceremoniously removed his long underwear, or *muthandies*, as Italians from "The Old Country" called them. No matter what the calendar said, it was officially spring whenever the family patriarch packed his *muthandies* in moth balls until next winter.

In an odd way, Rosanna was looking forward to picking up the coal spade when the November chill filled the rooms and Poppa declared it time to relight the furnace. She traced her fingers along the shovel, fitting her hand around the worn metal handle, feeling the heft of the tool. Soon enough, she would be shoveling coal again. Tiger always begged to help. This year, maybe she'd let him. This winter would be different, somehow more serene, she was sure of it. Rosanna lay the shovel back against the wall.

On an overhead shelf was an old radio. It had stood in the upstairs parlor when Rosanna was a girl. The family had gathered around it to hear the news, serials and comedy shows, each of the six children jockeying for position. Turning the dial, Rosanna wondered if it still worked. It did, but instead of hearing a rousing Sousa march or a sickly-sweet overture by Paul Whiteman and His Orchestra as she did in her youth, she heard Benny Goodman. The strains of "Stompin' at the Savoy" filled the cement room. She found herself humming along with the music as she made her way toward the chairs.

Perhaps this was why Rosanna didn't hear the footsteps on the stairs or sense the other body in the basement until it was too late. A strong, angry arm caught her around the neck and yanked her against a hard, washboard chest. Though she couldn't see the man's face, she could smell alcohol on his breath, could smell the filth of him. It was her husband.

Tony pressed his right arm into the spongy part of Rosanna's throat until she couldn't breathe. He had one crutch wedged under his left armpit, a wobbly third leg to stand upon. The other crutch was probably still upstairs, she guessed. Tony fell back against the cellar's rough wall, pulling Rosanna on top of him. With more leverage, he applied more pressure to her neck. Rosanna gasped for air like a goldfish on a Persian rug. "You fucking bitch," he snapped. "I'll teach you to make fun of me. And in front of my son, yet. How does it feel? Huh? How does it feel?"

With each question, Tony tightened his hold on her throat until Rosanna began to panic. Her eyes swirled from object to object, from baby buggy to tricycle, frantically searching for a weapon. She couldn't move, couldn't budge from his wrathful grasp. The sum of Tony's hate gushed to one place and his rage was directed at one person—her.

Rosanna dug her fingertips into his arm, feeling her short, cropped nails penetrate his skin. She forced her nails to pierce his flesh deeper, hanging on like a feral cat, but still Tony was unmoved. Rosanna flung her body against his and tried to throw him off balance. For a flash of a second, Tony's grip weakened and she broke free.

His arm dripped blood. "I don't understand," she said. "Just leave. Go. Please."

"You don't fucking understand is right," he spat at her. "Everything wrong with me is you. It's your fault."

In another time, Rosanna might have believed him. In another age, she might have broken down and cried, crumbled to the dirt floor and sobbed, and he would have left her there, perhaps even kicked her before he went, that is, if he'd had two solid legs to stand on. But this was not one of those times. "I'm not going without a fight," she warned him.

Tony lunged at Rosanna again, falling face-forward onto the ground. He clamored to his feet, dragging the cast behind him like it was something half-dead that refused to die completely. Tony hurled himself against his wife again. Rosanna shoved her elbow into his ribs as hard as she could. Tony doubled over, coughing. "You're nothing but a no-good, drunken bum," she said, turning for the stairs. "And I'm not scared of you anymore," she added.

Tony laughed wickedly. "Oh, yeah? Then why are you running?"

Rosanna stopped, turned and confronted him. Tony grabbed her by the hair and pulled her backwards. "And you're nothing but a fucking bitch," he snarled.

Tony threw Rosanna to the earthen floor and left her there. Her scar ached but she dared not let him know she was hurting. Tony loomed above her, ready to strike again. From the corner of her eye, Rosanna noticed the coal shovel leaning against the wall. Her hands shot out and sought it but Tony knocked it away with his crutch before she could reach it. The metal clanged against the furnace.

"You'll spend the rest of your life in jail," Rosanna told him, gasping. "Please just go. I won't tell anyone, I swear."

Tony stopped and thought for a moment. "I'll disappear so far into Coney, no one will ever find me. Not your fat cop friend. Not your sorry-ass brother-in-law. None of them. And believe me, it'll be well worth it."

"You think you can kill me?" Rosanna shouted. "Go ahead, kill me. It would be a relief. Then at least everyone would finally know the truth about you. But I'll tell you one thing, you're not going to get your hands on my kids."

"They're my kids, too!"

"You never acted like a father or a husband," she screamed. "Don't you think I remember what happened that night? Don't you think I told somebody? I just been biding my time, waiting for the right moment to..."

Tony shrieked like a wounded animal, the veins standing out on his lean neck. He pressed heavily on the crutch and wound back with his good foot, ready to give his beloved wife a good, swift kick. But before he could, Rosanna dove forward. She grabbed the end of Tony's crutch and yanked it as hard as she could. Rosanna saw a painful kaleidoscope of stars, then shook them away. She opened her eyes to see Tony crashing to the ground like a felled tree.

Tumbling backwards, first Tony's head cracked against the cinderblock wall behind him, then crashed sideways into the cast-iron furnace. Rosanna scrambled to her hands and knees in the dirt and grabbed the shovel. She straddled Tony's body, raising the spade high above her head until it clanked into the low ceiling, startling her.

That's when she noticed the blood that gathered beneath Tony's head. It leaked across the brown soil floor of the coal cellar and reached the tips of her shoes. Tony didn't move, didn't take a breath. But she just couldn't be sure. Rosanna shifted the shovel to her right side, preparing to take what her son would call a "Lou Gehrig shot." But she stopped. She stopped because she heard footsteps.

Sully and Harry came running down the basement's back steps and into the bowels of the coal cellar. "Bertha Rosenkrantz called in a complaint," Harry panted, out of breath. "Said she heard a lot of yelling."

When they saw Tony lying still and quiet in a pool of blood, they stopped short. Rosanna put down the shovel. "God bless Bertha Rosenkrantz," she said.

After the police came and went, after Sully and Harry managed to calm Poppa and Bridget, Rosanna and the children, after the medical examiner left and the funeral parlor removed Tony's body from the basement, life returned to a new kind of normal at the house.

The remaining Martinos ate their dinner, though the meal was quieter than usual, then retired to the radio in the parlor. Tiger didn't feel like going outside and playing "Hit the Penny" with Jimmy Burns. Since she'd been summoned from behind the candy counter at Kresge's that afternoon, Kewpie elected to stay home. She wanted, needed, to be with her family.

Rosanna darned socks while Kewpie read more of *Gone with the Wind* and half-listened to President Roosevelt's fireside chat on the radio. Tiger galloped his Niagara Falls horse, whom he decided to name "Coal" (this was before his father's unfortunate accident), from chair to sofa to chair again, trying to pay

attention to the good President's speech. F.D.R. seemed like
a decent fellow, and with his round specs, reminded Tiger of
Poppa. Mr. Roosevelt usually had something interesting to say.
There was always a new word or two for Tiger to add to his
ever-growing vocabulary. Chunks and pieces and wisps of Mr.
Roosevelt's speech stayed with Tiger, stayed with each of them,
and were a source of consolation that evening.

"I have been on a journey of husbandry..." the President
began. *"I saw drought devastation in nine states..."*

Rosanna pricked her finger on the needle but pulled the stitch
through the threadbare sock, undaunted.

*"I shall never forget the fields of wheat so blasted by heat that
they cannot be harvested. I shall never forget field after field of
corn stunted, earless and stripped of leaves, for what the sun left
the grasshoppers took..."*

Coal scraped his hooves across the coffee table until Rosanna
flashed him a corrective glance.

Mr. Roosevelt continued on about *"...indomitable American
farmers..."*

"Momma, what's 'indomitable' mean?" Tiger wondered, but
Rosanna wasn't paying attention and therefore didn't respond.

But Kewpie did. "It means strong," she told him. "Very
strong. Unconquerable."

It was a fine word, Tiger decided, and he would remember it.

*"...and stockmen and their wives and children who have
carried on through desperate days, and inspire us with their
self-reliance, their tenacity..."*

Before Tiger could ask, Kewpie told him, "Determination.
Drive. That's tenacity." And Tiger nodded.

Tiger looked at his mother. She was tenacious and more. Her
drive and determination had gotten them this far, even though
she was not the portrait of tenacity at this very moment, he knew
she would be again.

*"...and their courage. It was their fathers' task to make
homes; it is their task to keep those homes; it is our task to help
them with their fight."*

From the backyard rose the sound of water filling buckets,
of scrubbing, of raking. Sully and Harry returned to the house

after their shift to complete the ominous task of cleaning up the aftermath in the basement. Though the coal cellar's hard-packed, dirt floor had absorbed most of Tony's blood, there was a dark, ruby stain to the soil which they tried to wash away, scrape and otherwise obliterate. They approached this thoughtfully, as they would any mildly unpleasant task on the job. With their jackets and work shirts draped over the banister, Sully and Harry wore their work pants and under vests, which were ringed with grimy sweat. They resembled Dust Bowl farmers themselves, tilling an unyielding field, but with plenty of water instead of none.

The coal cellar was a muddy puddle at present but when the water dried thoroughly, the men were confident there wouldn't be much of a stain left, just a memory which would also fade in time. Harry continued raking. Sully picked up a broom and began taking long, even, sweeping strokes.

Upstairs, President Roosevelt went on about the drought:

"There are two reasons why I want to end by talking about reemployment. Tomorrow is Labor Day. The brave spirit with which so many millions of working people are winning their way out of depression deserves respect and admiration. It is like the courage of the farmers in the drought areas..."

Kewpie turned a page silently. Rosanna knotted and cut a long, black thread. Coal managed to remain cool clenched in Tiger's clammy hand.

"...There is no cleavage between white collar workers and manual workers, between artists and artisans, musicians and mechanics, lawyers and accountants and architects and miners," President Roosevelt insisted.

"Tomorrow, Labor Day, belongs to all of us. Tomorrow, Labor Day, symbolizes the hope of all Americans."

Needless to say, there was no Labor Day barbecue for these Americans that year, but instead, a funeral to plan.

40 A Wake

There was a saying Bridget was extremely fond of: you get the face you deserve. This was true in old age and in death. And it was especially true with her son-in-law.

No matter how Joe Bruno tried, he couldn't get the evil snarl off Tony's face. It seemed frozen there. Tony's teeth were permanently gritted. His mouth was set in an expression of rage, despite the efforts of Mr. Bruno, who was considered the best mortician in Borough Park, if not in all of Brooklyn. He tried stuffing Tony's mouth with cotton balls. He tried wires and pipe cleaners but nothing seemed to do the trick. Tony's lips kept retracting into a mean expression.

However, this didn't bother Mr. Bruno very much, even though he took great pride in his work. He'd gone to grade school with Tony so he knew exactly what kind of fellow he was: the kind who put lit firecrackers in your pocket, the kind who emptied an inkpot into your milk. Not a good kid, by any stretch of the imagination. And Joe had heard from neighborhood gossip that Tony hadn't grown into much of a man either.

Bruno & Sons was a rather sumptuous-looking structure of brick and white columns situated in the shadow of the El. Approaching the Fort Hamilton Parkway station, if you were headed toward Coney Island, just prior to the big curve in the rails that often made the wheels screech, you could even spot Bruno's from the train's dirty windows. It was convenient for the locals and easy for those unfamiliar with Borough Park to find.

Rosanna chose the smallest room Bruno's had and the most economical pine box they offered, even though what the Union gave would cover everything. As with most Italian wakes, the coffin lid was open so people could say their last good-byes face to face. Rosanna always suspected that the reason for this macabre tradition was because people wanted proof, evidence that the deceased was, in fact, actually dead. There was no way in hell she was having Tony laid out in the parlor like the old Guineas did. She wanted him out of the house as soon as possible.

Tony was waked the day after Labor Day. His wife was surprised by the number of people who came, many of whom she'd never met, others she hadn't seen in years. Kewpie and Tiger took dutiful posts in the seats beside Rosanna, looking suitably somber. Bridget and Poppa were always an arm's length away. Sully leaned against the back wall, near the doorway, as if standing guard.

The room was unadorned with flowers except for the arrangement from Tony's brother Paulie, who lived near Los Angeles, and couldn't make the trip in. He sent a "bleeding heart" array of red carnations with a trail of tiny tea roses meant to signify drops of blood.

Although there was a steady stream of visitors for Tony's send-off, there were no tears. Not from Rosanna, who positioned herself in a green Windsor-style chair in the middle of the front row of folding chairs, as was customary for the grieving widow. Many remarked that she looked more relieved than bereaved.

All of the neighbors showed up out of respect to the family. Even Violetta and Nunzi DeMeo from down the street, who never thought much of Tony. Mr. and Mrs. Lieberwitz. Mr. and Mrs. Wong. Bertha Rosenkrantz and Ti-Tu, sans violin. When no one was within earshot, Rosanna thanked Bertha profusely for calling the police two days earlier. "You saved my life," Rosanna whispered.

"My pleasure," Bertha told her.

Manny and his wife Consuelo came all the way from Fort Greene, as did a handful of Poppa's crew from the Navy Yard, who lived near Manny. It was odd that no one said "I'm sorry," but rather, they said, "Our thoughts are with you" or "God bless you." For most who knew Tony or knew of Tony also knew the type of guy he was.

There were motormen and conductors who came and politely explained to Rosanna who they were and how they knew her husband, and a representative from the Transport Workers Union, too. She felt a flush of embarrassment meeting these men especially, for if anyone was witness to how Tony had deceived her, how he had lied and cheated on her, they surely were. But none of it mattered now.

There was never a question about how Tony died. Sully and Harry attested to the "accident" in their police report. Tony had clearly been impaired, fell and cracked his skull. Mrs. Rosenkrantz and the other neighbors kept their lips buttoned about the shouting. It was a case of a drunken fall, plain and simple. The authorities accepted this explanation as well.

Rosanna borrowed a fine black dress from Astrid. It was pure silk and from Saks, with mesh cap sleeves and the same sheer black netting around the neckline. At first, Rosanna thought it too fancy for a widow but Astrid told her, "Pish-posh...you should be wearing a ball gown and throwing a party."

The high-heeled pumps came from Jo, who said that the humidity made her feet too swollen for heels. The black hose was from Camille. On Rosanna's head, Astrid pinned a small wreath of black roses trimmed with a veil that masked her eyes. "I whipped it up this morning," Astrid told Rosanna as she scraped the hatpin against her sister's scalp. It was perhaps the most tasteful hat Astrid had ever created.

At one point, a small, twisted woman made her way to Rosanna with the aid of a battered wooden cane. The gnarled figure seemed vaguely familiar but when the lady opened her mouth, Rosanna was absolutely certain of who she was. "Sure took the bastard long enough," the kindly gnome told her.

"Marie!" Rosanna exclaimed and then hugged her sister-in-law's small body close. "It's been years."

"I wouldn't miss this for the world," Marie Martino said. "I told him I'd never see him again while he was alive, and I meant it. Missed you and the kids like blazes, though." Marie pinched Tiger's cheeks for emphasis. It hurt.

"Kids, this is your Aunt Marie. Your father's sister," Rosanna told her son and daughter.

They each gave Marie a kiss on her wizened face. "Why haven't we met you before?" Kewpie wondered.

"It's a long, sad story," Marie told the girl. "I'll tell it to you someday." Marie rested her cane against a chair and held Rosanna at arm's length. "You look like shit," she told her sister-in-law. "Although I can imagine why."

"I been sick," Rosanna admitted. "But I'm getting better now."

"No doubt," Marie said.

Tony liked to call his sister "Crippled Marie" in all fondness, and to her face, at that. Marie had been born premature and was so tiny in fact, that they kept her in a peach crate by the furnace to keep her warm. As she grew older, she was still frail and sickly. Her bones didn't form properly. Little Marie was forever bent, had trouble walking and never married. And she never forgave Tony for the business with the trolley tracks, for that and other indignities.

Marie left her least favorite brother's wake immediately following a spell of gloating and promised to visit the family soon, though the stairs to their apartment would be a challenge. "I'll carry you up piggy back," Tiger suggested, and she pinched his cheek again, this time even harder.

Tony's brother Tommy also showed. Although Tommy was simple-minded, he was honest and hardworking. He shined shoes, did odd jobs and managed to eke by in that manner. Between Marie being of unsound body, Tommy being of unsound mind and Tony's wounded spirit, Rosanna always wondered if her mother-in-law Philomena's cold cruelty somehow slipped through the umbilical cord and poisoned her growing babies. Paulie was the only normal one and he had the sense to move far away to California.

Tommy knelt before his brother's coffin, head in his hands, moving his lips as he prayed intensely. He never learned to read or write but boy, he sure could pray. When he was through, Tommy approached Rosanna, cap in hand, nodding and sighing. He placed a hand on her shoulder and said, "There, there," and did the same to the children. The poor man tried his best to look presentable but his clothes were rags. "Stop by the house in a few days, Tommy," Rosanna told him. "I'll have some clothes for you. Your brother's things."

"Thank you, Roe. You always were good to me," Tommy told her as he backed away, bowing.

Rosanna's sisters held court, entertaining the neighbors, introducing fellow mourners to each other. In truth, Rosanna felt numb and out of her body, as though she were watching the proceedings from the back row of the funeral parlor. She observed a worn middle-aged woman in borrowed clothes, flanked by her two children, the pallid form of her husband in a coffin that was bordered by two ornate floor lamps. The woman was going through the motions, shaking hands, hugging people, kissing dry, unfamiliar cheeks. That woman was her.

When Tiger went off to talk with Jimmy Burns and Kewpie was busy with Augie, Jo slipped into the seat beside her sister. She took Rosanna's hand. "Seems a little unreal, doesn't it?" Jo asked. Rosanna nodded. "You'll be all right," Jo told her.

"I know I will," Rosanna said.

"The kids, too," Jo added. "They'll be just fine."

Jo and Rosanna sat there clutching hands, gazing up at Tony's coffin, silent for a few moments. Rosanna placed an open palm against her sister's slightly rounded belly. "So, when's the baby due?" Rosanna wondered.

"Is it that obvious?" Jo asked.

"Even Tiger suspects it," her sister smiled.

"I haven't told anyone yet, not Ma, no one."

Rosanna patted Jo's stomach. "Don't be afraid. This one will take. I know it."

Jo pressed her hand on top of her sister's. Harry watched from across the room and smiled. "I'm due in the middle of February," Jo told her.

"Ah, a Valentine's Day baby," Rosanna nodded. "Same as the other one."

"Hope. Her name was Hope," Jo said.

"Hope's a good name," Rosanna agreed.

Jo's eyes drifted to the front of the room. She squeezed her sister's hand when she noticed a blonde hunched over Tony's coffin. Rosanna immediately recognized her as the woman from the photographs her brother-in-law John had shown her. "Let's go for a walk," Jo suggested.

"No," Rosanna said. "I want to stay here."

The woman's hair looked freshly bleached, whitewashed so white that it wasn't really blonde at all. It was curled so tightly that the ringlets looked like they might snap off into pieces. Although the woman was wearing black, her outfit was inappropriate. The dress was bedecked with rhinestones and beadwork, meant more for the Copa than for a wake. The brassy outfit pulled tight across her swelling stomach. It must have taken some effort to button it closed. The woman teetered dangerously on a pair of black mules, which her feet seemed pressed into like sausages.

It's amazing the things you can tell about a person in a fleeting glance. This was not the sort of gal you'd imagine would know how to pray. But her lips were moving and she seemed to be saying something passionate and fervent that only she and Tony could hear. Rosanna studied the woman's profile. It was doughy and white, outlined heavily in make-up, blood-red lips, kohl eyes and rouge-encrusted cheeks. In her hand, the woman twisted a lace-trimmed handkerchief, also black, probably satin. The woman's fingernails were painted the same wounded shade as her lips. 'But I bet her underdrawers are dirty,' Rosanna thought.

The woman leaned closer to the coffin until she almost buried her face in it. At first, Rosanna thought she might kiss Tony, but instead, the woman parted her lips, swallowed hard and unleashed a big, audible glob of spit onto him, then another. Nobody moved. Not even Joe Bruno, who just watched impassively from the doorway, wondering what might happen next.

Finally satisfied, the blonde joined an older woman standing off to the side. Her mother? No, the older lady was wearing the conservative garb of an Orthodox Jew—long skirt, sheathed head, thick cotton hose, a tunic that covered her elbows.

This white blonde didn't stop to offer her condolences to Rosanna, who watched her intently as she passed. The woman watched Rosanna just as intently, and nodded, glaring at her. The woman left the room without saying a word. Her eyes were dry but crackling with anger.

Rosanna decided to have Tony waked at Bruno's for only one day, unheard of in those times. Most Italians waked their people at least three days. This was so that long-lost relatives from far and wide, sometimes as far as Long Island, could make the trip to pay their final respects. But Rosanna only wished to perform her duties and have them done with, that's all. No one argued with her decision, not even Joe Bruno, who was famous for treating the deceased with reverence. "The sooner he gets in the ground, the better," Camille's John snapped.

Tony's funeral was held on September 9th. Rosanna wore the same borrowed outfit. Kewpie wore another selection from Astrid's fine wardrobe. Tiger was dressed in a suit of Matthew's, the one Mattie had worn during his stint as ring bearer in the wedding of a Czech cousin once removed on Lettie's side. Tiger complained that the shorts were too tight and that the tie was choking him, but this was only after Kewpie told him that he looked like Freddie Bottle-Ass, and Poppa chuckled.

Mourners kept remarking that Kewpie looked beautiful, more like her father than like Rosanna. But these comments didn't seem to bother her as much as they did when Tony was alive. Camille whispered to her niece that she looked better in Astrid's clothes than Astrid did. Astrid wore a great deal of black "because it matched her personality," Sam joked.

All of Rosanna's brothers and sisters attended the funeral, except for Kelly, who offered to fly in from Arizona to support his sister. Only she convinced him not to because of the expense.

"Besides, you're here in spirit," she told him.

Julius, Lettie and the boys were due to leave for Julius' job in Mexico City two days later. Much to Poppa's protests, Julius arranged for his father to care for old Flossie until the family returned. "You'll be doing me a favor, Pop," Julius told him. "It's not charity," he insisted when his father kept objecting. "I should be paying you."

It all worked out well. At least Poppa didn't have to rely on public transportation to get to the Navy Yard for work the following day. Sully said he would be glad to take Julius's family back to Queens after the funeral. This way, he could visit his nephews, who lived nearby. Sully had gotten to see Irene and her husband Ray the day earlier when they attended Tony's wake but he hadn't seen the boys for a few weeks. (Rosanna insisted they didn't come back for the funeral.) Mattie had been looking forward to taking the El home to Sunnyside, which he rarely did, and was mildly disappointed, but he soon got over it.

Anthony Martino, Sr. was buried at Green-Wood Cemetery, after a short funeral service at St. Catherine's. Rosanna did this more for herself and her beliefs than for her husband's soul, which she knew was doomed anyway. Not many from the neighborhood came, for they had showed their respect elsewhere, and they would continue to show their respect in the ways of good neighbors and friends.

For her husband's final resting place, Rosanna chose a single plot at Green-Wood. Not so Tony would be eternally alone, but because she couldn't imagine spending eternity in the ground beside him or subjecting their children to that fate either. It was one of the cheapest she could find because there were no views of rolling hills, tranquil ponds or stately stands of weeping willows. It wasn't near any of the stone family mausoleums complete with Tiffany glass windows or monuments marking the graves of Civil War generals or Charles Feltman, inventor of the hot dog.

Instead, Tony's gravesite was on a stark hillside, overlooking the 38th Street train yard, not far from the intersection of Spruce Avenue and Public Lot 18372. If you stood on your toes and peered over the fence, you could see the far corner of the

Pink Pussycat. It seemed a fitting final resting place for a man like Tony.

A small, flat stone marked his grave, but no one visited. Ever.

Even the El turned its back on him.

Publisher's Note

While this book is inspired by real people, places and some actual events, *The El* is a work of fiction and is in no way meant to be a historical accounting. Any resemblance to persons, either living or dead, is purely coincidental. The book is intended solely for entertainment purposes.

Acknowledgements

I would like to thank the following people for their help and support:

First, my husband Peter, who is always there to calmly talk me off the writer's ledge, no matter how needy or pitiful I am.

To my parents, Teresa and Francis Gigante, who are both gone, but instilled in me a strong sense of self and truly believed that I could do anything I set out to do.

To my family, for their unconditional love and for sharing such wonderful stories around the dinner table.

To the nuns at St. Patrick's for teaching me the basics, and to Mildred McVay, my third-grade teacher at St. Pat's, for teaching me to love reading, and in turn, writing.

To my friends who suffered through this book in its early stages—Janet Farrell, Lisa Gilman, Pat Hurd, Maz Kessler, the Karp Klan (Joni, Joan and Bill) and Bobbi Wicks—and were a constant source of encouragement.

To Vinnie Corbo of Volossal, for his hearty "Hell yes" response when I asked if he might be interested in taking on my novel, and to Jacqueline for her friendship and support that has weathered the decades and the miles.

About the Author

Catherine Gigante-Brown has been a freelance writer of fiction, nonfiction and poetry for more than 30 years, since the ripe young age of fifteen. Her works have appeared in a variety of publications, including *Time Out New York*, *Essence*, *Seventeen* and *The Italian Journal of Wine and Food*. Along with Robert *"The Harrad Experiment"* Rimmer, she co-wrote two biographies for Prometheus Books (Mistress Jacqueline's *Whips & Kisses* and Jerry Butler's *Raw Talent*).

Her short stories appear in several fiction anthologies and her essay, "When I was Young," was included in Penguin Books' *Vietnam Voices*. A number of her screenplays have been produced by small, independent companies. Her essay "Autumn of 9/11" was awarded first prize in The Brooklyn Public Library's 2004 "My Brooklyn" contest. Her works, *Weekender* and *Moving Pictures*, were included in the Rosendale Theatre Collective's Short Play Festival in 2012 and 2013.

Gigante-Brown was born and bred in Brooklyn, New York, where she still lives with her husband and son. *The El* is her first published novel.

CPSIA information can be obtained
at www.ICGtesting.com
Printed in the USA
BVHW081723140820
586424BV00001B/23